"LIKE IT, MY LORD? WE CALL THIS SLOW DANCING."

"I can think of other names for it." He drew her even closer into his arms.

They weren't dancing anymore. They were just standing, simply standing. So why did she feel as if she were spinning in circles?

"Marcus?" Cassandra could hear her own heart beating in her ears. "Marcus? I don't know if I should bring this up, but we aren't dancing anymore."

"No, we're not, are we? But no matter. I believe I understand the moves. However, as long as we are here, I have just thought of another little experiment we might try. Another *comparison* we might make between your time and mine."

"Such as?"

"Such as, my dear Miss Kelley—has lovemaking shifted in its application as well as its constraints? In short, has this Sexual Revolution you spoke of not so long ago incorporated anything new into the world of lovemaking? Or are the rudiments basically unchanged?"

Cassandra's tongue pushed forward, to moisten her suddenly dry lips. "I—I think they're pretty much the same . . ."

OUT *of the* BLUE

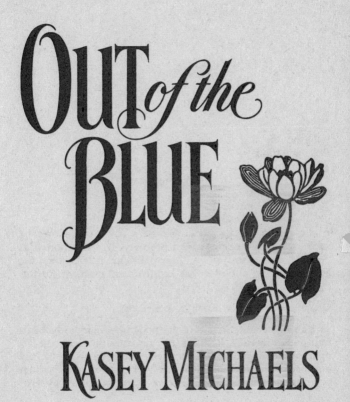

KASEY MICHAELS

A DELL BOOK

Published by
Dell Publishing
a division of
Bantam Doubleday Dell Publishing Group, Inc.
666 Fifth Avenue
New York, New York 10103

The trademark Dell® is registered in the U.S. Patent and Trademark Office.

ISBN: 0-440-21105-0

Printed in the United States of America

Published simultaneously in Canada

October 1992

10   9   8   7   6   5   4   3   2   1

To my niece, Nora Lynn Charles

Prologue

LONDON, 1483

The heavy wooden door slammed shut with a finality that echoed ominously through the high-ceilinged stone chamber. Its closing banished nearly all the thin daylight, along with the sight of any other humans—not that gaolers were necessarily human, at least not in the more lofty sense of the word. These particular gaolers, notably one Miles Forest, a man of such terrible brawn and rankness of flesh and mean beady eyes as to set fear in the hearts of even his fellow henchmen, were not to be missed.

Unless, of course, they did not show up again in time to serve dinner.

The young lad who had been thinking these thoughts began to whine and turned to his older brother, tugging on the boy's gored velvet sleeve. "We will eat, won't we, Ned? Would there be a kitchen here in the Garden Tower, d'ya think? I'm most frightfully hungry."

The older boy brushed his brother's hand away and began pacing the starkly furnished room. He stood a good half foot taller than his sibling and had a wonderfully straight spine that remained rigid even in these unwelcoming surroundings. Walking to the narrow arrow slit that served as the single window, he stood on tiptoe to look out over the Thames and the boat traffic that all but clogged the dirty water from shore to shore.

"Stop thinking of your stomach, Dickon," he commanded at last, turning to face the lad who had begun to snuffle in earnest. "We're royal prisoners. Royal prisoners don't think of their stomachs. They pray for their necks."

"Ned!" Dickon squeaked, covering his slim throat with both hands. "You don't suppose Uncle Gloucester will have us dragged out to the garden, like Lord Hastings, and chop off our heads?" The boy's lower lip quivered as hunger gave way to terror. "Would he stick them on pikes, and hang them from the rafters while he dined? He wouldn't do that, Ned. Uncle has always loved us, you know that. Besides, you're the king now. Mother told us so. You're King Edward V, and I am Richard, Duke of York."

Edward looked disdainfully at his brother before turning his head to peer into a dark corner where a hungry mouse scavenged for crumbs. He pointed to the rodent. "King, Dickon? Behold His Majesty the King's single subject save you, Your Royal Highness. Not much of a kingdom, do you think? Mother acted the fool to give us up to Uncle Gloucester, no matter how he loves us. Hastings warned her, but she believed our dearest uncle when he said he would be my Protector. When there is a crown in the picture it is better to take the word of the devil than a relative, I say."

"Never say so, Ned, I beg you. Uncle Gloucester won't harm us. And Mother will come, you'll see. And then we'll go to Westminster, and you'll be properly crowned, and you'll have Knights for the Body to guard us and Squires for the Body to dress and undress us and two dozen Squires for the Household, and we'll have candies and sweetmeats all day long, and—and you'll order the whole of the Tower of London razed to the ground and we'll never come to this cold, bloody terrible Garden Tower again!"

The young king held out his arms and his brother,

sobbing, fell into them. It could be difficult being a king, Edward realized, his own lip trembling, when one's years numbered only thirteen, one's father lay newly cold in his tomb, and one's mother, vain, ambitious fool of a Woodville or no, wasn't anywhere to be found.

As he patted Dickon's heaving back, Edward pondered this latest move on his uncle's part. It had been bad enough being confined to the royal apartments, and the move to the White Tower, combined with the disappearance of all their familiar servants, worried him more than he dared let on to his brother, but this latest maneuver on the part of his uncle had proved more than merely uncomfortable. It smacked of the ominous.

"Shhh, Dickon," Edward said comfortingly, hoping the good Lord wouldn't strike him down for his lie. "Everything will be fine. You'll see."

Three weeks passed, and the "ominous" maneuver had all but done its work, for the spartan tower, lack of servants, and poor food had reduced both Edward and Richard to naught but boys: dirty, sniffling children who —fearful for their lives—prayed almost incessantly and slept only in snatches.

Their gaolers, especially Miles Forest, gave them comfort by neither word nor deed, and the future seemed bleak—especially since Edward had overheard two of their gaolers discussing the rumored demotion of the two princes to bastard issue from an invalid marriage between their father and Elizabeth Woodville and Uncle Gloucester's supposed lavish coronation at Westminster, making him Richard III, King of all England.

England had need of a king, of that much Edward had been convinced since he had been old enough to sit up straight for his lessons. It did not, however, need two kings, or a runny-nosed Duke of York as heir first in line to the throne. Even if their uncle could move the Pope to declare them bastards, allowing Edward and his brother

Richard to continue to draw breath could only be considered a serious blunder, at least as long as there remained a single Woodville in all of England.

Their father's middle brother, the Duke of Clarence, had drowned in a butt of Malmsey wine some five years past, perishing in the Tower by way of that unhappy accident after being imprisoned for plotting against the king—and whether he had been helped to this untidy death or not remained a question. More important to Edward at the moment was the fact that Clarence's death had moved Richard, Duke of Gloucester, into the position of third in line to the throne behind Edward and Richard.

Removal of the two boys would make the Duke of Gloucester king in one single, clean stroke, although—if news of the coronation were true—Gloucester seemed to have already taken the matter into his own hands.

What else could Edward believe in, locked in this terrible room, hearing what he had heard, if not his once-beloved uncle's ambition? To the world outside the Tower, Edward and Richard must already be dead, not just declared bastards. All that remained was to feel the sharp sting of the headman's ax. Why was Uncle Gloucester waiting? It was dangerous. What did he hope to gain? If Edward were king, he knew he shouldn't delay for a moment in securing his throne.

Daily Edward's prayers lengthened as his time spent resting on the thin straw pallet grew shorter. To make matters worse, if this were possible, Richard had taken a chill and had begun coughing badly from morn till night.

Perhaps worry over Richard explained why Edward couldn't sleep, that or the strange feeling he had that this particular night out of so many nights seemed special. The stars appeared brighter, the night sky bluer, and Edward felt more invigorated than he had done since passing across the barbican at Lion's Gate and entering the Tower.

But if he were to say that the night felt magical, his brother would think his mind had slipped a notch, so Edward kept his thoughts to himself.

He turned away from the narrow window to look at Richard, who was sitting on one of the pallets, his spirit so broken that he no longer took the time to tie up his shoe points. The young king's resolve stiffened and he raised his head, tilted his chin, and stared defiantly at the door. Enough was enough! How dare they treat their king this way? The time had come for action. He had passed beyond fear, beyond pride, even beyond hope. If there were to be an end to this madness, he, Edward, would choose the moment.

And that moment was now.

Crossing to the door, Edward began beating his fists against the heavy oak, demanding to be brought before his uncle at once for an explanation behind this evil, traitorous imprisonment.

But his demands were answered only with curses and raucous laughter. At last, his small store of passion spent, Edward slumped to the floor, knowing that he would never see his uncle again. He and Dickon were doomed, and they were not even to be permitted a defense.

How long he sat on the cold stone he could not know, but it had grown fully dark when the door opened and two large men stepped inside.

"Where are ye, ye damned brats? Wake up, ye sleepy-heads. 'Tis time ta go."

Miles Forest. Edward recognized the man's rough voice in the darkness, as well as his grotesque, over-blown shape. Edward's heart fell. He had been right. This starry night would be special. It would be the night he and Dickon died.

The second man, slightly smaller, seemed to hesitate

at the doorway. "Oi don'ts loik this," he said in a small voice. "It ain't natural."

"Dub yer mummer, Green, ye sniveling dolt. We've got the keys from Brackenbury, bloodless coward that he is, and all the guards have been pulled away fer the night. I've already gots the chest fer stuffin' 'em in. Besides, we're actin' in the name of wot's right. We'll makes it quick and easy. Now fetch me a torch. It's too demmed dark in here."

Edward, who had slunk back against the wall and crawled to his brother's pallet, placing a hand over the boy's mouth, now quietly motioned for Richard to drop to his knees and follow him. Crawling their way out of a prison might not be noble, but it could only be considered highly preferable to the fate Green and Forest had in store for them.

Just as Green reentered the chamber with a torch held high over his head, Edward and Richard scampered out the door, heading for the staircase. Fear lent wings to their feet, fear and the sound of the two men hurtling down the steps behind them.

Having reached the ground floor, the brothers barreled out the unguarded doorway and turned right, heading toward the royal apartments, a plan already forming in Edward's head. It wouldn't do to try for any of the gates, for a dumb brute like Forest would expect them to do just that. The Tower was large, and filled with marvelous hiding places. They would find one and hide in it until Edward could think of another plan.

By fits and starts the boys made their way past the royal apartments, until they reached the steep, once-impregnable walls of the White Tower that William the Conqueror had ordered built to intimidate his not-so-loyal subjects. But the years had brought numerous changes to the White Tower, the most important being the addition of many wooden shelters and booths that leaned against its walls, clinging to its strength.

With Richard close behind him, one shoe already lost but no longer sniffling, Edward climbed from wooden building to rooftop, from stall to stall, until at last he and his brother had succeeded in gaining entrance to one of the lesser towers and, finally, the White Tower itself.

Their backs against the cold stone wall, their thin chests heaving from their exertion, the boys strained to catch their breath as they looked around the small chamber that appeared to house pieces of rusty armor and a few dozen broken lances.

"Now what, Ned?" Richard stood and looked around, spreading his arms. "We've naught but changed one prison for another. We should have made directly for the Watergate."

Edward shook his head. "It's a good thing I'm king then, Dickon, rather than a silly child like you. The Watergate has been shut up tight for the night. Besides, neither of us can swim a stroke. We only got this far because the guards have been pulled. No, we'll stay here while the hue and cry is raised, then slip out in the morning when everyone searches for us outside the walls."

Richard cocked his head to one side, as if considering this strategy. "But I'm hungry," he complained at last, heading for the door. "Come on, Ned, the guards are gone or asleep, and we can't be far from the kitchens."

Before Edward could tell Richard that an army might move on its belly but a king chose his movements only with his head, his brother had thrown open the door to the hall and stepped outside, and there remained nothing left for Edward to do but follow.

For a few minutes it seemed Richard had been right. From squire to servant, those in the White Tower appeared to be tucked in their beds, and no one challenged the boys' passage. But try as the royal princes might they could not locate the kitchens. Soon it would be dawn and the White Tower would come alive, and if they had not found another hidey-hole by then they would be captured once more. Edward pointed this out to his brother, but the boy just ran ahead, heading for a small hallway that seemed to have been sliced into the stone wall rather than built.

A curving staircase appeared at the end of the hallway, cut in a tight circle, with no arrow slits or lighted torches hanging from its bare walls. The terrible blackness was off-putting, but just then Richard's stomach growled demandingly, and he stepped forward fearlessly, into the dark.

Edward hesitated, sure that they would not find the kitchens buried deep in the bowels of the White Tower. Just as he opened his mouth to call to his brother, he heard the sound of heavy footsteps approaching behind him.

The ugly, pockmarked face of Miles Forest appeared around the corner of the hallway. "Green! Green! I found 'em! Oi told ye they'd be here somewheres."

Edward saw the shoe in Forest's hand and recognized it as Richard's. Sure he could only delay the inevitable, and wishing he'd had the foresight to arm himself with one of the broken lances so that he could at least give a good accounting of himself in a fight, the young king plunged into the darkness, his hands outstretched to balance himself against the narrow, curving walls as he followed where his younger brother had led.

He could hear Forest cursing as the heavy man struggled to negotiate the narrow, winding staircase, and he called out to his brother to hurry, for their capture was imminent. His feet all but flying, Edward ran forward, his palms scraped raw by the rough-cut ragstone, until he nearly overran Richard in his haste.

Grabbing the younger boy's hand, Edward pushed on, Forest and Green in close pursuit, the damnable, dark staircase seeming to have no end, until at last a small bluish light appeared below them.

"We're in the basket now," Edward told his brother, sure that the strange blue light came from torches held by soldiers loyal to his uncle.

Yet they continued down the staircase, for any fate had to be better than one to be found at the hands of Miles Forest, and they would much rather throw themselves on the swords of the king's guards than have their last sight on earth be the toothless grin of that same horrible man.

They reached the end of the staircase at last, to find themselves in a small, odd-shaped room that had no windows or doors. The light grew bluer and seemed to rise to meet them, swirling around their ankles like morning mist on a country pond, and Richard clung to his brother, his young eyes alight with unanswerable questions.

There were no windows, and yet there was light. There were no torches, no soldiers. They were alone in the strange chamber. Alone, safe from Green and Forest, who now stood frozen on the bottom step just outside the mist, watching, their mouths agape.

The blue mist swirled faster, rising to the boys' knees, past their waists, over their heads. They were enveloped by the cool mist, sheltered by it, comforted by it. Nothing existed beyond the mist, no stone walls, no gaolers, no thin gruel or straw pallets. The world outside the mist had ceased to exist.

Edward looked down at his brother, holding him as tight as he dared, for he could barely see him. Did Richard feel the peace that he felt? Did he feel the sense of adventure, adventure such as they had never known, growing deep in his chest? Fear fled, to be replaced by the sure knowledge that God, or their father, or some sorceress like Jane Shore, their father's beautiful mistress, had come to save them, to whisk them away to a better place.

"Feel it, Dickon. Feel it! We're safe now—safe at last!" Edward declared with all assurance, and then he threw back his head and laughed.

Chapter 1

LONDON, 1992

 "Ladies and gentlemen, good afternoon, and may I welcome you to Her Majesty's Royal Palace and Fortress, the Tower of London. If you will just step to your right and form a queue, a tour guide will join you presently." Bowing in dismissal, the plump, brightly dressed guard, who looked much like a red Delicious apple in a fuzzy top hat, turned to greet a group of camera-carrying Japanese tourists that was just straggling through the gate. "Ladies and gentlemen, good afternoon, and may I welcome you to Her Majesty's—"

Cassandra Kelley took her place in line behind Miss Smithers—a talkative, nearly oppressively cheerful retired librarian from Omaha currently on her third tour of England—careful to avoid the sharp point of the lady's umbrella, an accessory she herself had shunned in favor of optimism, which might not keep her dry if the unseasonably warm March day turned soggy, but at least did not have to be lugged from place to place in her already heavy bag.

Looking around the large yard at the sharp-eyed Tower ravens that seemed as numerous as molting pigeons in a Manhattan park, Cassandra grimaced, struck yet again by the curious English penchant for hanging starkly printed signs on everything from cannons to trees. Dungeons, she read on a forbidding-looking building off to her left. Be-

side it could be seen a similarly constructed sign that
pointed the way to the public rest rooms. The Tower
might once have been a forbidding fortress and terrible
prison, but the signs sure took a lot of the romance out
of the place.

Cassandra shifted her weight onto her right foot, silently cursing herself for thinking she could tramp across
London all day in high heels. She bent to rub her left
ankle, thankful the tour's next stop would be King's
Road, where she should be able to find a shoe store
somewhere among the trendy dress shops and sidewalks
littered with unisex creatures sporting spiked pink hair
and safety pins in their cheeks.

Cassandra, who hadn't been part of a group since
she'd daringly walked out on the National Honor Society
in her sophomore year of high school, felt uncomfortable being a member of this rigidly organized tour. She
would have preferred to investigate the city on her own
if only she had more time, probably giving the Tower a
miss, but she was in England for the London Book Fair,
and only for the weekend.

As the only editor from Wilmont at the Fair, she as-
sumed Sam Baxter had thought he was giving her a plum
assignment—though he was also killing two birds with
one rock. Cassandra had been given the trip as a bonus
for landing a hot prospect for a three-book contract, but
now she had to man their booth at the Book Fair. She
was smart enough to know that she'd better have her
happy, smiling face on show in front of the company
banner every minute the Fair was open. If she didn't,
she'd be sure to find herself Wilmont's representative at
the next writers' conference in Podunk, Kansas—popu-
lation eighty-three.

"All right, ladies and gentlemen. May I have your attention, please? My name is Olivia Hammond, and I shall
be your tour guide as we take a stroll through the Tower,

the shining bastion of nine hundred years of English history. Please step lively, as we have a good deal of territory to cover.''

Cassandra peered around Miss Smithers and saw a pert, rosy-cheeked teenager—the sort that could have peddled three hundred boxes of Girl Scout cookies without breaking a sweat—moving toward a wide flight of steps leading to, if she had heard correctly, the White Tower, an immense stone building that wasn't white at all. Adjusting the strap on her large canvas shoulder bag, Cassandra took a deep breath, fought back the urge to quit the tour, and followed.

Miss Hammond's staccato speech that sounded almost canned was nevertheless interesting, beginning with a stop at the base of a nondescript stone staircase, at which time she told of the renovation in the late 1600s that had yielded a large trunk containing the remains of two boys thought to be the Royal Princes, who had perished in the Garden Tower—now aptly dubbed the Bloody Tower—some centuries earlier.

The chest and bones were gone, of course, the bodies transferred to Westminster to be reinterred in the Chapel of King Henry VII, so there was little to see—except the prerequisite sign, of course.

A squat little woman at the back of the line could be heard lamenting the sad demise of the Royal Princes as her husband grunted, ''Oh, for Christ's sake, Alice. They've been dead for five hundred years. Who cares anymore? I want to see those damned jewels you've been hollering about.'' Cassandra smiled and shook her head, pitying Alice for having married the original Ugly American.

The guide's declaration that the princes supposedly had been murdered on the orders of King Richard III sparked a lively debate headed by Miss Smithers, who obviously did care. She championed Shakespeare's version of the king as a hunchbacked monster. Her initial declaration had prompted an immediate rebuttal from Stosh Polanski, a plumbing contractor from Pittsburgh. Stosh's money was on Henry Tudor as the man behind the deaths.

Cassandra, disliking the feeling that she was agreeing with Alice's husband, really couldn't have cared less either way. Medieval history, with all its various competing kings and beheadings, had always confused her. She had learned it all by rote for her college exams and then promptly forgotten it. All she really knew or cared about now was that there were a hell of a lot of steps inside the White Tower.

"If you will please follow me?" Miss Hammond chirped as the group began showing signs of becoming a mob. "There's much more to see, I promise you." The group set off once more, Alice's husband hanging behind, grumbling under his breath.

A half hour later, at the sight of yet another staircase, this one leading to an ancient chapel, Cassandra leaned against a sign calling attention to a particularly unappealing Elizabethan chair, waving Miss Smithers on her way as the woman looked back at her in question. "I'll just rest here a moment and then I'll join you when you come back down," Cassandra lied with a smile. She was not about to tell the librarian that she planned to desert the tour and go on the hunt for some Reeboks—half afraid that the energetic woman might volunteer to carry her on her back for the remainder of the tour.

Once the last tourist had disappeared up the spiral staircase, Cassandra lowered herself gingerly into the chair, sighing as the action relieved some of the pressure on her throbbing toes. She shivered; the air inside the large stone chamber was cold even on this sunny day in what passed for an early English spring.

As the footsteps of another small herd of tourists echoed from below, Cassandra stood, looking for one of the neatly printed EXIT signs, sure that the guide would frown on her plan to go off on her own. It was no good; the exit was also the entrance, and in a moment a new group would be upon her. Turning about, Cassandra saw a narrow hallway cordoned off by a velvet rope, a sign above the door stating that entrance was not permitted.

Cassandra hesitated. If she stepped around the rope she could hide in the hallway until the approaching tour joined her own group upstairs in the chapel, and then sneak out the way she had come. The plan seemed feasible—for Sheila Cranston, her friend all through grammar and high school. Sheila had possessed just the correct mixture of daring, larceny, and panache to carry off any sort of harebrained scheme.

But, Cassandra had learned to her sorrow, a person had to be born with those dubious virtues. They could not be learned. She always got caught. When she had skipped school to go to the local fair, the Ferris wheel had broken down—with Cassandra sitting in the highest gondola. When she had smoked her first cigarette in an alley behind Feinstein's Bakery, Father Burke had walked by, out on an evening stroll with his dog, Judas—who had shown his resemblance to his namesake by barking loudly until she had been forced from her hiding place to listen to a ten-minute sermon from the good priest, who then, not bound by the laws of the confessional, had damn near broken the sound barrier racing back to the rectory to telephone her mother.

Her luck hadn't gotten any better as she grew older. Hell, the night she had slipped Brad Renshaw into her dorm room, the damned building caught fire!

She shook her head. She wasn't ten anymore, or sixteen, or even twenty. She was twenty-five years old, had been living on her own in Manhattan for nearly four years, and had just been made a full editor at Wilmont, for crying out loud. She could do whatever she wanted! Cassandra made a face, knowing she was getting carried away. Well, maybe she couldn't do everything—like Sheila, who was training to be an astronaut—but she should at least be able to manage hiding in an out-of-bounds hallway without setting off an international incident.

With a toss of her head, done in imitation of Sheila, whose long, sleek, naturally blond hair did much more justice to the motion than Cassandra's cropped black curls, she hopped over the velvet rope—and nearly tumbled headfirst down the curving flight of stone steps hidden behind the first quick turn of the short hallway.

"That was very good, Grace—a daring acrobatic move accomplished with all your usual flair for the stupid," she grumbled as she looked down at her ruined pantyhose and scraped knees, then righted herself by bracing her hands against the narrow stone walls. Her voice echoed slightly in the depths below her and she leaned forward, trying to see into the darkness.

She took a single step ahead, then moved back two, her heart pounding. The staircase had a nearly overpowering appeal that she could not explain, especially as it was nearly pitch-black and she wasn't a particular fan of the dark. Remembering that curiosity—and horny "Brad the Bod" Renshaw—had gotten her put on probation for a whole semester, she fought the sudden, nearly overwhelming need to descend the staircase and see what lay at its end.

Behind her, she could hear the tour guide giving the new group of tourists the same word-for-word spiel as her guide had done earlier, waxing poetic over the Elizabethan chair that had, while Cassandra sat in it at least, proved to be extremely uncomfortable. No wonder those Elizabethans had had such good posture. It was impossible to slouch on such a hard chair without sliding ignominiously to the floor.

She could hear the group moving on toward the steps to the chapel. In just another minute she would be free to make her escape. She slowly counted to ten, nervously tapping one foot. "—nine, ten," she ended, willing her feet to move. She looked down at her toes. "Hey, fellas, I said—*ten.*"

It was no use. She was going somewhere all right, but it wasn't *up.* She had to know what lay at the bottom of this staircase.

Plunging a hand into her canvas bag, she pushed aside her two recently purchased guidebooks, her wallet, three lipsticks, a small zipper bag, two candy bars, the stale, opened pack of cigarettes she still carried in case she had a nicotine fit, and several miscellaneous items she was too lazy to sort through and discard, and finally located her lighter. She flicked it on, held it high above her head, and, her free hand braced against the rough stone, began the descent.

The narrow staircase turned in a tight circle to her right, with the stone steps coming out at an angle from the inside wall. Cassandra shivered in her vee-necked sweater and miniskirt as each step took her farther into the belly of the White Tower, away from the sunlight, and wished she hadn't left her jacket behind at the hotel. Her scraped knees stung with each step she took, but she had to go on, just like the courageous, dim-witted female in every bad Gothic novel she had ever read; the heroine who, all alone, and while the reader screamed "No! You *idiot,* don't go in there!" holds up her candle —or, in this case, her cigarette lighter—and enters the prerequisite *forbidden room.*

"When you get home, Cassie, you'd better make an appointment to see Mother's shrink," she told herself, speaking out loud in order to calm her racing heart, "because this is definitely getting *weird.*"

The lighter grew unbearably hot between her fingers and she let it go out, plunging herself into complete darkness. Anyone with a brain, she told herself, anyone with a single drop of common sense, would turn back now, locate sweet Miss Smithers and a couple of Band-Aids, and suffer through the rest of the tour.

It was impossible. She had to go on. The stairway had, ridiculously, become a small mountain to climb, on Cassandra's quest to prove to herself that she could at last get away with breaking the rules. At least that's what she told herself. She certainly wasn't going to dwell on the growing feeling that she was no longer the commander of this particular expedition.

Bracing her hands against the walls, her steps unsteady as she fumbled for footholds on the narrow, uneven stones, Cassandra continued her descent until, to her great relief, she detected a soft bluish glow somewhere below her, lighting her way. Her relief was quickly tempered by the realization that someone had to have turned on the light and that, once again, she was going to be caught doing something she shouldn't be doing.

"So, what else is new?" She gave another defiant toss of her head and pushed on. No one was going to yell at her, or clap her in irons in the dungeon next to the rest rooms. After all, she was an American, and everyone knew Americans were just a little crazy.

The blue light grew brighter, but it didn't hurt her eyes. It was a soft, nonthreatening blue, not in the least harsh, and it seemed to rise around her from all sides rather than shine up at her. She felt warmed and comforted by the light, yet strangely excited. *How New Age,* Cassandra thought wildly. *Shirley MacLaine would love it.*

Looking down, she realized that she could no longer see her feet, for the light had somehow changed to a cool blue mist. *I must be near the water,* she told herself, searching for an explanation that wouldn't send her screaming for Miss Hammond.

Cassandra took three more steps before realizing that she was no longer on the stone staircase but had reached a small, oddly shaped room that had no windows. She looked about for one of the handy-dandy signs that would tell her where she was, but the mist had risen above her head and she couldn't see anything but blue.

Oh, God, I've really done it this time. Shirley might get off on this stuff, Cassie, but your knees are rattling —so if you're going to get hysterical, now's the time. She drew in a quick breath, not daring to move as the mist invaded her nose, her mouth, her ears, smothering her.

And then she was floating, no longer able to feel the hard stone floor beneath her feet. Clapping her hands over her eyes, and fighting the impulse to call for her mommy, Cassandra Louise Kelley, twenty-five-year-old woman of the world, threw back her head and *screamed.*

Chapter 2

Peregrine Walton stood stock-still, his fists jammed on his hips. "Marcus, you're insane. Totally insane. You *do* know that, don't you? I mean, I just thought—seeing as I'm your best friend and all—I believe it behooves me to point out that sad fact to you. Besides, it's too demmed cold to be ghost hunting. What's it doing, snowing in March? It shouldn't snow in March."

Marcus Pendelton, Marquess of Eastbourne, never broke stride as he hastened toward the White Tower, his greatcoat billowing around his tall body in the damp breeze that blew off the Thames. "Of course I'm insane, Perry. We've both known it for years. Though, of course, that guard over there may still be sadly unenlightened. Perhaps you should repeat your declaration. Only this time, bellow it. The fellow might be hard of hearing. Now, are you coming with me or are you going to run back to the coach, and huddle beneath a blanket like some thin-blooded old woman, a hot brick at your toes?"

Perry sighed deeply, his sensibilities sorely abused, and broke into a half run to catch up with his friend. His short arms waving wildly, he persisted: "All right, Marcus, all right. So you found this diary of your ancestor's —old Ferdie. That was months ago."

"*Freddie,* one of Edward IV's most loyal Squires for the Body," Marcus corrected, lightly bounding up the wide shallow stairs. "And it was last Christmas at Eastbourne, more than a year ago."

"Freddie," Perry amended, beginning to breathe heavily, for he was a half foot shorter and three stone heavier than his friend, and all this hustle and bustle was beginning to wear on him. "Whatever his name was, his diary certainly isn't some heretofore undiscovered Gospel. My God, Marcus, three fourths of the thing is devoted to a recitation of his drinking and wenching—and the fact that he believed regular bathing a sacrilege to be avoided at all costs. They must have been a smelly lot back then. Just because he included some drivel he supposedly heard from a drunken guard—I mean, think on it, Marcus!"

The marquess nodded to the guards outside the doors before passing into the White Tower, his long strides eating up ground as his heels echoed hollowly through the cavernous chambers. He was a frequent visitor, permission for his explorations having been given by the Regent himself, so he was unchallenged as he bounded up a stone stairway, his destination firm in his mind. "I have thought on it, Perry. Green, the guard, wasn't drunk—he was dying, all but delirious with some terrible brain fever, and a fervent convert into the bargain. It was a deathbed confession of terrible guilt, the memory of which had brought him low. A man in his condition loses the ability to lie."

Perry wasn't convinced. "All right, so this man, this Green—this bloody *saint*—was about to stick his spoon in the wall. But what about your ancestor, *mm?* How about Filthy Ferdie?"

"Filthy Freddie," Marcus pointed out automatically, his long strides again leaving Perry behind.

"Ferdie, Freddie—the man was a sot—and, out of his own mouth, a smelly sot at that! Everyone knows Richard had the Princes smothered. Their bones are lying in

Westminster ever since King Charlie had them dug up. I can't believe this claptrap about Henry Tudor and this man Green and his cohort—this Woods fellow—''

"Not Woods, Perry. Forest."

"Woods—Forest. And what's it to the point anyway, I say. Don't interrupt. You can't really have swallowed this faradiddle about them killing two servant boys and stuffin' 'em in a trunk in order to save their own necks? Blue lights in the White Tower? Disappearing Princes? Where did they disappear to, I ask you? Can you answer me that? I'd sooner think the Earth revolves around the sun."

Marcus, his darkly handsome face splitting in a grin, turned to his friend. The perspiring, red-faced Perry stood just behind him, wiping his forehead with a large white handkerchief, exhausted from the necessity of being forced to talk and climb at the same time. "Much as it pains me to point this out, Perry, the Earth does revolve around the sun."

Perry *harrumphed,* then plopped heavily into a large brocade Elizabethan chair that stood against a wall in the upper chamber and began fanning himself with the handkerchief. "Stap me, Marcus, of course it does," he declared importantly. "I knew that. I was just trying to make a point. There's no need to get huffy."

The marquess wasn't listening. Looking around the room only to assure himself that it was empty—for his many trips to the Tower had made him familiar with all its buildings—he proceeded to the small arch marking a rude, narrow hallway leading to a circular staircase.

"This has to be it, Perry. The strange passageway. I decided it months ago. It's the only one I can think of in the whole of the Tower that serves no real purpose, has no easily defined use. There's nothing below here save a single, oddly shaped room."

Perry shook his head. "If you already know all about

it, Marcus, why did you insist on coming here again? What could be here today that wasn't here last week, or last year? I told you we should have stayed at Eastbourne. I hate London in the winter. There's nothing to do but stagger around this drafty old pile, waiting for my best friend to break under the strain. It's not a pretty picture, I have to tell you, and I should think you'd be concerned for my feelings in the matter, if not for your own sanity. Damme, but it's cold as a tomb in here. Lady Sefton has sent us both invitations for the month. You know what we should do, Marcus, old chum? We should leave at once. You know it will be jolly good fun. Even Prinny might attend."

"If our dear Regent plans to attend, no one will miss either of us. Besides, he'd be bound to quiz me as to how my search is faring. I had to tell him I was looking for ancient treasure to get his permission to dig around in here, and he's so purse-pinched he believes me. I'll probably have to produce a bag of pearls from my own stock or some such trinket sooner or later, just to quiet him. Now, come on, Perry. You must have caught your breath by now. I can't explain it, but I have this almost overpowering feeling that I am finally close to an answer to Green's little fairy tale, as you call it. And the answer lies somewhere in that room. You see, I have formulated this theory—"

"Yes, yes, a theory. Of course you have. How wonderful for you, Marcus. You must feel very gratified. Tell you what, if you promise not to share it with me, I'll be with you shortly." Perry leaned back in the chair and spread his legs out in front of him, the action nearly sending him sliding to the floor. "Stupid chair. I just want to rest here for a moment," he said, pulling himself upright on the hard overstuffed seat.

Without waiting for Perry, Marcus plunged down the

hallway, grabbing up a torch to light his way down the long, spiraling staircase to the small chamber.

Yes, he could feel it building, this strange urgency to see the chamber once more. His skin prickled, and he was aware of a certain light-headedness akin to the sensation he'd experienced at eighteen upon his initial sight of the dimpled Covent Garden warbler who eventually became his first mistress. Although he had learned to guard his emotions—and his purse—with more care in the ensuing dozen years, he could still remember the feeling. Something extraordinary awaited him in the chamber below. He would bet his best bays and curricle on it.

He was nearly to the bottom of the stairs when he heard it. Actually, he could have been at the top of the stairs—or possibly still outside—and not missed it, for it had to be the most prodigiously *loud* scream he had ever heard, bouncing wildly off the stone walls to assault his ears from every direction.

Three seconds later Perry cannoned into Marcus's back, nearly sending the two of them tumbling down the remainder of the steps. "My God! Marcus—what *was* that? Banshees? It sounded like a pig caught in a grate."

Marcus held the torch high and used his free hand to brace himself against the rough ragstone walls. "It was a female," he said, the pressure he'd felt in his chest all day nearly crushing him. He reached into his high-top Hessians and pulled out his stiletto. "Come on, Perry, stay close behind me."

"Well, if that don't beat the Dutch. And where did you think I was going to be—in *front* of you?" Perry, bent nearly in half, held on to Marcus's coattails as they negotiated the last turn in the staircase and entered the small chamber. Once his feet were safely on the stone floor he peeked out from behind Marcus, who had replaced the stiletto in his boot and was now standing very still and straight.

"Good Lord, Marcus," Perry exclaimed, bug-eyed as a strange blue mist evaporated into the air. "You were right. It is a woman. And the chit's *naked!*"

Cassandra heard a male voice and knew she had been discovered breaking the rules. She should have realized she wouldn't get away with it; she *never* got away with it. Still pressing her hands against her eyes, she struggled to envision how Sheila would have handled the situation, for as surely as Cassandra was freezing her pinched toes off in the damp room, facing possible disaster, Sheila give-'em-hell Cranston could have stepped in this same mud puddle of trouble and still come up smelling like a rose.

But she wasn't Sheila. She was Cassandra, and she'd have to fake it.

She lowered her hands to find that, thankfully, the strange, frightening blue mist had melted away and the small room was now lit by a brightly burning torch held by—"Oh, my God!"

Cassandra blinked, shook her head, then blinked again. She walked over to where the men were standing, the tall, handsome one very stiff and straight, the shorter, pudgy one seemingly trying to hide in the shadows behind his companion. "Hello there," she said, forcing a careless tone into her voice, hoping they would overlook her outburst. "I guess I'm out of bounds, aren't I, guys? I've heard of Mounties coming to the rescue, but we're not in Canada, are we? But don't you both look terrific! What are you dressed up for? I didn't know they gave performances here. Disney World comes to jolly old England, what?"

Cassandra shut her mouth, feeling as if she were giving her impersonation of Alice's Ugly American husband.

The men made no move to answer her, which convinced her she had been rude, if not unintelligible. Fear did that to a person, she reasoned, then pushed on, knowing she was behaving like a first-class idiot.

She inspected the two men and their anachronistic attire, walking fully around them before standing in front of them once more. "Regency Era, isn't it?" she asked conversationally, having taken note of their tight buckskins, trim jackets, and intricately tied starched neckcloths. "They're very good. I was an assistant editor of our Regency line for nearly two years, until just last month, actually, so that's why I recognize the clothes—from the cover art, you understand. Do you know it used to take those guys *hours* to get their neckcloths just right? You have to know a lot about that era in order to be an effective editor. I'm not surprised they chose to dress you in Regency clothes; it was quite a wonderful time in your history, wasn't it? Did you have to learn to tie them yourselves, or are those clip-ons—you know—like the ties?"

Still neither man spoke, although the tall one had begun to smile down at her in a most disconcerting way. The light cast by the torch he carried really wasn't very good and it cast weird, flickering shadows on the walls that were beginning to give her the creeps. The quiet, staring men were giving her the creeps. As a matter of fact, the whole cold, damp, dark place was getting on her nerves, and she longed for the bright lights and spiked pink hair of King's Road.

The men stood directly in front of the steps, keeping her from them, so Cassandra gave it another shot. "Did I tell you I'm an editor? A book editor, actually—the paperback kind. I work for Wilmont Publishing. In New York—that's in America. Silly me, you already knew that, didn't you? You probably haven't heard of us because we specialize in romances—no spy thrillers or anything—

for women, you understand. I've been moved to contemporaries now, but I really fell in love with England while working on our Mayfair line. I'm just here for the weekend, to peek in on your London Book Fair, but I'm coming back at the end of May with some friends of mine who—hey, look—I must be boring you. How about I come right to the point? I became separated from my tour group, and I seem to have lost my way while looking for the gift shop. I thought I'd buy a miniature headman's ax for my nephew, Todd. He's a bloodthirsty little bas—''

Cassandra's rambling monologue faltered, and she bit her lip a moment, struggling for composure. "You know, I had the strangest experience just now. It got all *foggy* in here and I couldn't see anything. I was really frightened—I may even have screamed.''

She wrinkled her nose as she grimaced. "All right, I admit it—I did scream. I guess you heard me and came charging to the rescue. Sorry about that. Well, anyway, as long as you're here, you guys wouldn't mind showing me the way to the gift shop, would you? You know, the *gift shop?* The *souvenir emporium?*''

This wasn't going well. As a matter of fact, it wasn't going anywhere at all. *"Um"*—she said timidly as the two men continued to stare at her as if she had been speaking a foreign language or something—"you *do* talk, don't you, fellas? Come to think of it, Mickey Mouse doesn't—speak, that is—he just dances around and has his picture taken with all the kids. That's a shame. I'd really love to hear you talk. I'm not arrested or anything, am I? Sam—Sam's my boss—well, anyway, he'll have a cow if I'm arrested. Oh, Lord, why can't I keep my mouth shut?''

The shorter man tugged on the other man's sleeve, looking up at his friend, his watery blue eyes wide. "You know what it is, Marcus—I think the chit's a witch. Do all witches talk so much? She's beginning to give me the headache. Do you think she'll turn us into toads?"

"Shut up, Perry," the taller man said quietly, still staring at Cassandra in a way that made her feel as if she were a particularly rare bug squashed between slides under a microscope. "Would you please be so kind as to give us your name, madam?"

Cassandra rolled her eyes. "Madam? Oh, brother, I *am* arrested. I knew it. I have to tell you something, guys, I don't think it's particularly sporting to have security guards dressed up like part of the show." She shook her head, disgusted with herself. "Here I am, all grown up, and I'm still getting called to the principal's office. Will I never learn? Madam! Nobody *ever* calls me madam."

"My apologies, *miss,*" the taller man amended promptly, handing the torch to the other man and removing his greatcoat, to place it around her shoulders. "Here, you must be cold, dressed as you are. And don't be frightened, my dear. You aren't under arrest."

"She should be, Marcus, tripping around London all but jay-naked like that. Either arrested or put to trod the stage. She's got nice enough legs for it, I'll give her that. If only she didn't talk so much."

"Perry, for God's sake, stifle yourself," the man called Marcus warned, smiling down at Cassandra, still with more assessing curiosity than kindness in his piercing green eyes. "Please excuse my friend, miss, as he has the most abominable habit of speaking before he thinks— when he bothers to think at all, having been forced to do it as a youth only to learn the process fatigued him most prodigiously. Allow me to handle the introductions. I'm Pendelton—Marquess of Eastbourne—and this is my very good friend, the Honorable Peregrine Walton. We're both perfectly harmless, I promise you. Tell me—who is this Mickey Mouse?"

He was the Marquess of Eastbourne? Sure, and she was

Madonna. *Who is Mickey Mouse?* What a silly question. Were these guys brought here from some time warp or something? Cassandra pulled the greatcoat more closely around her, Perry's avid stare making her feel decidedly underdressed. Was it her imagination, or had the temperature dropped thirty degrees?

"Thank you. My name is Kelley. Cassandra Kelley," she answered at last, believing she owed them at least that much.

Perry seemed to relax. "Irish, huh. That explains a lot. At least I guess it does. Never did know an Irishman that made a drop of sense, unless he was in his cups."

Cassandra gave the man a dirty look, then carefully hid her Irish temper. "I—I think I'd like to leave now, if you don't mind," she said, taking a step, terribly aware that she was all alone in the small room with two very strangely dressed men. "Miss Smithers will be missing me."

Marcus took a step as well, blocking her way. "Miss Smithers? Is she your chaperon, Miss Kelley? I'd like to meet her."

"My chaperon? Miss Smithers?" Cassandra laughed. "Hardly. She's a retired librarian from somewhere in Nebraska. No, I just met her today. Now, please, step aside."

"Nebraska? Precisely where in Ireland is that, Marcus, do you know? I don't think I've ever heard of the place." Perry, who had also taken a step forward, sighed, bent his head, and returned to his original spot. "I know, I know—'shut up, Perry.' I have to tell you, Marcus, this isn't the most jolly time you've ever shown me, stap me if it ain't. As a matter of fact, I might just go wait in the coach."

"Do that, Perry," Marcus said silkily.

"Don't do that, Perry," Cassandra warned quickly, grabbing at the man's arm and nearly dislodging the

torch as he shrank from her touch, "at least not without me. I, too, should like to wait in the coach. You do mean a bus, don't you? Is it a double-decker? I just arrived in London late last night and haven't had a chance to ride in one yet."

Did this Marcus, this mar*quess* or whatever he called himself, really believe she was going to stay in this dank room while his buddy, who seemed relatively harmless, took off? Right. Sure. She could see the headlines now: STUPID AMERICAN RAPED IN WHITE TOWER. No, thank you—not this stupid American!

Marcus held out his arm to block her way to the steps. "Not yet, I think, Miss Kelley. I have a few questions for you first."

Cassandra was getting angry. All right, so she had broken a rule. Big deal. Cervantes couldn't have had this much trouble with the whole of the Spanish Inquisition. Taking off the greatcoat, she threw it straight in Marcus's face. "Now, look, Mark, or whatever your name is, fun's fun and all that, but I want to leave now. I'm not entirely helpless, you know. I walk the streets of Manhattan alone. It's easy, you just walk with your head up and carry a big purse." She lifted her purse from her shoulder. "See? Big purse. Big, *heavy* purse. I have mace in here. Don't make me do something we'll both regret. Either arrest me or let me go—but either way, *I'm outta here.*"

"No, I don't think so, Miss Kelley," Marcus told her quietly and with enough conviction to make her long to choke him. "Not just yet. If you dare to step outside in those clothes, you'll either be hauled off to the nearest guardhouse or dragged away to Bedlam in your very own strait-waistcoat. Besides, you need me. We may need each other. I have been working on a scientific theory for quite some time now, and I think you may just have proved it. Humor me for a moment, if you please, my dear, and then I may allow you to leave. Tell me—what year is it?"

"What year is it?" Perry exclaimed in disgusted astonishment, slapping his palm against his forehead. "What *year* is it! Marcus—have you been drinking? It may only be March, but everyone knows it's the year of Our Lord, eighteen hundred and twelve!"

What? Cassandra thought her head would snap off, so quickly did she turn it about to gape at Peregrine Walton. She opened her mouth to speak, looked at Marcus—at his clothes—swallowed hard, and squeaked, *"Eighteen* —eighteen—*twelve?* Say, Perry, Marcus—you two haven't been smoking any funny cigarettes, have you?"

Marcus reached out a hand to steady her, his smile wide. He seemed to be extremely well pleased with her reaction to Perry's disclosure. "I'm right, Perry! It's just as I supposed! The 'benevolent blue mist' Green spoke of is the key, although I don't know why it appears when it does, or just how it *does* what it does. Green was right. Filthy Freddie was right. The Princes didn't die—they were merely whisked away to another, safer time!"

The Princes? Cassandra's head was spinning. He had to be talking about the Royal Princes, the ones who had been murdered in the Tower in—what had Miss Hammond said?—1480-something? Yes, Marcus had to be talking about the Royal Princes—only his theory was completely off the wall. Miss Smithers had said something about Richard III ordering the murders, but Stosh had argued his case for Henry Tudor—and she, fool that she was, hadn't seen a reason to care one way or the other.

Yet Marcus, the man now standing between her and the rest of the world, seemed to believe the Princes had been time travelers, and hadn't been murdered at all. Who said history was boring? Cassandra closed her eyes and put a hand to her mouth, praying she was really in her hotel room, having a bad dream.

"This isn't quite the time for a maidenly faint, Miss Kelley." Marcus was holding her by the shoulders again. "Pay attention. You came into the White Tower today— or whatever day it was—and then found your way down here, alone, to this room. I wonder why. Perhaps some supernatural force brought you here. I know I had the most overpowering need to come here today myself. You saw the blue mist. We glimpsed faint remnants of it ourselves. Are you listening, Miss Kelley? Am I right? You mentioned fog when we first stumbled upon you. It was a thick blue fog, wasn't it? *Wasn't it?*" Marcus gave her a single, quick shake.

She nodded vigorously, unable to find her voice. She'd have been sure she was dreaming, if Marcus's strong hands weren't holding her so tightly.

"Quickly, Miss Kelley—what year do *you* think it is? It has to be some years in the future, as your clothes are most extraordinary and unlike anything I've seen in any books. Are you from this planet?" He turned his head to address Perry. "There could be life on other planets, you know, Perry. I've studied all the writings on the subject. Or perhaps the moon—although I doubt it." He concentrated once more on Cassandra, who was trembling violently under his hands. "A year, Miss Kelley, I implore you—you must give me a year!"

"Humor him, Miss Kelley," Perry suggested, winking at her. "He never gives up, you know, once he has got his teeth into something."

Cassandra felt her head moving back and forth in mute denial. Marcus was lying to her—he had to be lying. My God, the man was talking about time travel! Nobody traveled through time—not really. Sure, Michael J. Fox had done it, but that was Hollywood magic, and she wasn't even sure what a DeLorean looked like! She couldn't have traveled through time. Okay—*Sheila*, maybe, but *not* her!

Cassandra opened her eyes, praying Marcus and Perry had disappeared. They hadn't. If this was a dream, it was a real doozy. "Take me upstairs," she ordered weakly, determined to find a way out of her nightmare.

She'd go up the steps, see the EXIT sign, and the sign over the uncomfortable Elizabethan chair, and all the signs out in the yard, and then she'd wake up.

"If that's what it takes." Marcus grabbed her hand, pulling her along after him willy-nilly as all three retraced their steps to the large chamber above them, Perry falling behind halfway up the steep steps to lean against the wall and catch his breath.

Once in the upper chamber, Marcus grabbed Cassandra by the shoulders once more and pushed her toward a nearby window. "If I'm correct, London should look different to you than it does to me, even if the only difference could be that Nash has finally stopped his infernal building from one end of the city to the other. Tell me what you see, Miss Kelley. Then tell me if this is what you expected to see."

Cassandra looked behind her and saw that there was no EXIT sign above the large archway, no second sign above the ugly Elizabethan chair. "Oh, God," she whispered, closing her eyes. "This isn't funny anymore. I *really* want to wake up now."

Marcus grabbed the back of her head and all but slammed her face into the thick windowpane. "Take a good look, Miss Kelley, and then tell me what year you think it is."

"*Um*, Marcus," Perry interrupted from behind them, "don't you think you're being a trifle rough with the girl? I mean, maybe she's just a little confused—perhaps slightly short of furnishings in her upper rooms? Possibly even dotty?"

Cassandra opened her eyes to look out at the city of London beyond the walls of the Tower.

There were no bright red double-decker buses wearing signs that said ENERGY IS OUR BUSINESS. BRITISH GAS AND ELECTRICITY.

There were no racing black cabs, no Royal Mail trucks with their golden crests.

There were no power lines, no traffic lights, no skyscrapers, no garish neon signs blinking at her from Piccadilly.

There was, in fact, barely any London, at least not as she could remember seeing it sprawled out in all directions as she had looked down from the airplane when they circled the city.

There was a lot of smoke, and a quantity of dirty snow, and a few carriages moving along the roadways.

Everything was different, very different. The only things that remained the same were the clothes of the guards and the number of squawking Tower ravens in the yard.

Cassandra pinched herself, hard. It hurt. It hurt because she wasn't asleep. She wasn't dreaming. She was lost in Regency England.

"Excuse me, please, but I think I'm going to be sick," she announced quietly, unable to tear her gaze from the unfamiliar scene.

"No, you're not, Miss Kelley," Marcus commanded, whirling her about to face him—just as if he could gain control over her stomach. "At least not until you tell me what year you believe it is."

Wildly, with no rhyme or reason, Cassandra remembered the first words Perry had spoken. "You don't burn witches anymore, do you? I mean, you're past that over here, aren't you? I think we stopped sometime in the sixteen or seventeen hundreds or so."

Marcus leaned down to look deep into her eyes.

"We're quite civilized for the most part, I assure you. Isn't that right, Perry? We don't burn witches above twice a week anymore."

"Marcus, for shame," Perry admonished, collapsing into the Elizabethan chair and grabbing at the arms so that he didn't slide to the floor. "Damme, if this chair ain't the most uncompromising bit of torture I've seen since last I visited my aunt's ancient pile in Surrey. Marcus, you mustn't tell such clankers. No, Miss Kelley, we don't burn witches anymore. Not unless you want us to, that is, although it puzzles me why anyone would want such a thing. It would have to be terribly uncomfortable, I should think—burning, that is."

"Perry is every inch the gentleman. He tells the truth, for one thing and, even if he does sit in the presence of a lady, he does it only because he is overcome with fatigue, and then makes sure he won't be comfortable." The marquess slipped his greatcoat around Cassandra's shoulders once more, whether because she was shivering in the cold or to hide her clothing from the view of any passersby, she wasn't sure. "I promise you, nothing bad will happen to you. As of now you are under my protection. Now, please, tell me what year you thought it was before you entered that chamber."

Cassandra looked up at Marcus, her head reeling. It fit. It all fit. Marcus's elegant speech. Perry's eccentricities. The scene outside the window. "It is—it *was* nineteen —*nineteen ninety-two*. March twelfth, nineteen ninety-two," Cassandra gasped quickly, just before she lost her lunch of fish and chips all over the Marquess of Eastbourne's shiny black Hessians.

Chapter 3

Cassandra sat on the edge of her seat in the large black coach, her head darting from side to side as she peered through the rapidly descending twilight at the buildings lining the slushy roadway. She was still frightened, for only a complete numskull wouldn't be, but she couldn't help being intrigued as well. It seemed as if every Regency novel she had ever edited had just sprung to life in full, living color.

The scene outside the coach reminded her of something out of a movie, except it looked more real than any movie she had ever seen. The beggars wore real rags, and the few well-dressed people she saw moved with regal grace, even as the ladies' hems dragged in the dirty snow and the men minced through icy puddles in shiny boots that reached to their knees.

She saw a peddler on one corner, his head topped by at least a dozen precariously balanced hats, and watched while a young boy, his dirty feet bare, ran ahead of a well-dressed man as they crossed an intersection, the lad sweeping a path clear for his customer. The smell of roasting chestnuts and not-too-fresh fish and a dozen other odors filtered into the coach. "Whew!" Cassandra reached into her pocket, pulled out a tissue, and held it to her nose.

Peregrine Walton, having been at last convinced that

Cassandra had been somehow brought to the Tower from another time, was now totally fascinated by her and had been staring at her unceasingly since they had departed some fifteen minutes earlier. "Did you see that, Marcus? Huh? Did you see that? Marvelous, ain't it? It can *smell!* You know, I've just had a thought. Strange you didn't think of it, Marcus, you being the smart one. Perhaps, in the interest of science, of course, don't you think you ought to begin writing these things down?"

Marcus sighed, adjusting his shirt cuffs. He should have been shivering from the cold, with Cassandra still in possession of his greatcoat, but he made no move to cover himself with the blanket that lay on the seat beside him. "I'll take your suggestion under consideration, Perry," he said quietly, then added, "and, Perry—Miss Kelley is a young lady, not an *it.*"

Cassandra hadn't heard the exchange, for she had spied a woman bustling hurriedly along the flagway, wrapped nearly head to foot in enough ermine to send the Animal Rights activists screaming to their congressmen. A small footman in a most outlandish red livery labored along behind, trying his best to keep up with her, his arms full of packages. "Oh, look at her! She may not be especially beautiful, but that fur had to cost a fortune. Is she a well-known hostess?"

Marcus leaned forward to peer out the window, then sat back, a smile teasing the corners of his mouth. "In a manner of speaking, Miss Kelley. That is Miss Harriette Wilson. She's a—well, let me see—how can I put this delicately?"

"Harriette Wilson? You're kidding!" Cassandra pressed her nose to the glass as the coach moved past the woman. "I remember her from one of the books I edited for Mayfair—that's the name of our Regency line, remember. And I've always loved learning about your country—or at least most of it, when I wasn't getting

confused on all your kings. I majored in English literature
in college, and minored in world history. Harriette Wilson. How about that! She's a courtesan, isn't she? A
strumpet—one of the Fashionable Impure—capital *F*,
capital *I*. She's the one Wellington told to 'publish and
be damned' when she threatened to write about their
affair in her memoirs.''

"Memoirs?" Perry sat forward so quickly he nearly
toppled to the floor. "Harriette's scribbling a book? Oh,
never say that, miss." He turned to Marcus. "Good old
Harry wouldn't really do anything so unsporting, would
she?"

Marcus smiled. "I don't know, Perry, but it seems Miss
Kelley does. Why don't you ask her?"

Cassandra rubbed at her forehead, trying to remember
everything she knew about Harriette Wilson. It wasn't
much. "It had to be some time after the war—once Wellington returned from Waterloo—when Harriette
needed money and decided to write a book, only she
wouldn't write about anyone who paid to buy her silence. That's when Wellington said—"

"After the war? Marcus, did you hear that? Miss Kelley
says the war is going to be over." Perry reached over to
tug at her arm, as she was already looking out the window once more, her curiosity completely overriding her
fear as with each turn of the coach's wheels more of the
history of Regency England rolled into her head. "Who
won, Miss Kelley? Us or Boney? I'm convinced we did—I
mean we will, because we didn't win yet, did we? Lord,
Marcus, but I'm confused."

Cassandra looked at Peregrine Walton, then at Marcus.
"Should I say?" she asked. "I mean, what if I shouldn't
be telling you what's going to happen? I might change
the course of history, or blow up the cosmos or something. I can remember what happened in *Back to the
Future* when Marty McFly messed around with history.

Everything worked out pretty well for him, but I might not be so lucky. After all, it's not as if I have a script-writer here with me, do I? I'm kind of winging it—God! I still can't believe this is really happening!"

Perry threw up his hands, clapping them over his ears. "Ask a simple question! There she goes again, Marcus, spouting gibberish. She's not going to be sick here in the coach, is she? I don't think I'd like that above half."

Cassandra reluctantly sat back in her seat. "No, Perry, I'm not going to be sick again. Why should I? I'm lost in the past, with no money, no clothes, and no way of getting back to where I belong." She shivered violently. "Lost in the past—it sounds like a book title. A *bad* book title. I still can't believe it. Even if I do somehow find my way back, I'm sure to miss the Book Fair—which will cost me my job—and if I were so stupid as to tell any-body the reason I missed it was because a blue fog landed me in Regency England, I'd be locked up some-where where all I'd get to do all day is weave baskets and rat on my mother about my supposedly dysfunc-tional childhood."

She dropped her forehead into her hands. "Oh, God, I really think I don't feel very well."

Marcus turned to look at his friend. "Happy now, Perry? All in all, Miss Kelley has enough on her plate without your questions. I suggest you do your best not to upset her further."

"Me?" Perry exploded, grabbing at his chest with both hands. *"I* upset her? Is that right? And I suppose I'm the one who whisked her out of the Tower and into this coach without so much as a by-your-leave, jabbering nineteen to the dozen about how you were taking her straight back to Grosvenor Square to *examine* her? I've seen the things you keep in those horrid bottles in your study, Marcus. I'm surprised the girl ain't fainting with fear."

Cassandra lowered her hands. "No, I was wrong. I'm not feeling sick. I think I'm actually beginning to feel hungry. I'd kill for a hamburger and fries, but I don't suppose you have those yet, do you? Never mind, of course you don't. Wait a minute—I'm sure I have a couple of candy bars in my purse. Pass it over to me, would you?"

Marcus shook his head. "Your satchel remains with me for the moment, Miss Kelley. I will want to examine and catalog everything inside it, in your presence, of course. In the interests of science."

Cassandra's stomach grumbled in protest. "In the interests of science, or in your interest? Now, look, Marcus, old sport—I mean, my lord—don't you think you're carrying this examining business a little far? It's only a Hershey bar—*chocolate candy,* for crying out loud—not a microfilm showing our missile bases in Western Europe."

Perry seemed to have taken in only as much of Cassandra's last statements as interested him, and quickly leaned over to make a grab for the canvas bag. "Candy, you say? Chocolate? You know what, Marcus, I don't think it would do any great harm if we each take a taste of it. I'll even go first."

Marcus pulled the purse out of Perry's reach. "Control yourself, Perry. Goodfellow will have our supper waiting when we reach Grosvenor Square."

Cassandra slumped into the corner, the fur wrap that had so excited her when she had first seen it pushed under her chin. "Nine to five it's baked eels in parsley sauce or some other weird Regency dish I've read about. I should have done my time traveling in Versailles. At least the French know how to cook," she grumbled, earning herself a commiserating smile from Perry, whose family's French chef—the one his late mother had been forced to let go years earlier when her husband ran

off to the West Indies with that hussy—had had a real
way with sauces.

A sooty darkness began to settle over London as the
coach turned yet another corner and finally halted in
front of a tall white portico, flambeaux burning at either
side of the wide doorway of the Eastbourne mansion.
After a liveried servant put down the steps, Marcus
alighted from the coach and reached up a hand to assist
Cassandra in her descent to the flagway. She moved to
step down and the greatcoat parted to the waist, exposing her bare legs to the servant, whose eyes all but
popped out of his head as he breathed, "Now 'ere's a
treat!" and broke into a wide, appreciative grin—doing
wonders for her ego.

A moment later the trio stepped inside the black-and-
white-tiled foyer of the mansion. Marcus barked orders
to a gray-haired man who began busily snapping his fingers at several young footmen already hastening to help
the gentlemen with their hats and gloves. Cassandra,
busily inspecting the chandelier that hung above a large
round table in the center of the foyer, thought that it
looked like the ones that hung in her favorite depart-
ment store in Manhattan—and immediately opened her
mouth and said so. When one of the footmen approached her, Marcus dismissed the lot of them, telling
only the gray-haired butler, Goodfellow, to remain.

"This is Miss Kelley," he told the butler before turning
to stare intently at Perry as he rushed through the lie he
had concocted on their way home. "She is Mr. Walton's
distant relation who has just arrived unexpectedly from
America—having escaped to one of our ships through
the blockade—and she has had a most terrible accident,
costing her all of her luggage as well as her chaperon,
and leaving her without a single change of clothes."

Goodfellow bowed to his master. "How terrible for
her, m'lord," he offered.

The marquess, Cassandra noticed out of the corner of her eye, had the good grace to blush. "Yes, well, thank you, Goodfellow. I assume my sister did not haul everything off with her when she married that mincing ignoramus and left for India? Good. In that case, I shall escort Miss Kelley to Lady Georgina's room and get her settled. I would like Rose to attend her within the hour."

Cassandra felt herself being guided toward a long staircase that led up to the first floor. Turning back to look at the butler, she added, "And please have Rose bring me something to eat—cold sliced beef and some bread, so I can make a sandwich—and also something cold to drink. Don't forget the salt and pepper if you have it, and some butter, since I don't know if you have mayonnaise. *Please,*" she reiterated sincerely as Marcus's hand pushed at the small of her back.

"Sir?" Goodfellow questioned, clearly not about to take orders from a woman, and a very strange woman at that.

"Do as she says, Goodfellow, please—and quickly," Marcus commanded tightly. "Impertinent little piece, aren't you?" he asked a moment later as they ascended the staircase.

"When my stomach's involved, yes," Cassandra answered, knowing she had probably shocked the butler, but she was still stinging under Marcus's refusal to hand over her Hershey bar. She allowed herself to be propelled along the hallway and into a room that appeared so achingly feminine that she fell in love with it on sight. She walked around the room, touching a Dresden figurine that sat on a side table, then peeked out one of the windows that overlooked the Square before turning back to Marcus, her dark eyes twinkling. "This belonged to Georgina—to your sister? It's lovely. We have our antiques in museums, and re-creations of this sort of furniture in my time, but nothing beats the real McCoy up close and personal, does it? I'll say one thing, my lord, I seem to have lucked out meeting you. I mean, just think of it—my first encounter could have been with a chimney sweep. This mansion. All those servants. You're filthy rich, aren't you?"

Marcus closed the door and locked it. "And you're unbelievably outspoken and vulgar, my dear, not to mention being most unbecomingly obsessed with money," he said pleasantly enough, walking toward a large cabinet that sat in one corner. "I can see that woman's basest human nature has been allowed its head in your time. Tell me, when was it that my sex so foolishly let go their grip on the reins?"

Cassandra longed to hit him. "And what makes you think you men were doing such a swell job? Two world wars, Korea, Vietnam—" she began heatedly before realizing that she must seem very forward to him. She wasn't a complete idiot—she knew she was a far cry from an ordinary Regency miss, from someone like his sister, Lady Georgina, who had probably grown up spending her days water painting and embroidering slippers and going for long walks with her governess.

She bowed her head, counted to ten, and tried again. "I'm sorry, my lord. I must have sounded like some money-grubbing monster, but I didn't mean it. I never did make a good first impression. I know a lot about you —about your time, I mean—but you don't know anything about me, or about my time. Women are considered the equals of men in the twentieth century—although we are still dealing with that 'glass ceiling' business and equal pay for equal work. As a matter of fact, England has even had a woman prime minister— and a damn good one, even if she did seem to have a schoolgirl crush on Ronnie Reagan."

Marcus's head snapped back as if he had been slapped. "A female PM? That's preposterous! A woman attempting the enormous job done by our Spencer Perceval? We Englishmen would never allow such ridiculousness. Miss Kelley, we can't help each other if you refuse to be serious. And here"—he tossed her a gown he had found in the cabinet—"go behind the screen and put this on before Rose comes knocking on the door. Servants talk, and I don't want word of your bizarre appearance to become the topic of conversation at every dinner table in town."

Cassandra deftly caught the sprigged muslin gown and held it up in front of her. It was typical of the time, she knew, a high-waisted, ankle-long concoction that would have looked more at home in a museum, or at a costume party. "Would you look at all those buttons? Zippers haven't been invented yet, have they? How am I supposed to do them up by myself?"

"Zippers? What are zippers?"

Cassandra sighed, wishing she had kept her thoughts to herself. She was beginning to feel like a walking encyclopedia, and she didn't much care for the feeling—especially on an empty stomach. Besides, her sore feet had traveled with her through time and she'd soon be willing to kill in order to be rid of her shoes. She walked over to Marcus, her hands going to the side zipper on her miniskirt. "Here. Watch this—the amazing Cassandra," she said, keeping the single button closed as she lowered and raised the zipper, laughing as Marcus bent down to examine the thin, plastic-toothed invention. "Opened—closed. Closed—opened! Boggles the mind, doesn't it?" she asked, stepping back as she closed the zipper one last time.

Marcus reached out to grab her arm. "That will be quite enough, Miss Kelley." He had seen the zipper move, opening and closing magically as she drew it up and down. He had also been given a brief glimpse of two small patches of soft white skin and a thin wisp of some silky material stretching crosswise seamlessly halfway between them. "I'm no prude, but I must suggest you step behind the screen before I am convinced the world you have come from consists solely of degenerates."

Too late, Cassandra realized what she had done: lowering the zipper had momentarily exposed her nearly bare hip and skimpy underpants.

Ready to apologize again, she stopped, knowing it would be a mistake. If Marcus was upset, that was his problem, not hers. Her French-cut swimsuit covered no more than her panties, and no one had ever found anything wrong with her swimsuit. If he insisted upon talking about degenerates, maybe he should look to his own time, an era that branded a woman an outcast if she dared to steal a single kiss in the gardens—while all the men paraded their mistresses at the opera.

She looked at Marcus levelly, recognizing for the first time that the dark-haired, green-eyed marquess was an extremely good-looking man. A real Regency hero. "Don't talk to me about degenerates, my lord. You're not even supposed to be in here," she told him coldly. "This *is* my bedroom—I mean, my bedchamber—now isn't it?"

"I want your clothing." Marcus uttered the statement from between clenched teeth, convincing Cassandra that she had at last succeeded in embarrassing him. "If you wish me to believe you are a lady, you'll go behind that screen and get undressed."

Cassandra cocked her head to one side, considering this latest order. He had been giving her orders ever since they met, as a matter of fact, and she was beginning to resent it. If, as she believed the Regency phrasing went, she hoped to "begin as she planned to go on," Cassandra knew she had reached an important moment in her relationship with Marcus Pendelton. For however long she might be trapped in this ridiculous time warp, be it a few hours or forever, their relationship would be based on this first important confrontation.

"All right, Marcus," she said sweetly, lifting her hands to her waist. "You want my clothing?" She tugged the sweater off over her head and threw it at him. "Here you go, sport—knock yourself out!"

Marcus caught the sweater automatically, then looked at Cassandra. She stood in front of him, the high swell of her breasts barely covered by a thin wisp of pink silk that left her stomach bare above the ridiculous scrap of wool that didn't reach as far as her knees. His mind took in the exquisite form of her body—her firm, high breasts rising above the strange, shortened chemise, her slim waist— and he smiled his appreciation.

He looked into Cassandra's eyes, eyes that had intrigued him at first sight, for they were such an odd shade, nearly violet in color, and were framed by absurdly long black lashes that he was sure weren't entirely natural. She was a pretty girl, or rather, a pretty woman, for she was at least two-and-twenty and certainly could not claim to be a debutante. Marcus smiled, happy to see that once he got past her odd dress, women had not changed much over the years, for he was an acknowledged admirer of the feminine form. But then he shrugged, realizing that it would be rather hard to improve on Mother Nature's perfection.

The unusual undergarment took his attention once more and he noticed that it had been fashioned very differently from the long, waist-hugging corsets worn by one of his former mistresses—he disremembered her name at the moment. He leaned forward, seeing that two semicircles of what seemed to be cloth-covered wire cupped Cassandra's breasts from below, raising them so that they thrust forward intriguingly, provocatively. He reached out to touch one of them, just to ascertain, he told himself, if it really was wire.

"Hey—knock it off!" Cassandra slapped his hand away and he looked up to see real fear in her eyes, fear such as the sort she had shown as she realized the blue mist had transported her to his time. "Just what the hell do you think you're doing, buster?" She looked down at herself, then back at him, her hands flying up to cover herself. "Oh, Lord, I must be out of my mind. What do you think *you're* doing? What do I think *I'm* doing!"

Marcus enjoyed the blush that had risen from Cassandra's breasts all the way into her cheeks. "I think, love, that you are showing me that no matter how things change, some things stay very much the same. But, please, Miss Kelley, don't stop now." He reached out to touch her waist. "Show me again how this zipper invention works."

Marcus didn't know how their little confrontation might have ended if there hadn't been a knock on the door and the sound of Rose's voice asking permission to enter. He flew into action, grabbing Cassandra by the elbow to propel her behind the screen. "We cannot allow the servants to see your clothing. Strip now, madam, or I'll do it for you," he commanded tersely, going over to the bed to retrieve his sister's dress. "Everything—to the buff—and then give it all to me."

He raced over to a burled cabinet and began rummaging through the compartments, unearthing undergarments and a chemise, which he tossed over the screen as he called to Rose to wait outside.

Cassandra stuck her head out from behind the screen, her violet eyes narrowed in temper as she threw Georgina's undergarments back at him. "You may have my clothes, you may have my purse, you may even have my Hershey bar, but I'll be damned if I'm going to give you my underwear! That's not science—that's sick!"

Rose knocked again, calling, "Is everythin' all right in there, m'lord? Goodfellow says yer got a woman in there. Should I be callin' fer yer aunt Cornelia?"

"God's teeth—Corny! I had forgotten all about her. That's all this farce needs." Marcus stuffed his sister's undergarments back in the chest. "No! That is, no thank you, Rose. There's no need to bother my aunt," he called loudly. "I'll be just a moment more."

Cassandra's head popped out from behind the screen once more. "Aunt Cornelia? I love it! Is she an eccentric, Marcus? The hero's relatives are usually eccentric in Regency romances. Does she constantly call for hartshorn and burnt feathers, or does she guzzle gin when no one is looking?"

Marcus, seeing Cassandra at last dressed in the gown, stepped behind the screen and began fumbling with the long row of buttons that ran up the back of the dress. "Tuck in those shoulder laces so that they don't show at the neckline. Hurry now. And you'll have to tell me more about these books of yours when we have time, Miss Kelley," he said, concentrating on fitting the small covered buttons into loops that appeared to have taken on a life of their own. "They seem to have given you a very twisted impression of my time in history. We have more serious pursuits than swooning, and sipping spirits, you know. There, that's done. Now turn around while I look at you."

Ignoring him, Cassandra walked out from behind the screen and busied herself looking into the large mirror that hung above the burled chest. She smiled at the vision of herself in his sister's gown. "I look nice, don't I?" she asked, turning about to curtsy in his direction. "Is there a comb anywhere so I can fix this rat's nest? Mine's in my purse, so I won't even bother asking for it."

"Rat's nest? You have a rat's nest in your bag? Whatever for?"

Cassandra laughed aloud, a throaty, totally unaffected laugh that Marcus liked very much. "My hair looks like a rat's nest—not that I've ever seen one, thank you. It's just a saying." She took the silver-backed brush he handed her. "Thank you, Marcus—my lord," she said and turned back to the mirror, running the brush through her hair.

"Rose could do that, since your maid didn't travel back in time with you."

Cassandra laid down the brush, to push at her hair with her fingers, making it, to Marcus's mind, just as disheveled as it had been before she combed it. "I don't have a maid, Marcus."

His left eyebrow rose a fraction. "No maid. No chaperon. I see," he said gravely. "We'll let that be our little secret, if you don't mind, Miss Kelley. I wouldn't want my household getting the wrong opinion of you."

Cassandra's reflection glared at him, her fingers halting in midair, a move that could only be looked upon by Marcus as a blessing, for her hair was beginning to look as if she had been caught in a stiff breeze. "And what opinion would that be, Marcus? Are you lumping me in with Harriette Wilson again?"

She turned around to face him. "Look, I know this Rose person is standing outside, but I think we have to clear something up between us before we go any further. Women in the twentieth century do not have maids or chaperons, at least not in America—or England either, for that matter, unless they're very, *very* rich. We're not considered loose, or *fallen*. We're considered liberated. I've been to college, have my own apartment, can do long division, support myself working at a job that I love —and I can walk and chew gum at the same time, which is more than can be said for at least one of our male presidents. I live alone, I drive a car—a carriage, to you —and have my own bank account. I even smoke, or at least I did until three weeks ago—God, could I use a cigarette right now.''

She stood up very straight, so that the hem of Georgina's gown dragged only three inches on the floor. "I am woman, Marcus—hear me roar!"

And then, seeing his confused frown, she shook her head in exasperation. "Oh, forget it. Just go open the door."

Marcus walked across the room to stand close in front of her, looking down into her flashing violet eyes. "I've made you angry with my assumptions, haven't I?"

"Go to the head of the class, Lord Eastbourne. You got that in one," she answered, pushing the lacy straps of her bra beneath the fabric of the gown.

He reached out to tip up her chin with his hand. "I didn't mean to upset you, Cassandra Kelley," he said softly. "I've been searching for so long, forever it seems, for answers to my questions about the room—the blue mist—and now that I am finding them I'm rushing my fences and making impulsive leaps of logic when I should be taking my time, content to learn as I go. You will forgive me, won't you?"

He watched as her gaze shifted rapidly from side to side, searching each of his eyes individually, as if attempting to look past those eyes and into his soul. She brought out her tongue to wet her lips. "We have gotten off on the wrong foot, haven't we, Marcus?" she asked, her voice faintly husky as he allowed his fingers to begin stroking her cheek. "I always act like an idiot when I'm frightened. And I am frightened. More than I can tell you."

He smiled, remembering how her body looked beneath his sister's demure gown. "Don't be frightened, love," he told her, moving a step closer. "Perhaps it will help if we two cry friends. After all, we're all we've got in this, aren't we?"

She looked up at him and smiled. "There's always your companion—my *cousin* Perry," she said, her violet eyes laughing. Her moods seemed to change with each tick of the mantel clock. "Although I have to tell you, Marcus, I don't think the man would be much of a brick in a crisis."

Marcus chuckled softly beneath his breath, then lowered his head to within an inch of Cassandra's. She stared up at him, seemingly holding her breath. Marcus sobered, knowing he was going to kiss her; he was sure of it.

"Perry will be discreet," he promised, his voice low and intimate. All his attention centered on Cassandra's full red mouth. "Cassandra, I—"

"M'lord!" Rose's voice pierced the solid oak of the door, shattering the moment into a thousand embarrassing pieces. "Goodfellow has sent a tray fer the lady, and Mister Walton says fer me ta tell yer that his stomach's wonderin' if his throat's been cut, he's that hungry, beggin' yer pardon, m'lord."

Marcus watched as Cassandra's eyelids lowered, concealing the expression in her violet eyes, before she stepped away from him to seat herself in a nearby chair, her hands folded in her lap, her shoes covered by the overlong gown. "I'd feel greatly relieved, Cassandra, if I didn't already know that demure pose to be just that—a pose. You may be *woman,* as you call yourself, but, please, for all our sakes, try to *roar* as little as possible while Rose is in the room. It's enough that you've already shocked poor Goodfellow down to his toes."

Gathering up her clothing from behind the screen, he crossed to the door and opened it to admit Rose, a small, thin girl who staggered into the room beneath the weight of a heavy silver tray.

"Lord love a duck, m'lord, but I thought ye'd never answer," said Rose as she hefted the tray onto a nearby table before turning to peer inquisitively at Cassandra. "Hullo, miss," she said, curtsying. "Ain't that Miss Georgina's gown, m'lord? It's too small in all the wrong places, and more than a mite too long, if I'm any judge."

Marcus rubbed his eyes, suddenly very weary. "Thank you, Rose, we already know. Just serve the food, please, get fresh water for the pitcher, light some more candles, and turn back the bed so that Miss Kelley can retire once you've found her a proper nightgown. We'll take steps to remedy her wardrobe in the morning, when we're all rested."

"But, Marcus—I mean, my lord—it can't be more than six o'clock. I don't want to go to bed."

Marcus heard Rose's sharp intake of breath upon hearing Cassandra's frank, strangely accented speech. Did the girl have no brain at all, questioning him in his own house, in front of his own servant? He bowed in her direction. "I am otherwise committed this evening, Miss Kelley, or else I would bear you company until today's trying events bring you to your knees, begging for the comfort of a warm bed. But if you promise to be good, I shall see about escorting you to Bond Street in the morning."

"Bond Street?" Cassandra seemed to perk up. "That's where all the best shops are, isn't it?" She leaned back in the chair, smiling. "That could prove interesting. All right, my lord, I'll be a good little Regency miss and go to bed early. And if I'm still here tomorrow morning, we'll go shopping."

"If she's still here?" Rose turned to look at her employer, clearly confused, and perhaps more than a little frightened. "Where would she be goin ta, m'lord?"

Marcus shifted the small bundle of clothing under his arm, looking meaningfully at Cassandra. "Miss Kelley isn't going anywhere, Rose, at least not if she knows what's good for her," he said firmly, turning on his heel to join Perry downstairs in the study.

Cassandra, he was amused to see as he passed a large wall mirror on his way out of the room, stuck out her tongue at his departing back.

Chapter 4

Following Rose's directions, Cassandra found her way to the ground-floor study at the rear of the Grosvenor Square mansion, knocked twice on the paneled door, and entered.

"Good morning, Miss Kelley," the Marquess of Eastbourne said, rising from his chair behind a wide mahogany desk situated in front of a triple bank of impressive windows draped in floor-to-ceiling burgundy velvet. Her purse sat on the desktop, the contents placed in neatly spaced piles beside it. Marcus appeared to be as cool, as calmly collected, as he had been yesterday in the White Tower before their interlude in his sister's bedchamber—before he had called her Cassandra and almost kissed her. "I trust you slept well."

Slept well? Was he nuts? Cassandra was frightened. Frightened, and alone, and totally out of her element. Good God! Just a few minutes earlier she had cleaned her teeth with a laughable contraption Rose had called a toothbrush and then spent ten minutes explaining to that same servant that she could dress herself, only to learn that, thanks to the oddness of some of the garments, she couldn't even put on her own underwear. She wanted nothing more than to sit herself down someplace and quietly unravel.

But she couldn't do that. She wouldn't do that. There

was only one avenue open to her, and that was anger.
Anger, and maybe a dash of bravado. Any other reaction
could lead only to madness, a complete meltdown of her
mental faculties. She sniffed contemptuously at Marcus's
fairly innocuous statement as she deliberately swaggered
across the room, ruining the effect by tripping over the
hem of her sprigged muslin morning gown and nearly
ending up lying flat on her face. "Did I sleep well? How
can you ask that, Marcus? Tell me—strictly as a conversation starter, you understand—do you think I'm stupid?
Lamebrained? As you Regency fellows say—'totally to let
in the attic'?"

"No. Of course not," he countered soberly, although
she couldn't miss the glint of humor in his eyes.

" 'Of course not,' you say." She flung her hands wide
in mingled disgust and despair. "So how in hell can you
possibly ask if I slept well? Only a complete *idiot* could
be in my position—in this asinine predicament—and still
sleep well!" She looked around the room distractedly,
noticing and just as quickly dismissing the glass jars filled
with, as Perry had said, some particularly disgusting
specimens. "Oh, God. I need to sit down."

"Allow me," Marcus said, motioning to a nearby chair.
But Cassandra had rebounded, sighting two packs of cigarettes on the desktop. She had forgotten that a second,
unopened pack had been in her makeup case. Close to
forty marvelous, nerve-soothing cancer sticks lay just
outside her reach.

"There is a God!" she exclaimed, sweeping past the
marquess and lunging for the opened pack before he
could stop her in the name of "science." Grabbing the
pack, she quickly rummaged through the remainder of
her possessions, unearthing the disposable lighter. A moment later, her chin tipped up, her eyes closed in bliss,
she exhaled a thin blue stream of smoke. "Oh, I needed

that," she said, turning to smile at Marcus, at least temporarily in charity with the world.

Her smile faded at the look of mingled horror and revulsion on his handsome face.

"What? And don't tell me women in the Regency never smoke, because I won't believe you. At least two of my writers' heroines experimented with cigars." She inhaled again, dancing out of his reach behind the desk, just in case he thought he was going to relieve her of the one pleasure she'd had since being dumped into this unbelievable mess.

She looked down at the desktop, slightly embarrassed to see that he had spread out all her private possessions and snatched up the slim pink plastic case that looked like a holder for a pocket comb, but in reality held something very different. A moment later the case containing her birth control pills disappeared into the pocket of her gown.

"I won't tell you anything of the sort, Miss Kelley— Cassandra. But if I might broach a suggestion? If you plan to blow a cloud in public, be prepared to step lightly as you do, in order to avoid being toppled upon by the swooning matrons," the marquess told her in his deep-throated, cultured English voice. His smile reminded her that Marcus Pendelton was one extremely handsome man. Real cover-art material, with slashing black eyebrows over his sexy emerald eyes, intriguing high cheekbones, aristocratic nose, and a bedroom smile meant to melt hearts. It was amazing. His teeth were so straight and white she couldn't believe that orthodontics hadn't yet been invented.

And that body! He was no Arnold Schwarzenegger, thank goodness, for Cassandra had never understood the fuss some women made over muscle-bound men, but he had broad shoulders and a narrow waist, and his pantaloons and skintight hose showed his long legs to advantage. Objectively speaking, she'd take him over any current thick-necked Hulk Hogan look-alike cover model without so much as a blink!

Cassandra inhaled a third time, only to realize that after three weeks without regularly feeding nicotine into her system, she was beginning to feel light-headed. Maybe even a tad nauseated. She crushed the cigarette out in a small dish that sat on the desk and collapsed into a chair. "There," she said, glaring at the marquess. "I've put it out. Don't ever say I never did anything nice for you. Happy now?"

"Ecstatic," Marcus answered blandly, holding out his hand so that, hating herself for giving in, she could place the lighter in it. "And, if I may be so bold—the strange case," he prompted, pocketing the lighter. "In the interests of science, you understand."

"I'd rather die," Cassandra retorted quickly, then spread her hands to encompass the remainder of the items lying on the desk. "You're free to rummage through the rest of it. I mean, hey—knock yourself out. I was lying. I don't really have mace. But this case is mine. You—you haven't examined it yet, have you?"

Marcus took a seat in one of the chairs placed in front of the desk. "Don't you mean, am I aware that you are not a virgin, Miss Kelley? That is what those tablets are, isn't it? A strange method of avoiding pregnancy. *Lo Ovral*, I believe, was the name I read on the printed paper inside the case. You cannot begin to fathom the length and breadth of the questions I have been contemplating since discovering that piece of paper."

Cassandra didn't know whether to blush or pick up the small silver inkwell and bean him with it. "So now I'm Harriette Wilson all over again, aren't I? That's a real open mind you've got there, Marcus. And you call yourself a man of science?"

"Then I'm incorrect? Shame on me. Forgive me for

leaping to conclusions. You're right, of course. I am not being scientific."

Cassandra sighed, searching for the best way to attack the subject, not that anything she said could possibly make a dent in Marcus's poor opinion of her, his poor opinion of the women of her time in general. "Look, Marcus—my lord. The world has changed a lot since your time. I mean—a *lot!*" She grimaced, knowing anything she said would be an understatement. "A *whole* lot. What seems normal to me has got to be so off-the-wall to you—I mean, so extremely peculiar to you—that it would take me years to explain it all. Oh, brother. I can't believe we're having this conversation. I was sure I'd wake up this morning back in 1992. Rose blew that theory straight to hell when she showed up in my room with hot chocolate and a chamber pot. Thank God she told me about the new 'water closet' you've had installed. I quit the Girl Scouts because of the outhouses at summer camp. I'm just not the back-to-nature type. Of course, if I'm going to be lost in time, I guess I should consider myself lucky. I could just as easily have landed in prehistoric times, or popped up as the only female on a Greek freighter. Oh, God, Marcus, stop me. I'm babbling again."

Marcus nodded, then rose and walked to a corner of the room where he pulled a cord, summoning one of the servants who must have been camped just outside the door. "Coffee for two, please," he ordered, dismissing the servant before returning to sit in front of Cassandra once more. "You do have coffee in your time, don't you? Many of our ladies prefer tea, but somehow I believe you might drink coffee. Perhaps I should write that information down as well. For Perry's sake, you understand. I believe he harbors the thought that people in your time dine exclusively on chocolate and other delicacies. Spent most of last night telling me he thought he might enjoy living in such an enlightened age.''

Cassandra smiled weakly and then nodded, aware that he was giving her time to collect her thoughts. "Thank you, Marcus," she said, in appreciation of both his offer of coffee and his kindness. She leaned forward, searching through the items on the desk top until she found a small tin of aspirin. "These are for pain," she said, opening the tin. "I have a headache and I'm going to take two of these tablets when the coffee gets here. Don't try to talk me out of it, okay?"

"I wouldn't dream of such a thing," Marcus answered. "Are you going to take one of the other tablets as well? You should, you know. The literature I read on the printed paper points out that you are to take the tablets religiously until they are finished."

Cassandra's laugh was more of a sniff. "Oh, yes, Marcus, you're right. After all, you never know when I might decide to jump one of the footmen. We modern women are real animals." She knew she was at the end of her cycle and that the remaining pills were all placebos, but didn't think she owed the marquess that much of an explanation.

"You're angry again," the marquess pointed out needlessly. "Women of your time must be extremely volatile. I suggest that if we are ever to hope for a pleasant association we get this matter of morals out of the way. Now, please, Cassandra, tell me about the tablets."

Before Cassandra could speak, the servant returned, placed a heavy silver tea service on a nearby table, then retired. Marcus quickly poured them each a cup of coffee, inquired as to whether or not she took cream, and then placed a cup in front of her. "Take your time, Cassandra. After all, we may have years and years together in which to discuss everything."

"Years and years. Gee, thanks for cheering me up,

Marcus," Cassandra said bitterly, downing two aspirin with a sip of hot coffee. "That's just the sort of news to make a girl want to jump right up and dance." Replacing the cup in the saucer, she looked piercingly at the marquess, gauging his ability to understand what she had to say. "All right," she said at last. "Let's talk about women in my time. As I've already told you, things are a lot different. We can go to college. We live away from home —without chaperons. We work as teachers, politicians, secretaries, doctors, police officers, lawyers—solicitors, to you—why, I even have a friend who's training to be an astronaut, not that you'd know what that is. In short, we can do anything a man can do—backward, and in high heels."

"Hence the female PM," Marcus cut in, his expression of dismay almost comical. "How endlessly fascinating. Do you fight in wars?"

Cassandra nodded. "In America women do almost everything in the services, and in some countries women fight in combat. American women will also go into all areas of combat soon, if we have our way. After all, if we're going to have bombs dropped on us we should be able to fight back, right?"

"Amazing." She noticed that the marquess had taken up a notebook and was busily scribbling in it. "Have you fought in a war, Cassandra?"

"No, not unless you count riding the subways. But we'll leave war for another time, okay? It would only open another can of worms, what with smart missiles and nuclear weapons. Let's get back to the women of my time. The majority of us don't have come-out balls and Seasons and that sort of thing, and we wouldn't want them. We go to work, at eighteen, or after college—at about twenty-two. We pull our own weight. We don't marry right away either, at least a lot of us don't."

"Why not? All women wish to make an advantageous

marriage. It is what they are raised to expect. My sister, Georgina, began planning her marriage in the nursery. Has marriage fallen out of favor?''

Cassandra's head was aching behind her eyes. This was impossible. She couldn't possibly explain her life-style to him. Not this morning. Not today. Not in the years and years he spoke of so glibly. No one could. ''No, marriage has not fallen out of favor. We women still want marriage. But not right away. We have our careers to consider. Many women don't get married until they're in their thirties, then go on to have children into their forties.''

Her last statement seemed to have gotten Marcus's full attention, so that he stopped as he was about to dip his pen into the inkwell once more. ''Their forties? But that's positively ancient! Oh, Sally Jersey may have attempted it, but—Miss Kelley, I must insist you tell me the truth. It won't do either of us any good for you to spite me by spinning fanciful tales.''

Cassandra instinctively reached for the opened pack of cigarettes, then thought better of it. ''I *am* telling you the truth. We're talking about one hundred and eighty years of progress here, Marcus. Thanks to modern medi-cine, people routinely live into their seventies and eight-ies. There's plenty of time for marriage and children— although my mother has never agreed with that theory. She insists that I'm destined to be an old maid. Last sum-mer, on my twenty-fifth birthday, she showed up at my party dressed all in black, saying she'll never be a grand-mother.''

''You're five-and-twenty?'' Marcus questioned, shaking his head. ''That won't do. That won't do at all. We'll have to keep your age our little secret, I'm afraid, as I've al-ready informed my aunt that I wish to launch you into Society next month, as part of my experiments, you un-derstand. But if Corny finds out you're at your last prayers she'll insist we put you in caps and seat you with the dowagers. We have been acquainted less than twenty-four hours, Cassandra, but I am already convinced that your place is most definitely not among the dowagers."

Cassandra finally found something to laugh about. "Your aunt Cornelia and my mother would get along swimmingly, Marcus. Of course, your aunt would get a little upset when my mother started to talk about her idea of my becoming a single parent, as she has all but given up the idea I'll ever marry. She read somewhere that I have as much chance of getting married as I do of being abducted by little green men from Mars."

Marcus shook his head. "Stop, Cassandra. Please, stop. This discussion is getting out of hand. We are simply going to have to form some sort of agenda for speaking of individual subjects. This random accounting you are spouting is getting us nowhere at all. Now, if I accept the notion that women of your time do not marry until much later in life, can we get back to the discussion of those tablets hidden in your pocket? As an unmarried woman and, as you assert, a woman not to be lumped with the Harriette Wilsons of this world—why in blazes are you carrying those tablets?"

"You aren't going to give up, are you, Marcus?" Cassandra took another sip of the now tepid coffee, then came to a decision. "All right. I'll tell you the truth, even though I know it will blow your mind. You said I wasn't to talk about anything but the pills, but I must tell you that we had a different sort of war in the last twenty or thirty years—my years, not yours. It was called the Sexual Revolution. Women figured out that barefoot and pregnant wasn't all it was cracked up to be. We went to college, we went to work, we fought for equality, and—and you're really going to have to pay attention now, Marcus—we decided that women can have sex without marriage just as you men have been doing since the beginning of time. We know all about sex. We teach it in school, as a matter of fact. So, no, Marcus, I am *not* a virgin. 'Brad the Bod' Renshaw took care of that little bit of my education during my third year of college. And surprise, surprise, it wasn't all that great, so I gave it up. I take birth control pills—those 'tablets'—because I live and work in Manhattan, and a girl could get raped living in Manhattan.''

Her speech completed, and her entire body shaking with nerves, Cassandra sat back in the chair and waited for Marcus to explode and maybe order her out of his house before she could contaminate the rest of the inhabitants, and to hell with his intention of "experimenting" with her.

But he surprised her.

"I see," Marcus said after a long, pregnant pause. "I think I understand now, Cassandra. Women of your age —your *time*—have decided to be just like men. You go to university, you fight wars, and you live alone and work in places so dangerous that you must take preventative tablets for fear of being violated. And the name you give to all of this is 'equality'?''

"Right." Cassandra grimaced. "Only it doesn't sound quite as logical the way you say it. *Um*—did I mention that we've gotten the right to vote in elections?''

Marcus laid down his notebook. "No, Cassandra, you have not mentioned that. My felicitations on yet another feminine accomplishment. But I think I've heard enough for this morning. Before I ask any more questions I will comprise a list from which to draw on. For now, I think we must prepare to introduce you to the rest of the family. You've already met Peregrine Walton, my good friend who has been living with me since his parents died, leaving him penniless. He is a good sort, but rather simple, so that I wouldn't want you to tax his mind with too many stories of your time. I would ask the same consideration of my aunt Cornelia—actually, she is not my aunt, but I call her 'Aunt.' She would doubtless have a strong attack of the vapors if you were to apprise her of the truth of your circumstances.''

"Of course," Cassandra answered automatically, watching as Marcus rose and began pacing the carpet, his hands clasped behind his back. Did he have to be so very handsome? Modern men could learn a lot from the way Marcus spoke and carried himself—and the way his pantaloons, or whatever they were called, clung to his shapely legs. "I won't give myself away. I'm to be Perry's American cousin. Nothing more."

"Very good. It also goes without saying that Perry and I are to be the only two people who know the truth about you. It could be dangerous if the wrong sort of person were to discover the true circumstances behind your appearance in London. In order to be assured that you will not bring undue attention to yourself, thus putting all of us at risk of being declared insane and locked away in some asylum, you will spend the next few weeks under my tutelage, learning the ways of young misses in what you call Regency England."

He stopped pacing and looked at her piercingly. "Why do you call it Regency England, Cassandra? What is England called in 1992?"

Cassandra felt herself beginning to relax. Marcus hadn't liked hearing about her lack of virginity but, by and large, she believed he had taken the news rather well. "As I've explained, Marcus, I work as an editor. A book editor. Many of the books I edited—until my promotion, that is—were romance novels about England during this time. You know, like Jane Austen? She has been published by now, hasn't she? Good. Anyway, these particular books are set in the time the Prince of

Wales was Regent, from 1811 until he became king—around 1820, I believe."

Marcus looked somber. "I see. So poor mad George does eventually die. There are many of us who have begun to believe he will live forever, locked away in his own world, unknowing of what goes on around him." He was silent a moment longer, then asked, "But why would anyone write romantic novels about England in our time? Lord, woman, we're at war!"

Cassandra smiled. "Yes, Marcus, but it was a romantic war. Any war one does not fight in personally is a romantic war, didn't you know that? Besides, there were so many lovely things about the Regency Era. Your fashions; your wits and eccentric characters, like Beau Brummell and the others; the lovely lives you led, full of balls and parties; the great works of literature, with Byron, Shelley, and the rest—oh, I don't know, Marcus. But they are lovely books in our Mayfair line, with lots of humor and, of course, happy endings."

"Eccentrics. I believe you mentioned that word last night. You seem to have a fixation with the word. I agree that we have a few strange characters stumbling about the place. Poodle Byng. The Green Man. Romeo Coates. But doesn't every age have its share of eccentrics?"

Now Cassandra laughed out loud. "We've got Michael Jackson and Zsa Zsa Gabor but, trust me, it's not the same. Besides, you English are still full of eccentrics, even in 1992. Almost every story of eccentrics to make the news either comes from California—if it's about aliens or weird religions—or from England. Yours usually have to do with pigs, oddly shaped vegetables, or crop circles. Marcus? May I meet your aunt Cornelia now?"

The marquess shook his head. "I told you I had spoken with her, but that was last night. Corny doesn't rise before noon, and leaves her chamber at two or three. You'll meet her later, before dinner. For now, I suggest we adjourn to Bond Street and a modiste I have favored in the past.''

"For your mistresses, Marcus?" Cassandra heard herself asking before she could think to guard her tongue. "Do you keep a Covent Garden warbler, or do you run with married women who have already given their husbands an heir?"

She watched, bemused, as Marcus's face filled with color. It was obvious he had not flushed in embarrassment, but in anger. Righteous anger. "You impertinent little chit! Surely, if you have any knowledge of this time in history, you know that you should not speak that way to me. No—don't interrupt. You cannot claim ignorance in this matter, even if, in your time, you consider yourself free to do or say anything your *emancipated* mind can conjure up. And if you were to say something like that in public! You would be immediately ostracized, which would do my planned experiments no good at all. But I refuse to allow your willfulness to defeat me. Perhaps I should send Perry out to bruit it about that you are pretty enough, but no more than an amicable dunce. It would certainly save me a lot of trouble."

Cassandra felt her chin begin to wobble as both her courage and her bravado melted under the heat of Marcus's anger, leaving only her fear. How could she be so difficult? After all, it wasn't his fault that she had traveled through time and landed on his doorstep. It was her own stupidity, her own decision to break the rules, that had landed her in Regency England. At least Marcus seemed to believe there was some reason behind her trip through time. She needed him. She couldn't cope with any of this without him.

"I—I'm sorry, Marcus," she said, rising and walking around the desk to face him head on. "Truly. I've been an ass."

"You don't say *ass*," he said from between clenched

teeth, his green eyes flashing. "You don't smoke those strange cigars, you don't swear, you don't let on that you know the war is going to end or that King George will die. You don't yell 'fire' if you are standing in the middle of a blazing room. In short, you are to keep your mouth shut tight unless I am by your side, at which time you will speak only when spoken to and *think* before you so much as say 'thank you' when someone offers you food. Do you understand?"

"I understand, *my lord*," Cassandra responded, nodding and trying desperately to keep from bursting into tears. She delved into her store of Regency phrasing. "I am to be a pattern-card Regency miss, a 'milk-and-water puss,' a well-behaved creature who has feathers for brains and has nothing more weighty on her mind than her outfit for the next ball and the wish to catch herself a suitable husband. God—and people think the Regency was romantic? I might as well be in jail!"

Marcus put a finger beneath her chin and tilted her head up to his, so that she felt an unexpected shiver climb her spine. "It will get better, Cassandra, I promise you. I will teach you. And in turn, you will teach me. And then, between us, we might be able to find some rhyme and reason for your presence in that room in the White Tower and, with that knowledge, find a way to send you back to your own time."

Cassandra's chin wobbled once more. "Don't be too nice to me, Marcus," she warned, trying to smile. "I think I can carry this off, if only you aren't too nice to me. Otherwise, I might just start blubbering." She took a deep, steadying breath, then continued, "Can we go to Bond Street now? Maybe if I were to have some clothes that fit I might feel more like the Regency miss you want me to be. I promise to be good—and quiet."

Marcus bowed, then smiled in a most sympathetic way and held out his arm to her. "We'll have one of the footmen fetch your cape and your abigail, my dear Miss Kelley, and be on our way."

She longed to throw herself against him, weeping. Blinking back tears, Cassandra allowed herself to be directed down the hallway toward the foyer. "Marcus?" she questioned as they walked along. "Why do you call it the White Tower? It isn't white, not in my time, and not now."

Marcus motioned to one of the footmen, who sprang into action as if he knew exactly what his master required. "It's simple, my dear. When William the Conqueror came to England, he ordered the tower erected to impress the local populace of his intention to stay as their ruler. Although the structure is of ragstone and limestone, and very impressive, once it was finished he had the whole thing whitewashed. He said that white would make the tower appear larger and even more imposing."

Cassandra giggled as Rose appeared with a cape and draped it over her shoulders. "And old Willie was right," she whispered to the visibly baffled marquess as they stepped out into the gray London day. "It's the same argument I used on my mother last summer when she wanted to buy white slacks."

Chapter 5

Cassandra was floating at least a full inch off the ground as she descended the wide, winding staircase and crossed the foyer just as the dinner gong rang, and headed for the footmen guarding the doors to the drawing room. It had been a long day, but it had certainly not been boring.

From the moment she and the marquess (and Rose, serving as her abigail) stepped onto the flagway and climbed into the waiting carriage, Cassandra's senses had been inundated with sights, sounds, and smells so rich in the history she loved that she had completely forgotten the fact that she didn't want to be here. No wonder historians called London "the Metropolis," the center of the world. None of her necessary reading and research for her duties as editor of the Mayfair line, not even any of her best authors' works had prepared her for the reality of the London streets.

Grosvenor Square seemed to be a haven of order and quiet, lined on all sides with many-storied mansions, and in the center was a fenced circular garden around which people traveled to or from their destinations by carriage, on horseback, or on foot. The dirty snow that clogged the gutters and the pall of chimney smoke that hung over the area did nothing to cool her enchantment.

Once out of the Square the scene changed rapidly, the streets now clogged with horse-drawn vehicles of every size and description, the coarse shouts of drivers taking the place of blaring taxi horns in this Regency Era version of a rush-hour traffic jam.

And then they were riding down Bond Street, and the marquess was pointing out buildings of interest as well as commenting on the fact that London was "rather thin of company" at this time of year, although this was changing, as carriage loads of debutantes and their hopeful mamas were descending on Mayfair daily, to ready themselves for the spring Season.

Stepping out of the carriage in front of a rather nondescript-looking building near the bottom of Old Bond Street, Marcus was quick to usher Cassandra inside a tall building no more than twenty feet in width. It was a small pocket of feminine delight neatly tucked between two larger buildings, one of them housing an art gallery and the other a haberdashery.

Marcus was immediately greeted like visiting royalty by a middle-aged Frenchwoman whose fading beauty was artfully masked by a heavy application of paint and powder. Cassandra was left with no choice but to stand quietly by as the two had a rapid-fire conversation that quickly outstripped her thin repertoire of high-school-freshman conversational French.

It was the last moment of peace Cassandra was to have for the next three hours.

Halfway through her conversation with the marquess Mme. Gerard whirled to face Cassandra, visually measuring her up and down with, to Cassandra's mind, all the cold calculation of a racetrack tout.

"From 'er head to 'er foots, m'lord?" Mme. Gerard questioned, walking fully around Cassandra, lifting a lock of her short, shaggy cut and *tsk-tsk*ing as if Cassandra's forty-dollar splurge for a haircut on Fifth Avenue just the previous week had been a terrible mistake.

"And from the skin out, Mme. Gerard," the marquess

said in English, glaring at Cassandra as if to dare her to contradict him. "Hats, gloves, shoes, hose, walking dresses, riding habits, ball gowns—*undergarments*. We will need at least three complete outfits today from your stock, more if you have them, and half the total order in a sennight. The rest must be completed within the month."

This statement brought another torrent of nearly indecipherable French from Mme. Gerard. Cassandra was only able to catch a few words, such as *"Impossible! Inconcevable! Outrageux!"* and, lastly, *"How* much, m'lord? *Oui,* m'lord. *Naturellement, bien entendu.* Of course, of course."

Yes, it was true. Cassandra had landed herself in Regency England. But she had obviously also landed herself in one of the deepest "gravy boats" in all of Mayfair.

Now, dressed "from the skin out" in beautiful silk undergarments, soft kid slippers, and a hastily altered high-waisted gown of palest green batiste originally fashioned for some poor lady who hadn't yet paid her bill to Mme. Gerard, Cassandra felt as if she had stepped into a fairy tale. A very lovely fairy tale. And she was the beautiful princess. As a matter of fact, she had been humming snatches of "I Enjoy Being a Girl" for most of the afternoon.

Her hair had been combed over something Rose had called a curling stick, so that her black locks curled toward her face and caressed her nape, tickling her whenever she moved. Over Rose's objections, Cassandra had lightly brushed her cheeks with the blusher from her purse and applied mascara to her lashes, the marquess having granted her possession of her "satchel" once more—holding back only her lighter, her cigarettes, and her wallet, as he wished to study the snapshots of her family, which he, to her amusement, had termed to be "modern art."

The footman, whom she recognized as the one who had helped her from the carriage the previous evening, now inclined his head to her and pushed open one of the double doors, bidding her to enter the impressively furnished and rather dauntingly immense drawing room.

Immediately upon entering she searched the room nervously for the marquess, suddenly aware that she was once more out of her element. He was nowhere in sight.

But that didn't mean that the large room was unoccupied. There was a rustle of movement to her left and suddenly Peregrine Walton was in front of her, his round face flushed with excitement as he made a great business of bowing over her hand—the hand she had unconsciously extended, thinking he would shake it. When she realized that he was about to kiss her hand, she began to snatch it back, then thought better of the notion and extended it again, just as Peregrine had lifted his head to look at her quizzically. The end result of this strange dance of manners being that Cassandra's index finger poked the mannerly Mr. Walton squarely in the eye.

"Oh, damn," Cassandra exploded in dismay, immediately taking his head between her hands and peering into his eyes, inspecting him for damage. "Sorry, Perry. I've always been known for my social graces. Does it hurt?"

One eye squeezed tightly closed, Perry attempted to shake his head. "No, no. I've had worse, I assure you." He then leaned closer to her and whispered, "But Marcus won't like it above half if you swear, Miss Kelley, I mean Cassandra. Being you're m'cousin now, I have to call you Cassandra. Wouldn't make much sense to call you Miss Kelley, would it, us being related and all. Corny would smell a rat in a moment. But, anyway, please don't swear anymore because Aunt Cornelia is just over there, beside the fire, and she wouldn't understand that you new people talk so plain. Oh, and by the by, you look

fine as ninepence tonight, Cassandra. Better by far than
you did walking about half-naked.''

Cassandra smiled her thanks for this backhanded compliment, then looked past Peregrine and saw that Aunt
Cornelia was just where he said she would be, sitting
beside the fire, her head bent low over what looked to
be a Bible. ''Thank you, Perry,'' she said absently, taking
his hand as if his presence could lend her strength. ''I'll
try to keep my swearing to a minimum, I promise. And,
Perry—could you bring yourself to call me Cassie? Only
my mother and a couple of my teachers from grade
school ever called me Cassandra. Now, come on. I think
it's time you introduced me to what I hope will be the
resident eccentric.''

The little the marquess had told Cassandra about the
woman he called Aunt Cornelia had served to make her
believe his ''Corny'' would be a lovable little old lady
who wore purple turbans and constantly misplaced her
spectacles, but it was obvious at first glance that she had
been wrong in her conclusion.

The woman seated on a green-and-white brocade satin
settee looked to be neither very old nor very cuddly.
Even seated, it was obvious the woman was tall, probably taller than Perry, and her steel-gray hair and stubborn
chin framed a tightly drawn aristocratic face that, unless
Cassandra missed her guess, looked as if the woman had
just finished sucking on a lemon.

Her gown was of dull lavender watered silk and
sported a starched white collar so high and tight that her
watery blue eyes seemed to be about to bulge right out
of her head from the pressure. In short, Aunt Cornelia
looked like every child's nightmare vision of a wicked
stepmother, and Cassandra's heart dropped to her toes.

''Um—Aunt Cornelia?'' Peregrine questioned in a tentative voice, his grin almost a grimace of anguish.
''There's someone here to meet you.''

Nothing.

As Cassandra stood beside Peregrine, wishing she could shake the feeling that she was back in third grade and had just been called to the principal's office for something Sheila Cranston had talked her into doing, and while Peregrine stood beside her, running a finger around his suddenly too-tight collar, Aunt Cornelia remained as still as a statue. Only her eyes moved back and forth rhythmically as she read down the page of what was definitely a Bible.

"Aunt Cornelia? Did you hear me? It's m'cousin, Cassandra Kelley, arrived last night from America, remember?"

Still nothing. Zilch. Zip. *Nada.* It was uncanny. As far as the woman seemed to be concerned, Cassandra and Peregrine did not exist.

"How do you do, Aunt Cornelia," Cassandra said, extending her hand and wishing she knew the woman's last name so that she didn't have to call her Aunt Cornelia. As a matter of fact, she wished she didn't have to call her anything. She wished she were a thousand miles away, or at least one hundred and eighty years away, and safely behind the Wilmont Publishing booth at the London Book Fair, smiling at freebie-grabbing wholesalers.

"Amen," Aunt Cornelia said at last, sighing deeply before closing the Bible with a firm *snap* and looking up at Cassandra.

"Amen," Cassandra echoed automatically, longing to disappear into the deep Aubusson carpet at her feet.

"What? Yes. Yes, of course. Amen. You're quite right, Cassie. Amen it is. Amen, *Amen!*" Peregrine all but shouted as Cassandra gave his hand a warning squeeze.

"Oh, stifle, Perry," Aunt Cornelia said in a low, mannish, and rapid-fire voice, shaking her head. "I swear, you're the most bird-witted creature God ever created. And what are you doing standing here, holding this child's hand as if you're frightened to death she might fly away? Introduce me—or don't you remember her name? Perhaps you should scribble it on your shirt cuff, along with your address, not that you've been home in years, since you prefer to slip your legs under m'nephew's table as if you live here.''

"But I do live here, Aunt Cornelia, remember?" Peregrine shot Cassandra a look that told her that if a great hole were to open in the carpet in front of them, she would have to fight him off if she wanted to jump in first. "Marcus invited me years ago. Got my own rooms and everything.''

"Of course I remember, you dolt. I just find it amusing to watch you squirm from time to time. I'm old now, and take my pleasures when I can. Now introduce me to this young lady I'm to present this Season, as if I have nothing better to do with my time than play ape-leader to another simpering miss. That's what's wrong with today's girls. No gumption. Not like in my day, when we took in balls in our riding dress. Ah, those were the days. We had spleen then. Look at her, standing there, staring at me as if I were about to eat her.''

Aunt Cornelia leaned forward and tapped Cassandra's hand with the Bible. "What's the matter, gel—scared of me? Good. Shows you're not entirely without furnishings in your brain box. Must be a distant relative of Perry's, and escaped the taint. This boy has more hair than wit and would starve in a gutter if it weren't for Marcus's tender heart. Now, speak up, gel. What's your name?''

Cassandra smothered a giggle as she looked down at the imposing Aunt Cornelia. And Marcus had told her he didn't believe England was crowded with eccentrics? What did he call Perry—and now this lady, if he did not call them eccentrics?

"How do you do, ma'am," she said, extending her hand once again. This time the woman took it, squeezing so firmly that Cassandra was hard pressed not to wince. "My name is Cassandra Kelley. Are you reading that Bible hoping you'll discover some way to be as nasty as you can be during this life and still sneak into heaven when you die?"

Aunt Cornelia's sharp bark of laughter nearly smothered Peregrine Walton's dismayed gasp. "Perry!" she exclaimed, squeezing Cassandra's hand yet again, nearly bringing tears to her eyes. "You didn't tell me the gel's got a head on her shoulders. Neither did Marcus, come to think of it. All he did was mumble something about her being very different, having grown up around wild Indians and the like, so that I'm not supposed to pay too much attention to anything she says. This might not be so terrible after all. Looks, a decent posture, and a brain. Yes, we might just scrape by, even if she is American. Anything we can do about that accent, gel? It's atrocious, you know."

"Take it, Perry," Cassandra said, grinning, figuratively tossing the question to him. "She's not supposed to listen to me."

Peregrine sputtered helplessly for a few moments, then spread his hands as if unable to find the proper words to answer the woman. "Marcus says he's going to be her tutor, ma'am, so I imagine he'll do something about her speech." And then, as if finally realizing that Aunt Cornelia had accepted Cassandra, he smiled broadly and asked rhetorically, "So you like her, Aunt Cornelia?"

This inquiry brought another frown to the hatchet face of the older woman. "And how should I know that, you ignoramus? I've barely met her. One fine-feathered swallow doesn't make a summer, you know. Besides, it hardly matters if I *like* her. I ain't going to buy her, you know, only present her. Now go away, Perry, and let the two of us get acquainted. Here, you—gel. Sit down beside me. Marcus and the Reverend Mr. Austin will be here shortly, so we won't have much time to talk. Mr. Austin is the most obnoxious buffoon in fifty miles, but Christian duty requires that we entertain him at least once a month. If it weren't for eating other people's food, the man would probably starve, his sermons are so paltry. Bother the man. I've been boning up on the Apostles all the afternoon. Tripped me up last month, he did. Mark, Matthew—what difference does it make, I ask you? They're all in the same book. Well, speak up, gel—what do you think of my nephew? Don't set your sights on him, I warn you. He'll never marry. I should know. I've been parading eligible young ladies past him for years."

"Years and years and years," Marcus Pendelton said from just inside the doorway, so that Cassandra, who had been listening to Aunt Cornelia in growing fascination and apprehension, gratefully turned to smile at him. "Good evening, Aunt, Miss Kelley—Perry. You'll have to excuse my tardiness, but I was reading in my study and lost track of the time."

"Marcus!" Cassandra didn't know if she cried out his name because he was the one sane, seemingly reliable person she had met since being zapped back in time or because, dressed in his evening clothes, he was the most handsome, desirable man she had *ever* seen, but she knew she had never been so happy to see anyone in her life. She left Aunt Cornelia to sit alone on the settee silently mouthing "Marcus" as if attempting to reconcile Cassandra's familiar use of her nephew's Christian name with her notion of respectability and all but raced to the marquess's side. Stopping a few feet in front of him, she inquired quietly, "Do I look more like a Regency miss now, my lord?"

"That depends," Marcus answered, lifting one expressive eyebrow. "At first sight you seem tolerably presentable, but is it necessary for you to *gallop* across the room, my dear? I've seen shorter strides on a racehorse."

Cassandra felt as if he had slapped her. "Gee, and I'm crazy about you, too, Marcus," she said, looking him up and down, searching in vain for some flaw in his appearance. There wasn't even one. She longed to hate him.

"You've met Aunt Cornelia," Marcus said, slipping her arm through his and leisurely strolling in the direction of the fireplace and the woman sitting so stiffly on the settee, the woman looking as if she had the fireplace poker stuck up her back. "She was quite the belle in her day, although she never married. What was it, Aunt, true love gone sadly wrong?"

"Impudent puppy," Aunt Cornelia countered, her tone severe, although Cassandra felt sure she saw a gleam of affection in the woman's eyes. "You know very well that I was—I am—too independent ever to allow myself or my destiny to be placed totally in the hands of any man. I came to live with you only because you need someone sane about the place to ride herd on your nonsense. Found any great chests of jewels and gold plate at the Tower yet, Marcus, or are you going to have to dig into your own coffers to placate Prinny now that you've got him all heated up about buried treasure? You've done some harebrained things in the past, Marcus, but this latest business is dangerous. It isn't wise to wave the prospect of fortune under the nose of that great revenue-devouring ape we call our Regent."

Cassandra's eyes slid sideways, to gauge Marcus's reaction to Aunt Cornelia's scolding. He smiled indulgently, inclining his head in the older woman's direction. "I cannot tell you how much easier my rest is, knowing that I have succeeded in keeping you up nights, worrying about me. But, to answer your question—yes, I believe I am making considerable progress in my search. Only yesterday I discovered a diamond in the White Tower." The marquess looked down at Cassandra, who felt herself blushing. "A rare blue diamond. It is rather rough, and needs a bit of polish, but it shows great promise."

"We did?" Perry questioned, his brow furrowed. "Oh —oh yes! Of course! Lovely creature—er—lovely *thing!* You ought to see it, Aunt Cornelia. Isn't that right, Marcus?"

"No, Perry, that is not correct," Marcus said stiffly as his aunt sat forward, looking eager. "If you will recall, I have already decided to keep the jewel hidden until such time as I can present it in its best light. You do remember that, don't you, Perry?"

As Perry stumbled about, trying to extricate himself from his verbal misstep, and Cassandra bit her bottom lip in the hope she wouldn't burst into laughter, a footman entered the room to declare: "My lord, ladies and sir. The Reverend Ignatius Austin."

"Oh, Aunt, not again," Cassandra heard the marquess utter in noticeable exasperation before he turned to greet the man now striding into the drawing room. "Ignatius! Grand to see you!"

"Liar," Cassandra whispered before he left her standing in the middle of the room to walk to the clergyman, his hand outstretched in greeting. Taking up her seat beside Aunt Cornelia once more, she took a moment to inspect this newest player in what she could only look upon as a typical Regency Era drawing room farce.

It took her only a moment to place the man, or at least the type of man the Reverend Ignatius Austin seemed to represent. He looked almost exactly like a drawing she had once seen of the character Ichabod Crane, from Washington Irving's *The Legend of Sleepy Hollow.* Tall, rail thin, and dressed head to toe in a funereal black suit that showed entirely too much of both his cuffs and his heavily patched stockings, the man had the look of a lean and hungry ferret: his nose extended a full two inches farther than his nearly nonexistent chin. And his dark eyes seemed to glow red as if lit by either religious fervor or, she thought, fanatical zealotry. She didn't know whether to be amused or revolted.

"Pitiful creature, ain't he?" Aunt Cornelia whispered *sotto voce*, nudging Cassandra with one pointy elbow. "Still, having him here to dinner once a month is a world easier than sitting through his sermons every Sunday. Wait until you see him at table. Eats as if the universe will come to an end before dessert. It is a compromise I've made with God, you understand. As you so astutely pointed out—I must do all my possible to secure a position in heaven. This little bit of charity ought to get me a good seat, don't you think?"

"Front row, center," Cassandra agreed, relaxing completely. Aunt Cornelia might put on a stern air, and her appearance certainly was enough to put a girl on her best behavior, but the woman was all right. With a little work, they might even become friends. Cassandra frowned, considering her last thought. Well, maybe not *best* friends—but at least she wasn't afraid of the lady.

"Mr. Austin," Cassandra heard the marquess say, calling her back to attention, "may I have the honor of presenting Peregrine's American cousin, Miss Cassandra Kelley, who is to be with us for an indefinite stay."

With Aunt Cornelia's pointed elbow prodding her on, Cassandra extended her hand while murmuring a simple, safe "How d'you do?" A moment later the vicar was bending over her hand, kissing it with what she could only consider to be fish lips. Cold. Almost slimy. "It is nice to make your acquaintance, sir."

"May the good Lord watch over and protect you, Miss Kelley, and keep you from the temptations of the flesh and the devil," Mr. Austin intoned in his rusty-hinge baritone. He then dismissed her and turned back to Marcus and Peregrine, inquiring as to whether it was possible to anticipate his dinner with a judicious glass of sherry.

"Of course, Ignatius," Marcus answered, moving toward the drinks table that stood at one side of the room. "Perry? Aunt? Cassandra?"

"Nothing for me, Marcus," Perry answered, leaning his chubby body against the marble mantelpiece with the air of a man whose dearest wish was to fade into the woodwork.

"Ratafia, Nephew," Aunt Cornelia instructed offhandedly, belatedly noticing the Bible in her lap and hastily stuffing it between the cushions of the settee.

"Scotch and water, please, Marcus. On the rocks," Cassandra replied, busily assisting the older woman in her attempt to hide the evidence of her "cramming" as if for a test.

"I beg your pardon?"

Marcus's steely tone sliced through Cassandra and she slapped a hand to her mouth. *"Um—er—*I mean—" She looked at the marquess in naked terror, knowing she had really blown it this time. *"Um—*it's an American drink," she inserted hastily. "Much like wine. That's it. I'll have a glass of wine, thank you, Marcus."

"You'll have ratafia, missy, and like it," Aunt Cornelia supplied testily. "Savage Indians, and now I learn the gel drinks like a demmed flounder. Marcus, must you continue to plague an old woman out of her mind with these strays of yours?"

Marcus approached, carrying two crystal glasses on a small silver tray. Bending over Aunt Cornelia, he whispered, "You dare to complain, Aunt, with that death's head on a mop stick you've got cluttering up my drawing room?"

"Yes, well, I suppose you might have a point," Aunt Cornelia conceded, turning to Cassandra. "Sorry, little girl. I suppose things are quite different in the colonies.

But don't you worry. We'll get you up to snuff before the Season. Good Lord!'' she exclaimed in astonished tones, although she kept her voice low. "Gel—uncross those legs! You're showing your limbs to anyone who cares to look. Do you want to send the vicar into an apoplexy?"

"Forgive me, ma'am. It—it's another dreadful American custom.'' Cassandra quickly uncrossed her legs, glaring up at Marcus as if daring him to say anything. After all, he had told her to keep her mouth closed. He hadn't said anything about how she was to sit. "May I have my drink now, please?"

"If you can promise me you won't try to toss it off in one gulp, yes,'' Marcus told her as Aunt Cornelia turned to skewer Peregrine with a depressing look and began reading him a pithy lecture on the merits of good posture. "Although I am not yet totally conversant with this supposed equality you spoke of earlier, may I most earnestly beg that you also refrain from belching at table or requesting to blow a cloud in the gardens with Perry and me after dinner?"

"I know I goofed, Marcus. Now why not give it a rest?'' Cassandra grumbled just as Goodfellow entered the room to announce that dinner was served.

Dinner passed without incident, Cassandra's mother having firmly instructed her in the *why's* and *wherefore's* of multilayered serving utensils and the myriad courses served at exclusive dinners, just as if any of the Kelleys were in momentary anticipation of being invited to the White House for an inaugural banquet. Seated on Marcus's right, and across from Peregrine, who was barely visible above a large, ornate silver epergne, she had nothing to do except remember not to slurp her soup and to nod occasionally as the Reverend Mr. Austin expounded at great length, and in mind-numbing detail, on the wages of sin.

However, as the meal progressed, and the servings of wine varied from course to course, the vicar's speech became more and more slurred, until he at last lapsed into a near coma, allowing Marcus and Peregrine to carry on an intelligent discussion of England's latest victory on the Peninsula. Knowing that anything she could say on that subject would probably only confuse the issue, Cassandra turned to Aunt Cornelia. The older woman had graciously allowed her to call her by this name, tempering her generosity with the information that she abhorred being called Miss Haskins, and took the opportunity of offering her first, rudimentary lessons in conduct befitting a young miss about to make her debut.

This information was couched in the frankest of terms and had a lot to do with "the social pitfalls inherent in allowing oneself to be cornered in some dark garden with an overly ambitious fortune hunter" or "daring to step into the dance with the same partner more than twice in one evening." Cassandra began to wonder if she had slipped through time to Regency England only to be landed in a bizarre sort of convent where she must take a vow of stupidity.

Aunt Cornelia's rather peppery comments and recitations of social strictures lasted past the time she and Cassandra excused themselves from the table, leaving the gentlemen to their port and cigars. The lecture did not end until nearly an hour later, when the men rejoined them in the drawing room for tea and evening prayers, by which time Cassandra had been able to build up a dangerously short temper.

"Find yourself a comfortable seat once the vicar finishes slopping down his second cup of tea, m'dear," Aunt Cornelia warned Cassandra after concluding a homily on the indelicacy of some young girls who actually dared to wear bright colors rather than the favored white or pastels. "That's when he gets his second wind and takes over evening prayers, calling down God's wrath on all the sinful. Goes down the list one by one, you know, touching on thieves, murderers, card players, blasphemers, wanton women, devil worshipers—on and on and on. I think he means to bore them all into repentance, or to death. I know I've contemplated putting a period to my own existence a time or two, listening to him prose.''

Cassandra shook her head. "Is paradise worth this, ma'am?" she asked, for she was already heartily sick of Ignatius Austin and sensed that the rest of the company felt much the same way. "Perhaps a large monetary donation would serve your purpose just as well?"

Aunt Cornelia's ever-present pointed elbow jabbed once more into Cassandra's tender ribs. "What? And spoil the fun of watching Marcus squirm, falling all over himself trying to be polite when he'd like nothing better than to have the man landed on his scrawny rump on the flagway? Every time he allows that walking cadaver to cross his threshold, he is telling me that he loves me. A woman my age, and in my precarious monetary position, needs occasional reassurance. I'm only a courtesy aunt, you know, gel, at least three times removed. No money, no title, and no prospects for these past thirty years. Doesn't pay to be bitter, but there it is. Maybe I should have married dearest Harold when he asked, but as his breath would have felled a calvary officer and he has been below ground these twenty years, I don't see as how I should refine on *might-have-been's*, do you? It's enough that the dear boy cares for me. Why, if he should one day deny that doomsday merchant the house, I should know that I'm no longer wanted."

"Marcus would never throw you out, Aunt Cornelia," Cassandra said, looking across the room to where the marquess—a tic visible in his left cheek—stood listening to the Reverend Mr. Austin. "I realize I've only known him for little more than twenty-four hours, but he seems to be a kind man." As she spoke, Marcus turned his head in her direction and surprised her by winking. "A very kind man."

Aunt Cornelia sniffed, obviously seeing Marcus's playful gesture. "And a bloody handsome fellow—and rich as Croesus into the bargain, isn't that right, Cassandra? As I told you before, you'd be hunting mares' nests, trying to catch that one in the parson's mousetrap. That is what that paper-skulled Walton is planning, isn't it? Cementing his position by marrying his cousin off to his best friend? I didn't come down in the last rain, gel, and I already know who's footing the bill for this debut of yours. Strange. Hadn't thought Walton to be such a downy one."

Cassandra, who had been staring at Marcus this whole time, trying to decide if her attraction to him had been born in gratitude for his rescue of her or if her reaction to him was of a more basic, physical nature, was surprised to hear Aunt Cornelia's opinion of her presence in Grosvenor Square. "Is that all you people think about? Marriage? From the moment we met, all through dinner, and again now. Can't a young woman have anything else to occupy her time, her *mind?*"

"Her mind?" Aunt Cornelia laughed out loud, a harsh, horsey laugh. "And what else is there, I ask you? Oh, maybe in my day, when we were freer in our ways. A few of us raced our own carriages, and gambled deep in private salons. But what else is there, when you get right down to it? What else is a young lady of quality raised to do besides catch herself a suitable husband and breed the next generation of rich, useless gentlemen and giggling, witless twits?"

"What else?" Cassandra—caught up in her argument and goaded by the sickening thought that she, a liberated female, might be trapped forever in this stupid time warp—was quick to point out what, to her, was the obvious. "Women have brains, Aunt Cornelia. *You* have a brain. It's obvious every time you open your mouth. Yet instead of standing up for yourself, finding a way to make yourself independent, you play silly games, teasing Marcus with a bloodsucking evangelist who would make our worst television preachers blush. And then you perpetuate your insecurities by denying young women an education that would lead to independence. Well, let me tell you something—I'll be damned if *I'm* going to sit around here doing nothing more than looking pretty and praying some man who's been raised to think he's God's gift to women will take care of me. Remember, Aunt Cornelia—a woman needs a man as much as a fish needs a bicycle!"

Cassandra's voice had risen as her temper climbed—both at an alarming rate. All her promises to be good and her acknowledgment of the need to hide the true circumstances behind her appearance in Regency London had been forgotten. She nearly jumped out of her skin when the Reverend Mr. Austin, who had come up beside her as she spoke, broke the silence, his rusty baritone resounding throughout the room.

"She-demon! Blasphemer! Taking the good Lord's name in vain! Vile, vile creature!" he ejaculated, one hand to his heart and the other pointing straight at Cassandra, damning her. "Miss Pendelton, your lordship—you are harboring a snake in your bosoms. Begone, Satan's spawn. Begone!"

"She-demon?" Cassandra lifted a hand to wipe some of the agitated preacher's spittle from her cheek. The man was a first-class mental case. "Now look here, Ichabod, or Ignatius, or whatever the hell your name is, why don't you go take a flying—"

"Cassandra!" Marcus interrupted before she could say anything more and compound their problems. "Ignatius, you'll have to forgive the girl. She has had a most traumatic crossing, you understand, losing all her belongings and her abigail as well during a storm just before landing at Dover. Perry's uncle sent along a letter informing us that Miss Kelley is rather high-strung, with unusual views, but I feel sure that she will learn to temper these feelings once she is made to understand that she is in England now, and away from the radical thoughts rampant in our former colonies." He leveled a stare directly at Cassandra. "Isn't that right, Miss Kelley?" he questioned from between clenched teeth.

She was tempted to contradict him. *Very* tempted. All her earlier enthusiasm at seeing London and being outfitted with new clothing had fled as, with nearly each word she spoke, Aunt Cornelia had brought home the daunting fact that she, Cassandra Louise Kelley, was no more than a piece of meat to these people. A piece of meat to be dressed up, toted about, and then married off to the first eligible male. She had been reduced, in the space of a day, from a young woman with a promising career to a milk-and-water puss with no brain, no feelings of any account, no ambitions of her own, and no say in her future.

"No, that's not right. It's no good. I hate this, Marcus," she told him, hoping he'd understand. "You want me to live a lie. I can't pull it off. Every time I stray from the truth a house falls on my head. Trust me, I know what I'm talking about. How do you think I ended up here in the first place?"

"Marcus? What is this chit talking about?" Aunt Cornelia had repositioned herself at the far end of the settee, as if trying to distance herself as far as she could from possible contamination.

"And what's a tell—a-vision?" Peregrine asked, peeking his head out from around Marcus's shoulder. "And a bi-cycle? It sounds like something you'd ride. Is it anything like a hobbyhorse? How would a fish ride on a hobbyhorse?"

"Perry," the Marquess said firmly, "go have some tea. *Now.*"

"Miss Haskins," the vicar implored, having recovered his breath after his emotional outburst, "move away, do, before you are lost. I have been watching this female all evening. She is possessed, I tell you. Possessed. Perhaps she is even a witch. Did she bring a cat with her from America? They use cats as familiars, you know. They have a third teat, from which their familiars suckle. Move away, Miss Haskins, I beg you, if you have a care for your immortal soul!"

Cassandra began to tremble at the Reverend Mr. Austin's reference to witches. Now she had really done it! Why did she have to have such a big mouth? Aunt Cornelia wouldn't have been saying anything out of the ordinary if she had been talking to a real Regency miss. It wasn't the older woman's fault that she was really talking to a nineties female who would rather die than be involved in an 1812 version of *The Dating Game*. Besides—who said she was even going to be stuck in this time warp long enough to be presented in April? It was only March, for crying out loud. Fun was fun and all that, and she did like the gowns and the novelty of the whole business, but to believe she would still be sipping tea and wearing high-waisted gowns in April was enough to make anyone blaspheme.

Cassandra rallied at last, glaring at the Reverend Mr. Austin. "I am *not* a witch. I'm not any kind of a witch. I'm—"

"—tired," the marquess put in strongly, sending her signals with his eyes that told her she had better let him handle this. "Aren't you, Cassandra? Very, very tired."

"Yes—*um*—I guess I'm tired," she answered at last, hating herself for needing him to bail her out of the trouble she'd gotten herself into. "Maybe even exhausted?" she added, trying to be helpful.

"Definitely exhausted," Marcus offered, taking her hand, so that she rose and stood beside him. "And light-headed."

God! Did he have to look at her that way—as if he could mentally burrow straight through her, bending her to his will? "Light-headed? All right," she conceded, giving up the fight. "I'll play along. I'm light-headed. Must be something I ate?"

"Possibly. As a matter of fact, Cassandra," he went on, squeezing her hand in warning, "you might just be about to swoon dead away."

"Oh, now really, Marcus—" Cassandra began in sudden exasperation, at last understanding exactly what he had in mind. But a quick look at the vicar, who was at that moment holding his index fingers in front of her, crossing them to make the age-old sign against the evil eye, kept her from saying more. "Okay. It's your drawing room."

Peregrine Walton stood nearby, his fist shoved firmly into his mouth. Aunt Cornelia, a very astute woman, began chuckling into her handkerchief. And the Reverend Mr. Austin pulled out a prayer book and began to read aloud from the Twenty-third Psalm as Cassandra purposely rolled her eyes up into her head and directed her gracefully "swooning" body straight into Marcus's waiting arms.

Chapter 6

Using the heel of one booted foot, Marcus kicked the door to his sister's bedchamber closed behind him with considerable force and walked to the bed before rudely dumping Cassandra's slim body onto the satin coverlet. "Now, madam," he said, keeping his temper under control with what even he could only term superhuman effort, "would you mind telling me exactly what purpose you had for that distasteful display?"

Cassandra struggled onto her elbows, glaring up at him in a way that told him that, incredibly, *she* believed herself to be the injured party. "Purpose? I have to give you a *reason?* You mean beyond the fact that your domineering aunt is already planning to marry me off, Perry is about as useless as pockets on a giraffe, the *Reverend* Mr. Austin should be under close guard somewhere, playing with finger paints, and you—yes, *you*—barely lifted a finger to help me tonight, so that of course I got into trouble? Is that what you mean, Marcus? Because, if it is, I think you owe me an apology."

"I owe *you* an apology?" The cheek of the girl! Marcus couldn't believe what he was hearing. Not only was the girl an incorrigible nuisance, but she was ludicrous into the bargain. He was gratified that his theory of time travel had proved correct—but couldn't a kind providence have sent him a *man?* A man would readily be

reconciled with his precarious position. A man would do all his possible to insure the secrecy so necessary to a successful experiment. A man would *understand*. How was he supposed to deal with this headstrong female? "I owe you an apology?" he repeated, unable to believe Cassandra could be serious.

"Thank you, Marcus," Cassandra said, slipping from the high tester bed and beginning to pace in front of him. Her grin told him that she knew full well that he hadn't offered his apologies. "I forgive you. Now—what are we going to do about Mr. Austin? You'll be able to handle Corny and Perry. But do you think icky old Ignatius honestly believes I'm a witch, or was he just milking his audience for all it was worth? How much influence does he have? Do people really listen to him, or are they all like Aunt Cornelia, paying him lip service and nothing more? He could be dangerous, I suppose, but I doubt it."

She stopped pacing and stood in front of him, her hands on her hips, her eyes searching his face as if for answers. "Well? What do you think?"

Would this maddening creature ever cease to amaze him? "I think," the marquess said, measuring his words, "that you might have made a tolerable general, as you don't waste your time worrying about what is past, but concentrate on what is to come next. Tolerable, I said— not great. The Reverend Mr. Austin could pose some problem, but you're correct—it's nothing a generous contribution to his personal bank account won't take care of. Aunt Cornelia, however, is another matter entirely. Don't underestimate the woman. We'll have to let her in on our little secret now, or she'll have my liver for saddling her with an incorrigible minx whose antics will most probably lead her, and all of us, to an early grave."

"Thanks for the compliment, Marcus."

Cassandra's smile, her straight white teeth, and those glorious, laughing violet eyes did something strange to his insides. Strange, but not entirely unfamiliar. Only he hadn't expected to have this reaction to Cassandra Kelley. His was a scientific interest only. Or at least he had supposed so, up until the moment she had stepped from the fitting room at Mme. Gerard's, dressed head to toe in the latest fashion, and figuratively delivered a crushing blow to his senses.

He watched as she hopped back onto the bed, allowing her legs to dangle over the side, her shapely ankles visible for his inspection and delight. "In my time we call it 'damage control.' Politicians use it all the time, within minutes of being discovered with their hand either in the till or under some centerfold's skirt. Whoops! Sorry about that. I'm shocking you again, aren't I? Well, never mind. The other reason my mind works this way is because of my job. I have to read every manuscript for plot flaws, for missed *what if's.* Anyway, what will you tell Corny?"

Reluctantly drawing his attention away from Cassandra's ankles, Marcus said, "First of all, I will tell her that you are not insane. I am convinced that will keep her from bolting her bedchamber door and stationing a footman outside it with a blunderbuss in his hands."

"Good point," Cassandra admitted, wincing. "For all her bluster, she looked about to faint herself when I threw my tantrum. It was a tantrum, Marcus. I'm willing to admit that. But you have no idea how frightening it was to listen to her go on and on about how she's going to present me to Society and find me a suitable husband. I don't want a suitable husband. I don't want to *be* here next month. I've got a job to go back to—a career. And, yes, although I'd never tell the vicar, I have to go back to Satchmo, my cat. Poor Satch. What will the kennel do to him when I don't pick him up? I only paid for six days of boarding. And my parents? What about them, Marcus? Sam and Stella are still visiting my uncle Joe in Florida and Mom got involved in some canasta tournament—but she calls at least once a week, just to remind me that I'm still single. What will they think when I don't show up in Manhattan next week? Marcus—I have to go back. I have to!''

She looked so young, so small, so very frightened. Marcus longed to go to her, gather her into his arms, tell her everything would be just fine—but he couldn't. He had thought only as far as to decide the blue mist had something to do with travel through time. He was still woefully ignorant as to the true mechanics of the thing, the *why's* and the *wherefore's*. For instance, had it been no more than a fluke that he had been in the White Tower when Cassandra made her appearance, when she had slipped through some strange crack in time and came to rest in what she called Regency England—or was there some deeper reason for his presence there?

Yet from that point on, that sublime moment when Cassandra had appeared in front of him as if by magic, he had done nothing but think about how wonderful it was that his theories had been proved correct. He hadn't considered that she might serve any purpose other than to enlarge his knowledge and feed his curiosity. And one thing more—occasionally to bemoan the fact that she wasn't a male. He couldn't help wishing that his life did not have to be turned upside down with trying to fit her into Society's notion of an unexceptional female. He wasn't by nature a bitter man, but he did not really believe himself up to dealing with Cassandra's fits and starts for an indefinite time simply for the interests of science.

But he also knew Cassandra wasn't just a subject for him to study. Her situation, her plight, was more than a matter of intellectual interest. She was a human being, a very delightful, delectable human being, and she was frightened. How would he react, should he find himself in a similar circumstance? What if he had stumbled into the blue mist and been whisked forward, to her time? Would he now be coping better than she? He doubted it.

"Marcus?"

"Yes, Cassandra? What is it?"

"You're staring at me. No, let me rephrase that. You're staring straight through me. Look, I'm sorry if I'm somewhat hysterical, but I don't think I can help it. It's like something I read somewhere. The five stages of impending death, or something like that. I think I'm a textbook case. Even if it isn't death I'm facing, you've got to admit, it's close. Denial comes first. I took care of that in the White Tower—all over your boots, if you remember. Then comes anger. I think I've just done that one in spades in the drawing room. Next is guilt, then fear—or grief—and, finally, acceptance."

She lifted her chin, her smile so tremulous, her posture so immensely brave, that he was hard pressed not to go to her, hold her tight in his arms, and offer to "die" in her place.

"Cassandra, I—" he began, only to have her cut him off.

"I think I'd be wise to stick with anger, don't you? Otherwise"—her voice broke—"otherwise I'll have to think about how I only landed here because I broke the rules. That would take care of the guilt, of course, but then all that I'd have left is the grief. Acceptance is completely out of the question, because I can never accept the idea that I might be trapped here forever. I can't accept that. I just can't!"

She looked away, off into the middle distance, then back to him, her violet eyes shimmering with tears. "I didn't want to do this. I promised myself I wouldn't fall apart, but—oh, God, Marcus, hold me. I'm scared. I'm so damned scared."

Abandoning any thoughts as to the right or the wrong

of the thing, Marcus sat beside Cassandra on the side of the bed and, gathering her close against his chest, allowed her to cry all over his pristine cravat.

She sobbed for several minutes, her slim shoulders shaking under the strain of her grief, her fear. He didn't talk, didn't try to dissuade her from giving in to her emotions, but only continued to hold her, gently stroking her back, pressing his chin against the top of her head, rocking slowly, absorbing as much of her pain as he could.

At last, her head still pressed tightly against him, she mumbled a request for a handkerchief, which he gratefully produced, hoping the worst was over. He might consider himself to be a man of the world, but he'd had precious little contact with weeping women. Now he knew why. Weeping women made him nervous. Cassandra made him nervous. She made him feel inadequate, because he knew he could do nothing to help her. And he wanted to help her more than he wanted anything else in this world. He wanted to ease her pain, calm her fears, share his strength with her, gift her with his protection.

He also wanted to get out of Georgina's bedchamber, Cassandra's bedchamber, the bedchamber of a single, unattached female, just as quickly as possible, before Aunt Cornelia, once she had rid herself of the Reverend Mr. Austin, came to investigate the reason behind Marcus's prolonged absence. He had enough on his plate without Corny barging through the door to discover him and Cassandra locked in what only could be called a compromising position.

"Cassandra?" he said at last, attempting to disengage himself from her nearly painful embrace. "Are you feeling more the thing now?"

"If by that you mean am I feeling better, then yes, I think I am. A little," she mumbled into his cravat, her grip tightening on his body. "You aren't going to leave me, are you? I don't want to be alone."

He lifted his hands to her shoulders and gently pressed her back against the mattress. "I'll send for Rose. She'll stay with you."

As he attempted to leave her she reached up, grabbing his forearms with a strength that surprised him, and pulled him down beside her. He could see the apprehension that lingered in her eyes.

"No! I don't want Rose. You should have seen her face this morning when she saw my bra—my undergarments —before I could hide them. I want you. I can speak freely in front of you. You're the only one who understands. Please, Marcus. *Please* don't leave me."

"Cassandra," he began reasonably, "as you told me yesterday, you know enough about this time in history to be aware that you are in dire peril of being compromised, don't you? I shouldn't be here. I shouldn't have been here." Even as he delivered this very proper speech, even as he used it to remind himself that he was not behaving in Cassandra's best interests, Marcus already knew he wasn't going anywhere. He was going to continue to lie here, his body pressed, neck to knees, against this beautiful, vulnerable, trusting, yet disturbingly *forward* young woman for as long as she wished. Maybe longer.

"Oh, all right, madam. You win." Shifting his position so that he was lying on his side, his head braced by one bent arm, he used the tip of one finger to trace the tracks of still-wet tears on Cassandra's cheeks. "Rest now, Cassandra. I won't leave you until you've fallen asleep, all right?"

"Promise?" Cassandra's bottom lip quivered as she asked this question, and it struck the marquess that it was remarkable how much stronger she appeared to him when she allowed her weakness to show. She might have done all that she could to impress him with her independence, with her frank speech, with that business about living alone and working for her daily bread. But now that her veneer of bravado had been scraped away, he could see that no matter how much women might have changed over the years, some things remained the same. They still had the power to bring any man to his knees with their tears.

"Yes, imp, I promise," he told her, his hand now stroking her dark, silky curls, much in the way he would comfort a child, although he was very much aware that Cassandra was no child—and that his feelings were not in the least paternal.

She seemed to relax slowly, her body curving toward his as if seeking his warmth, his strength. "You're a nice man, Marcus," she told him, reaching out a hand and tugging at his badly compromised cravat. "I told Aunt Cornelia as much, you know, but I think I mean it more now than I did before. You're a nice, kind, caring man—not exactly Alan Alda—but a good man. A man a woman instinctively trusts."

Looking down to where her fingers were tangling in the folds of his cravat, he was mesmerized by her informality, her seeming ease with this unusual intimacy. "Who—er—who is Alan Alda?" he asked, hating himself for having to know. "Is he one of your *beaux?*"

Cassandra's laugh was low, husky, and, he could tell, entirely at his expense. "No, Marcus, I don't even know the man. He's—he's an actor. Women in my time think he's 'sensitive.' "

Marcus frowned, unable to understand. "Sensitive? That doesn't sound in the least attractive to me. What is he sensitive about, Cassandra? His looks? His performances? Why would women be attracted to a man who is so thin-skinned?"

The fingers were still moving along his chest, her fingertips tracing the line of his waistcoat. "He's sensitive to a woman's feelings, silly," he heard her say through the roar of his own blood pounding in his ears. "He plays characters who really care about how a woman feels, who aren't afraid to show their own feelings. Even cry."

Marcus's upper lip curled in disdain. "Cry? First you inform me that women of your time want to be like men, and then you tell me that you want the men of your time to be like women. Tell me this, do men in your time wear skirts and carry reticules?"

Cassandra's throaty laugh accelerated into an out-and-out giggle. "Some of them, yes. And earrings. And women wear slacks—pantaloons. Oh, Marcus, it's really very normal. It's only when I see my time through your eyes that it all seems so ludicrous, so backward."

"Yes, of course," Marcus answered, still confused and rather embarrassed for the men of the twentieth century. But at least his questions seemed to have taken Cassandra's mind off her predicament. He didn't think he'd like it if she turned into a watering pot on him again. Why, he might then be pushed to take her completely in his arms and kiss her. And then where would he be? Where would they both be?

Cassandra was quiet for some moments, her hand stilling in its travels over his chest, so that he could feel the tension growing between them in the nearly dark chamber. There were only a few small candles burning in a holder across the room and he was becoming increasingly aware of their intimate positioning on the bed. This wasn't right. Nothing about this was right. Cassandra might not be a virgin, but she was no strumpet either, by her standards or his. Reluctantly, yet knowing he had no choice, he began to disentangle himself, preparing to rise.

"Marcus?"

"Yes, Cassandra?" he didn't like the tone of her voice. It was too low, too tremulous. Too inviting.

The hand was back on his cravat. He could feel the heat of her through to his skin. "Could you do me a favor?"

"A favor?"

"Well, not *exactly* a favor, actually. Could you make me a promise?"

A promise? A bargain? A commitment? At this moment he would offer her anything, if only she would stop touching him; if only she would go on touching him. "Of course, Cassandra," he answered, inwardly praying she wouldn't ask him to allow her to treat him like an older brother, or an uncle—protecting her from the world.

"Thank you, Marcus," she answered, looking up into his eyes, her own eyes twinkling with a mischief so alien to the fear he had seen there earlier that if he were a more prudent man, it should have sent him running from the room. "You're not only nice—you're very trusting. Maybe too trusting, considering the fact that you don't know what I'm going to ask. Marcus"—she hesitated for a moment, a lifetime during which he became excruciatingly aware of the soft curve of her full lips, the extreme delicacy of her complexion—"will you promise to always treat me as an equal? I don't know how long I'll be here. I could be gone by tomorrow morning, I suppose, or I might be here forever. But one thing will never change. I've had twenty-five years to become my own person, and I know I'll never be able to sit quietly and embroider handkerchiefs, or water paint, or wait for someone to speak before saying anything, or be told how to dress or how to sit or what to eat or drink. I just can't. If I have to be on my best behavior seven days a week, twenty-four hours a day, I'll probably explode. I need you to allow me to be me. I'll need to have time alone with you, to let my hair down, to say what's on my mind—to blow off steam. We could go riding—I do ride, you know—or go out walking, or stay up late and talk in your study. Otherwise, this business with the vicar tonight is going to end up looking like a walk in the park next to what I might do in the future.''

"Aunt Cornelia won't understand, Cassandra," he pointed out reasonably, "even if I can convince her that you've traveled here from another time—and I dread that conversation more than you could understand. I know Corny, and she'll give short shrift to any notion that the two of us should be allowed to go off on our own. She'll insist on chaperoning us."

"I already thought of that. But you know something, Marcus? I'll bet there's a way around her—if we just put our minds to it." He felt her fingertips on his chin, tracing the line of his jaw. The minx! He knew, just knew, that she was totally aware of what she was doing, aware of her effect on him. In fact, she looked so innocent that he was sure she was about to say something totally outrageous.

"I know about the rules of Regency Society, Marcus," she said, somehow inching her body even closer to his. "But the rules are a little more relaxed for engaged couples. Betrothed couples are allowed to be alone, aren't they?"

"Betrothed couples?" Yes, she had definitely said something outrageous. Sometimes Marcus wished he wasn't always right. He felt a shiver run down his spine, his instinctive reaction to the threat she had just proposed. What maggot had the girl taken into her head now? Yes, he had mentioned the word *compromise* to her, had reminded her that what they were doing—what she was doing—was not only dangerous but unacceptable, but it was a giant leap from that innocent observation to a betrothal. "Cassandra, you can't mean—"

"Can't I?" Suddenly she was gone, jackknifing into a

sitting position and then slipping from the bed, leaving him lying there alone feeling and, he was sure, looking ridiculous. Her face, her entire body, were so animated, that he was sure she believed she had come up with what, to her at least, was a near-divine inspiration, a remarkably wonderful solution to her problem.

Her next words proved his worst fears. "It would be like something straight out of one of my authors' plots—only not as permanent. Think about it, Marcus. As Perry's American cousin I am vulnerable to all sorts of trouble—most especially Aunt Cornelia's determined matchmaking. Trust me, Marcus, she was building up a real head of steam about it downstairs. Can you imagine the trouble I could cause on what you people call the Marriage Mart? But as your affianced, why, there is nothing I could do that wouldn't be forgiven. Even the Reverend Mr. Austin would have to keep his big mouth shut. You're a marquess, for crying out loud. You're rich, and powerful, and probably very, very important. Nobody would dare to say a word. And, as I already said, it would only be temporary. I'm *not* staying, remember?"

Marcus sat up, scratching behind one ear as he considered the matter. "It might be a workable solution," he said, then frowned at his own stupidity. What was he thinking? "No. No, it won't suit. It won't suit at all."

Cassandra jammed her fists on her hips—a distastefully mannish mannerism that he would have to rid her of during their lessons. "And why not, Marcus? Chicken? It's not like I'd really expect you to marry me."

"And that, my dear termagant, is exactly what is wrong with your plan," he said, tapping the tip of her straight little nose as he walked past her to seat himself in a small slipper chair. "Think about it a moment, if you please. If I am to announce our betrothal—which would shock all of London, as we have just met, but which would be a nine-days' wonder, lasting only until another scandal rears its head, which in London is depressingly often—and then you were to disappear without warning, what would happen then, I ask you? Will I be hanged for your murder? And if we could explain your absence, would I be destined to become a laughing-stock, having been thrown over by a mere slip of an American? And, to take this forward to the next logical step, what if you were to remain locked in my time— what then? Would we have to marry, no matter what our separate feelings in the matter? Would you jilt me, or would I have to play the cad?''

She whirled to face him, her expression one of dawn-ing dismay, but when she spoke he realized it was not his carefully pointed out *situation* that bothered her— but his heart. "Why didn't I think of this before? You're already in love with someone. Oh, Marcus—what a mess. How are you going to explain me to the woman? No wonder you said I was to be Perry's cousin. But what's going to happen to me when you marry? Perry and I can't continue to live here, that's for sure."

Then her expression cleared and her eyes narrowed. "Wait. Something's wrong here. I think I'd better back up a minute. Aunt Cornelia told me you'll never marry. She was adamant about that. And you're not—well, never mind what you're not, but I can tell that you're not. Women know these things. What's wrong, Marcus? Do you hate all women? Did some woman turn you down, break your heart—and now you've sworn never to marry?"

Marcus rose, standing stiffly, with all the dignity he could muster. In truth, he would have liked nothing bet-ter than to throw Cassandra over his knee and thrash her for her insolence. Did she honestly believe that he didn't know she had nearly catalogued him as a man-milliner, a lover of men? "You, Miss Kelley, are the most perni-cious, nosy, *indelicate* female it has ever been my displeasure to encounter. No, I have not been disappointed in love. I have merely found my life less encumbered without having to deal with feminine whims and wiles—feminine whims and wiles women of your time, Miss Kelley, seem to have elevated to an art form.''

He walked to the door, laying a hand on the knob as he paused to put in a parting shot, a crushing setdown meant to put this topic of conversation to rest once and for all. ''I have no need to set up a nursery, as I have an odiously wealthy, passably responsible distant cousin to whom I will be grateful to turn over my title and any entailed estates upon my death. This house, my favorite estate in Surrey, and a generous allowance will go to Perry, so that he will never want for anything.

''I have had—and I know this plain speech will not put you to the blush—and will continue to have suitable arrangements with discreet, willing women who accommodate my needs. I am leading a life that I enjoy, pursuing my studies and interests to the top of my bent. In short, I have a comfortable, pleasing existence. I see no need to clutter that life with a wife. And *that,* Miss Kelley, ends this discussion.''

He bowed deeply from the waist, then added, ''Oh, and by the by, Miss Kelley—I am *not* chickenhearted. If I were I should have stood back and let the Reverend Mr. Austin harangue you into insensibility, then had you dragged off to Bedlam so that you could no longer plague me out of my mind. And now, good night. Please ring for Rose to help you out of your gown and get a good night's rest. We begin our lessons in the morning at nine in my study. You are to be prompt.''

''But, Marcus—''

He didn't wait to hear what she had to say, what insanely logical argument her quick, entirely too intelligent, inventive mind had come up with while he had been speaking, but only opened the door and all but barreled through it, slamming it behind him. And he had actually considered kissing the woman? He could count upon less entanglement if he were to embrace an octopus!

Peregrine was just outside in the hallway, pacing, and nibbling at one side of his left index finger. "Hullo there, Marcus," he said, his grin sheepish. "About time you showed your face. You've been closeted in there for nearly an hour, do you know that?"

"Yes, actually, I did. But thank you *so* much for that most intriguing bit of information. I believe I shouldn't know what to do without you about to point out the obvious. What are you doing here, Perry, other than counting off the minutes?" Marcus asked, longing for the solitude of his study and his decanter of brandy.

"Me? Well, that's simple enough. There's no need to put your back up, Marcus. Corny shooed me up here to find out what's keeping you. You should have been downstairs with us, you know. We had a devil of a time ousting the vicar. There's a fellow who'd come for the wedding and stay for the christening, as my father used to say. It wasn't until Corny thought to offer him that nearly full snifter of your best brandy from your study that he got off his knees and stopped ranting and raving about the devil's doings coming to Mayfair. Creepy sort of fellow, the vicar is. Ran from the house clutching the decanter to his breast, completely ignored Corny's arguments that she had offered him a snifter—and not the whole piece."

Marcus's curse was low and impassioned.

"Bother you, eh, Marcus? Heirloom, ain't it? Aunt Cornelia says it's too bad, seeing as how the decanter has been in the family for ages, but she says it's a small price to pay for being rid of the vicar. Anyway, Corny's gone stomping off to bed with the headache, so you're safe for now. But she also said to tell you she'll be waiting in the

drawing room at three tomorrow, ready to tear a strip off
your hide for bringing home another stray. I can't say I
like that above half, Marcus, being called a stray. And
don't say she didn't mean me as well as Cassandra because it won't fadge. Lord knows she takes every chance
she gets to jab at me.''

Peregrine's expression was so woebegone and his tan-
gled recital so absurd that the marquess, whose nerves
had been stretched almost to the snapping point, could
only throw back his head and laugh out loud at the
mental image of the righteously holy Ignatius Austin
chasing himself down the street, the filched brandy decanter tucked up under one bony arm.

He laughed for some moments, clutching his arms to
his waist and shaking his head until, once more gaining
control of himself, he belatedly sought to soothe his
friend's injured sensibilities. Taking only a moment to
look back at Cassandra's closed door, he slipped a com-
panionable arm around Peregrine's shoulders and began
leading the other man back down the hallway. ''Corny
doesn't mean any harm, Perry. She just likes to remind
you now and again that, although she considers herself
also to be a stray, at least she is a connection of mine.
Would you like me to adopt you, old friend? That should
serve to spike her guns.''

''Adopt me? Marcus, if that don't beat the Dutch. First
I'm saddled with an American cousin, and now you want
to sweep me into the bosom of your family. In the space
of one day and night you've thoroughly bungled my family tree, you know that? We Waltons are not so shabby on
our own, you know. I can trace m'ancestors back to
Prince Charlie—even if it is on the wrong side of the
blanket. But thank you anyway.''

As they neared the staircase Perry looked back down
the hallway. ''How is she? Fainted dead away, didn't she?
I hadn't thought she was the sort, although I have to

own it, the Reverend Mr. Austin is enough to make *my* knees shake like dry bones in a sack."

"Miss Kelley is bearing up nicely under the strain of making an utter fool of herself, thank you," Marcus replied, only vaguely ashamed of himself for speaking flippantly of his beleaguered time traveler. "And she is not slow to come up with ways to protect herself. She suggested we become betrothed, in order to shield her from Corny's matchmaking attempts—and as a way to be alone with me, out of sight of people who might not understand her ways."

Peregrine tripped on the stairs and would have fallen if the marquess had not swiftly steadied him. "Betrothed? You? Oh, Marcus, that is rich, isn't it? You? Married?"

"And what would be so odd about that?" Marcus felt stung into replying. He might not wish to marry, but he did not quite care to hear that his good friend found the notion laughable. "Am I such a poor candidate for a husband?"

Now it was Peregrine's turn to collapse into laughter, and he leaned against the curving wall that stood to one side of the wide staircase. "The worst, Marcus. The absolute worst! Racing about the countryside whenever the whim takes you, digging up moldy ruins or picking weeds to see if they'd make good medicines, and losing yourself in books for days on end, either reading them or writing them. And what about those bottles in your study? What woman of any sense would want jars stuffed with birds' eggs and creepy, crawling things cluttering up her household?"

Marcus brushed past Peregrine and continued down the staircase at a rapid clip so that his friend had to hurry along or be left behind. "Intellectual pursuits, Perry, all of them. I served my country with Nelson, I have taken up my seat in Parliament, I am a good landlord to my tenants at my estates in Sussex and Surrey. It isn't every man who is content to be a drawing room ornament, or happy riding neck or nothing to hounds, or committed to dedicating himself to gaming too deep."

"That's true enough, I suppose," Peregrine said. He held tightly to the bottom of the banister and swung partway around, landing gracefully on the tiled foyer floor, then followed the marquess as that man headed for the rear of the mansion and his private study. "The ladies don't much like any of that business above half. Now that I think on it, there's a precious lot of things the ladies don't like. My aunt Lillian once chased my uncle Henry halfway around the downstairs, waving his own dueling pistol at him because she found a bill for a diamond necklace he gave to one of his Covent Garden dancers."

"And that's another thing," Marcus persisted, pushing past the hovering Goodfellow and into his study. "I keep but one mistress at a time—and very discreetly, I must add—and am conversant with the social graces. My face is not such that it sends young children running for their nurses when I ride in the park, my dress is unexceptional, even according to Beau's standards, and I never drink myself into a stupor. And—and to top it all off, I'm sensitive. *Damned* sensitive!" He collapsed into a leather wing chair, ending, "I have all the makings of an exemplary husband."

Perry, pulling at his collar as if the action would facilitate regaining the breath he had lost in this mad chase his friend had led him on through the house, sank into a facing chair. "Well, now that you put it that way, Marcus," he offered apologetically, "I suppose you're right. Cassandra is right. Isn't it above everything wonderful how that all worked out? My felicitations to you both."

Peregrine's last words brought Marcus back to full attention. He longed for an end to this conversation but, knowing Peregrine, if he didn't make himself clear he would wake one morning to see that his friend, acting as Cassandra's cousin, had sent out notices of the betrothal to the newspapers. "Felicitations? Perry, there are times when you are a great disappointment to me. Haven't you been listening? I am not going to become betrothed to Miss Kelley. I'm not even sure if I *like* the young woman. She's entirely too argumentative for my taste, for one thing, and considerably forward in her manner."

"Really, Marcus?" Peregrine shook his head. "Seems nice enough to me. Warned me about Harriette and her memoirs, you know."

Marcus sighed. "Perry, in all the years I've known you, you've never so much as said boo to Harriette Wilson— or any of her sisters."

"I know that, Marcus," the other man answered testily. "But I might have. Someday. Only now I won't, of course. See how much trouble Cassie has saved me?"

"Cassie?" Marcus didn't like the sound of that. It sounded entirely too familiar.

Peregrine nodded, grinning. "Gave me her permission. Wouldn't be so free otherwise, for I'm up to snuff on the social graces m'self, you know. Stands to reason, though, me being her cousin and all. *Cassie.* You couldn't be so familiar, of course, as you're not related. Cousin Cassie. Cousin Cassie. Nice. Has a bit of a ring to it, yes?"

It had been a very long day, which was probably why Marcus felt pushed to retort hotly, "Much as I appreciate the wholeheartedness of your commitment to this endeavor, Perry, may I remind you that Cassandra is *not* your cousin? She isn't *anybody's* cousin—at least not anybody who will be born for more than another hundred and fifty years."

Perry smiled—quite smugly, or so Marcus thought— and folded his arms across his pudgy middle. "No need to fly into the boughs, my friend. You could call her Cassie, too, if you were betrothed to her, that is. Yes, the more I refine on it, Cousin Cassie has come up with a splendid notion. Might even be the making of you, Marcus. Shall we talk about it awhile—especially about how we'll go about breaking the news to Corny? Call me a stray, will she? Now I'm to be a member of the family— and you won't have to go to the bother of adopting me.''

The marquess, a student of strategy since his days sailing with Nelson, was aware of the benefits of diversion, especially when he knew that any other course could end only with his rising from his chair and flailing his good friend heavily about the head and shoulders until he had beaten some semblance of sense into the man. "You know, *Cousin* Perry," he said conversationally, "with all that has transpired in the past twenty-four hours, I believe I have forgotten to mention an extremely interesting book on ancient mazes that I discovered in one of the book stalls the other day. There is a certain passage in it concerning the Troy Town maze that I found particularly interesting. Would you care to have me read it to you?''

Perry came out of his chair like a shot fired from a cannon. "Love to, Marcus. Truly. Mazes? Interesting. Absolutely top rate. But I just remembered—I promised Georgie Frankenham I'd meet him at Boodle's for a late round of cards. Can't imagine how it slipped my mind. Not polite, is it, when you're making up the fourth? See you in the morning?''

"In the morning," Marcus agreed, watching Peregrine's departing back before reaching to the table beside him and picking up one of the two strangely put together books he had found in Cassandra's purse. The books, called *Travel Guides*, one concentrating on London and the other a general compendium to all of England, had kept him busy most of that afternoon, engrossing him with their strange pictures and stranger words until well after the dinner gong rang. He had read nearly half of the London guide before Goodfellow came looking for him, discreetly pointing out that the family had all been gathered in the drawing room for some time.

Now, at last convinced he would not be disturbed for the remainder of the evening, he pushed away all thoughts of Peregrine, Aunt Cornelia, Cassandra, and her outrageous proposal, and opened the larger of the two booklets, the one dealing with England in general. A few minutes later Goodfellow tiptoed in, placed a fresh decanter of brandy on the table beside his master, and tiptoed out again. The marquess did not even notice his presence. Turning page after page, Marcus at last came to a section on Sussex.

Later, just as the tall clock in the far corner of the room struck the hour of twelve, Marcus Pendelton, Marquess of Eastbourne, placed a slightly trembling finger on page 214 and traced each and every word once, then twice, and then a third time. *Cassandra has told me that she is frightened, and justly so,* he thought. *Would it reassure her, I wonder, to learn that she is no longer the only person in this house to be experiencing some niggling concern for the future and their place in it?*

Chapter 7

"Where does a two-thousand-pound canary sit?"

Marcus looked up from his notes and peered at her across the desk. "I haven't the foggiest notion, Cassandra," he answered in the same slightly exasperated tone he might use when dealing with a precocious but well-loved child. "Where *does* a two-thousand-pound canary sit?"

Grinning, for she had been trying without visible success to gain his attention for the past twenty minutes, Cassandra fell back in her chair, spread her arms wide, and announced gleefully, "Anywhere he wants to!"

Marcus directed a long, dispassionate stare at her. "And this passes for amusement in your time? Interesting." With that, and still remarkably straight-faced, he returned his attention to the papers on the desk.

"Well, I for one don't understand," Aunt Cornelia said a moment later from her own perch on the window seat. "Why wouldn't it sit in the trees? You make precious little sense at times, gel."

Cassandra hopped out of the chair and looked at each of them in turn; then shrugged, taking her comedic failure in stride. "Tough room," she remarked as if to herself as she approached the desk and picked up a small jar holding what appeared to be a long-dead frog. "I could trot out a little Eddie Murphy, I suppose, but I don't think you guys are ready for that yet.''

"If this Murphy fellow is anything like that woman, Lucille Ball, whose Italian vineyard antics you reported to me yesterday, then no, Cassandra, I do not believe we English are as yet 'ready' for such humor." Marcus stabbed one of the papers with his forefinger. "For now, I should like to get back to our discussion of twentieth-century architecture, if you please. We spoke of skyscrapers yesterday, but I am still having some trouble imagining the form. Perhaps if you'd draw one for me?"

"I hear and obey, O master," she said as she bowed in his direction. Her smile fading, Cassandra dutifully picked up the sketchbook Marcus had given her and a stick of charcoal and retired to the opposite end of the window seat, which was still occupied by Aunt Cornelia, her self-appointed chaperon and near-constant companion these past three weeks.

And what a wild three weeks they had been, beginning with Marcus's confession to his relative that they were harboring a bona fide time traveler beneath their roof. After that flabbergasted woman had recovered from her swoon, it had taken her no more than a few days to pass from disbelief to concern, then to out-and-out delight. She had pestered Cassandra nearly every waking moment with penetrating questions about people, fashions, and scandals that might be of interest to "an old woman who must take her delights where she can."

Peregrine Walton, relieved of his position of "cousin," at least within the confines of the Grosvenor Square mansion, had become a good friend. He was always there to save Cassandra from herself whenever, as she still did, she suffered a mental lapse and went groping for a light switch as she entered a darkened room, or forgot herself and asked one of the servants if she could have a Coke with her dinner. Although obviously still nervous around her, Peregrine had announced only the other day that he believed Cassandra to be "a ripping good sport about the thing," for he, if landed in a similar situation, "should surely have slipped my wits by now."

And there had been times when Cassandra might have agreed with Peregrine's assessment of the effects of time travel. As March gave way to early April, she had wondered more than once whether this whole affair was nothing more than a bad dream, and she had been the victim of some freak accident—like walking in front of a bus—and she was actually lying in a coma somewhere.

But that wasn't her only theory. After all, the characters who resided in Grosvenor Square with her could have been drawn from any of several dozen characters she had read about as she edited books for the Mayfair line. Perhaps her familiarity with the architecture, the furnishings, the food, the fashions—and, most especially, the eccentric characters of the time—had combined with her presence in London to make her believe she had actually traveled through time, when all she had really done was to take a nose dive down those curving stairs in the White Tower. She might really be confined to an asylum and was mistaking the nurses and doctors for real Regency people.

For some reason the idea of an asylum seemed preferable to being locked in a coma in a hospital. At least she was eating well.

It was only Marcus's presence in her life that kept her from putting too much credence in either theory. Yes, she might have dreamed up a devastatingly handsome Regency hero along with all the others, but Marcus was unlike any Regency hero she had ever encountered in her authors' books. Regency heroes, after all, were by and large arrogant sorts and spent their time going to balls, and sparring with Gentleman Jackson, and going to cockfights, and caring more for their wardrobes and their mistresses and their horseflesh than they did about the effect of sunlight on mushrooms or the reason Roman roads still survived while many newer, English-built roads were constantly in need of repair.

In short, the man was a bottomless pit of curiosity on every subject from war to morals to literature to politics to imagining the possibility of traveling through time. In the past three weeks she had more than once felt as if she had been turned inside out and upside down by his questions, his constant probing, his insatiable appetite for learning all he could about her world. And he had absorbed the information she had given him like a thirsty sponge; he had assimilated knowledge with an ease that fascinated her. Patiently, and while taking copious notes on all she said, he had led her through the subjects of electricity, transportation, television, the two world wars, the latest antibiotics, organ transplantation, the diminishing rain forests, and even nuclear energy and space travel.

He did, however, become upset when she could not go into detail on some subject that interested him— resorting to taunts as to the quality of the college education she had received in "the colonies." When he had laid her solar calculator in front of her and demanded she explain how it worked, she had apologized through clenched teeth that she had not had the foresight to bring a set of encyclopedias with her when she entered the blue mist, a remark that had only led him to pick up his pen once more and inquire into what advancements had been made in the area of publishing.

Between questions concerning her "time," she received lessons from Aunt Cornelia and Marcus in the proper behavior of a young lady in Regency times— schooling her in matters of deportment, the importance of titles, and explaining the intricacies of morning visits and calling cards. Cassandra had fallen into bed each night exhausted, too tired to cry, too worn out to worry as to whether or not her stay in Regency England was indeed to be permanent.

Her gorgeous new wardrobe had arrived, but that didn't mean that Marcus had allowed her any more fresh air than she could breathe while pacing like a prisoner inside his walled garden. Her only contacts with the outside world had been the half dozen or so merchants summoned to the house to supplement her wardrobe with various pelisses, reticules, scarves, gloves, boots, and bits of intimate apparel, and a French hairdresser who had wrung his hands at the sad state of her hair for nearly an hour before taking ten or twelve infinitesimal snips at it, standing back, and announcing that she was now *ravissante*.

She had become accustomed to the formality of their everyday meals, the pomp and ceremony that accompanied the serving of each lush course, and she now believed being served hot chocolate in bed every morning and stepping straight from her prepared tub—to be wrapped in a fluffy, warmed towel before being led to a dressing table where Rose lovingly dried and brushed her hair—beat the hell out of grabbing a quick shower and wolfing down a strawberry Pop Tart before racing for the subway.

But, as Cassandra well knew, she was not a happy camper, no matter how luxurious her life had become from the moment she stepped out of the marquess's carriage in front of the stone steps that led up to the mansion in Grosvenor Square.

For she was a prisoner, not only in time, but in this same mansion. Her outburst that first day—she knew her behavior at the time had been shocking—had led her to make Marcus a startling proposition, and now, three weeks later, she was still waiting for an answer. Yes, their possible betrothal had been a spur-of-the-moment inspiration and, yes, she had known how forward she was, lying on the bed with him, deliberately toying with his cravat and his emotions, but she had been desperate.

She was still desperate, and Marcus had avoided being alone with her ever since that night, as if she might attack him if neither Aunt Cornelia nor Peregrine were present.

The whole situation was beginning to prey on her nerves.

"There," she announced at last, rising from the window seat to take the sketchbook to Marcus. "One skyscraper—two actually—for I drew one of the Twin Towers at the Trade Center. Satisfied?"

Marcus took the sketchbook and studied the drawing carefully before looking up at her severely. "I believe I recall telling you that I don't appreciate being fobbed off with fanciful fibs whenever you become bored with my questions. It was bad enough when you tried to tell me that you can send printed pages from one country to another through wires—"

"It's called a fax machine, Marcus, and it does work," Cassandra protested, interrupting him. "I'm sorry if I can't tell you how, but it does."

"Don't attempt to distract me," he warned, turning the sketchbook upside down, as if looking at it from another angle might improve matters. "This is not a building, Cassandra. This is nothing but a rectangle with squares inside it."

"Those aren't squares, Marcus, they're windows. The whole building is almost nothing but windows. And nearly all skyscrapers look like rectangles."

He eyed her quizzically. "Where are the columns, the pediments, the buttresses, the domes? This is all so unremittingly plain, so ugly. And you call this progress?" He shook his head, throwing down the book.

Cassandra agreed with him, but she wasn't going to

give him the satisfaction of admitting it. "Hey, you asked" was all she said as she took her seat in front of the desk.

"She's right, you know, Marcus," Aunt Cornelia said from the window seat. "I don't know why you go on and on, day in, day out, about such unimportant matters. I haven't given up my lifelong habit of staying abed until noon to hear about obese canaries. Now, if you ask me, Sally Jersey's fate is much more to the point. My dear gel, can't you recall what happened to her?"

Cassandra turned to look at the older woman, once more amazed by her erect posture and stern features, a façade of sophistication that, if she were to have been born in the twentieth century, would have hidden the heart of an avid reader of supermarket tabloids. "Sorry, Aunt Cornelia. All I can remember is that she once had an affair with your Regent, people called her 'Silence' because she talked all the time, and she was a patroness of Almack's. Marcus," she said, turning back to him in sudden anticipation, "will you be able to get me a voucher to Almack's? I'd kill to see that place."

"I doubt you will have to resort to bloodshed, my dear, as I do, for my sins, travel in the first circles," Marcus answered, his tone so calm, so controlled, that Cassandra longed to jolt him into awareness of her by doing something totally outrageous. She settled for crossing her legs so that her ankle showed below her hem, a move she had already learned seemed to rob Marcus of some of his thirst for knowledge. It worked. Turning away, he said, "Cassandra, please," as if this was sufficient to correct her wanton behavior. "I thought you had come to understand at least the rudiments of correct posture."

"I've committed them all to memory, my lord," she answered, deliberately swinging her leg, her toes pointed inside her soft kid shoes. "What you haven't asked me is if I give a flying flip about them. Because I don't. In spades, I don't." And then, knowing she was making an ass of herself, she uncrossed her legs and folded her hands in her lap.

"I am, of course, shattered to hear this confession," Marcus returned coldly, picking up his papers and laying them in a drawer. "However, we have been at this all morning, haven't we? Aunt, it would appear that the child has had enough of questions for the moment. Perhaps she should have a lie-down before dinner?"

Aunt Cornelia rose, approaching the desk. "But, Marcus," she said, frowning, "I thought the gel was to have her first dancing lesson this afternoon? I've already told that chuckleheaded Peregrine Walton to wait upon you in the music room."

Cassandra, who had begun to think going to her room for a while might be a good idea, immediately sprang to attention. "Dancing lessons? All right, Marcus, now we're getting somewhere! Have you hired a French dancing master, or is Perry to be my partner?"

Marcus moved out from behind the desk, his tall, impeccably clad body having the same impact on her senses as it did whenever he came within three feet of her. "Perry? If you prefer him, of course Perry shall partner you. Aunt, we will see you at dinner?"

Aunt Cornelia, who had earlier announced her intention to have the carriage brought round at precisely five o'clock, in time for a judicious jaunt through the park to see who else of the top two thousand had come toddling back to town, repeated that information. Then, with an uncharacteristic wink to Cassandra, she sailed out of the room, leaving the pair unchaperoned and causing Cassandra to wonder if she might have gained an ally in her notion to talk Marcus into a mock engagement.

"Marcus?" Cassandra said as the two of them also headed for the door.

"Yes, my dear?"

"Am I wrong, or were you surprised when I asked if Perry was to be my partner? I mean, *you* weren't planning to teach me yourself were you?"

"Is the prospect so impossible to conceive, Cassandra? I do have a nodding acquaintance with the steps, you know."

Cassandra could have kicked herself for jumping to conclusions, but it was too late to do anything about it. Marcus, by the simple act of never being alone with her after that first night, had made it perfectly clear that he wished their association to remain that of teacher and student or, even worse, professor and scientific oddity. She'd had to bite her tongue more than once so that she wouldn't call him "Professor Henry Higgins" and then offer to recite "The rain in Spain stays mainly on the plain" in an exaggerated cockney voice.

"Even the waltz, Marcus?" she countered at last, taking refuge in sarcasm. "Or is that one too scandalous for a fine, upstanding gentleman like yourself?" she asked as they crossed the threshold into the music room, to see Peregrine sitting at the piano, looking as if he'd rather be somewhere else. Anywhere else.

"While it is not generally accepted throughout society in its purest form, I have danced it minus the allemande a time or two at private parties. However, today we will begin with a simple Scottish reel. Ah, here, as promised, is the so estimable Mr. Walton, come to assist us. Perry?" he asked. His friend rose, backing away from the piano as if it might bite him. "Are you ready for our first lesson? There has been a slight change of plan. I will play and you will partner your 'cousin.' Is that agreeable?"

Perry nodded, cleared his throat, and nodded again. "I suppose I'm ready, although I have to own it, I ain't exactly brimming over with joy at the prospect," he said at last, wincing. "Not really my strongest suit, you know,

Marcus. Dancing, that is. Couldn't be, or else why would my partners keep telling me they'd much rather I fetched them a cup of lemonade when I show up to claim my dance?''

"Oh, poor Perry," Cassandra said sympathetically, slipping her arm through his. "Two left feet, huh? Well, don't worry. I can teach you a dance where you won't step on anyone's toes. There's no bowing, or circling each other, or touching of any kind. Would you like to try it?''

Peregrine brightened. "No touching? None? Not that I've ever hazarded the waltz, you understand, but those Scottish reels can be the very devil, with all that hopping about and *to*ing and *fro*ing. Marcus? What do you think? Could we give it a go? You're always wanting to know about Cassie's time.''

Cassandra turned her head, smothering a grin by biting on the inside of her cheek, waiting for the marquess to answer. Peregrine had hit on just the proper argument, she knew—reminding Marcus of his unending thirst for knowledge.

"All right," Marcus said at last. "In the interests of science. If Cassandra agrees.''

"Oh, Cassandra most definitely agrees, Marcus," she said, quickly seating herself at the piano before he could change his mind. "Luckily, my mother insisted on piano lessons, although this isn't technically a piano, is it? Well, close enough, I suppose, though I'm used to eighty-eight keys. Marcus, if I play a few chords and a simple melody, do you think you can pick it up? You played so beautifully last night after dinner.''

"I doubt it will be too taxing," he answered from behind her. He leaned forward to peer over her shoulder, and her fingers trembled slightly as she touched them to the keys.

She ran a few scales, just to limber up, then hesitated,

deciding on a tune. She didn't want to try anything too complicated, although the urge to rip off a quick rendition of the introduction to one of Billy Joel's raucous piano solos was almost unbearable. She settled at last for a simple set of chords and a toned-down version of a recent "top ten hit," her senses leaping at the sound of the familiar upbeat melody. She played it through three times, adding more passion each time, closing her eyes as she gave herself up to the music, the beat, the memories the song evoked of the free, unfettered life she had left behind not a month ago.

When she had finished (not without a suitable flourish) she opened her eyes and saw that Perry had covered his ears, his expression one of absolute horror. As he slowly realized that the music had stopped, he tentatively removed his hands, saying, "Are you done? Did you break it? Marcus, I think she broke it. It never sounded like that before."

"The piano isn't broken, Perry," Cassandra said, laughing. "Oh, I'll admit it didn't sound as good as it would have on a real piano, but it wasn't half bad. Was it, Marcus?"

"That depends, my dear," the marquess replied, helping her to rise so that he could take her place in front of the keyboard. "If it was supposed to put a person in mind of a riot in progress, I would have to say you've succeeded admirably." He extended his left hand and flawlessly executed the succession of chords she had just played. "Amazing." A moment later he added his right hand, struggling for a few bars, his right hand dragging along slightly behind his left. Then he smiled as he finally got it right.

Cassandra found herself longing to throw her arms around him and kiss him. He was so interested in everything, so open to new ideas.

"Absolutely amazing, Perry—isn't it amazing?" Marcus said. "So alive, so vibrant."

Peregrine puffed out his cheeks and exhaled in a rush. "Sounds like an army on the move, Marcus, if you ask me. Dear God! Cassie—what are you doing?"

Marcus had continued to play, and Cassandra found herself tapping one foot along with the rhythm, her eyes once more shut in ecstasy. It took only a moment for her tapping foot to send impulses to the rest of her body, and she began to dance, her head and shoulders moving to the beat, her hips swaying, her feet shuffling against the polished wooden floor, her arms raised, her fingers snapping in time with the music.

It was good. It wasn't great, but it was good. She could imagine the song as it was played on her compact-disc player, almost hear Paul McCartney's voice as he belted out the lyrics. With her eyes closed, she was back in her Manhattan apartment, her compact-disc player turned up loud as she sang and danced her way through her weekly house-cleaning.

Cassandra's daydream splintered as Marcus brought down both hands in a discordant crash of sound. Blinking her way back to reality, she turned to look at him, her arms still raised above her head, and saw that a tic had begun to work in his cheek. "Hey! Marcus? What's your problem?"

"Well, that's easy enough to answer," Peregrine supplied when Marcus didn't say anything. "He's worried about you, Cassie, that's all. So was I, for that matter. You looked about to take a fit. You all right now?"

"That will do, Perry," Marcus said softly, rising from the velvet-topped bench. "Cassandra was not about to 'take a fit.' I believe, as a matter of fact, that she was dancing. An—an interesting set of maneuvers, wasn't it?"

"Interesting?" Clearly Peregrine was aghast. *"Interesting?* She was shaking all over like a blancmange!"

Yes, Cassandra thought, feeling rather pleased with herself, Perry was definitely aghast. What pleased her more was that Marcus wasn't aghast. He might be upset, but he wasn't aghast. He was *interested.* What a shame she had been forced to dance in this silly, juvenile sprigged muslin gown. Imagine how *interested* Marcus would have been if he could have seen her dance in her black leather slacks and white lace camisole! And wasn't it nice to see that his *interest* in her could be more than academic?

Hey, a girl might be lost in time, but that didn't mean she didn't like to feel attractive, did it?

"Let me guess. We've concluded this particular experiment, haven't we?" she asked when Peregrine took refuge on a nearby chair, fanning himself with a large white handkerchief. "Unless you'd like to see our version of the waltz?" she ended, thinking of no other way to explain "slow dancing."

Peregrine hopped to his feet once more. "The waltz? I don't know about that, Cassie. I might step on your hem or something. I do that a lot, you know. Clarissa Felton slapped me with her fan last season when I tripped over her flounce—broke two of its sticks on my forehead. Hurt like the very devil. Don't know why she hit me. Not my fault, after all. I told her I couldn't do it."

Marcus, who had been quiet, almost too quiet, stepped forward. "I agree, Perry. You are not at your best in the waltz. But we must get on with Cassandra's lessons, as the Season is already embarked on its first, tentative flush of activity. Perhaps you would like to play for us while I test Cassandra's proficiency?"

"You, Marcus?" Cassandra's eyes were twinkling. She just knew they were twinkling. "But what of my demonstration of my sort of waltz? I really would like to show it to you. It might go a long way toward explaining my culture to you.''

"Later, Cassandra," Marcus said, looking at her levelly as he took her hand and led her to the center of the room. "First your lesson, all right? Perry? If you would be so kind?"

"Are you sure, Marcus? I mean, the waltz is rather, *um*, intimate, and we are alone here, aren't we? Corny wouldn't like it above half."

Still looking at Cassandra, Marcus replied, "You've become damned moral now that you have a female cousin, haven't you, Perry? Close your eyes as you play if you would seek to spare your blushes. Now, if you please, Perry? We're waiting. Cassandra, if you would pretend that you are wearing one of your best gowns and reach down—delicately, my dear—and hold out your skirt with your right hand, just here, where your hand falls naturally when you hold your arm at your side. Ah, that's it. And now, a curtsy, if you please, just as Corny has taught you—lift your chin high and hold out your left hand to me as I bow."

It was like something out of a dream, a scene from an old movie, a romantic novel. Cassandra, delicately holding out her skirt as she extended her left hand, put one foot back and sank into a curtsy. Marcus's right hand steadied her as she looked up into his clear emerald eyes. A moment later Peregrine began to play and Marcus drew her to her feet with the power of his gaze, laid his hand lightly on her waist, and led her into the first steps of the dance—at the same time sweeping her into a fantasy land of long-ago elegance and manners and romance.

She followed him effortlessly, her mother's insistence that she attend ballroom dance classes at the local women's club at last bearing fruit. With her right hand barely touching his left, all her attention, all her feeling, was centered in that small, favored place on her back where his right hand deftly instructed her as to the direction of the next steps in the dance.

Her hand burned where it touched his sleeve just below his shoulder, and although they were a good two feet apart, she felt that they had never been closer, that no two people on this earth had ever been closer. His back was so straight, his shoulders so broad; he moved with the grace of a panther, a dancer, a god, leading her with the caressing whip-touch of his hands, the magnetic pull of his eyes, the heady power of his presence.

They dipped and swayed with the music, twirling round and round the small circle of bare floor, Cassandra's heart beating in tune with Peregrine's playing. She was Cinderella at the ball, Miss America wearing her crown for the first time as she drifted down the runway and into the throng of applauding subjects. She was Princess Di, opening a ball with her Prince, Grace Kelly in her role in *High Society,* Eliza Doolittle dancing all night in *My Fair Lady*.

Was the Regency Era a good time frame for romance novels? Yes. Yes! Oh, God, *yes.*

They made one more turn and came to a halt in front of Peregrine as the waltz ended. Noting the small, instructive inclination of his head, Cassandra took a step back and dropped into another curtsy as Marcus bowed over her hand. The quick, slight touch of his lips against her skin nearly sent her crashing inelegantly to the floor, almost unable to deal with such ecstasy and remain upright at the same time.

"Thank you, Perry." She heard Marcus's voice as if from a distance, then watched as Peregrine beat a hasty retreat from the room, looking for all the world as if he needed a good dose of fresh air. She could readily understand why. The atmosphere in the music room was full of tension, of electricity, perhaps even a hint of passion.

"Cassandra, that was—adequate. Quite good, actually. It's a comfort to know that not all of our customs have fallen into disuse. Would you care to retire to your chamber for a rest before dinner?"

Retire? Leave? Go away? Allow this bubble of happiness to burst? Was he crazy? Was the man out of his mind?

"But—but, Marcus," Cassandra said, stepping in front of him as he turned toward the door, "you said I could show you how we waltz in 1992, remember?"

"Vividly, Cassandra, vividly," Marcus replied, the intensity of his tone doing wonders for her ego. "However, after viewing your earlier demonstration, I have concluded that anything you might show me would be a crushing disappointment. Therefore—"

Cassandra tipped her head to one side challengingly. She had him on the ropes now, and she wasn't about to let him get away. He *was* attracted to her; she was sure of it. At least half as sure as she was that she was attracted to him. "Chicken*hearted*, Marcus?" she teased, employing his version of the age-old taunt. "Come on. What could it hurt?"

"We have no accompaniment," he pointed out a moment later, and she knew she had won.

"We don't need any," she told him, taking his hand and leading him once more to the center of the room. "You can hum, can't you? Now, let's take up our positions."

Marcus took a step back, prepared to bow, but she held out a hand, stopping him.

"No, you don't have to do that. Let me explain. We are at a dance—I guess you'd call it a ball—and you have just seen me standing across the room. You don't know who I am but you like the way I look, and when you catch my eye I smile at you—like this." She tilted her head and smiled at him, exaggeratedly batting her eyelashes. "The music starts. You hotfoot it across the floor and ask me if I'd like to dance.''

"Without being properly introduced? Impossible!"

"Wrong. Very possible. Even probable, considering the fact that if people in New York waited for proper introductions the marriage and birth rate would both drop sixty percent. Now, you've asked me to dance and I've accepted. We walk onto the dance floor separately—after all, we don't really know each other—and you turn to me. I walk into your arms."

"I beg your pardon?" Marcus's tone was frosty. Positively glacial. And his left eyebrow had nearly climbed to the top of his forehead. "We enter the dance floor separately because you don't know me and you *walk* into my *arms?*"

"Now you've got it," Cassandra replied, enjoying herself more by the moment. "Here, I'll show you. Start humming, Marcus."

His frosty manner melted marginally and a twinkle entered his eyes, temporarily unnerving her. Maybe she wasn't upsetting him as much as she had hoped. Maybe he was even beginning to enjoy himself. It was a daunting yet exhilarating thought.

"All right, here we go," she said, stepping forward until she was standing chin to chest with him, close enough to smell his cologne or whatever it was he wore, close enough to feel his warm breath on her cheek, close enough to want to be even closer. Taking hold of his hands, she moved them forward, placing them, palms down, on her waist, then lifted her own hands and rested them on his shoulders as she laid her head against his lapel.

They stood that way, pressed together intimately from chest to knee, motionless, for several seconds.

"Marcus, you aren't humming."

His spread fingers moved slightly lower, burning into

the soft flesh covering her spine just below her waist. "That, my dear girl," he growled from somewhere above her left ear, "is merely your opinion."

This small triumph made Cassandra even bolder, goading her on to further heights, further advances. "Now we move our feet, Marcus. One foot at a time, and slowly, like an old man shuffling along the sidewalk—the flagway. Two steps forward, two steps back. And hum."

He did as she had instructed. Their bodies moved in unison, their proximity causing her to be increasingly aware of his body against hers, her thigh becoming more familiar with the intoxicating bulge of his manhood with each slow step of the dance. Instinctively seeking to be closer, she slid her arms up, up and around his neck, then leaned back, to look into his eyes.

He stopped humming.

"Like it, my lord? We call this slow dancing."

He peered down at her, his chin crinkling endearingly as it collided with his high shirt collar. "I can think of other names for it," he said, drawing her even closer into his arms.

They weren't dancing anymore. They were just standing; simply standing. So why did she feel as if she were spinning in circles?

"Marcus?" Cassandra could hear her own heart beating in her ears. This wasn't a game anymore, a ploy to make him notice her, a lighthearted flirtation to keep her mind off the fact that she was one very displaced person. "Marcus? I don't know if I should bring this up, but we aren't dancing anymore."

"No, we're not, are we? But no matter. I believe I understand the moves. However, as long as we are here, I have just thought of another little experiment we might try. Another *comparison* we might make between your time and mine."

"Such as?" Cassandra was uneasy. When had the

power slipped from her hands into his? His hands, that were so intimately pressed against her waist, holding her tight against him.

"Such as, my dear Miss Kelley—has lovemaking shifted in its application as well as its constraints? In short, has this Sexual Revolution you spoke of not so long ago incorporated anything new into the world of lovemaking? Or are the rudiments basically unchanged?"

Cassandra's tongue pushed forward and moistened her suddenly dry lips. "I—I think they're pretty much the same," she said, hating herself for having suddenly lost her nineties air of sophistication and becoming a nervous, fumbling adolescent in the presence of—she suddenly decided—a master of the art of seduction. She should have known the marquess had not spent all his time studying. He was too handsome, for one thing. Women had probably been throwing themselves at him since he was twelve, for crying out loud. Oh, Lord, what were his hands doing now? She could feel his fingers moving, kneading, splaying themselves lower, cupping her buttocks. She stiffened. "Marcus?"

"Hmm?" he questioned, his tone absentminded, as if he were distracted, his attention centered elsewhere. Slowly he lowered his head, his eyes never leaving her face. "Since that first day, that first hour, I have wondered what it would be like to hold you, to kiss you. You possess such energy, Cassandra, such life, such spirit. Even when you are angry—especially when you are angry. You delight me even as my mind tells me that you could be very dangerous to my peace of mind, to my purpose in life."

"Well, if you feel that way, Marcus, perhaps we'd better call this off now, before I corrupt you entirely." Cassandra braced her hands against his upper arms, preparing to push him away.

He shook his head. "Too late, my dear. My intellectual curiosity has been aroused."

Pressing her forehead against his chest, Cassandra muttered softly, "And that's not all that's been aroused." She lifted her head once more, still wondering why she was fighting him when she had been wanting this for weeks. Then she decided that she understood. "Marcus? You're trying to scare me into behaving myself, aren't you?"

"Perhaps. Am I succeeding?"

She looked at him a long time, admiring the way an errant lock of his coal black hair fell forward over his brow, drinking in the sculpted planes and angles of his handsome, smiling face, delighting in the mischievous twinkle that she saw in his eyes. She felt a smile tickle at the corners of her own mouth. Oh, what the hell. It didn't matter why he was doing what he was doing. Just as long as he didn't stop. "I don't think so. Maybe you should try harder?"

"Why, Miss Kelley—what a splendid idea," she heard him say just before he captured her mouth with his own.

Chapter 8

Her mouth tasted of youth, and springtime, and just faintly of the strawberry jam she had partaken of earlier in the breakfast room. And, for all her talk of that unscrupulous bastard, Somebody Renshaw, Cassandra Kelley also tasted very much of innocence.

Marcus could feel her trembling beneath his hands, hands that held her tightly against his manhood, crushing her softness to his hard, heated body as he bowed her body backward, forcing her to cling to his shoulders to support herself.

How long had he dreamed of holding her this way, tasting her, touching her, learning her? From that first day, when she had taunted him with a maddeningly brief glimpse of her satin-smooth hip, he had been experiencing the tortures of the damned whenever she smiled. Lying beside her on her bed had been an exercise in frustration he had relived nightly, his fertile imagination changing the details, enlarging upon them until he'd been forced to seek solace in a snifter of brandy.

Ever since that night, ever since she had astonished him with that harebrained scheme of a mock betrothal, he had gone out of his way not to be alone with her, not to give in to the longings he felt to be inappropriate, not only because he would be taking advantage of her vulnerability but because they shared an uncertain future. It wouldn't be fair to her if they were to tumble into love, only to be torn apart by time. Or by an untimely death. And so he had resolved to remain aloof, distant, unmindful of her seeming determination to tease him into declaring himself.

But now, after all his fine promises to himself, she was here, in his arms, where he'd always wanted her to be, and he no longer gave a damn about what was right and what was wrong. He was kissing Cassandra Kelley, and he wanted to go on kissing her until his time, her time, all time melted away into oblivion.

Clasping one hand firmly at the base of her spine, he let the other roam free, moving up her back, his sensitized fingers smoothing the fabric of her gown before giving in to the temptation of inching forward to gently cup one small, firm breast. He could feel her blossom through the thin fabric of the gown as he rubbed the pad of his thumb over her sweetly erect nipple. *Exquisite.*

He moved his mouth from hers—reluctantly yet eager for further investigation—to travel down the length of her throat. He allowed his teeth and tongue only a single small detour along the way, to play with one shell-like ear and blow soft breaths against her skin. But sweeter territory beckoned—the smooth expanse of skin above the modest cut of her gown. He felt his lips seared by their contact with that smooth flesh, causing a frisson of passion to skip down his spine.

She wasn't fighting him, thank God, for he couldn't stop now. He just couldn't. Not if he didn't want to die, to become a sacrifice to his own desires. But what was this? He felt her hand leave his shoulder, to move beside his, guiding him, helping him to free her breast from the bodice of her gown. Oh, God. Marcus opened his eyes for a moment, to gaze at the perfection before him. Oh, God. *Oh, dear God!*

His mouth closed over her nipple and he began to suckle gently, drawing it inside his mouth so that he could tease it with the rough side of his tongue and feel her flower for him. Cassandra moaned low in her throat, the soft sound encouraging him to new intimacies, so that he slipped his other hand fully onto her buttocks, moving his own hips forward so that she could not help understanding his need, his desire. It was heaven. It was everything he had ever hoped for or dreamed.

But it wasn't enough.

He wanted more; he wanted all of her, all she would give, everything she would allow him to take. He wanted to sweep her into his arms and carry her off to his private chambers, lay her on his bed, slowly divest her of this damnable gown, and make slow, burning love to every delectable inch of her body for the remainder of this day and all through the night.

Even that wouldn't be enough.

He wanted her for a lifetime. Her lifetime. His lifetime.

And that, he knew, just might prove to be impossible.

Reluctantly, and silently cursing himself for having been reared as a gentleman—although a true gentleman would never have done what he had just dared—Marcus drew the gown back up over Cassandra's breast, then cradled her head against his chest while he tried to regulate his rasping breath.

"Marcus?" Her tone was soft, tremulous, and not a little apprehensive as she pulled away to look up at him, her eyes swimming with tears. "What's wrong? Why did you stop? Oh, God—you hate me, don't you? You think I'm loose, or fast, or whatever it is you call women like me."

He stroked her dark curls and dropped a kiss on her forehead. "No, my sweet love. It isn't anything like that. It isn't anything remotely like that."

"But I did lead you on, Marcus," she said, grimacing.

"Let's not kid. each other here. I've been flirting and teasing you every chance I could for the past three weeks, although until today I didn't think I was getting anywhere. Face it, Marcus. I chased you until you caught me." She buried her head against his chest. "God, Marcus, I'm so ashamed."

He was getting himself back under control. It wasn't easy, for Cassandra's body seemed to touch him in every vulnerable place—her hip still very much in contact with his manhood, her breasts burning against his chest. "Stop it, Cassandra," he ordered quietly but firmly. "I'm no green-as-grass boy. I know what you were about. I've known from the beginning, and I was—and remain—flattered. You are an engaging minx, you know. Extremely engaging. And—and I've grown quite fond of you."

His last statement seemed to return the spark to her bewitching violet eyes. Leaning back so that she could smile up at him, she said, "Really, Marcus? How fond?"

"Don't push the matter, imp," he responded, stepping away from her, putting a bit of distance between himself and the temptation she presented. "I am also fond of Shakespeare."

She took a single step toward him, her smile wide and unaffected—although its effect on him was proving to be nothing short of extraordinary. "Yes, Marcus, of course. But did you ever want to kiss a copy of *Romeo and Juliet?* Have you ever struggled with the temptation of making mad, passionate love to *Macbeth?*"

"Cassandra," he intoned warningly, "we have to be reasonable here. Obviously we are drawn to each other. Quite drawn to each other. But you may not be here much longer. There are considerations that must be—*er* —that must be *considered,* and possible consequences of our feelings that could complicate matters. If we were to do anything momentous, anything that might commit us irrevocably to each other, we could—*Cassandra!*"

He caught her just as her eyes rolled up in her head and she fainted.

As he had been talking, taking more backward steps, and as she had been smiling, and matching each of his backward steps with a forward step of her own, her expression had begun to change. At first he thought he had insulted her again, so that he had kept on speaking, digging himself a figurative hole that had grown wider and deeper with each ridiculous word.

But, he realized as he carried her to a nearby couch and gently laid her down, she probably hadn't heard anything he'd said. She hadn't even been listening. She had been lost in her own world, her eyes wide and unblinking, her complexion starkly white.

"Cassandra?" he prompted, kneeling beside her and stroking her cheek. She was so still, so motionless, so small and vulnerable. Were there rules to this business of time traveling, boundaries that shouldn't be crossed? Had he taken the chance of emotional involvement, only to stumble blindly into one of those boundaries, causing Cassandra irreparable harm? "Cassandra? Oh, God, what has happened? What have I done?"

Marcus was torn between wanting to stay with her and knowing that he should be summoning assistance, calling for hartshorn and burnt feathers in the hope of reviving her. If she could be revived.

Just as he had decided that he could leave her long enough to summon Goodfellow, Cassandra rolled her head from side to side and moaned.

"Cassandra? Darling? Come back to me. Please, come back to me!"

"Marcus?" Cassandra opened her eyes and looked up at him questioningly. Her voice was weak, her tone puzzled. "What happened? How did I get here? Why am I lying on this couch?"

He took her hand, rubbing it against his cheek. "You fainted, my dear. One minute we were talking, and the next—but it is of no real importance. It will all come back to you in a moment."

"Fainted?" Cassandra pushed his hands away and struggled to sit up, holding a hand to her head as if she had the headache. "Well, how about that. I knew you were good, Marcus, but I never expected to—oh, no! Now I remember. Marcus—the stairs!"

She launched herself into his arms and he could feel her tremble as she squeezed him so tightly his stickpin dug into his chest. "The stairs? What stairs?" he asked, his heart sinking. He knew what she was talking about. She was talking about the staircase in the White Tower.

Damn it! He never should have kissed her! To kiss her, to love her, was to take the chance of losing her. Why did this one theory, of all the theories he had toyed with in the past three weeks, have to be correct? He had worried whether or not Cassandra's physical presence in his time could withstand an emotional involvement. Obviously not. She had to remain detached in order to exist in his time. To fall in love with her, to have her fall in love with him, was to lose her.

"I don't know how it happened," she was telling him, so that he brought himself back to attention, listening closely. "One minute you were talking—preaching, actually, as I remember it—and the next all I could see was that twisting staircase. I was standing at the bottom step, looking up. All I wanted to do was climb those stairs. I wanted it so badly I could taste it. Oh, Marcus, what does it mean?"

Marcus stilled his hands in their soothing motion of gently stroking her back as he was struck by a swift shaft of clarity. A blinding ray of hope. *"Up,* Cassandra? You were looking up? Not down? Are you sure? Are you quite sure?"

"Yes, I'm sure. I kept looking up, straining to see past the first curve in the staircase, longing to see something, feeling as if something completely unknown yet absolutely wonderful was waiting for me just around the first turning, out of sight. I was overcome with this terrible *longing*, Marcus, and then . . . and then—"

Marcus caught her face between his hands. "Cassandra! Darling! You were going *up!*"

She was looking at him strangely, almost as if he had slipped his wits, a thought that had occurred to him on many occasions since discovering Cassandra in the White Tower.

"Yes, Marcus. *Up*. And I don't see why it's anything to laugh about. It probably means I'm going to travel back to my own time soon. The staircase was a symbol, Marcus. I've seen it in books, in movies. Sometimes people lose strength, or they have weird dreams—but it all means the same thing. I'm getting ready to travel through time again." Her bottom lip quivered and tears sparkled in her eyes. "Oh, Marcus. It isn't fair. All I've been thinking of for weeks is how much I wanted to get back to my own time. But now everything has changed. I don't want to leave you. Not now. Not ever."

He leaned forward and kissed her, not passionately, but tenderly, as if she were made of fragile porcelain. "You aren't going to leave me, Cassandra. I thought so, but I was wrong. Thank God, I was wrong! If you had said you saw the top of the staircase, I would have to say that you were being given a sign that you must go back to the White Tower and go down the stairs, back into your own time. But you were still at the bottom of the staircase, my love, climbing upward, toward adventure— toward *me*—just as I was drawn to those same stairs, needing to travel down them, in order to find you. Cassandra, nothing is ending. We have only just embarked upon this adventure. Today, this moment, is our real beginning.''

She covered his hands with her own, tears now running freely down her face. "Do you think so? Do you *really* think so?"

Marcus sobered, remembering what he had read in Cassandra's guidebook. It wouldn't do to go into any of that now. She was already frightened. "Yes, my love, I really think so."

Her smile nearly destroyed him. " 'My love,' " she repeated. "What a wonderful expression, Marcus." Then she frowned. "But for how long?" she remarked vaguely as Marcus helped her to her feet. He kept a supporting hand beneath her elbow as he led her toward the doorway. She was obviously still feeling the effects of her swoon, or he wouldn't have been able to fob her off so quickly with only a few kisses and a general explanation. Later, however, when she had totally recovered her strength, he was sure she would bombard him with questions.

But it was time they left the solitude of the music room, and the temptation that solitude offered them, behind. "I don't know, my love," he said as they walked toward the foyer and passed by the butler, Goodfellow's silent censure making him want to laugh, or weep. "But we should do our utmost to make the most of whatever time we have, don't you think? Now why don't you go upstairs and lie down for a while, and then, as Perry seems to have deserted us, I shall treat you to a ride through the park."

Cassandra's smile was weak and slightly forced, but then, bless her, she rallied. Her strength of will, one of the first things that had attracted him to her, was coming to the forefront. "Hyde Park? For the Promenade? Do you mean it? Am I finally going to be allowed out in public? Aunt Cornelia said Beau Brummell has come back to town. I'm dying to see that guy. Gosh, Marcus, maybe I ought to faint more often.'' Before he could stop her, she stood on tiptoe, wrapped her arms about his neck, and planted a firm kiss on his lips. ''Five o'clock, my lord? I wouldn't want to miss a moment of the Promenade!''

And then she was gone, running up the staircase, her skirts indelicately raised above her ankles, and he was free to retire to his study, to read through more of the guidebook on London, searching for the answer to a question he still did not know how to ask.

As Aunt Cornelia had already put in her bid for the closed carriage, Cassandra and Marcus were reduced to riding in his high-perch phaeton, which exposed them to a damp breeze that was only partly dispelled by a thin, watery English sun.

But Cassandra didn't mind, not when she had the chance to show off her new navy-blue pelisse and cossack hat. Her lap was covered by a carriage wrap, but she didn't really need it to keep her cozy as long as Marcus continued to sit beside her on the high seat, his warm gaze mentally transporting her to the height of summertime.

She was falling in love. There was no denying the feeling. She was falling in love with Marcus Pendelton, Marquess of Eastbourne. And he was falling in love with her. Life was strange but wonderful.

Marcus looked marvelous as he tooled the reins, handling his horses with a sure hand and understated elegance that told Cassandra that she was in no danger of becoming one of the major parties in a road accident. Marcus, she believed, also looked marvelous—simply because he *was* marvelous. Wonderful. Kind. Sweet. Protective. And sexy as hell!

No modern-day cover artist had ever successfully captured the real Regency hero, not if "her" marquess could be an example of the species. He wore his curly-brimmed beaver at a rakish angle over his ebony curls, and his many-caped driving coat was not only flattering, it was a minor sensation: it accentuated his broad shoulders yet revealed just enough of his fawn pantaloons and high-top Hessians to allow him to cut a dashing figure. He looked authentic enough to grace a Currier and Ives print, handsome enough to pose for a centerfold in *Playgirl*, and sexy enough to have her looking forward to the evening, and the moment Aunt Cornelia bade the rest of them good night, so that she and Marcus could be alone.

Not that she told Marcus any of this, for he would only ask her to explain the first two thoughts, totally breaking the mood—and the last thought might make her appear just a mite calculating. But that didn't mean a girl couldn't hope, did it?

They had traveled only a little over three blocks when Cassandra saw Hyde Park, which reminded her vaguely of the nicer areas of Central Park—minus the muggers. "Are we in time for the Promenade?" she asked Marcus, turning about on the plank seat to see that they were now making up what seemed to be a small traffic jam of curricles, coaches, phaetons, and other yellow-wheeled, high-sided vehicles, all of which appeared to be heading in the same direction.

"Cassandra," Marcus said, his tone low but, thankfully, amused, "much as I am sure you are wont to do so, I must point out that it is not considered polite to goggle. Remember our lessons? Rather than make a spectacle of yourself, like some green country girl in town for her first Season, you are to sit very still, your chin raised, and your expression faintly bored. You will nod to passersby, but only enough to acknowledge them, and not enough to encourage them to stop, for it plays the devil with the horses. We are here, my love, only to see and be seen. Understood?"

Cassandra giggled. "I've got it, Marcus. It's sort of like we used to do back home in New Jersey when I was in high school—only we called it 'cruising.' There were nights we put seventy or eighty miles on my dad's car, just cruising up one street and down the other, checking out the kids in the other cars. Funny, I thought we were so original, yet you guys were doing the same thing more than a century before any of us were born. I could have used that argument on my dad after I put eighty miles on his Buick one night before Jimmy Marino admitted he really couldn't turn back the odometer."

"Seventy or eighty miles," Marcus repeated in an awed tone. "No matter how often you tell me these things, my dear, I still have difficulty believing them. I should like very much to see these cars you speak of, and the airplanes. Yes, I would very much like to see a jet. Tell me again about this one you call the Concorde."

Cassandra pushed aside the question with an impatient wave of her hand as she watched an enormous black carriage pass by and tried her best to catch a glimpse of its occupants. "Later, Marcus, later. It's my turn to ask questions."

"Ah, the 'liberated female.' Her exemplary manners are an unending delight," Marcus said, easing his equipage into the line of vehicles that were making their way down the *route du roi*, that name long ago corrupted to Rotten Row. "What is it you wish to know, imp?"

With the tip of her tongue poking through her lips, Cassandra concentrated on the people moving toward them. She scanned each passerby anxiously in the hope she might see Beau Brummell, or the Green Man, or even another Fashionable Impure. Living in Manhattan, where it wasn't unusual to see famous people walking the streets or even jogging through the park, Cassandra had become marginally blasé about celebrities. But these people weren't just celebrities—they were the stuff of which history had been made! "Who's that?" she asked eagerly, pointing at an extremely handsome young gentleman astride a large gray horse. "Is he anybody?"

Marcus turned and waved at the man, who smiled broadly as he passed by. "That, my dear, is the Marquess of Anglesey. I've heard that he is off to join our troops next week." He shook his head. "So many of our best are leaving, and Anglesey is one of our brightest."

Cassandra's smile slowly evaporated and her head drooped toward her breast as she abruptly lost much of her enthusiasm for the ride. "The Marquess of Anglesey. Marcus—he loses a leg at Waterloo," she said dully. "I still remember his name because he had the leg buried on the battlefield and then wrote a poem about it. One of my authors used it in her book about the battle."

She looked up at Marcus, tears standing in her eyes. "It was a great poem, Marcus—funny and optimistic. I can still remember the last stanza. 'And now in England, just as gay as in the battle brave, he goes to rout, review and play, with one foot in the grave.' Damn! I don't think I like this anymore. Can we go home now? Marcus?"

"In a moment, my dear," he answered, his voice tight, his light touch on the reins urging the horses forward along the drive. Obviously her information had disturbed him. "It will take some time to get free of this traffic."

They rode in silence for some minutes. Cassandra's delight in a scene filled with rotund, rouged dowagers in turbans and elegant dandies wearing outlandish greatcoats that sported buttons as big as dinner plates was dampened by the knowledge that everyone she saw— each man, each woman, and even the occasional child— was already dead. Their fate had been decided more than a century before Cassandra had been born. They would die in battles that might have been prevented, from simple diseases for which there was not yet a cure, or as a result of natural disasters about which they had no fore-knowledge. Their lives, their hopes, their dreams, their sorrows—they were all nothing more than dry data recorded in books. These people weren't alive. Not really. They were history. They just didn't know it.

Like the handsome, smiling Marquess of Anglesey. If only the English and their allies had guarded Bonaparte better on his first island prison—then he would not have escaped, and there never would have been a Waterloo. Think of the lives that could have been saved!

Cassandra laid a hand on Marcus's arm. "Can't we change any of it, Marcus? Isn't there anything we can do?"

"I don't know," he answered solemnly. "I just don't know. That's the most damnable part about this entire business. I don't really know why you're here. I don't know why I seem to have been chosen to become a part of your adventure. Are you here to change history—or to become a part of it? Or have we merely met by accident, inexorably drawn to each other over the centuries? I would like to believe that, but it might be too simple, too selfish on my part." He looked at her, his dark eyes troubled. "I just don't know."

Cassandra felt herself becoming mulish—or at least that was the expression her mother used whenever she saw Cassandra's lips compressed into a tight line and her eyes narrowed into slits. "You know what, Marcus?" she asked, looking across the park to where the Marquess of Anglesey was conversing with a pretty young thing dressed from head to toe in sunny yellow. "I don't care. Oh, I *did.* But not now, not anymore. I just don't give a good goddamn about any deep-seated reason behind my presence. I'm here, Marcus—and as long as I am, I'm going to try to help these people."

"Is that so, Cassandra?" Marcus's face had also

changed—he had tilted his head belligerently and raised his brows in question. "And how do you propose to go about 'helping these people'? I confess, I am at a loss as to how to begin."

Cassandra could barely contain herself. Idea after idea exploded in her brain, then took a number and got in line to announce themselves out of her mouth. "I could tell them about how stupid it is to go around bleeding people who have already damn near bled to death. I could teach the women Lamaze—I edited a book on Lamaze, you know—and maybe teach physicians to wash their hands so there wouldn't be so many women dying in childbirth. I could get them started on experiments with moldy bread, so they could discover penicillin. Marcus, you remember what I told you about modern medicine, don't you? I could even help them set up a Social Security system that would give them money for their old age; then so many soldiers and older people and sick children wouldn't have to live on the streets. I could explain that war is no real answer. I could—"

"Enough!"

Cassandra looked at Marcus, and saw that he was very, very angry. What was the matter with him? He had questioned why she was here. Well, now she was telling him. "Enough? It's not nearly enough. I'm just getting started! For crying out loud, Marcus, can't you see? Don't you understand? I could *save* these people! Me, little old Cassandra Kelley from Edison, New Jersey! God, Marcus—this is terrific!"

"Are you quite through?"

Cassandra shrugged. "For the moment," she said, wondering why she had never noticed how stern Marcus could look—almost more imposing than her high school principal, and that guy could freeze lava at fifty paces. "What's the matter, Marcus—jealous? I mean, you've got all those bottles and books and theories back in your study, and so far you haven't been able to do anything to change the world. Does it bother you that I can do what you can't?''

Marcus pulled the phaeton out of line and stopped it beneath a tree, using one booted foot to press on the wooden brake lever before turning to her, a tic working in his left cheek. "You ignorant, insufferable little chit," he ground out from between clenched teeth. "Haven't you learned anything in the weeks we've been together? And it was you who told me that time travelers can't change anything.''

Cassandra rolled her eyes in exasperation. "Is that all? That was in the movies, Marcus. Nobody has ever traveled through time before—not really. Anything I said about changing things comes from books or movies. *Fiction,* Marcus. But this isn't fiction. We're talking *facts* here, buddy. I was born in 1967 and I'm living in 1812! This is a first—a breakthrough.''

"And the Princes? Have you forgotten the Royal Princes, the reason I was investigating that room in the White Tower in the first place?''

He almost had her stumped, but Cassandra rallied. "Okay, so maybe I'm not the first—if that really happened. I mean, except for that old diary, you have absolutely no proof the Princes really traveled through time. Surely there would be some other evidence somewhere. And two bodies were found buried beneath the stairs.''

"Two bodies, yes," Marcus argued reasonably, "but two bodies that were never actually proved to be those of the Princes. Remember my ancestor's diary, Cassandra. According to it, the bodies were of two innocent servant boys the gaolers killed in order to cover the fact that they'd bungled their mission that night. Think about it a moment, Cassandra. Can you truly envision Green and Forest reporting to their superiors, saying that—just as they were about to do the dirty deed—a strange blue mist came rolling in and whisked the Princes away? Oh, yes. Oh, yes, indeed. I can certainly see how their superiors would have taken that bit of news. No! Green and Forest valued their necks too much to try to fob anyone off with such an impossible story.''

"Yeah, well, maybe," Cassandra admitted, hating his rationality in the midst of her euphoria. "But that doesn't really prove anything. I still think I can change history. And I still say you're *jealous!*"

"I will not dignify that assertion with a denial, Cassandra. But I will ask you a question, if I may. While you were indulging yourself in your juvenile ranting and raving, you mentioned something about being able to help the elderly, the ill, and—was it the soldiers? Yes, I believe it was the soldiers, such as those we passed on the way to the park, men who have lost limbs or eyes in the war and have been reduced to living in the gutter. Are you saying that your generation, your age, has succeeded in solving these problems? There are no hungry walking your streets, no children begging on the corners, no wandering men without homes?"

Why did Marcus always have to be so nit-picking, so quick to poke at every little detail? "No," Cassandra countered angrily, "I'm *not* saying that we've solved all of those problems—but at least we care, which is more than I can say for most of the people in your time. At least we know it's wrong to allow innocent people to suffer just because they're old, or sick, or . . . or—oh, you know what I mean."

Marcus raised his gaze to the sky, as if seeking an answer to his questions there. "I see. People in your time are still suffering. But they are better off than the same sort of people are in *my* time, because more of your populace *care* for the plight of these distressed individuals. And does *caring* fill their bellies, Cassandra? Does *caring* give them their own hearth and home? Does *car-*

ing provide them with medicine? Or could it be that your age and mine share many of the same problems and that in nearly two hundred years of progress, you have taken no more than one step forward—multiplying the *care* you feel for these unfortunates—yet, in reality, changing nothing.''

"God, you're insufferable!" Cassandra longed to hit him. Not simply because he was insufferable, but because he was sharp as a tack. "Oh, all right," she admitted at last, "so maybe we haven't got all the answers. Maybe we're not perfect. But if we could go back—start earlier—maybe 1992 would be different. Maybe, if I can change history in 1812, the problem will have been *solved* by 1992. Now do you understand, Marcus?"

He frowned. "I'll consider it," he said stiffly, his back still so ramrod straight that she knew he was still angry. Whether he was angry with his own confusion or the fact that she had dared to argue with him wasn't clear to her. All she really knew was that their kisses in the music room now seemed to have taken place a long time ago. "But for now, we should be heading back to Grosvenor Square. You must be chilled to the bone now that the sun is fading."

Cassandra smiled, moving on the seat so that she snuggled closer to his shoulder. "Only my nose, Marcus," she said, laughing. "The rest of me is warm as toast. I like a good argument."

"I would never have guessed it," Marcus answered, his tone dry, his intention obviously sarcastic, so that for the first time since they had left Grosvenor Square Cassandra felt a distinct chill in the air. He lifted the reins to prompt the horses into movement, then dropped them. "God's teeth!" he exclaimed feelingly. "Damn and blast! Here come Lady Blakewell and that idiot Austin. Cassandra, if you have a modicum of sense left in your argumentative head, for the love of heaven, *keep your mouth shut.*"

"The Reverend Mr. Austin?" Just what she didn't need. Cassandra groaned as she looked to her left and saw the minister approaching on foot, his long strides all but chewing up the ground, his pencil-thin body wrapped in a voluminous black cloak. He looked like one of the Tower ravens, only hungrier. "Who's Lady Blakewell?" she asked directing her attention to the almost grotesquely fat woman doing her best to keep up with the vicar. Her painted face and outlandish purple cape and matching turban reminded Cassandra of the guy who played the dancing bunch of grapes in one of the Fruit of the Loom underwear commercials. "Is she another old lady trying to buy her way into heaven?"

"If it were only that easy," Marcus said, already removing his hat and doing his best to bow from a sitting position. "Lady Blakewell is a renowned hostess, most probably because it is easier to appear at one of her functions than to discover the next morning that your absence made you her latest target for gossip. And she is highly ambitious. I believe she has her eye on becoming the Regent's next inamorata. He likes them old, you see, and plump. Now be quiet, Cassandra, and we may yet get out of this with a whole skin."

"My *dear* marquess!" Lady Blakewell, visibly struggling to regain her breath, rested one gloved hand against a wheel of the phaeton and smiled up at its occupants. "How perfectly coincidental to have found you here, just as the good Reverend Mr. Austin was telling me that you have a stranger under your roof. Is this she? Lovely child. You must bring her with you tonight when you come to my little party. But first you must introduce us. Come, come, my dear man. Do the pretty as your dear late mother taught you."

While the marquess handled the introductions, Cas-

sandra dutifully kept her mouth shut and peeked down
at the vicar from beneath her lashes, unable to ignore his
sly, insinuating smile. Been talking about her to Lady
Blakewell, had he? Oh, and Cassandra could just bet she
knew what he had been saying. *Call me a witch, will
you?* she thought, her eyes narrowing. *I'll bet you're
standing there now, longing for me to say something
stupid, just to prove your theory. Well, fat chance, Ichabod. I am not about to make your day.*

"Kelley, you say? Kelley," Lady Blakewell ruminated,
tilting her head as she looked up at Cassandra, her long
nose quivering like a bloodhound trying to pick up a
scent. "I don't believe I recognize the name. And you say
she is a cousin of Walton's? Well, I imagine that explains
it, doesn't it, my lord? Peregrine is a lovely man, truly,
but he certainly is not in the least distinguished. And
rather nervous, too, into the bargain. Ah, well, I suppose
you must bring him along, considering that it is only a
small party. Miss Collingswood is to play her harp, Lady
Miranda will delight us with a song or two, and Mr.
Throckmorton has agreed to regale us with his latest
poetic tribute to His Majesty. And then, to top off the
evening, the Reverend Mr. Austin is going to save our
souls by way of some preliminary readings from his
planned Easter sermon. Aren't you, Ignatius?"

Cassandra, who moments earlier had been overjoyed
to hear that she had been invited to an actual *ton* party,
gave Marcus a discreet nudge in the ribs, hoping he'd
figure some way to get them out of the evening. A harp?
Singing? A poetry reading? What was this—amateur
night in Mayfair? Besides, she'd rather have a root canal
than listen to another of Ignatius Austin's sermons.

But the marquess, it seemed, was impervious to hints.
"What a charming evening, Lady Blakewell," he said, deliberately moving his arm so that she couldn't poke him
again with her elbow. "My aunt has other plans, but

Miss Kelley, Peregrine, and I will be sure to be there. Isn't that correct, Miss Kelley?''

Cassandra pasted a painfully false smile on her face. "Wouldn't miss it for the world," she said brightly. "And if we're really lucky, Cousin Perry might treat you to a viewing of his clever shadow puppets. He does a wonderful rabbit, doesn't he, my lord?"

She was rewarded by the slight twitch of humor that tickled the corners of Marcus's mouth before he added, "You are looking chilled, Miss Kelley. I have been remiss keeping you out and about for so long. Lady Blakewell, Mr. Austin," he said, inclining his head in their general direction, "you will forgive us if we toddle off now, won't you?"

The Reverend Mr. Austin, who hadn't said more than three words since the marquess completed the introductions, quickly removed his black hat and executed a rusty bow, taking hold of Lady Blakewell's arm as they both drew clear of the phaeton. Cassandra relaxed completely, knowing she had done fairly well, all things considered, and turned to wave good-bye as Marcus flicked the reins, giving the horses the office to start.

"Oh, Miss Kelley," the vicar called after them just as Cassandra turned back to Marcus to demand that he compliment her on her good behavior, "you never said. How did you come to England?"

While Rose helped her dress for dinner, long after the short, pithy lecture the marquess read to her concerning the absolute lunacy—not to mention inherent danger— of speaking before thinking, Cassandra still shivered whenever she remembered how she had smiled over her shoulder at the vicar and replied in painfully honest stupidity, "How? Why, I flew straight in to Heathrow."

Chapter 9

Marcus stabbed his fork into another french fry before holding it in front of him, eyeing the length of crisp, browned potato as if it might bite him. He really liked french fries; almost as much as he favored the finely chopped fried beef cakes Cassandra called hamburgers—even though there wasn't a bit of ham in them.

Ever since Cassandra's visit to the kitchens the week before, the eating habits of the residents of the Grosvenor Square mansion had undergone a radical change. For one thing, his chef had thrown a monumental French fit and refused to leave his rooms for three days, until cajoled from his sulk by a plate of these same french fries. Cassandra now spent several hours each day in the kitchens, and the resultant dishes that appeared nightly on his dinner table had run the gamut from mildly interesting, such as "lasagna," to downright ridiculous, such as "chicken fingers." Fingers? What was the world coming to when grown men, supposedly civilized human beings, were expected to eat poultry with their hands?

But the french fries had become his favorite, no matter how often Cassandra told him he hadn't *really* tasted french fries until he had eaten at a "fast food" restaurant. "They're nothing without the chemicals, preservatives, and additives, I guess," she had told him, licking her fingers after downing an entire plateful of the greasy po-

tatoes as she sat in the window seat in his study, her legs
tucked beneath her skirts.

Marcus ate the last french fry, then pushed his plate to
the far side of his desk, remembering that the kitchen
was not the only place Cassandra was leaving her mark.
Only yesterday he had walked into the music room to
see Cassandra, Rose, and a half dozen other housemaids
jumping and twisting in something Cassandra called
"aerobics, Marcus. Got to keep the old heart pumping,
you know. Try it!"

The marquess had politely declined, then retreated
rapidly to his study, where Peregrine Walton was happily
involved in practicing the steps to a dance Cassandra had
called "the moonwalk."

"Jolly fine, ain't it?" Perry commented, beaming as he
seemed to slide backward effortlessly across the highly
polished floor. "Showed Henry Jamieson down at Boodle's, and he said I looked absolutely splendid. What's
the trouble, Marcus? You look as if your ship just came in
while you were waiting at the airport."

"Perry!" Marcus remembered shouting (yes, unfortunately, he had been reduced to shouting in his own
household). "How many times must I remind you not to
use Cassandra's ridiculous cant? You could land us all in
the basket."

"Oh, cool it, Marcus," Perry had replied, grinning.
"You'll get yourself all strummed out."

"That's *stressed* out, you nincompoop," Marcus had
corrected wearily, deliberately sitting at his desk and
opening a book, burying his head, and his anxieties, in
the pages of Milton's *Paradise Lost*—and some *good* English.

Now, looking at his empty plate, Marcus came to a
decision. He had to find something for Cassandra to do,
something that would keep her out of trouble, yet some-

thing that would preserve his household from any more of her "improvements."

The evening at Lady Blakewell's had not been an actual disaster, for Cassandra's behavior—as a result of her horror over her nearly fatal faux pas in the park—had become considerably subdued. But it had not been a success, either, thanks to Lady Blakewell's overbearing presence. The woman had pumped Cassandra for most of the evening, asking her probing questions about America, the war, and her knowledge of *ton* personalities—all done with the Reverend Mr. Austin hovering just behind her, smiling thinly as he rocked back and forth on his heels. It was an interrogation, nothing more, nothing less, and by the end of the evening Cassandra had been near to weeping with anxiety and fatigue.

Their argument in the park had not been touched upon again these past two weeks, presumably (he hoped) because Lady Blakewell's probing questions had shown Cassandra the inherent danger in going about London trying to act the savior. But it seemed as if their romantic interlude in the music room had been similarly banished to the realm of forgetfulness.

And that, Marcus believed, was a damnable pity.

Where once he had done his best never to be alone with Cassandra, it was now she who shunned his company. She involved herself with Aunt Cornelia, Perry, and the staff of the mansion, regaling them with her amusing parlor tricks and sopping up knowledge from each of them like a thirsty sponge. She made fewer and fewer mistakes these days, leaving that sort of thing to Perry. He had become enamored of her ludicrous sayings and most vigorously with the concept of flight, which, considering how ill he had become merely watching a balloon's ascension, seemed totally out of character.

But then Cassandra Kelley had a way of creating immensely attractive word pictures. Her stories of New York, of America, of the inventions and strides of the twentieth century, were like a siren song not only to Perry but to Marcus as well. He would gladly give anything he had to be able to see for himself these wonderful inventions Cassandra had told him about: to pilot a jet, to program a computer, to watch television, to drive an automobile. Ah, if only he were able to walk the corridors of the Metropolitan Museum, to stand at the top floor of the Empire State Building and look out on the city, to ride on the subways, buried deep under the streets, and visit the library at Columbia University where he could immerse himself in the knowledge of the ages.

And then he and Cassandra would travel to the Grand Canyon, to glory in its magnificence (and perhaps to spit in it, as Cassandra had done as a child), then on to California, and Disneyland, and to Hawaii, to see the volcanoes and the beaches of white, pink, and even black sand.

He and Cassandra. Cassandra and he. All his daydreams included her, all his hopes revolved around her, and all his fears concerned her. He had to find some way to return her to her own time, this laughing, loving, argumentative, maddeningly adorable spirit who had come into his house and captured his heart, all their hearts. She could not stay here, she must not. It was too dangerous, and it would become even more so if he were to believe what he had read in one of her guidebooks.

Pushing his troublesome thoughts aside for the moment, Marcus reached for the London guidebook he had been ignoring for the past weeks, let it fall open on the desktop, and began reading.

Fifteen minutes later, when Cassandra entered the room, he was so absorbed he did not notice her until the enticing fragrance of her floral-based perfume reached his nostrils. He raised his head and saw her standing just on the other side of his desk, her slim body clad in the same gown she had worn that momentous day in the music room, her violet eyes twinkling with some hidden amusement.

"Hello there, Marcus," she said, seating herself on the edge of the desk just as if she hadn't been warned a dozen times—a thousand times—that such behavior was unfeminine. "Busy solving the world's problems again this afternoon, are you? It's time for my refresher lesson in titles, remember? I think we're up to barons. Perry promised to join us shortly—although at the moment he's pretty busy in the drawing room, making paper airplanes. He's really getting the hang of sailing them, although Corny didn't appreciate it too much when one of them landed in her soup plate."

Marcus waved his hand, dismissing Perry, his relative, and the paper airplanes. "Cassandra," he asked, closing the guidebook, "you said you entered the room in the White Tower at about three in the afternoon, didn't you?"

Cassandra rolled her eyes. "Are we back to that? I thought you didn't want to talk about time travel anymore. At least not with me. Perry says you talk about it all the time with him. So why are you asking me about it again? What have you discovered? You've already told me that you think I'll travel back to my own time eventually—not that you've explained why you think so. Oh, no. Not the great Marcus. He doesn't discuss. He *pronounces*. He *teases*. And then he *ignores*."

Marcus rose from his seat and began pacing behind the desk. "Is that what's been bothering you, Cassandra?" he asked, turning to face her. "Is that why you've been avoiding me? Because I haven't been entirely open with you?"

She tilted her head and smiled at him—evilly, he thought. "And Perry said you were slow," she said, stepping back from the desk. "Hell, Marcus—haven't you learned yet that I don't appreciate being treated like a child?"

"Don't swear, Cassandra," the marquess corrected her mildly, remembering that she did very well in her role of Regency miss—but only when she wanted to. There were still times, regrettably, when she—

"The *hell* I won't, Marcus," Cassandra said, her fists jammed on her hips. "And there's nothing you can do to stop me. Hell, I said, Marcus—hell, hell, *hell!*"

It would be so easy to fall into a slanging match with her, Marcus knew, for he had come to enjoy her temper, but now was not the time, no matter how sure he was that she was deliberately baiting him. He had discovered something—rediscovered it, actually, for he had been through the guidebook several times—and he wanted to discuss his findings with Cassandra before Perry barged into the room.

"Feel better now?" he asked when it appeared as if she had concluded her outburst. He looked at her, seeing her flushed cheeks, the way her breasts rose and fell in anger, and he had to fight down the impulse to take her in his arms and kiss her into a better humor. *Later*, he silently promised himself. This overwhelming attraction, this passion he believed to be entirely mutual, would have to be dealt with—but not now—no matter how she provoked him. He had waited these past two weeks; he could wait another day. "I think I have discovered a way to test the reason for your presence here."

"No kidding? You mean besides the thought that I might have been drawn here to meet you, for all the good it's doing me?" She was immediately all attention. Slipping into a nearby chair, she placed both feet flat on the floor and folded her hands delicately in her lap—the model of Regency perfection. The pose didn't fool him for a moment. "Go on," she said tightly, her intelligent eyes unblinking. "What have you found?"

Ah, those clever violet eyes. They could see through any artifice. Marcus winced and scratched a spot behind his left ear. "I don't know where to begin," he admitted, carefully measuring his words so that he wouldn't say too much. "Do you remember what we discussed the day I took you driving in the park?"

"You mean before or after I told the Reverend Mr. Austin that I *flew* to England?" Cassandra asked, grimacing. "And you told *me* not to swear! I'm not kidding, Marcus, you could have blistered paint with some of the words you used on our way home. And then, once we were alone in your study—"

"I have already apologized for my language, Cassandra," Marcus interrupted her. He sat on the edge of the desk, aware that he had to anchor himself somewhere sooner or later and get down to business. "And you were very good at Lady Blakewell's later that evening."

"I was too frightened to be anything else *but* good, the way that woman was milking me for information. I'm sure the vicar has convinced her that I'm a witch," she said self-deprecatingly, sitting forward in her chair. "But that's what I came to talk to you about this afternoon— and why I sent Perry chasing off to Bond Street with Aunt Cornelia. I lied when I said he'd be joining us. Marcus"—she hesitated, then went on after a moment— "I've figured something out these past two weeks. I've figured out that while I do know some things about Regency England, I know only enough to make me dangerous. Dangerous to you, and dangerous to myself. You're right not to allow me out in company, Marcus, and I was wrong to think I could help people like that poor Marquess of Anglesey, much as I wish I could."

She leaned back in the chair and spread her hands.

"So, now that I've admitted what an idiot I've been, why don't you forgive me and tell me what you've discovered? What sort of test? And why do we need a test?"

Would she ever cease to amaze him with her clear, if slightly belated, deductive reasoning? "We need a test because what we are dealing with is a theory, and theories must by rule be tested," the marquess answered, picking up the guidebook and opening it to the page he had already marked. "Here, Cassandra—read this. And read it out loud, if you please."

"Out loud?" Cassandra put out her hand, accepting the guidebook with all the wariness of a person being handed a loaded pistol. "Here? Where you've marked the page? All right. It says 'Known as the New Palace of Westminster, the Houses of Parliament continue to rank as a royal palace even though it has not been in use as such since the reign of Henry VIII, who moved to Whitehall Palace. In 1547 the Royal Chapel of St. Stephen, as was the case with all private chapels, became secularized, and by 1550 the building took on the name Palace of Westminster and was used as the meeting place of the Commons. The Chapel was a tall, two-storied edifice and, as it had no aisle, it was wonderfully suited to its new use as a debating chamber. The Members were seated in choir stalls and the Speaker's chair was positioned where the altar had formerly been. Indeed, the custom of bowing to the Speaker's chair can most probably be traced to the genuflection to the altar.' Marcus? This is all very interesting, but—"

"Keep reading, Cassandra," Marcus intoned gravely, suppressing the need to rise and begin pacing once more.

"All right. 'Once the canons of St. Stephen's were dismissed in 1547 and, considering that the Palace was no longer a royal residence, Members and officials of both the House of Commons and the House of Lords began to occupy many of the vacant chambers in the huge building. This continued until 1834, when the building was all but destroyed by fire. The existing Parliament, including the Clock Tower, home of Big Ben, was not completed until 1858, and the House of Commons sustained extensive damage during bombing in 1941, when it was rebuilt once more.' Marcus? Other than to prove what I've been saying about World War Two, and learning that the Parliament I saw was not the one that exists now—what am I supposed to be reading here?''

He rose, going to the drinks table to pour them each a glass of wine. "Go to the last paragraph, if you please."

Cassandra read silently for a few moments, then turned the page, reading aloud once more. " '—And on May 11, 1812, at the height of the Napoleonic Wars, Prime Minister and Tory manager Spencer Perceval was assassinated in the lobby of the House of Commons by a bankrupt broker who had come to St. Stephen's to kill one Leveson Gower, whom he blamed for his financial problems. As Gower was not available, the man shot the Prime Minister instead, thus throwing the government into upheaval.' *May eleventh, 1812? Oh, wow!*''

"Indeed," Marcus said, handing her one of the glasses. "Perceval dies in less than a month—unless we can prevent it. A pity your guidebook doesn't name the assassin. It certainly would make our job easier."

Cassandra absently sipped at the wine. "Yeah, well, Marcus, you can't have everything. So—are you saying that I was sent here to help you prevent this guy's murder? No—no, you're not, are you? You called it a 'test.' Marcus—are you planning to use this murder to see if we can change history?"

He nodded, knowing he was getting to the more difficult part of his theory. "If—if we can stop Perceval's murder, perhaps we can change—change another bit of history as well."

"But not the Marquess of Anglesey, or any of those people I've seen in the park? I'm not here to save the world, but only one person? That's what you're saying, isn't it? Bottom line, Marcus," Cassandra said, pinning him to the carpet with her violet gaze. *"Whose* history are we supposed to be changing?"

He broke eye contact with her, not without some effort. "This might be terribly self-serving, but I'd like to think it's mine," he said quietly. "According to everything I've read in the guidebooks, it is my conclusion that I am to die on the last day of May."

"Die? You?" She sprang from the chair in one fluid movement, the wineglass dropping from her hand, its contents making a puddle on the pale carpet. A deep red stain, like spilled blood. "Oh, God, Marcus—how? *Why?"*

"Frankly, my dear, I don't know." Marcus bent to pick up the glass and placed it on the desk beside his own. "I have no enemies that would want to see me dead, or at least I don't believe that I do. Perhaps I walk in front of a carriage, or choke on a peach pit. I have no idea. But according to your guidebook, the one that is a general informational pamphlet on rural England, Eastbourne, my family seat in Sussex, reverts to the Crown on May thirty-first, 1812, upon the death of the fifth marquess. I, my dear, am the fifth marquess. What happens to my cousin and heir I cannot know, any more than I know what happens to me. It is my theory—indeed, my devout hope—that you have been sent to me as a most personal messenger, delivering a warning that will prevent history from taking its course."

She put her hand on his arm, her eyes brimming with tears. "You mean that I have been sent through time, not to be with you—but to *save* you?"

"Possibly. As I said, this is only a theory, and scarcely scientific. I have been aware of the Perceval information for some time. If we can save the Prime Minister, it would stand to reason that we can alter my future—or should I say, my seeming *lack* of a future. And if we can't save Perceval—"

"—if the Prime Minister dies, you die. *Oh, Marcus*—how could you have kept this a secret from me? We've wasted so much time!" The marquess stood very still as Cassandra wrapped her arms around him and pressed her head against his chest.

"And," he continued stiffly, "that is why I have decided—hoped, actually—that you will travel back to your own time on or before the last day of May, an event we must begin to prepare for now, so that Perry can help you if I'm no longer able to be of assistance. I cannot conceive of your remaining in my time once I am not here. The fates wouldn't be that unkind."

He put his arms around her and held her close to him, shamelessly feeding on her youth and her strength, jealously seeking her love when he knew it to be the height of selfishness. But Cassandra broke from him and began pacing the carpet as he had done not so many minutes ago. Her forehead was creased in a thoughtful frown.

"All right, Marcus, let's see what we've got here," she said dispassionately, delighting him with her lack of feminine hysterics. "It's only the second week of April. We've got time—plenty of time. First things first. We've got to save this Perceval guy. May eleventh, you said. Okay, let's suppose we can do that. From the way it's described in the guidebook, all we'll have to do is stake out the lobby of the House of Commons, looking for a wild-eyed guy with a bulge in his jacket—the gun, you understand. Then what?"

Marcus leaned against the desk, smiling as he watched Cassandra. He could almost hear her brain working, its gears whirling about, seeking questions, weighing theories, searching out answers. How could he have waited all this time to tell her? Why had he allowed her to avoid him, when all he wanted, all he needed, was to have her by his side, on his side, working with him toward what, he hoped with all his heart, might be their shared future? "Then what?" he repeated, picking up his wineglass and draining its contents. "Why, I suppose we will just have to take it one day at a time, until the thirty-first."

She ran across the room and took hold of his arms, shaking him. "Are you nuts? It's obvious you haven't watched detective shows on television. Boy, could you have used a few episodes of Miss Marple or Perry Mason. We can't just sit back and wait. I mean, you could die, waiting for the thirty-first. You could be shot tomorrow —today—and not die from your wound until the end of May. You didn't think of that one, did you, Marcus? You could be challenged to a duel, or run afoul of some desperate French spy, or stumble onto a plot to overthrow the Prince Regent—or even be poisoned by your supposed heir. Or perhaps your mistress will hire someone to slit your throat. Those things happen in books all the time. And don't tell me you don't have a mistress, because Perry has already told me her name. Marianne Carruthers—so there! Although Perry says you haven't visited her since I dropped in on you—which only gives her more reason to want to see you dead. You see?"

She shook him again. "There's a whole world waiting out there to kill you. I'm not kidding. We have to be on our toes all the time, Marcus. Marcus? Are you listening to me?"

"You know about Marianne?" He couldn't believe Perry would be so indiscreet. No wonder Cassandra had been avoiding him, the man who had all but seduced her in the music room. She knew about Marianne. "What do you know?"

"Ooooh!" Cassandra let go of Marcus's arms and

punched him squarely in the chest. "I don't *believe* you! Haven't you been listening to anything I've said?"

Marcus snapped himself back to attention, rubbing a hand across his chest. Cassandra might be little, but she was strong. Must be those "aerobics" of hers. "Of course I've been paying attention, my dear. I'm a target for everyone from Boney on down. I can't imagine how I shall have the courage to lay my head on my pillow tonight, for fear someone will jump out of the shadows to destroy me by way of some terrible wound that will lead to a long, lingering, undoubtedly unpleasant death."

She dipped her head. "You think I'm being ridiculous, don't you?"

"Only slightly," he said, putting a finger under her chin and tipping her head up so that he could look into her eyes. "But I do appreciate your concern."

She shifted her gaze, eluding his. "Yeah, well—don't go reading too much into it, okay, Marcus? It's just the way I am. I'm kind to dumb animals too. I mean—"

"Cassandra," he said, slipping his arms around her waist, "don't spoil it. You care. That's enough."

She looked up at him, tears once more standing in her eyes. "You're really going to die if we can't change history, Marcus? Is that why you've been avoiding me? After that day in the music room, I thought—I thought—well, you have to know what I thought. What I hoped. But then there was that mess at the park, and Lady Blakewell's questions, and—well, I thought you had decided I was more trouble than I was worth."

"So you, in turn, began avoiding being alone with me," Marcus said, helping her with her explanation. "And Marianne Carruthers had nothing to do with it?"

She wrinkled her nose. "Maybe a little. But not much. I can't blame you for what you did before you met me. No man lives like a monk, I suppose. Besides, Perry has promised me that you haven't seen her in weeks. Perry is right, isn't he?"

"And if he isn't?" He was teasing her, he was sure she knew it.

"That's simple enough. If he isn't, *I'll* murder you, and I won't wait until the last day of May to do it," Cassandra replied, reaching up to stroke his cheek. "I may be liberated, Marcus, but I'm not generous. I was always getting into trouble in grammar school because I wouldn't 'share.' "

The slight trembling of her fingers on his cheek told him that she was nervous, perhaps even as nervous as he was. He pulled her almost roughly against his chest, threading his fingers through her short curls. "Cassandra —do you remember that I was apprehensive about your ability to have an emotional involvement during your stay in my time? And do you remember, since you saw yourself standing at the bottom of the stairs, longing to climb upward, that I believed you had wanted to come to my time—to me?"

He felt her nod her head and he took a deep breath, knowing that they were about to take a giant step forward, yet not knowing if they were moving toward a greater happiness or a yawning abyss. "I want you, Cassandra. I want to be with you, I want to love you, for as long or as short a time as we are allowed." He moved his hand so that she could tip back her head and look at him. "Is that selfish? Am I asking too much? Or am I right, and do you want me as much as I want you?"

He watched as a single tear escaped her eye and slowly traveled down her cheek. "For as long as we have, Marcus," she said just before he drew her completely into his embrace.

"Marcus, you won't believe who I saw on Bond—well, hullo! That's Cassie I see behind you, isn't it? Have I interrupted something? Sorry. I'll just close the door and go away again. Pretend I wasn't here. And I didn't see anything, honestly I didn't. No. Not me. And if I did, I certainly wouldn't tell your aunt. Not Corny. Not at all. Wouldn't want to be anywhere near when that lady flew up into the boughs. Well, I'll be off now—"

Marcus, whose back had been turned toward the door, released Cassandra but held her close to his side as he turned to see a red-faced Peregrine standing just inside the room. "Come in, Perry," he said smoothly, doing his best to ignore Cassandra's giggle. "We have no secrets from you. At least not until I can remember to lock my door."

Peregrine advanced into the room and flung himself into a nearby chair. "Well, I suppose not, Marcus, old friend. Dashed difficult keeping secrets if you're going to be playing April and May all over the house, where just anybody could walk in on you. Hullo, Cassie. *Um*— pretty gown."

"Thank you, Perry," Cassandra said politely, moving away from Marcus but still holding his hand and not breaking contact with him until she stepped out of his reach. "Now, if you gentlemen will excuse me? I believe I'll go to my chamber for a while. I—I have some thinking to do."

"Thinking?" Peregrine shook his head. "Is that all you people do? Think? No, I suppose not—considering what I just walked in on. Isn't that right, Marcus? Not that I'll breathe a word of it, you understand. What are you going to be thinking about, Cassie? Did Marcus tell you about the reception at Carlton House tomorrow night? You aren't thinking you won't go, are you? That would be a pity, seeing as how Marcus has already decided to let you wear his mother's pearls. You did say the pearls, didn't you, Marcus? I'm sure it was the pearls."

"Perry," Marcus asked wearily, "aren't you thirsty? I'm convinced I'd be thirsty if I had talked only half as much as you have since entering this room. Why don't you fetch yourself a drink?''

Perry looked from Marcus to Cassandra, and then back at his good friend. "Why don't I go drown myself, you mean," he said, pushing himself to his feet. "Sorry, Cassie. I didn't mean to spoil the surprise. But you will go, won't you? You said you were dying to see Prinny.''

Cassandra's smile did something very strange to Marcus's equilibrium, filled as it was with a mixture of happiness and sorrow. "I suppose I'll go, Perry," she answered, "although suddenly, seeing the Prince Regent just isn't all that important. Is it, Marcus?''

"Not important?" Perry exclaimed, nearly dropping the wine decanter. "Well, if that don't beat the Dutch. For weeks you've been beating me over the head, pestering me to get Marcus to take you someplace, and now that he is willing to take you, you say it ain't important. Women! No wonder I've decided never to marry. A wife would have me running straight to Bedlam within a fortnight. Stap me if she wouldn't.''

Cassandra walked over to Peregrine and kissed him on the cheek. "I'm sorry, Perry. Of course I'm delighted by the prospect of seeing Prinny. As a matter of fact, I'm so delighted that I think I will take special care not to tire myself anymore today with lessons, or playing cards with you and Aunt Cornelia after dinner. No, I've decided to be a good little Regency miss and take a warm bath after my meal and then go straight to bed at ten o'clock, so that I'm well rested for tomorrow night." She turned to look meaningfully at Marcus. "Don't you think that's a good idea, my lord?''

The minx! She had as good as invited him to her bed, although, thankfully, Peregrine—just then downing a glass of wine—remained happily unaware of that fact. Marcus looked past his friend and smiled at the woman he loved, the woman who loved him—even if neither of them had as yet said the words. "I think that is an excellent idea, my dear. So good, in fact, that I believe I shall do much the same thing. The Season is not yet three weeks old and I've already had too many late nights."

Her blush delighted him as Marcus watched Cassandra sweep out of the room.

Perry replaced his empty glass on the table, frowning as he, too, watched her go. "Leaving me to spend the evening losing all my money to Corny, are you? Plays a wicked game of cards, your aunt. Oh, no. Thank you for the warning, Marcus. I believe I'll be off now, to have dinner at my club. You can tell Corny I'll be very, *very* late!"

Marcus waved his friend on his way, then took up his seat behind his desk once more, no longer interested in theories, or guidebooks, or possible disasters. His entire mind was concentrated on moving the hands on the mantel clock until they reached the hour of ten.

Cassandra was able to reach the privacy of her bedchamber before breaking down, throwing herself onto the satin coverlet, and muffling her sobs with one of the pillows. Her hands shook; her stomach felt queasy after holding her emotions in check for so long—putting up a front of courage for Marcus, exhibiting a bravery and an optimism she didn't feel.

Marcus was in danger. Terrible danger. She hadn't even thought to doubt him, to ask to see the guidebook for herself in the hope of disproving his statement that he would die on the last day of May unless, together, they found some way to change history.

But they would find that way, she tried to assure herself. Deliberately cutting her tears short, she slipped from the bed and dashed cold water on her face. Why else would she have traveled back in time, if not to save the man she loved—the man she hadn't known even existed until a little more than a month ago?

After drying her face she put down the towel and wandered over to a window. She pushed back the drapery and looked out over the Square. How she had come to love this place, this mansion, this Square, this hustling, bustling city, this glorious time in history. If it weren't for the fact that her parents must be beside themselves, wondering where she had disappeared to, she wouldn't ever want to go back. "Although I'd have to find some way to invent Coca-Cola," she thought out loud, turning away from the window. "And Twinkies. And Dove bars. Lord, yes, definitely Dove bars."

She shook her head, wondering why she couldn't keep her mind on the subject. It certainly was an important enough subject. She would have to take this one step at a time. "One—Marcus is supposed to die the last day of May. Two—Marcus believes I may have been sent to help him avoid that death. Three—I either go back to my time on the last day of May, mission accomplished, leaving a healthy Marcus behind, to live out the rest of his life without me, or, God forbid, Marcus dies and I'm either sent back to my time anyway or I'm left trapped here, with Marcus gone."

She pressed her hands to her cheeks and they came away wet with her tears. "Four—no wonder I'm still crying!"

Locking the door to the hallway, Cassandra pulled a chair over to the armoire and reached up to feel about for the pack of cigarettes and the lighter she had stolen from Marcus's study and hidden behind the raised, ornamental wood carving. The time had definitely come for a healthy—or unhealthy—infusion of nicotine to the brain, a sort of jump-start to her thinking processes.

A flick of her lighter and a deep breath sent the smoke into her lungs and the nicotine into her bloodstream. It hit her brain cells in a short, satisfying seven seconds—at least, according to an article she had read a while before, that was the accepted progression of events. Unfortunately, it took only one more drag and about fifteen seconds for the chemicals to hit her stomach, and once more she felt the light-headedness and queasiness she had experienced that first morning in Marcus's study. She felt as if she were back behind Feinstein's Bakery, turning green as she tried to inhale one of her father's unfiltered Pall Malls.

This time she fought it, finishing one cigarette and quickly lighting another, the ashes deposited in the washbasin she must remember to empty out the window before Rose found them. As she smoked, she thought about Marcus and his admission that he loved her. Well, not that he loved her. Not exactly. He had said that he *wanted* her. That was close enough for now, because she wanted him, too, and had wanted him, it seemed, forever.

She butted the second cigarette in the washbasin and returned to the bed to lie on it, a small smile playing at the corners of her mouth. He would come to her tonight, after everyone else was sleeping, and they would begin their future. It was only April. They had time; they had lots of time. Between them, they'd figure out a way to save Spencer Perceval, and then they'd figure out a way to save Marcus. That wasn't theory; that was *fact*. Because he wasn't infallible, her dear, handsome, desirable Regency scientist and gentleman of the world. He wasn't infallible, because she, Cassandra Louise Kelley, had absolutely no intention of losing the man.

Not now.

Not on the last day of May.

Not ever.

Chapter 10

The clock at the head of the stairs struck the hour of eleven. Cassandra sat in the middle of the large bed, propped against a half dozen pillows, and furtively watched the closed door to the hallway. She had carefully set the scene with a few strategically placed candles, a small fire burning in the fireplace, one of the draperies drawn back to allow a spill of moonlight to fall across the bed. But now it seemed so staged, so artificial—like something out of an old Bette Davis movie—that she had gone from nervous excitement to just plain scared.

Dressed in a lovely white nightgown trimmed with fine Mechlin lace and sheer enough to have come straight out of a Victoria's Secret catalog, she had felt marvelously seductive when she slipped between the sheets to await her "lover." But an hour's wait, now more than an hour's wait, had found her rethinking her fantasy.

Perhaps she shouldn't be *in* the bed when Marcus entered. That was sort of pushing things. Perhaps she should be seated at her writing desk, a paisley shawl all but falling off her shoulders, a pen in her hand, as if she were writing a letter, or some lines of poetry?

Or she could be sitting at her dressing table, brushing her hair. Then Marcus could enter—dressed in his banyan, which was what Regency types called their bathrobes—and come up behind her, pull back her hair, and plant a kiss on her exposed neck. No. She didn't have enough hair to carry off that particular scenario.

One thing was certain. She couldn't stay in this bed, like some sort of sacrificial lamb or some sort of predator awaiting her prey. Throwing back the covers, she slid to the edge of the mattress, her nightgown hiked up near her hips, and began searching the floor for her slippers. She would go to the window, the one with the pulled-back draperies, and stand staring through the panes at the stars. That would be romantic, without pushing the point.

"Where the hell are my slippers?" she questioned aloud in exasperation, hopping from the bed. She dropped to her knees and began searching under it. Candlelight might be romantic, but she sure could use a flashlight. With her rump pointing skyward, she stuck her head under the bed frame and extended one hand, sweeping it back and forth over the bare floorboards. "Damn it—what did they do, go for a walk?"

At the slight squeaking of an opening door she froze, her hand just closing around one of the elusive slippers, and she became embarrassingly aware of her undignified position. Dropping her forehead to the cool floorboards, and thankful that the bed ruffle covered her head, she mumbled bleakly, "Marcus?"

"As a matter of fact, yes," came the deep-throated, obviously amused answer from somewhere behind her. "However, if you're looking for me under the bed, I have to tell you that I'm not there. Or have you changed your mind, and are you in the act of hiding from me?"

She lifted her head from the floor, then softly banged it against the wood three times. "Dumb, dumb, *dumb*. Oh, God—I'm such a klutz!" she murmured before carefully backing out from under the bed ruffle and slowly getting to her feet. "Hi there. I lost my slippers—but I've found one of them—see," she said brightly, much too brightly, giving him a small wave with the hand holding the slipper before wrapping her arms around her body, trying to pretend she wasn't standing directly in front of a small brace of candles whose light had undoubtedly turned her nightgown into little more than a revealing veil of cobwebs.

"Congratulations, my dear," Marcus answered as she dared to look at him, seeing that he was indeed dressed in his nightclothes, a deep burgundy silk banyan tied tightly at his waist. He looked so good. So big. So handsome. He held out his hand and she automatically placed the slipper in it. "I think we can dispense with your search for its mate, don't you? Unless you plan to go for a stroll?"

She shook her head. "A stroll? Me? Now? Nope, I don't think so," she said quickly, the words tumbling over each other as she dared a peek at the bed and then all but dived under the covers, pulling them up to her neck. *Oh, boy,* she thought, wincing, as she realized what she had done. *Great work, Sherlock. You're right back where you started.*

His smile nearly destroyed her, for she was convinced he was laughing at her, seeing her for what she really was—an inept, clumsy, disaster-prone idiot who couldn't pull off a romantic assignation if she had a week to prepare for it. A year!

"I've taken the liberty of bringing us some wine," Marcus said, using the slipper to point across the room, so that for the first time she noticed the silver tray holding a decanter and glasses that sat on her desk. "Shall I pour you a measure?"

Her tongue cleaving to the roof of her mouth, she only nodded, wildly wondering how Sheila Cranston would handle this particular situation. *One whole hell of lot better than you're doing, sweetcakes,* her brain announced in mocking tones, so that Cassandra felt tears stinging behind her eyes. What was wrong with her? She loved Marcus, truly loved him. Why was she carrying off this interlude with all the panache of a hippopotamus stuck in an elevator?

Marcus, now minus the slipper and holding two filled glasses, perched himself on the side of the bed, his position not in the least threatening, even if his proximity had her toes curling under the covers. "Here you are, my dear. I suggest you sip it."

She took the glass and downed its contents in one long gulp, wishing it were Scotch and water—not that she was ever a heavy drinker. "So much for suggestions," she said, handing him the empty glass. "Marcus —I'm not too clear on this point, so I'll ask you, okay? Is England prone to earthquakes?"

He leaned forward to place the wineglasses on the nightstand, then looked at her, frowning in the moonlight. "Earthquakes? We've had a few. Why?"

Cassandra nervously plucked at the bedcovers. "No reason. Well, that's not quite true. There is a reason. You see, I never get away with anything. Honestly. You already know about Brad the Bod. Well, the first—the first *time* we, you know, the first real *time,* my dormitory caught on fire. And then—and then there was the time I had this crush on Josh McCabe in the ninth grade. We were taking an English exam and I was whipping right through that test, when all of a sudden Josh poked me in the back and handed me a note asking for the answer to number seven. I knew it, of course—and I gave it to him. I figured he'd appreciate it so much he wouldn't notice the braces on my teeth, or the fact that I hadn't really *developed* as much as the other girls in my class."

"But?" Marcus prompted, resting his hand on top of hers as her nervous plucking had begun to wreak havoc with one of the embroidered roses.

"See? Even you knew there had to be a 'but' involved in anything I do. *But* Mr. Hendricks saw me pass the note back to Josh and I got sent to the principal's office for cheating. *Me!* Not Josh. The other kids made fun of me for days, and Josh took Melissa Sanderson to the freshman mixer anyway—that's a dance, Marcus. God, how I hated Melissa and her straight teeth and her thirty-six-C cup. Anyway, what I'm trying to say here is that I just can't get away with anything. I don't know how to pull it off, I guess. I always end up in some kind of trouble."

"Hence your question about earthquakes," Marcus said, lifting her hand to his lips. "Do you really believe that making love with me will cause this house, perhaps even this entire city, to tumble down around our heads?"

She felt the imprint of his lips burning on her skin, so that her throat constricted, making it difficult to swallow. She pulled her hand away and pressed it against her cheek. "Possibly—at least figuratively. I just think it's only fair that I warn you. I mean, look how we met in the first place, for crying out loud. I was breaking the rules when I stumbled down that rabbit hole of a flight of stairs and into the blue mist. Every time I break the rules it's like I'm *begging* for some sort of disaster to strike. And then tonight—tonight"—her voice broke on a small sob—"tonight I wanted everything to be *so* perfect. You don't know how I planned for this, Marcus. It all seemed so good in theory, but in practice? Think about it, Marcus—you came in here tonight expecting to find a woman waiting for you, and instead you stumbled over an idiot stuck half under her bed, bobbing for slippers. God, Marcus," she wailed, falling back against the pillows and pulling the covers up over her head, "How can you be depending on me to save your life? I can't do *anything* right!"

She lay very still, waiting for him to leave the room, disgusted with her, and had to bite back a sob when she felt the bed shift beneath her as he stood up. Counting to ten, waiting for the sound of a door opening and closing again behind him, she held her breath, expelling it only when the mattress shifted once more and she became aware of the fact that he was now lying on the bed, beside her.

A moment later he had removed the covers from her face, slowly sliding them down until they rested just above her breasts. "Much as I appreciate your warning, Cassandra, I've decided I like living dangerously," he said, the back of his knuckles softly stroking her cheek.

She looked over at him and saw that his banyan was gone, as were the rest of his nightclothes. His long body was stretched out on top of the covers for her examination, and with the help of the candlelight and moonlight that spilled across the bed she drank in the sight of his bared chest, his long, straight legs, his—

"Oh, you're good, Marcus," she whispered hoarsely, raising her eyes to his face, to his wonderfully handsome, lovable, and openly loving face. "I don't have much in the way of personal experience, but I've seen all of Kevin Costner's movies, and I can tell you this— you're very, *very* good."

"And you talk too much," he responded, inching closer to her so that he could place small kisses on her bared arm, then moving his lips provocatively from her elbow to her shoulder.

Cassandra closed her eyes and pressed her head back against the pillows as his lips began blazing a trail across her shoulder and up the length of her throat, lingering just at her ear, his tongue and teeth doing things to her equilibrium that she hadn't believed possible while she was lying flat on her back in bed.

She felt the covers receding from her body and her

nervousness ebbed along with them, exposing her to his view, exposing her to the heat of his body as he moved marginally, pressing himself against her hip, and then ever further, searing the soft skin of her belly through the sheer material of her nightgown, branding her as his own.

And then he moved again, his actions swift yet tender. A moment later her nightgown was gone, discarded right along with the remainder of her inhibitions.

Cassandra had never felt less gauche, less inclined to disaster, than she did as Marcus tilted her head toward his with his fingertips and claimed her mouth. She opened her lips to him, and he took up the invitation, his tongue making rapid inroads on her belief that sex, while really not all that bad with Brad, probably hadn't ever really lived up to its advertisements.

His hands were everywhere, but not in the wildly groping way she had experienced with Brad. This was a man who knew what he was about, whose lovemaking was just that—a sharing of love, and not a taking of territory; an action born of desire, and not a selfish indulgence in which she might as well be nothing more than a mildly interested spectator.

Marcus moved his fingers around the fullness of her breasts, across the sensitive skin of her rib cage, and into the moist nest between her legs. Cassandra felt beautiful, cherished, as he spoke sweet love words in her ear before he moved to her breasts, his mouth claiming one tightly budded nipple, then the other, coaxing them into full flower as he cupped, kneaded, caressed, with his hand.

She opened her legs as she was no longer able to keep up a show of feminine modesty, of typical Regency "missish" prudency. Marcus was magically lighting small fires of desire with every light stroke of his fingers as he gently probed her most secret parts. The fires built, glowing white-hot behind her tightly closed lids as they combined to make a single all-consuming conflagration, so that she felt almost feverish with desire.

It was all so beautiful, so dazzling, so perfect—but it was not enough. She needed *him,* needed him deep inside her, holding her tightly in his strong arms, quenching the fires with the power of his love or burning them both to a crisp with the flames of his passion. It didn't matter. Nothing mattered. Not as long as they perished together, soared above the constraints of the flesh together—were reborn together, as the phoenix had risen from the ashes.

She raised her arms and moved to hold Marcus closer, to feel his heated skin beneath her fingers as she slid her hands over his shoulders and down his smoothly muscled back. So strong. So perfect. So unbelievably, heartbreakingly wonderful.

And now, now that she held him, a new sensation built deep within her and intensified her desire a thousandfold. This was more than lovemaking, more than a mere delight of the senses. She could feel it growing, crowding out everything save the awareness of a yawning emptiness that only Marcus could fill, an expanding hunger that mere food would never satisfy. It had taken her twenty-five years and a time leap of nearly two centuries, but at last she knew why she had been born. Not only to save Marcus, but to love him.

To be loved by him.

Forever.

Without conscious thought she began to move her hips, and she rubbed herself against his hardness—feeling his hand on her breast was no longer adequate to her newly discovered but rapidly mushrooming needs. His mouth was driving her steadily toward ecstasy—steadily, yet not fast enough. She moved her hands lower, to his buttocks, guiding him fully on top of her, so that she could wrap her legs around his.

He lifted his head, looking down at her through the moonlight, the soft candlelight—his dark eyes questioning. "Cassandra, my sweet darling—so soon?"

The old Cassandra would have been embarrassed, and instantly awkward, mumbling something inane and digging herself a figurative hole to throw herself into. But this was the new Cassandra, reborn only moments earlier, in this room, in this man's arms, and she had never been more sure of herself, of anything, in either her old life or this new, enlightened incarnation.

She gazed up at Marcus, loving the way his dark hair tumbled forward onto his forehead, loving the way she could actually see his pulse beating frantically in his throat, loving the way he looked down at her as if she were the most precious, wonderful creature he had ever seen. Loving *him.*

"Do you love me, Marcus?" she asked, shuddering as his thumb lightly grazed her nipple, sending blissful, shivering signals to her nether regions. "Will you always love me, no matter what the future has in store for us?"

His smile almost broke her heart. "I will love you, Cassandra Kelley, until there is no past, no present, and no future. I will love you forever."

Laughing, crying, she opened herself to him completely, saying, "In that case, my darling marquess, it can never be too soon for us. We have the rest of the night, the rest of our lives, to take it slow."

It was only as dawn began to break over Grosvenor Square that Marcus gathered up his nightclothes, kissed Cassandra one last, lingering time, and slipped back to his own bedchamber. Snuggling deep under the covers, her body still warm from his loving, she realized her most beloved marquess had been wrong. There *had* been an earthquake in the mansion last night, a devastating, heart-stopping, truly glorious shifting of the earth—only the phenomenon had been confined to Cassandra's room and the high, wide tester bed.

Chapter 11

"Well, I hope you're satisfied, gel," Aunt Cornelia said, nudging the feathered headdress that had slipped a notch as she pushed her way through the crowded hallway. Cassandra followed along behind, stopping every few moments to gawk at yet another artistic extravagance the Prince Regent had on display in every nook and cranny. "I never saw such a sad crush this early in the year. Everyone and his wife must have come back to town for the evening. See and be seen, my sainted aunt Mary! If one more person trods on my hem, the entire *ton* will be seeing me *in naturabilis*, for my gown will be stripped from my body! Don't dawdle, child—the gentlemen are waiting."

"Yes, ma'am," Cassandra answered dutifully, taking one last peek over her shoulder. She was sure the painting she had glimpsed was a Constable. Strange, she hadn't thought he had been well received in England until much later. Obviously the Prince Regent made his own decisions concerning what he liked.

And, she thought as she followed the nodding purple plume stuck in Aunt Cornelia's headdress, the Prince Regent seemed to like almost everything. No wonder the man was in debt up to his eyeballs. From the moment she, Aunt Cornelia, Marcus, and Peregrine had passed beyond the fine Corinthian portico and into a large, ab-

solutely splendid hall lined with Ionic columns fashioned, so Marcus told her, of the finest brown Siena marble, Cassandra had been hard pressed to remember to
keep her mouth closed. She knew she was in danger of
making a complete jerk of herself by oohing and aahing
like some hick tourist set loose in the big city for the first
time.

The hall had eventually opened onto an octagon and a
magnificent double staircase that led, she soon discovered, up to the state apartments. Because of the crush of
people, it took over an hour to ascend to the first floor
(added to the two hours it took for their carriage to inch
its way through the clogged streets to the front door in
the first place). Cassandra learned that the entire reason
for this expedition was to be greeted by their host, walk
from one room to the other in an orderly procession,
and then leave again. There would be no dancing, no
card playing, and very little in the way of refreshments.
Marcus called it a rout. Cassandra called it asinine and
couldn't wait to get home to tell Marcus that the Prince
Regent had later ordered Carlton House torn down because it wasn't magnificent enough for him.

After a few minutes spent waiting to see the Regent,
who had already deserted his post at the top of the stairs
in favor of a comfortable chair in the drawing room (his
corset was probably giving him the devil, Peregrine
whispered into Cassandra's ear), Aunt Cornelia announced in stentorian tones that she was in need of inspecting one of His Highness's innovative water closets
or else there'd be no accounting for what tragedy might
befall them all on the way back to Grosvenor Square.

And so Cassandra had found herself trailing after Aunt
Cornelia, who seemed to know her way around the large
building. Marcus and Peregrine were left to do their best
to waylay one of the wandering servants and procure

some wine before they were pushed into the next room and down the staircase again, into the street.

Cassandra and Aunt Cornelia elbowed and squeezed their way back through the overheated rooms and the throng of jeweled, perfumed, and elegantly attired denizens of High Society. Cassandra became increasingly aware that although their clothing was of the finest and their jewels dazzling to the eye, there were several of the *haut ton* who probably had little more than a nodding acquaintance with soap and water.

Now, with Aunt Cornelia's mission accomplished, Cassandra was more than happy to locate Marcus and Peregrine and escape all this Regency grandeur before she suffocated. Hanging back momentarily, she took another quick peek at herself in one of the many mirrors that lined the withdrawing room. She adored the gown Marcus had chosen for her this evening and delighted in the way the soft, blush-pink muslin gown flattered her figure. She had become increasingly aware of her figure since last night, when Marcus had called it "perfect." She raised a hand to her throat, touching the triple strand of pearls he had presented to her this afternoon and knowing that if she were to lose them in this crowd she'd never forgive herself.

Once assured that the diamond-encrusted clasp still held tight, she turned to follow Aunt Cornelia, only to realize that the woman was nowhere in sight. All around her were fleshy arms, suffocating scents, elaborate headdresses, and enough feminine chatter to drown out any polite attempt to call Corny's name.

For the first time since being introduced to the soft ballet-type heelless slippers that were an everyday part of her wardrobe, Cassandra longed for her old, uncomfortable high heels, for she wasn't tall enough to see over the heads of the dozen or so women who clogged the hallway that led back to the main rooms. Great! Now she'd done it, she thought, hopping up and down, hoping to see a familiar face. How was she ever supposed to locate Corny or Marcus in this crowd? She was lost, cut off from the only people she knew, and she hadn't the faintest idea how she'd ever get back to Grosvenor Square.

As she moved forward, trying to appear nonchalant and faintly bored—Marcus's prescription for looking as if she belonged and not calling attention to herself—and keeping a wary eye out for Aunt Cornelia's distinctive purple plumes, she felt a hand close over her forearm. "Marcus?" she asked, whirling about hopefully.

" 'Marcus'? Why, my dear girl, has your association progressed to the informal? I had no idea."

Cassandra felt her heart, and her hopes, plummet to her toes. How could she have forgotten? She did know somebody else in London. "Good evening, Lady Blakewell," she said quietly. "How nice to see you again." Yeah, right. About as nice as walking stark naked into her shower stall, only to come face to face with a cockroach big enough to be sporting a saddle!

Lady Blakewell, her immense girth draped in a red low-cut gown that looked as if she had hidden the Pillsbury doughboy in the bodice, leaned close enough to Cassandra that she could see the scum on the woman's crooked front teeth. "*Alone*, my dear? How enterprising of dearest Cornelia Haskins to allow you off the leash. Is this how she plans to launch you—setting you loose to strike up conversations with gentlemen in the hope notoriety might gain for you what your breeding does not? Oh, not that Walton's isn't an unexceptionable enough ancestry, but he hasn't a feather to fly with, and all the *ton* knows it. Or has that so clever Peregrine prevailed upon dearest Marcus to provide a dowry?"

Cassandra had once asked Sheila Cranston how she got rid of people who seemed to feel it their duty to make her life miserable by questioning her life-style. This had been an important question both for Sheila, the aspiring astronaut, and Cassandra, who wanted to live alone in Manhattan. Cassandra had always argued with the people, which seemed to get her nowhere, while Sheila somehow got the busybodies of Edison, New Jersey, to see her point. "I don't know why you bother talking to them, Cassie," Sheila had said. "Why should I let some jerk give me grief about wanting to orbit the earth with a bunch of men in a tin can? What do *I* say to them? Well, I've always found a simple 'fuck off' to work pretty well."

But that was Sheila, and Sheila wasn't standing smack in the middle of the Prince Regent's private home, being leered at by the most vicious gossip in all of London. If Cassandra had learned anything since her first two meetings with Lady Blakewell, it was to keep her mouth shut —much as she longed to take a page out of Sheila's book and tell the old bitch to go screw herself. She'd have to try for a little of Marcus's sort of mild arrogance.

"Dear me, I have no idea what provisions have been made for my future, Lady Blakewell, although I imagine you might apply to the marquess for an answer if you wish. Or would you like me to present your comments and questions to his lordship and have him get back to you?" she inquired sweetly, opening the fan that hung around her wrist and beginning to wave it in front of her face while she watched the older woman flush with anger and frustration. This wasn't so bad, this business of putting people in their place by politely calling their bluff. "But, no matter. Perhaps you can help me. I'm afraid I tarried too long in the withdrawing room, and now I seem to have misplaced dearest Miss Haskins."

"Of course I shall help you, my dear child, although I must tell you that, in this sad crush, we shall be lucky to locate either Miss Haskins or the marquess, who have doubtless already been carried away by the tide. You must allow me to offer you my carriage." Lady Blakewell's smile oozed malicious delight, and Cassandra was sure the woman would have the news of the Marquess of Eastbourne's lax care of his guest spread all over Mayfair by tomorrow morning. But she was desperate, so she allowed the woman to steer her in the direction everyone else seemed to be going—like lemmings mindlessly heading for the cliffs.

They had traveled through one large drawing room and entered another before Lady Blakewell steered Cassandra toward a tall, blond, handsome man dressed in the height of fashion—rigged out in exactly the bright hues and ornate trappings of starched, too-high neckcloth and flashing jewelry that both Beau Brummell and Marcus Pendelton so wisely shunned.

"Reggie! Look what I have found," Lady Blakewell called, pulling Cassandra forward and making her feel as if she were some sort of prize the old woman had just discovered in a box of Cracker Jacks. "It is Miss Kelley, whom the Reverend Mr. Austin and I have told you *so* much about. Marcus has misplaced her, the naughty boy. Isn't this above all things wonderful?"

Reggie struck a pose, then ran long, thin fingers down the length of black grosgrain ribbon hung around his neck and lifted the gilt-edged quizzing glass suspended from it to his right eye. Still holding on to the glass, he trailed his eyes over Cassandra, then lifted his chin, looking extremely bored. "Just so, madam. And I had so hoped you had located refreshments somewhere in this great barn. What do you propose to do with her now that you have found her?"

"Reggie, don't be difficult," Lady Blakewell simpered. Yes, Cassandra decided, the woman was positively simpering. It was disgusting to watch. But the older woman recovered herself shortly and introduced Cassandra to her nephew, Reginald Hawtrey, whose belated bow was impeded only slightly by the corset he wore in order to obtain a wasp-thin waist.

"Delighted to make your acquaintance," Reginald said, leering at her as if contemplating how she might taste if he were to take a bite out of her. "Would you like me to bring you into fashion, Miss Kelley? I shouldn't wish to brag, but I have that power. One word from me and you will become the pivot of the Social Season. Lamentably, you are not blond, which is this year's color, but I shouldn't think I would have trouble surmounting that little shortcoming. Now, if you were to be a red-head—" He shuddered, as if that possibility was too much to be borne.

Cassandra was fascinated in spite of herself. From his impeccably curled (and probably dyed) hair to his elegantly embroidered waistcoats (he wore two), to his red-heeled shoes, she knew she was standing face-to-face with her first honest-to-God Regency dandy. Give him a silk shirt, a gold chain, and a leased Mercedes and he could be any of the lounge lizards she avoided on her infrequent visits to Manhattan's singles bars. The guy's ego was nearly as big as the gold buckles on his shoes.

"Oh, Mr. Autry," she gushed in her best Scarlett O'Hara imitation, deliberately batting her eyelashes at him as she fanned herself frantically, "you'd do all that for little old me? I'd be ever so grateful, truly I would." She turned to face Lady Blakewell. "How fortunate I am, dear madam, to have been rescued by such a kind lady as yourself. Just think—Marcus has been fretting without reason. Why, with Mr. Autry to introduce me, I shall have no worries whatsoever. Isn't that true, Mr. Autry?"

"That's *Haw*trey, Miss Kelley," Reginald responded. Something in his not unintelligent blue eyes alerted her to the fact that she hadn't exactly dazzled him with her show of naïve adoration. Perhaps purposely mispronouncing his name had been taking things too far.

Cassandra giggled and pressed her fan to her lips. "Oh, silly me," she said, casting her gaze about the crowded room, still hoping Marcus would come riding to the rescue but beginning to doubt it. Fighting his way through this unending river of people would be like trying to navigate upstream without a paddle. "*Um*, could we possibly leave now? Perhaps Marcus and the others are waiting for me at the bottom of the stairs, and then you will be spared the chore of giving me a lift—I mean, a *ride* back to Grosvenor Square."

Reginald exchanged glances with his aunt before smiling at Cassandra, making her flesh creep. How could a man be so basically handsome, yet positively ooze oily pseudosophistication? "I am your servant, Miss Kelley— but I must beg a favor before I move so much as an inch from this spot. You will drive out with me tomorrow afternoon, won't you? We must begin planning if I am to make you the sensation you deserve to be. Isn't that correct, Aunt Agnes?"

Lady Blakewell clapped her hands like a gleeful child who had just been offered her very own Barbie doll. "Correct indeed, you dear boy. Oh, I knew it the moment I saw Miss Kelley again. She is perfect for you, Reggie—or am I wrong, and it is only my wishful thinking that sees the twinkle of attraction winking at me from your eyes?"

Cassandra's smile became strained as she looked from aunt to nephew. Something was wrong; she could sense it. Lady Blakewell was too interested in her, and the nephew's attitude was so patently false that even he seemed to be having difficulty keeping up the charade. She saw him glance at a petite, blond-haired young thing who was discreetly waving in his direction, then he reluctantly looked back at her.

"Perhaps Miss Haskins and the marquess have other plans for me, Mr. Hawtrey," she said, beginning to feel desperate as she scanned the crowd, inwardly cursing Marcus for not mounting a white charger and coming to her rescue. Didn't he know what kind of trouble she could get into? Hadn't he told her often enough that she still didn't have all the "town polish" he would like her to have before agreeing to set her loose in society? How pleased he'd be that she had proved him correct.

And then she saw him. Not Marcus, but one of history's more interesting Regency characters, one she had seen portraits of, and she forgot everything except the possibility of meeting the man in the flesh. "Oh, look—isn't that Lord Byron over there? Yes! It has to be Byron. Mr. Hawtrey, you simply have to introduce us!"

His quizzing glass coming into play once more, Reginald Hawtrey turned his head (but carefully, for his shirt points were so high and so starched that a quicker pivot might end with his slicing off an ear), then looked back at Cassandra. "Go out driving with me tomorrow, Miss Kelley," he said with the convincing air of a used car salesman swearing to the sterling mechanical condition of a six-year-old Yugo, "and I shall introduce you to the world—starting with my dear friend Byron."

"Oh, Reggie, you're so droll!" Lady Blakewell exclaimed, rapping his forearm with her closed fan, a move that earned her a fleeting look of utter hostility from her nephew before his quick smile drew attention away from what Cassandra was sure was a thinly veiled hatred of the older woman.

Anxious not to get involved in a family fight, which might end with her being left to find her own way home, heaven only knew how, Cassandra quickly agreed to the proposed drive in the park, then slipped her hand through Mr. Hawtrey's arm to be led to Byron's side.

"Hawtrey?" Byron asked, looking pained once the introductions were completed. "Didn't I decline your invitation to dine last week? Scrope," he said, turning to his friend, who had been introduced as Scrope Davies, a smallish man whose even good looks paled beside the flamboyant beauty of Byron's fallen-god features, "surely we declined, didn't we? I shouldn't hope I was so in my cups that I accepted."

Scrope hid a smile behind his hand, then grinned broadly as he saw Cassandra's quick understanding of Byron's insult. "So, Hawtrey here says our friend Marcus has misplaced you," he said, stepping forward to bow over her hand. "Well, Marcus's loss can only be seen as our gain, Miss Kelley. We must speak of America, for I am endlessly interested in such things."

"Looking for another hidey hole if your creditors become too much for you, Scrope?" Byron said teasingly. "What would you do in America, old friend, with all those wild Indians about? I for one prefer the continent. I have even thought of traveling to Greece again one day."

"Greece?" Cassandra racked her brain. Byron's words had set off alarm bells in her head. Then she remembered. Lord Byron was to leave England under a cloud of scandal in a few years, contract malaria while fighting in some war in Greece, and die there. "Don't do it, my lord," she blurted without thinking. "Especially Missolonghi. Whatever you do, stay away from Missolonghi!"

Lord Byron, who had been affecting an air of bored indifference, looked at Cassandra with some intensity. "Missolonghi? I don't believe I have ever heard the name, much less entertained the thought of traveling to such a place. But to be so impassioned, Miss Kelley? Why, it's almost as if you had looked into my future, and discovered tragedy."

Now she'd done it! Open mouth, insert foot. Why, sometimes it seemed as if the only time she opened her mouth was to change feet. Oh, yes, Marcus was going to be *ecstatic.* She took a small backward step, planning her escape—the hell with figuring out how she'd get back to Grosvenor Square without Lady Blakewell. "It's nothing, my lord," Cassandra stammered. "Honestly. I—*um*—I just sometimes get these—*um*—these *feelings.* Yes, that's it—feelings. They never amount to anything."

Lady Blakewell's jowls were quivering as she leaned across Cassandra, speaking directly to her nephew, all but drooling in her excitement. *"Feelings,* Reggie. Did you hear that? The girl gets *feelings.* Didn't I tell you that the Reverend Mr. Austin said she was strange? That she spoke in tongues, saying words unknown in any language?" She turned to Cassandra, her eyes gleaming. "You're Irish, Miss Kelley. My mother's dresser was Irish, and she had the second sight. She could find lost jewelry, tell us when it was coming on to rain—all that sort of thing. You're fey, aren't you? The Reverend Mr. Austin, fool that he is, thinks you're possessed of the devil. But you're not. You have the second sight. You might even be able to tell the future."

"Aunt, please," Reginald interrupted, his tone deadly.

"Foretell the future?" Lord Byron laughed, and Scrope Davies laughed along with him. "Well, that settles it, dear man," he said. "I shall not dare set foot in Missolonghi—wherever it is. I shall just have to stay here, sponging on my dear friend Scrope—and harassing the public with my poor scribblings."

"Miss Kelley!"

Cassandra flinched, then whirled about to see Marcus descending on their small group, that telltale tic working in his left cheek. And what was he so angry about? *She* hadn't gone off and left *him.*

By the time he had elbowed his way through the crowd, he seemed to have regained his good humor. Bowing a welcome to Lord Byron and Scrope Davies, he turned to thank Lady Blakewell and her nephew for taking such good care of his errant "ward." Cassandra, a smile likewise plastered to her face, leaned close to him and, while nodding agreement to his statements, gritted out from between clenched teeth, "Marcus—get me the *hell* out of here. *Now.*"

"Good as it has been to see you," the marquess, still not looking at Cassandra, went on smoothly after Lord Byron good-naturedly needled him about misplacing his house guest, "I'm afraid we'll have to be leaving now. I've sent Perry on ahead with my Miss Haskins to secure the carriage. Good night."

Mr. Hawtrey, his quizzing glass stuck to his eye for a third time, effectively stopped Marcus in his tracks, saying, "Good night, Miss Kelley. And remember your promise. I shall not sleep a wink in anticipation of our drive tomorrow—at three?"

Cassandra avoided Marcus's eyes, concentrating on refolding her fan. Not that he'd kill her here. There were too many witnesses. But she knew she wouldn't give two cents for her chances once they were safely back in the carriage.

"Miss Kelley has agreed to drive out with you, Hawtrey?" Marcus inquired, his fingers digging into the soft skin just above her elbow. "I don't know if that is convenient."

Lord Byron threw back his head and laughed. He laughed a lot, Cassandra thought, for a man who had such tragedy lurking in his future. "Oh, Marcus, how utterly gothic of you. You sound like a hen with one chick, afraid to let her out of your sight. Or are you fearful of poachers?"

Goaded, Marcus reacted like any man. "Nonsense, George. I was merely reviewing Miss Kelley's hectic schedule. This is her first Season, you know."

Lord Byron nudged his friend Davies. "What do you

think, Scrope? Is Marcus putting it on too thick and rare? Anyone would think Hawtrey here was a dangerous criminal.'' He leaned forward, to peer at the dandy. ''What say you, Hawtrey? Are you dangerous?''

''Dangerous? Oh, your lordship, if that isn't above everything silly!'' Lady Blakewell trilled, using her fan on Lord Byron's arm. The move brought a look of intelligent cunning to his lordship's eyes that Cassandra would not appreciate having directed her way, for she had just remembered that Byron slept with a loaded pistol under his pillow. ''My Reggie is a saint,'' the older woman continued, ''and all know it. Why, he has agreed to introduce Miss Kelley to all the best people. Isn't that correct, Miss Kelley?''

Cassandra's smile, she knew, was sickly to the point of expiration. ''Well, he did say *something*—but, I don't know . . .'' she trailed off weakly, looking up at Marcus, who was looking down at her with something very close to disgust in his dark eyes. Wait a minute! He was *disgusted* with her? Oh, *really?* Did he think she was going to go into her ''Harriette Wilson mode'' or something and jump good old Reggie's bones? Or did he just think she was too stupid to carry off a simple carriage ride through the park? Well, she'd show him!

''Actually,'' she said, brightening, and hoping Marcus choked on his overprotective instincts, ''now that I think about it, I should be most pleased to ride in the park with you tomorrow, Mr. Hawtrey. Heaven knows I could use the fresh air.''

''Then it's settled!'' Lady Blakewell leaned forward, kissing the air beside Cassandra's cheek, and a moment later Marcus had extracted his ''ward'' from the group and was steering her into the flow of people heading toward the next room, his hand once more a vise on her elbow.

Cassandra took refuge in speech, hoping to prolong

the inevitable. "Did you see that, Marcus? Lord Byron! Me—Cassandra Kelley, talking to Lord Byron! God, I never thought I could be a groupie, but that guy has really got something. I mean, he just *oozes* sexiness— kind of like Jim Morrison of The Doors. No wonder Caro Lamb went crazy over him. 'She walks in beauty, like the night of cloudless climes and starry skies—' Oh, could that man write poetry! Marcus, do you think I'll be seeing him again? I'd just love to talk to him about—"

Marcus sliced her a look that convinced her that it might be wise if she shut up—immediately. "Let me take a wild guess here, Marcus—Byron hasn't written that yet, has he?"

"How utterly remarkable," Marcus countered, pushing past an elderly couple to reach the head of the stairs. "At last, and eons too late, the woman *thinks*. How could you have let yourself become separated from Aunt Cornelia? A *dog* knows how to heel, Cassandra. I should be grateful that you have at last shown at least a slight awareness of the difficulties you could have landed in this evening, if only I could decide which would be the lesser of two evils—having you found out for a time traveler, or having to extricate you from one of Hawtrey's orgies."

He pulled her down the stairs and out onto the flagway, where a worried-looking Perry was standing beside the open carriage door, her evening cloak folded over his arm.

"Orgies?" Cassandra asked as Perry laid the cloak over her shoulders and bustled her up the two steps to the carriage. "That wimp? You have got to be kidding. I'd have given you odds he was gay."

Perry, his cheeks flushed, collapsed on the seat next to her. "Gay? Who's gay, Marcus? I didn't think anybody looked best pleased to be here tonight. What a sad crush. Sorry we lost you, Cassie."

"What happened?" Aunt Cornelia asked from the opposite seat. She directed her question to Marcus, who was sitting as still as a statue, glaring at Cassandra through the darkness. "Did the gel disgrace us? I tell you now as I told you before, Marcus, she was there one moment and gone the next. I had absolutely nothing to do with it. It wasn't my idea to bring her, remember. I wash my hands of the whole business."

"Well, thanks a heap, Pontius," Cassandra was stung into retorting. "Marcus," she continued, pointing at the marquess, "before you start on me again, I want to say something here, okay? I think you're overreacting."

"Really?"

"Yes, *really*," she countered, becoming more and more incensed by his coldness. Was this the same man who had held her in his arms last night, loving her? The same man she had given herself to, body and soul? The man whose uncertain fate had become more important to her than her own dilemma? This same man—who was now acting as if she had just committed a capital crime? "I only agreed to go out driving with Reginald Hawtrey, not marry the guy."

Peregrine groaned. "Hawtrey? Marry Reggie Hawtrey? Oh, good grief, Cousin Cassie, what would you want with a fellow like him? Not that he doesn't move in the best circles, because he does, thanks to his aunt, who dotes on him. But Reggie Hawtrey? No. No, I won't allow it. Not *my* cousin."

"Perry," Cassandra reminded him as the carriage stopped outside the mansion in Grosvenor Square, "I am *not* your cousin."

"And it's a good thing, too," Peregrine said with some satisfaction as he helped her down the steps once more and onto the flagway, "because no cousin of mine would be so addlebrained as to set her cap at Reggie Hawtrey. Not a nice man, Cassie, not a nice man at all."

"Marcus," Cassandra said, abandoning Peregrine and lifting her skirts to run after the marquess, who was escorting his aunt into the foyer, "can't we talk about this? Okay, so things didn't go too well tonight. I didn't even get to see Prinny—but it wasn't the disaster you're trying to paint it either. I made one little slip, but there wasn't any real harm done. Lady Blakewell just thinks I can see the future—something about having the second sight because I'm Irish. It's no big deal. Hell, Lady Blakewell doesn't have both oars in the water—anybody can tell that."

Aunt Cornelia turned to look at Cassandra, then sighed and headed for the staircase as if she didn't have the energy to explain how foolish Cassandra's statements were.

"Marcus?" While Cassandra had been watching Aunt Cornelia, the marquess had relieved himself of his cloak and was now heading for his study, with Peregrine not five steps behind him. She pushed past the hovering Goodfellow and took several steps toward the hallway, then stopped. "Marcus—listen to me!"

He turned, slowly, deliberately, skewering her with his dark gaze. "Fascinated as I am by the sound of your voice, Miss Kelley, I believe we have said all that can be said this evening. It is after two, and I suggest that you concentrate on getting a good night's rest if you wish to look your best for Mr. Hawtrey tomorrow. Good night."

And then he was gone, Perry with him, and she and Goodfellow were alone in the foyer. She smiled at the butler, who had never seemed to be as friendly and supportive as beloved family retainers always were in Wilmont Publishing's Mayfair Regency romances. She beat a hasty retreat to her bedchamber, wondering why she had always thought "conflict" was a necessary ingredient in romance novels. Didn't anybody ever get to the "happily ever after" without having a monkey wrench thrown into the works somewhere around the sixth chapter?

Obviously not.

Chapter 12

"Good morning, my lord. Sleep well, I hope —*not*," Cassandra said, striding into the study, her arms swinging, and then perched on the edge of the Marquess's desk. She knew he hated it when she did that.

He did not lift his head, but only continued to concentrate on some figures he was feeding into her solar calculator. It really blew her mind how he had mastered the calculator, even the memory buttons, which still gave her fits. Of course, it shouldn't have surprised her, for Marcus could do anything.

Well, almost anything. Obviously he still hadn't learned how to apologize. He hadn't come to her room last night—not that she had really expected him to, but he had also been absent from the breakfast room this morning. She and a decidedly nervous Perry had spent a desultory half hour pushing eggs and ham (or, in Perry's case, eggs and kippers) around their plates, eating little and talking about everything except one Reginald Hawtrey and Cassandra's engagement to go driving with him in the park today at three.

And then Perry had gone, mumbling something about looking in at Tatt's. "Not that my blunt runs to setting up m'own stable, of course," he explained, "but just for the fun of watching all the gamesters settling up by selling their horseflesh." She was left to wander the mansion alone, wondering whether she had it in her to wait it out, to let Marcus make the first move.

Five minutes earlier she'd had her answer. In this particular battle of wills she had decided to be the loser. She hadn't dwelled on that for long, as she preferred to believe that of the two of them, she was being a grown-up about the thing.

"Hey, Marcus—your hair is on fire," she said after a few moments of strained silence.

He looked up at her, his eyebrows raised as if to say that yes, he had heard her, but no, he didn't plan to speak to her. Then he returned to his figures, punching in numbers from a list he had scribbled on a piece of paper.

"You know, Marcus, if this was April 1992 and America, I could understand it, because your income taxes would be due. I don't have to pay any this year, so I filed early. Got eight hundred and fifty big ones back. I should have put it in the bank, but I blew it on a round-trip plane ticket to London. Now there was money wasted, wasn't it? *Marcus!* Talk to me, damn it!"

Marcus hit the total button, frowned, wrote the figure at the bottom of the page, snapped the plastic cover over the calculator, folded his hands in front of him on the desk, and looked up at her, his expression bland. "I had hoped, taking into account normal calendar changes, and figuring in the vagaries of February, I could come up with a formula that would show that, given the difference of one hundred and eighty years, May thirty-first and March twelfth might actually be the same day, but they are not. Ah well, it was only a theory. Were you speaking to me, Miss Kelley? Strange, I should have thought you'd be upstairs, primping for your drive with Reginald Hawtrey."

Cassandra looked at him in amazement, dismissing his

ramblings about dates—none of that was important at the moment. "I don't believe it. You're *jealous!*"

He averted his eyes, then pushed back his chair and stood. Turning his back on her, he stared out the window at the mews. "Don't be more ignorant than you can help, Cassandra," he said cuttingly, clasping and unclasping his hands behind his back. "I am only concerned about the consequences. Hawtrey is all but promised to Susannah Winterson, a considerable heiress who, like you, is not known for her willingness to 'share.' Driving out in public with you will jeopardize his chances with the girl. His insufferable aunt and known benefactor is in on this business, I know it. I just can't figure out what her motive is." He whirled about to face her, narrowing his dark eyes. "Why is the woman so interested in you?"

Cassandra pulled a face, shrugging. "She likes me? Some people do, you know."

"Hardly. Lady Blakewell doesn't *like* anybody. She only uses them to better her own position. Besides, the woman barely knows you. There has been something havey-cavey about this business from the very beginning."

"The Reverend Mr. Austin?" Cassandra asked rhetorically as Marcus stepped out from behind the desk and began to pace up and down. Hopping down from the desk, she leaned against it with her hands folded at her waist. She loved the way he moved, softly, sleekly, soundlessly, like a panther. And he was, too, jealous. She wouldn't tease him about it—but he was. "He was with her that first day at Hyde Park, and again at her house that night, grilling me."

The marquess stopped, to look at her as if he were seeing her for the first time. "You're wearing a riding habit. I thought Hawtrey said he was taking you for a drive."

"He sent a note this morning, saying he'd rather we went riding. I told you I could ride, not that you've ever taken me up on it." She grabbed a bit of material on each side of the divided skirt and whirled about in a circle. "Isn't it terrific? I just love Regency fashions."

"I see," Marcus said, that telltale tic beginning in his left cheek so that she knew he was just dying to forbid her to see Hawtrey. "I should have realized sooner. My apologies, Cassandra. It is only that we don't have a sidesaddle in the stables anymore, not since Georgina left."

Cassandra winced. "A sidesaddle? Oh, God, Marcus, I don't know how to use a sidesaddle. I wouldn't even know how to get on one! What am I going to do?"

Marcus had been busying himself getting them each a glass of wine from the drinks table. He handed a glass to Cassandra and leaned against the desk beside her, his eyes twinkling. "Are you asking my advice, Cassandra? How novel. A pity you didn't think to do that last night, before accepting Hawtrey's invitation."

"You're loving this, aren't you? You're just loving it," Cassandra snapped, taking a sip of the wine.

"If by that you mean, am I enjoying your predicament, then yes, my love, I do find myself to be marginally amused, although it doesn't make up for the night I've had. I thought we were dealing with more important issues than a childish effort on your part to make me jealous—as if anyone could be jealous of Reggie Hawtrey."

Cassandra slammed the glass on the desktop and glared at the marquess. "How many times must I tell you that it wasn't my fault? I got separated from Aunt Cornelia, Marcus, and Lady Blakewell promised to take me home. The rest—well, the rest just happened. Besides, you were the one who wanted me out in public, remember, as part of your damned 'experiments.' "

"Those experiments have not been a part of my agenda for some weeks, Cassandra, and I wished for you to be presented only so that I could gauge your reactions to the people you met, and perhaps learn from you. But now we have discovered the reason for your presence in my time. I thought we would concentrate on trying to save me from whoever or whatever appears to want to put a nasty period to my existence on the last day of May. I—foolishly, perhaps—believed that you would now wish to concentrate on a plan to save Spencer Perceval, as a prelude to changing my not-too-distant future. But if you would rather spend your time riding about the city with Reginald Hawtrey, far be it from me to—"

"Oh, Marcus, how I adore you!" Cassandra exploded, throwing herself at him so that they nearly tumbled to the floor. Her arms around his neck, she showered his face with quick kisses, loving him more now that he had shown her that he was not always the perfect marquess, the genius she had imagined him. He was as human as any man. He was jealous. And, bless his arrogant heart, he loved her!

It didn't take him long to begin to return her kisses. Their lips were locked together as he slipped his arms around her waist, crushing her against him. All the love, all the passion, all the longing they had felt only two nights before and missed so much when it was absent last night flooded to the surface. Within moments Marcus had slipped an arm beneath Cassandra's knees and lifted her, their mouths still fused, and carried her to a nearby wide couch.

He put her down gently and then sat beside her. His smile brought tears to her eyes as he said, "I've been an idiot, darling. Please forgive me. It's just that I was so anxious when I saw Corny and you weren't with her. I went charging from room to room like a mad animal—pushing straight past Prinny, who must think I'm trying to avoid him because I haven't found any treasure in the White Tower. I feared the worst, I feared that you were terrified to be on your own. And then—''

She lifted a hand to stroke his smooth cheek. "And then you found me, and I was chatting happily with Lord Byron and looking as if I hadn't a care in the world. Actually, Marcus, now that I look at it from your position, I'm surprised you didn't leave me to find my own way home. Oh, darling, I'm so sorry.''

He began fumbling with the small covered buttons at the neck of her riding habit. "We could waste precious moments discussing who is to blame, my sweet, but I prefer to spend our time engaging in other, more appealing, pursuits. God, Cassandra, how lonely I've been without you. I didn't sleep a wink all night.''

"Me neither,'' Cassandra admitted, her grammar slipping as the heat of Marcus's body reached her through the fabric of her gown and inflamed her senses. "And the last thing I want to do this afternoon is to go riding, or driving, or whatever, with Reggie Hawtrey. I don't want to waste a moment of our time together, Marcus. Marcus?''

One moment he had been holding her. One moment he had been deftly opening the buttons of her jacket, exposing her breasts. One moment she had been willingly responding to his urgency, not caring that yet again the door was not locked. Let Perry walk in on them. Let Corny and Goodfellow and the whole damn household walk in on them—let them sell tickets if they wanted to. Marcus was loving her, and she was loving him back. But now—now he was gone. Gone from her; gone from the wide couch, and standing above her, looking down at her, so that she shivered and began nervously rebuttoning her jacket, feeling as if a bucket of cold water had just been poured on her raging desires. "Marcus? What's wrong now? If you're worried about someone walking in on us—"

He shook his head and ran a hand through his dark hair. "No, it's nothing like that, although I certainly should have taken such a possibility into account. My mind ceases to function clearly whenever you're near. It's Hawtrey, Cassandra. I think you have to see him to-day."

Cassandra swung her feet to the floor and glared up at him as she finished rebuttoning her jacket. "You've got to be kidding." When he didn't answer she frowned, biting her bottom lip. "You're not kidding. You really think Lady Blakewell suspects something? Marcus, the woman isn't that smart."

Marcus lifted his wineglass from the desk and drained its contents. "No, my darling, she's not. However, as someone we both know very well said to me recently, she knows just enough to be dangerous. If you cancel your appointment with her nephew at the last moment, it will seem to her as if we are attempting to conceal something. We have enough to keep us busy for the next six weeks without looking over our shoulders to see what Lady Blakewell is doing. Much as I dislike saying this, you must keep your appointment with Reginald Hawtrey at three."

Cassandra sat on the bench seat of Reginald Hawtrey's high-perch phaeton and held on for dear life as they entered Hyde Park. "Is he anybody?" she asked, daring to lift one hand to point at a well-dressed man standing quite alone just inside the gate, his expression announcing that he was totally bored watching the procession of carriages, curricles, phaetons, and showy horseflesh on parade.

Hawtrey, who was having a bit of difficulty handling his high-strung pair of snow-white geldings (he certainly wasn't the whip Marcus was), took a moment to follow the direction of Cassandra's discreetly pointed finger. "Brummell? Only to himself, my dear Miss Kelley, only to himself. Especially now that he doesn't have our Prince Regent so deeply in his pocket anymore. *I* am much more the thing, you know."

As the phaeton moved away Cassandra looked back to see the famous Beau Brummell and, giving in to impulse, smiled broadly and waved at him. And the Beau, bless him, waved back! Cassandra's smile wavered, for she knew the Beau's history well. After this first falling out with Prinny, the Beau remained in London until 1816 when, plagued by debts, and without the protection of the Regent, he was forced to flee to Calais. Two dozen years later the man who had brought hygiene, wit, and elegant fashion to the world died, slovenly and insane, in a French asylum—a broken man, betrayed by all he'd helped and entertained.

Cassandra turned back to Hawtrey, hiding a sneer as she looked at the man who had dared to look down his nose at one of her heroes. Hawtrey, dressed in a puce morning coat, his waistcoat of canary yellow, his high shirt points digging into his earlobes, was a cartoon figure whose reputation would not outlive him, while Beau Brummell's name still meant fashion in 1992. "You'd have loved polyester, Mr. Hawtrey," she said, hanging on tightly to the seat once more as the horses took exception to a passing coach.

"Polly Ester? I don't believe I've heard of the lady, Miss Kelley." Hawtrey shrugged, the even dozen capes of his bottle-green driving coat all but obscuring his chin. "But no matter. If I have not heard of Miss Ester, she is nothing. Ah, but here comes someone I do know, although I should not say so, should I? Such a lovely woman, the widow Carruthers, although she is looking faintly down pin these days, as she has been without male companionship these past weeks."

You slimy bastard, Cassandra thought, following the direction of Hawtrey's unsubtle pointing finger, to see an open carriage drawing near from the other direction. The woman inside the carriage was stylishly dressed in a pink confection with a straw hat tied beneath her chin. She was about thirty years of age, had blond hair and blue eyes, and was startlingly beautiful. Cassandra hated her on sight.

Hawtrey pulled the phaeton to a stop, causing the coachman directly behind him to begin cursing his driving. But Hawtrey ignored him. Bowing from the waist while he tipped his hat, and very nearly letting go of the reins—Cassandra, muttering under her breath, reached between them and engaged the wooden brake as she had seen Marcus do—Hawtrey went about the business of introducing Cassandra to Marcus's former mistress.

"Laws, Reggie, I should thank you for condescending to stop, truly I should, as I have heard so much about Perry's little American cousin." Marianne Carruthers's simper set Cassandra's teeth on edge. "Hello, my child. Are you enjoying your stay in your mother country? And isn't Reggie wonderful for taking you up in his phaeton? It isn't everyone he allows the privilege, you know. But then, some of us are in more need of borrowed consequence, aren't we?"

This was Marcus's former mistress? He actually went to bed with this bitch? Cassandra wished that once, just this once, she could come up with a really sarcastic line, just to watch the woman turn white under her artfully applied rouge. Cassandra knew Marianne's type. If the woman had been born in 1960 she would have played tennis at the local country club, slept with her husband's boss, and shopped exclusively at Bloomie's—and her nickname would have been Buffy. "La, yes, Mrs. Carruthers," Cassandra answered at last, as Hawtrey snickered beside her, "I am indeed blessed. But then, as they say, *youth* has its privileges. Doesn't it, *Mrs.* Carruthers?"

Marianne's cornflower-blue eyes narrowed to slits, but she recovered quickly. Smiling, she inclined her head to Cassandra. "Ah, the kitten has claws. No wonder Marcus is diverted—for the moment. Reginald, you will bring her to my party next week, won't you? I should like to get to know our little American better. But now we must move on, for I see that my horses are on the fret. Good day, Miss Kelley."

"Good day, Mrs. Carruthers," Cassandra answered as the two equipages moved off in opposite directions, and not a moment too soon for the coachman driving the closed coach behind them. Cassandra heard the man say none too quietly, "And about time, too, ya bloomin' pop-injay. I wuz soon goin' ta let m'cattle take a bite outta yer rump!"

Once they were moving again Hawtrey (who seemed to have lost much of his former good humor when Cassandra defended herself against Marianne Carruthers) inclined his head in her direction—turning his head could lead only to disaster, for neither his shirt points nor his death grip on the reins allowed such a movement.

"My Lord Eastbourne seemed a tad put out that I have usurped his duty to bring you into fashion," he said conversationally after a few minutes, obviously trying a new way to draw blood. "I shouldn't know why, for I am highly presentable. Or perhaps he has more than an altruistic interest in his lovely ward?"

"The marquess?" Cassandra asked, forcing a laugh, for she was still smarting over Mrs. Carruther's well-aimed darts. Tonight, probably just after midnight, Cassandra was sure she'd come up with half a dozen smart answers she could have given—maybe even a full dozen. That was how it always happened. Yet, all things considered, she didn't think she had done too badly. "Don't be silly, Mr. Hawtrey," she assured him, trying to concentrate on the matter at hand. "All he cares for are his intellectual pursuits, and those disgusting specimens he keeps in jars in his study."

She shivered delicately, remembering that she was supposed to be fishing for Hawtrey's reason for paying so much attention to her. "I cannot tell you how grateful Cousin Perry and I are that you have condescended to drive out with me, lending me your considerable consequence. Why, Perry says this one drive will absolutely *make* my Season. It must be gratifying to wield such power, Mr. Hawtrey. Even Mrs. Carruthers remarked on it."

Gag me, Cassandra thought, pretending an interest in the passersby in order to hide her distaste. Being a pattern-card Regency miss was rather like running for political office—you'd say anything to get elected.

"Please, Miss Kelley, you don't have to thank me," Hawtrey drawled, inclining his head to a man and woman approaching from the opposite direction, their combined bulk as they sat on the bench seat of their phaeton prompting Cassandra to wonder if they had used a winch to raise themselves onto the seat, the way the Prince Regent used a winch to hoist himself onto a horse.

"Perhaps it is time I took the gloves off. You see," he continued silkily, "I have been fascinated with the stories my dear aunt, Lady Blakewell, has been prattling on about these past weeks—fantastical tales of speaking in tongues and second sight and the like. Not to wrap this business up in fine linen, I'm afraid the Reverend Mr. Austin has quite a hold on my aunt's pocketbook, which I vow I cannot like, and I wish to prove his theories incorrect. Yes, the man needs his comeuppance. Hence my interest in you. So sorry, my dear, if you were holding hopes in that quarter. I do not wish to bruise your tender heart but, alas, matrimonially, I am otherwise committed.''

He smiled at her, and Cassandra's flesh crawled. This guy could give vanity lessons to Donald Trump! "Although I must say," he continued, "I wasn't best pleased last evening when you told Byron that little faradiddle about Missolonghi. You made absolutely no impression upon him, I fear, but to my aunt? Well, let us just say that the woman has ambitions.''

Here it was, the reason Hawtrey had invited her out for a drive, and the reason she had accepted. Marcus was right. Lady Blakewell *was* up to something, and she knew just enough to cause trouble if she should start going all over town blabbing about Cassandra's warning to Byron. Thank God she hadn't told Marcus what she had said.

"Ambitions, Mr. Hawtrey? I don't understand."

"Of course you don't, my dear," Hawtrey answered as, thankfully, they completed the circuit and he moved the phaeton toward one of the exits. "I shouldn't imagine that you do, although you should, if my aunt's conclusions were correct—which, of course, they are not. My aunt, you see, believes she has a chance to replace Lady Hertford in Prinny's affections—the two women being much of a pair in girth, if not in intellect.

"My dear aunt, you must understand, is smart enough, but she lacks intelligence. If she should be able to whisper in Prinny's ear, tell him of the future—ah, that would go far in evening the odds. Of course, she would assure him *she* had seen into the future. It wouldn't do to tell him she had gleaned her information from a fey Irish nobody from the colonies. God's teeth, Miss Kelley, whoever heard of an Irish oracle?''

Cassandra pressed her hands to her cheeks, nearly toppling from the seat as Hawtrey's cow-handed driving took the off wheel through a muddy ditch on the side of the road. Hawtrey didn't think his aunt was smart? "You've got to be pulling my—I mean—my dear Mr. Hawtrey, you mustn't tease me so! Lady Blakewell wants *me* to tell her the future? I wouldn't do such a thing, even if I could, which I can't. *Nobody* can!"

The phaeton turned into Grosvenor Square and Cassandra bit her bottom lip, determined not to say another word until they reached the mansion. But Hawtrey pulled the horses to a halt just inside the square, a good five hundred yards from the mansion, although Cassandra didn't notice this at first. She was still too angry over Hawtrey's Regency Era Irish jokes.

"And this business about flying, Miss Kelley?" he persisted, his sly smile making her see red. "You were funning with the good vicar with that ridiculous clunker, weren't you?"

So much for resolutions. The guy was really beginning to get to her. "No kidding, Reggie," she blurted, looking down at the roadway and mentally gauging the distance from seat to street. It wouldn't be a graceful descent, but she could manage it. "That idiot preacher needed his guns spiked, so I made it up. It served him right. Now, are you going to drive on, or am I going to have to jump for it?"

"Jump, Miss Kelley? Don't be ridiculous. We will move on in a moment. Directly after you tell me about Missolonghi. As I recall, you told Byron you occasionally get 'feelings.' Precisely what sort of feelings, Miss Kelley? You realize I must return to my aunt with a full reporting of all you have said, or else we shall be forced to do this again. Come, come now, tell me about these feelings, and then I will deposit you back in the bosom of your family. You're so close to that family, aren't you, my poor, dear Miss Kelley, so close and yet so far."

Cassandra made a fist of her right hand. Boy, would

she like to pop this guy one, square in his grinning, self-satisfied face. "I'll give you this much, Reggie—you're a real piece of work. Tell me, when you were younger, did you get your kicks pulling wings off flies?" She knew she was losing her temper, but she just didn't care anymore. "You might think you're hot sh—hot stuff, trying to bully a woman, but you don't scare me. You're nothing but a joke. You act as if you're God's gift, but you can't move without asking your aunt first. You can't do *anything*. Yes, you talk big, and you get off playing your sick little games, but when Auntie says jump, you ask 'How high?'"

Oh, she was on a roll now. Sheila would have been proud of her. Reggie Hawtrey was sitting completely still, his mouth hanging open. She didn't have to wait until midnight to get this guy. She had the snappy lines all ready for him—and he was going to hear them all! "You want answers, buddy? Okay—I'll give you answers. I'm a witch, Reggie baby. A broom-flying, cauldron-stirring, future-telling, card-carrying *witch!* I'd turn you into a toad, to prove it to you, but somebody already beat me to it. But don't come near me again, buster—*ever*—or I'll make your nose grow. Let's see how fast you'd marry a fortune then. Oh, yeah, and one more thing—*you dress funny!*"

Before he could answer, and before she could think of anything else to say, Cassandra felt someone tapping her on the shoulder. *"Now what?"* she demanded in exasperation. She turned quickly, angry enough to curse whoever was bothering her, and saw Peregrine Walton standing beside the phaeton, his cane raised like a sword. She had never been so happy to see anyone in her life. "Perry!"

"Yes, it's me. Hullo, Cousin Cassie," Peregrine responded, frowning. "What are you doing sitting up there, in the middle of the Square? We live over there, you know," he said, using the cane to point down the Square toward the mansion. "Hawtrey, you picked her up. Should have known that, shouldn't you, even if m'cousin don't? She's Irish, you know, and can't help it. At least that's what Marcus told me to say whenever she acts queer."

Hawtrey opened his mouth to speak, but Cassandra wasn't about to let him get a word in sideways. "Never mind that now, Perry," she said, holding out a hand to him. Reaction was setting in. She felt as if she was shaking all over. "Just help me down. Mr. Hawtrey has an important appointment with his aunt, and doesn't dare be late." She landed gracefully—at least, she thought, gracefully for her—and turned to look up at the man, deliberately crossing her eyes, as if she had been possessed by spirits or something. "Isn't that right, Mr. Hawtrey?"

He was staring down at her, bug-eyed. It was great to watch his Adam's apple ride up and down his throat as he struggled to locate his voice. "A-an appointment? Oh —oh, yes! An appointment! Walton—will you be so kind as to escort Miss Kelley home?"

Peregrine slammed his fists onto his hips, shaking his head, and stumbled backward as Hawtrey drove off. The oaf had nearly run over Perry's toes in his haste. "Well, if that don't beat the Dutch. You'd think the devil himself was after him, wouldn't you, Cousin Cassie? Told you I don't like him. Don't like him above half."

As they turned toward the mansion, Cassandra slipped her arm through Peregrine's and laid her head against his sleeve, seeking his comfort. "You're so brilliant, Perry," she said, smiling up at him. "And such a great judge of character. Now, please—let's go home! Oh, and Perry— we'll keep this our little secret, okay? There's no reason to worry Marcus about it, is there? I'll tell him all he needs to know." *Marcus will blow his top if I tell him everything,* she thought. *So I won't, that's all. I just won't. If Peregrine cooperates, that is.*

And, luckily, Peregrine was most cooperative.

"Marcus?" The rotund little man rolled his eyes in comedic terror. "Wouldn't tell him anything, Cousin. Not about Hawtrey. He's been prowling his study like a caged beast, growling at everybody, waiting for you—which is why I went out for a stroll. No, least said, soonest mended, I always say. Or was it m'mother who said that? Never mind. Shall we be off, Cousin?"

Chapter 13

Cassandra lay on her bed, her hands tucked behind her head, a small smile playing around her lips as she watched Marcus untie his banyan. For the past two weeks it had been as if they were married—at least until it was dawn, and time for him to return to his own room.

Marcus had accepted her explanation for Lady Blakewell's interest in her, for she had told him the truth about the woman's belief that Cassandra's "feelings" might give her an entry to Prinny's affections. He had been angry but Cassandra convinced him that she had lost her taste for moving about in London Society, and he had at last agreed not to confront either Lady Blakewell or Reginald Hawtrey with that anger. He opted instead for allowing Aunt Cornelia to tell everyone that Miss Kelley was "ill, most probably a reaction to her uncomfortable crossing."

And Cassandra had not lied to the marquess. The novelty of living in Regency England, if novelty was the proper word for it, had more than worn off, thanks mostly to Reginald Hawtrey. She couldn't face going into public again, couldn't chance meeting up with either him or his meddling aunt, even if they didn't dare say too much to other members of the *ton*. Marcus was too powerful, and Lady Blakewell was too conscious of that power.

No, as long as she stayed within the four walls of the Grosvenor Square mansion she was safe. Besides, she wanted to spend every moment with Marcus, the man she loved, the man who loved her. They had to plan to save Spencer Perceval, had to prove that it was possible to change history. They had to, or else Marcus was doomed.

But she wouldn't think of that at this moment, not when Marcus had now stripped to the skin and joined her under the covers. Cassandra lived for the night, for the moment Marcus came to her and, with his sweet loving, transported her beyond worries, beyond time.

"You're looking pleased with yourself this evening, my dearest," Marcus said now, pressing a kiss on her bare shoulder. "I should be concerned, if you had not been so well behaved these past weeks. Confining yourself to strolls within the Square, allowing Aunt Cornelia to teach you embroidery, spending countless hours with me in my study, answering all my questions without ever pouting. You haven't even teased Goodfellow above twice. Are you ill, darling? You are being so very good that perhaps I should be worried. Are you planning some sort of mischief?"

Cassandra snuggled close to him, running her fingers through the mat of hair on his broad chest. "I could be, Marcus," she said teasingly. "What sort of mischief would you like? I'm open to suggestions."

"Minx." His hands disappeared under the covers to begin tickling the sensitive skin at her waist so that she writhed on the bed, giggling, breathlessly begging him to stop. "Stop, is it? Yes, I suppose so," he said, collapsing against the pillows. "After that *mischief* you showed me last night, I think you should be too exhausted to plan anything except a good night's rest." He sat up, throwing back the covers. "Shall I leave you to it?"

She grabbed his shoulders and pulled him back across

her legs, then bent over him, her face close to his. "You wouldn't dare! Only think, Marcus, if you leave me, I may cry. I may wail and sob so loudly that Corny will be forced to come in here to see for herself what is wrong with me. She's crazy about me these days, you know, and not just because I'm such a good pupil at that stupid embroidery. I tell her about the future, about Byron's troubles with Lady Caroline Lamb, about poor Brummell's fall from grace, about the celebrations after Waterloo. She is ever so grateful to her informative Regency miss. Why, if I were to be unhappy she might blame you, Marcus. I don't think you'd like that. Corny is a woman who could make any man's life a living hell if she put her mind to it."

He looked up at her, grinning, boyish in his good humor. "Corny doesn't hold a candle to you in that particular endeavor, imp," he said, slipping a hand behind her neck and slowly pulling her down so that their lips met in a sweet, encouraging kiss.

And then, as always, the passion that simmered all day, carefully tamped down while they were in his study and while they sat at table with Peregrine and Aunt Cornelia, exploded between them. In these last weeks Cassandra had discovered that lovemaking *was* all she'd heard it had been cracked up to be—if you were with the right man.

Marcus had taught her so much, and her education continued tonight. Locked in his arms, she flowered beneath his hands, taking and giving and climbing to the heights, heights she hadn't dreamed existed.

They had come together that first night in white-hot passion, and that passion showed no signs of burning out, although they had learned to draw out their pleasure, to take the time to talk with each other, to tease each other, to indulge in the leisure of lying side by side in the dark, watching the fire slowly die in the hearth, sharing their dreams, their hopes, their fears.

It was those fears that kept their lovemaking new, exciting, and, at times, desperate. It was already May. Soon they would go together to the House of Commons, to change history—if it could be changed. Their plans had been made, with Peregrine taken into their confidence. All that remained was to execute those plans.

Time. It was their friend, until the last day of the month; it allowed them to be together, to love.

Time. It was their enemy, each tick of the clock bringing them closer to that same last day in May, drawing them inexorably closer to the moment when Marcus would either cheat the fates or be outwitted by them.

Her arms wrapped tightly around Marcus's back, his body buried deeply within hers, his fevered breath rasping against her cheek, Cassandra strained to hold him tighter, closer—willing time to stop. And as she held him, as the fever built, time did stop, hovering on the precipice, dancing just out of reach, before, together, she and Marcus went tumbling down, down into the pleasant valley below, and they slept, still locked in each other's arms.

And the clock ticked on.

"No! Marcus, no! Oh, God, no!"

Marcus awoke in an instant and saw that Cassandra was sitting upright in bed, her violet eyes wide as she sightlessly stared into the predawn darkness. He put his arms around her, but she was rigid—he couldn't move her even though he could feel her trembling beneath his hands.

"Cassandra! Darling! What is it?"

"The stairs," she said, although he knew she wasn't speaking in answer to his question. "Oh, God, please, not the stairs!" She began to rock in his embrace, back and forth, back and forth, like an old woman he had seen mourning in the street, kneeling over a child run down by a carriage. "Not yet. Oh, please, not yet. Too soon. Too soon! Marcus, where are you? *Marcus!*"

"Hush, darling, I'm here," Marcus crooned over and over, desperately trying to break through Cassandra's nightmare. Her terror was palpable. "I'm here. I'll always be here."

"Marcus?" Cassandra was suddenly still, before she turned in one swift movement and threw her arms around his shoulders, burying her head against his chest. "Oh, Marcus! It was horrible! I was in the White Tower, standing at the entrance to that small passageway—the passageway that leads to the stairs, to that room. Oh, God, Marcus, I was walking toward the *top* of the stairs!"

He kissed her hair, her temple, her cheek, tasting the salt of the tears that streamed down her cheeks now that she had come completely awake. "Hush, darling. It was a dream, Cassandra. Only a dream. I'm here."

She pushed herself out of his arms and scrambled off the bed. Picking up her nightgown, she pulled it over her head, then began pacing, hugging herself, her slim figure outlined by the dying light of the fire. "Yes, Marcus, you're here. I'm here. But for how long? You seemed so sure that I'd be here until the end of May, that I'd be here to help you change history. But the dream—it was so *real*, Marcus!"

He slipped from the bed, shrugging into his banyan. "Tell me about it, Cassandra. Tell me everything."

She stopped pacing and put a hand to her head. "There's nothing to tell. I was there, the stairs were there. It was just the way it was the first time." Her bottom lip began to quiver. "Oh, God, Marcus, I can't go. I can't leave you. What would I do without you?"

He took hold of her shoulders, giving her a small

shake, daring to hope. "Just the way it was the *first* time, Cassandra? Tell me, what were you wearing?"

She shook her head, as if shaking away his questions, then looked up at him, her eyes widening. "Marcus! I was wearing my own clothes! You were right, it was a dream. I was reliving the day I first met you. It was just a dream!"

Marcus sighed, pulling her against him, cradling her shuddering body, thanking whatever gods there were for this reprieve. For she hadn't been the only one to be frightened. He had been planning for the last day of May, hoping for the best, but that did not mean his theory would be proved correct. Cassandra's nightmare had brought home the fact that he was fallible, that things might not go as he had planned, as he was still planning. Thank heaven he hadn't told her all of his theories. There was no point in encouraging her to hope.

"Come back to bed, darling," he said now, running his hand along her spine, feeling the warmth of her skin beneath the thin nightgown. "It will be morning soon, but I want to know that you are sleeping before I leave you."

She sat on the edge of the bed, but would not let go of his hands. "Don't go, Marcus," she pleaded, squeezing his fingers. "I don't think I could stand being alone right now." She smiled, running her thumbs across his palms. "Besides, this is stupid. Why are we hiding like this? Perry already knows about us, and so does Goodfellow. I can tell because he's looking down his nose at me even more these days. If Goodfellow knows, Rose knows—all the servants know. Can't we just tell Corny and get it over with?"

He sat down beside her, inwardly admitting that her arguments made sense. It was the height of ridiculousness, sneaking about like a green youth, hiding what he was about. Yet to tell Corny would be to open an avenue of discussion he wished to remain blocked. "We can't tell Corny, Cassandra. She'd start making wedding plans, and neither of us will be here long enough to walk down the aisle." The moment the words were out he knew he had made a mistake.

"Oh, Marcus!" Cassandra wailed, throwing herself into his arms once more. "How can you be so rational about this? You're talking about your possible death the same way you'd talk about one of your damned experiments. I love you, Marcus, but there are times I really could hit you."

He chuckled under his breath. Maybe he hadn't said the wrong thing. Cassandra was angry now, and an angry Cassandra was much preferable to a weeping Cassandra. "I'm sorry, darling," he said. "Perhaps you'd rather I moaned and gnashed my teeth? I can't see where that would help either of us, but I would, of course, do anything to oblige you."

"Creep!" She sat up, giving him a playful punch on his arm before using the hem of her nightgown to wipe her eyes one last time. "You know I'd fall apart if you weren't so strong." She pushed herself back against the pillows, throwing the covers over her legs and folding her hands in her lap. "You promised to stay here until I fell asleep again. Tell me a bedtime story, okay?"

"Incorrigible imp." Marcus chuckled in real amusement, seeing the light of humor in Cassandra's lovely violet eyes. She would never cease to amaze him, not if they were to be granted a lifetime together. He smoothed the covers over her legs, then leaned back against one of the high bedposts. "What sort of bedtime story, darling?"

She shrugged, snuggling beneath the covers, for the morning was cool. "I don't know. Tell me more about London. God knows I haven't seen much of it lately."

"Very well," Marcus answered, slanting a look at the

mantel clock, for it had grown light enough for him to see it, even from this distance. He'd have to be quick about this, or the whole household would see him scurrying back to his own rooms, his bare legs sticking out under his banyan. And wouldn't that be a pretty picture! "Shall I tell you about a typical evening at Almack's? You refused to use the voucher I procured for you, not that I can say I'm sorry, for never was there a duller place than that."

She shook her head, smiling, and Marcus suddenly knew that she had a particular subject in mind. He also had the niggling feeling that he wasn't going to like hearing what it was. "I heard Perry telling Goodfellow the other day that he had been to the White House, and was sorry he hadn't looked in at Brooks's instead. But when I asked Perry what the White House is, he just turned red and stammered something about having to keep an excruciatingly important appointment with his hatter. So you can tell me. What's the White House, Marcus? We have one you know, in Washington. You guys burn it down sometime during the war you're going to start soon. You remember what I told you about that?"

"I remember. You also told me that nobody will win this particular war, my dear," Marcus said tightly, for he still bristled when she reminded him that the United States, and not England, was the mightiest military country in her world. Imagine! To be known for pink-haired youths, eccentrics, and musical plays! It was insulting, especially to a man who had cut his wisdom teeth at Trafalgar. "But much as you must already know that you shouldn't be asking this particular question, I will answer you. Perry did not want to say anything to you because our White House—unlike your government building—is a discreet, very discreet, brothel."

Cassandra giggled. "A *brothel?* And our White House

is different? Oh, Marcus, I wouldn't touch *that* line with a ten-foot pole!''

Marcus frowned, then smiled when he realized that Cassandra no longer seemed frightened. Actually, if that was her toe, just now pushing intimately against his thigh, she seemed to have made a most miraculous recovery from her nightmare. But though he was inclined to take up her invitation, he knew he must leave.

He was leaning forward, to kiss Cassandra one last time, when the door to her bedchamber opened. He all but leaped from the bed, cursing as he stubbed his toe on the night table and hoping against hope that it was only Rose coming to relight the fire. Then he heard Aunt Cornelia say, ''Cassandra, my dear, I couldn't sleep a wink last night thinking about our plans for your latest project. I believe we should begin at once, which entails an early excursion to my favorite shop for embroidery thread. . . . *Marcus!* Is that you? Whatever are you about? My stars—are those your *feet?''*

''Don't look now, but methinks the jig is up, old sport,'' Cassandra whispered, then ducked under the covers, leaving him to explain as best he could.

He took refuge in a lie. ''Cassandra cried out in a nightmare, Aunt, just as I was passing by her door on my way down to my study to retrieve a book I had been reading,'' he said, avoiding her eyes. ''I have just finished calming her and was about to return to my own chamber. Isn't that right, Cassandra?'' he said between clenched teeth.

She peeked out from beneath the covers. ''If you say so, Marcus,'' she said, winking at him so that he longed to bend her over his knee and spank her.

Aunt Cornelia approached the bed. Her ramrod-straight body was wrapped in a heavy dressing gown and a ridiculous frilled cap covered her rag-tied curls. She looked more imposing than any uniformed, gold-braid-

festooned general he had ever seen, and twice as nasty.
Aunt Cornelia gazed at him levelly for a long while, so
that he could feel his toes digging into the carpet, just as
if he were ten years old once more and had been caught
trying to filch sugarplums from his mother's candy dish
in the drawing room at Eastbourne.

"I see," she said, and Marcus knew that she did see.
She saw all too much, including his nightclothes, which
he suddenly realized were still sprawled at the foot of
the bed, where he had carelessly dropped them before
joining Cassandra under the covers. Obviously Cassandra
saw them, too, for she had begun giggling again,
wretched child that she was.

"Corny—I mean, Aunt Cornelia," Marcus heard himself babble, "I can explain."

"And it is an explanation I shall look forward to with
great anticipation, Marcus." Aunt Cornelia turned on her
heel, dragging the hem of her dressing gown and her
dignity behind her, and headed for the door. "Your
study, Marcus. *Alone.* Ten o'clock. I would advise you
not to be late," he heard her say just before the door
closed on her departing back.

Marcus collapsed onto the bed, at last beginning to
appreciate the humor of the situation—which he considered to be a good thing, for Cassandra was all but dis-
solved in mirth. He didn't want to appear too stiff-
backed about the business. After all, he was not a
naughty child. This was his house. As a matter of fact,
this was his bedchamber, if one wanted to nitpick.

"Oh, Marcus, did you see her *face?*" Cassandra said,
gasping for breath. "Poor Corny. I don't know whether
she's upset at finding us, or angry because she didn't
suspect it long ago. What are you doing?"

Marcus had stood to untie the sash at his waist. "Doing? What does it look as if I'm doing, my dearest? I'm
preparing to join you. That is what you've been wanting

all along, isn't it—for the two of us to be open about our deepened association? The way I see the situation now —with the interview I have to endure in a few short hours—I may as well be hanged for a sheep as a lamb.''

Cassandra looked toward the door, frowning, then back to him, a slow smile beginning to tug at the corners of her mouth. "Oh, Marcus, I *do* love you!" she exclaimed, sitting up in order to pull her nightgown over her head.

"Of course you do, imp," he answered, slipping his long frame under the covers and reaching out to pull her down on top of him. "I wouldn't have it any other way."

"All right, Perry," Marcus said, using his fruit knife to point at the soup tureen. "Watch and listen carefully. This is the House of Commons."

Perry closed his eyes and sniffed, shaking his head. "Do you really think we should be using turbot, Marcus? I don't suppose I would like it above half if you compared me with a fish. Couldn't we call back the roast beef?"

"Perry," Marcus intoned tightly.

Perry held up his hands. "All right, all right. It was merely a suggestion, that's all. Please continue, Marcus. The House of Commons is fish soup. It is very clear to me now. What are those wilting pieces of carrot you've got propped up next to the tureen?"

Cassandra leaned forward, peering at the carrots. "I know," she exclaimed, smiling at Marcus. "Those are the columns in the lobby, aren't they, darling?"

"Cassandra, please," Aunt Cornelia cautioned in a hissing whisper, inclining her head toward Goodfellow, who was discreetly hovering in a corner of the dining room, being the only servant Marcus would allow to attend them at this meal. "There are rumors enough belowstairs without you spouting ridiculous endearments every other moment. 'The better part of valor is discretion,' my dear."

"Who said that, Cassandra? That Kennedy fella you told us about? Or was it Churchill, our own hero? I suppose I like it, but not half as well as his 'we shall fight on the beaches, we shall fight on the landing grounds, we shall fight in the fields and in the streets, we shall fight in the hills; we shall never surrender!' Lord, Marcus, ain't that the most inspiring thing you've ever heard?" Peregrine grinned, proud of his great memory, then picked up one of the carrot columns, nearly taking a bite out of it before Marcus snatched it from his hand and replaced it on the table.

Cassandra applauded softly. "Very good, Perry. I had to learn that speech for my public speaking contest in high school, but I've never done it so well. You're a quick learner. Only Churchill didn't say that business about discretion being the better part of valor. And the Kennedy quote was, 'Ask not what your country can do for you, but what you can do for your country.' "

"Then who talked about this discretion business?" Perry asked, clearly confused. "I'm sure I've heard it somewhere."

"Will Shakespeare, you brainless twit!" Aunt Cornelia exploded, nearly beaning Peregrine with an apple she had snatched from the fruit bowl. "Cassandra, I don't know why you bother with the man. It's clear as the vacant grin on his face that he understands next to nothing. Now pay attention, Perry, if you can apply yourself for a moment. Marcus is about to show us how we're going to save Perceval."

"Thank you, Aunt," Marcus said, inclining his head in her direction. He didn't know how he had ended up allowing his relative to be a part of their rescue plan, but his interview with her in his study the preceding week would most probably always be a little hazy in his memory. All he knew was that he had been speaking about his love for Cassandra and his growing apprehensions, and somehow Aunt Cornelia had wheedled the whole of it out of him.

It was vaguely depressing, this new feeling of vulnerability, but he knew he should welcome it, for it told him that he was human. He had Cassandra to thank for that. For years he had concerned himself almost exclusively with his experiments, his theories, his writing, burying himself in books and research. Now, facing death, he felt more alive than he had done in years.

When he had mentioned this new exhilaration to Cassandra she had only nodded, saying it had something to do with the thrill of "living on the edge." She hadn't seemed too pleased, though, and added that it was "just like a man to get his jollies thinking about matters of life and death," whatever that meant. Her further statements about sky diving and something called bungee jumping he chose to ignore, for the moment. Later, if his plans worked out, he would ask her about them again.

"Perceval is never alone," Marcus explained, reaching into his pocket and extracting some tin soldiers that had been the playthings of his youth and placing them on the table. "I have been watching his movements for several days so that I have learned his habits. Thankfully, he never varies from his routine. He arrives at the St. Stephen's Chapel entrance at eight each morning, leaves again between noon and one thirty of the clock, and returns from three until six. The assault could take place during any of those times, for he always enters and departs through the main lobby. Any questions so far?"

Peregrine tentatively raised his hand, as if afraid to be called upon to speak. "I have one, Marcus. Why don't we just tell the man? You said the murderer only shot him because he was there—which, by the by, seems to be a very silly reason for blowing a hole in anyone. Well, anyway, it stands to reason then that if Perceval *weren't* there, he wouldn't be shot." He turned to Cassandra, who was busily setting up the soldiers near the carrot columns. "Ain't that right, Cousin?"

"Marcus already explained that, Perry," she answered, positioning the last soldier, the one with an *X* painted on its chest in black. "We can't tell Mr. Perceval anything because we don't really know anything. There's no plot to murder him. He just happened to be in the wrong place at the wrong time. There's no French plot, no uprising of the people. Just dumb bad luck. He'd never believe us. We might," she finished, looking up at Marcus, "even end up in trouble ourselves. Isn't that right, darling?"

"There she goes again. *Darling,*" Aunt Cornelia said, sighing. "State secrets are one thing. Traveling through time is another. But a hole-and-corner affair, taking place right under their noses? This can't be overlooked. Oh, the servants will have a field day with this! We'll be a part of dinner table gossip all over Mayfair, with me to blame because I am in residence. Oh, the shame!"

"Oh, cut line, Corny," Peregrine said, quickly snatching up one of the carrots and sticking it in his mouth before Marcus could act. "Only Goodfellow knows for sure, and mayhap Cousin Cassie's abigail, and both of them know to keep their yappers shut. Ain't that right, Goodfellow?" he asked, calling to the butler, who still hovered in the corner. "You wouldn't cry rope on the marquess, now would you?"

Goodfellow rolled his eyes as he bowed in his lordship's direction, then returned to his job of slicing the ham that made up the rest of the third course. Obviously, to the loyal butler's mind, Peregrine's question did not deserve an answer.

Peregrine chomped on the carrot, satisfied on two heads—his reading of the butler and his success at claiming one of the carrots for his own. "See? What did I tell you, Corny? You're going to worry yourself half to Bedlam if you don't stop, you know that? Now let's get on with it. Marcus—you were saying?"

The marquess opened his mouth to speak, but Cassandra beat him to it. "All right, Perry, Aunt Cornelia—here's the plan. We will go to the House of Commons at the crack of dawn—"

"The crack of dawn!" Aunt Cornelia interrupted. "Impossible! I never rise before noon."

"You did a fairly good impression of someone rising at dawn one day last week, Aunt, as I recall," Marcus interjected meanly before reaching for a restorative sip from his wineglass. When had he lost control of this meeting?

"We position ourselves inside the lobby as soon as the doors open. Marcus's consequence will see to that. No one will dare to deny him entry," Cassandra continued, avoiding his eyes as she struggled to control a laugh. Obviously it still amused her that he had been read a stern lecture by his aunt, like a schoolboy remiss at his sums. "Marcus, would you like to use your toy soldiers to show us how you plan to place us?"

He stepped forward once more, leaning down to pick up one of the soldiers. "I beg you to bear in mind that these are not toys, Cassandra, any more than we are indulging in a game, much as I seem to be the only one cognizant of that most pertinent fact."

"Oh, lighten up, Marcus," Cassandra retaliated, leaning her head against his sleeve. "There are four of us and only one shooter—the shooter is the guy with the gun. That's what they're called—shooters. Anyway, we know he's coming, but he doesn't know we'll be there. It doesn't take a brain surgeon to figure out that the odds are all in our favor."

Marcus looked at the other occupants of the room in turn. Corny, who certainly could not be counted upon to wrestle the man to the ground if he should appear beside her; Perry, whose intentions were good, but who had never seen action more dangerous than crossing the street when the stage was coming in to the White Horse; and Cassandra, who seemed to think that the whole dangerous business was a great adventure, and would most probably try to save Perceval herself, and end by getting in his way when he went to disarm the "shooter."

"Goodfellow," Marcus said, motioning for the old man to join him at the table, "you served some time in the army, didn't you?"

"Yes, my lord. Served king and country for six long years, I did," the butler said proudly, then bowed his head. "But that was a long time since, my lord. The rheumatism has slowed me down a bit. But I would be proud to make up one of your party, my lord." He raised his hand in salute, wincing as the swift movement gave him pain. "For king and country, my lord!"

"Oh, good grief," Cassandra muttered, resting her head in her hands. "Why not recruit Rose as well, Marcus? She could hit the shooter over the head with my purse. Or, better yet, why not your wonderful French cook? Raoul would probably delight in taking a meat cleaver to the fellow. Or one of the footmen. They could—"

"Enough!" Marcus brought his fist down on the table, the force of the blow toppling the carrot columns and scattering the tin soldiers. "Aunt, you and Goodfellow are dismissed. No arguments. Just go—please," he ended, his tone softening. "I have decided that Perry and I will do this on our own. Each person we add only multiplies the possibility of disaster."

Aunt Cornelia allowed the butler to help her rise from her chair. "We're old now, Goodfellow," she said, leaning heavily on his arm as he led her toward the door.

"Old and unwanted. Would you like a glass of sherry, Goodfellow? I think we deserve a treat, don't you?"

"Poor Aunt Cornelia," Cassandra remarked, smiling as she watched Aunt Cornelia and the butler leave. Then she frowned. "Whoa! You and Perry? Hold it just one darn minute here," she exploded. A moment later she was on her feet, her hands jammed down on her hips—a now familiar warning that she was about to do battle. "Haven't you forgotten someone, Marcus? What about *me?* What am I supposed to do—sit here twiddling my thumbs while you and Perry rescue Perceval? Well, think again, buster. I'm going with you!"

Marcus smiled as he put his hands on her shoulders, pushing her back down in her chair and kissing her heated cheek. "Of course you are, my darling. I wouldn't dream of leaving you behind—at least not unless I had personally tied you to your bedpost with a stout rope." His smile faded, to be replaced by a knowing frown. "You'd only sneak out of here the moment I was gone and hire a hack to take you to the House of Commons, and arrive just in time to ruin everything."

"Well, I guess you might have a point," Cassandra admitted, wincing. "But I couldn't stand being left behind. This is too important. It means everything, Marcus. It means your life!"

"Precisely," he answered, picking up the soldiers once more and rescuing another of the carrot columns from Perry's fist. "Now, might I suggest that we get on with it?"

Chapter 14

It was raining, and the fog was nearly impenetrable, more of the soggy gray mist creeping into the lobby each time the large double doors opened. The foul, damp weather was not an unusual occurrence in early morning London, but Marcus, who had taken up his position just inside the doors, cursed it anyway.

It gave him something to do.

Peregrine leaned against one of the nearby columns, his hand raised to his mouth as he stifled a yawn. Marcus had been up all of last night, figuring and refiguring how he would go about this business of altering history, but Peregrine, who had promised to attend Lady Hertford's ball, had not straggled in until after three, to fall asleep in one of the chairs in the study. Even now, still clad in his evening dress and flat-heeled black slippers, he was hardly an imposing sight in this most august of foyers.

And yet, Cassandra having told him all about the battle of Waterloo, Marcus could only ask himself how many of the soldiers had been attending the Duchess of Richmond's ball in Brussels and had raced to the battlefield still dressed in their finest evening clothes? His countrymen had won that battle, hadn't they?

"Of course," he mumbled under his breath, "dear, good-hearted, dimwitted Peregrine is most probably not destined to fight at Waterloo."

Marcus looked to his left, where Cassandra, clad in the underfootman's Sunday best, was surreptitiously shoving a stray lock of her short, dark hair back under her cap. His gaze slid to her legs, her shapely calves revealed by the much-mended hose, and he swallowed down hard on the apprehension rising in his throat. How had he let himself be talked into allowing her to don men's clothing? Better still, why had he not tied her to the bedpost, leaving her behind entirely?

She looked at him, her violet eyes wide and alert, then ran her index finger down the side of her nose, a silent signal she had explained to mean that everything was "aces," that things were going as planned.

Marcus returned the gesture, then passed it along to Peregrine, who seemed inordinately pleased to repeat the movement, going so far as to perform the signal twice, as if for emphasis.

It had just gone eight of the clock, and gentlemen were beginning to enter in small groups, shaking the rain from their hats and greatcoats as they moved through the foyer and speaking quietly so that their words would not echo in the high-ceilinged chamber. Several of the men recognized the marquess and nodded solemnly in his direction, some of them frowning, for they knew his place was in the House of Lords, not that he had graced that hall in weeks. Not since Cassandra Kelley had come into his life.

"My Lord Eastbourne, good morning," a gentleman Marcus recognized as one of Perceval's aides said. The man approached him, bowing as he removed his hat. "You've shown a marked interest in this foyer these past days. Is there something the Prime Minister should know?"

"No," Marcus answered, looking past the man as Perceval entered the foyer, surrounded by a group of solemn-faced men. ''Just an Englishman's healthy interest in government, my good man.''

The man bowed again, then followed the Prime Minister, looking back over his shoulder as the group disappeared into the former church of St. Stephen's to go about the business of governing the people.

Wishing he were not so tall and so readily recognizable, Marcus breathed a sigh of relief, then signaled to Cassandra and Peregrine that they could relax. Perceval would not be back in the foyer until noon at the earliest. He leaned against the column beside him, prepared to remain on guard all day, his blood running hot, his hopes high.

He slipped his hand into the pocket of his greatcoat and felt the comforting solidity of the pistol that he had put there that morning. It was all right. Everything was going to be all right.

The day they had waited for all these weeks had at last begun.

Cassandra's feet hurt. The underfootman's heavy wooden clogs were a good three sizes too big, but that didn't mean that her toes, pushed forward in the shoes, weren't throbbing. She shifted her position slightly as she stood tucked out of the way in a corner of the foyer, waiting for Perceval to appear, hoping she wasn't developing blisters on her big toe. It seemed a shame that such a mundane complaint should mean anything today, when they were about to save a man's life, but facts were facts, and her feet were killing her.

She slipped a hand into her pocket to pull out her watch and covertly peeked at it only to learn that no more than five minutes had passed since the last time she had checked it. Eleven o'clock. God, would this morning never end?

She hadn't felt well when she awoke this morning,

alone in the big tester bed for the first time in over a week as Marcus had never come upstairs. As it worked out it was a good thing, though, for her stomach had turned and she had prudently run for the never-before-used chamber pot within seconds of lifting her head from the pillow.

Nerves, she had told herself as she rinsed her mouth a few minutes later. It had to be nerves.

She felt perfectly fine now—she had shunned her morning chocolate for a cup of tea and a few pieces of dry toast—but if Marcus had found her sick he would have jumped at the chance to keep her at home, away from the action.

And that she could not have borne. This day was so important, the most critical day of her life, for today would tell her whether or not they could change history, and to hell with all the book proposals she had read that said it couldn't be done. What did those writers know? All they had going for them was imagination. She'd bet none of *them* had ever blundered into a blue mist and been transported to Regency England!

She sneaked a look at Marcus out of the corner of her eye, loving his erect, alert posture, the tired lines under his eyes, even the intensity with which he approached this most crucial project.

She had teased him unmercifully these past days, pretending to make light of all his plans to save Perceval, but she'd felt she had no other choice. If she didn't tease him, divert him, the entire household would be thrown into gloom, especially poor Aunt Cornelia, the lady with the steely outside that hid a center of softest marshmallow, whom Cassandra had discovered one morning in the music room, sniffling into a handkerchief.

Marcus, Cassandra had learned as Aunt Cornelia struggled to speak through her tears, had just left her after telling her that he had prepared a letter to his solicitor providing for her in the event of his untimely death. He had mentioned that she was already named in his will, but he felt the need to make additional arrangements in the event he left no heir.

"Which is totally ridiculous," Aunt Cornelia said, struggling to control herself. "Richard is only thirty, and quite odiously healthy. He has yet to marry and set up his nursery, however, and Marcus has entreated me to travel to Richard's country estate next week, to convince the boy it is time he gave some thought to his own heir. Oh, Cassandra, this is terrible. Just terrible! Marcus's son should be the next marquess—Marcus's and your son— and not that odious Richard. He's such a country bumpkin. Imagine, he has yet to come to town for a Season! However shall I go on, having to deal with such a green goose? He's so mad for hunting that I wouldn't be the least surprised if he insisted upon mounting me on one of his smelly horses and taking me haring across country, chasing some mangy fox—as if I would, because I wouldn't, not even if Marcus refused to provide for me and I ended by sleeping under the hedgerows."

Cassandra smiled now as she attempted to picture the straight-backed, straitlaced Aunt Cornelia bouncing up and down atop a rawboned horse as they galloped across the countryside. Poor Corny. She had been a brick thus far, even going so far as to give Marcus and Cassandra her blessings, although she would much rather have had their engagement announced in the papers and begun planning a hasty wedding.

"You're nothing but an old romantic," Cassandra had said teasingly, hugging Aunt Cornelia. Although it didn't seem exactly proper, the older woman said, she would turn her head and pretend she did not know what was going on under the roof in the mansion. Still, she could not understand how Marcus, usually such a rational man, could have allowed himself to become a part of a clandestine liaison.

"Must be my bad nineteen-nineties influence, Aunt Cornelia," Cassandra had suggested, kissing Corny's papery cheek. And that had been the end of it.

Cassandra looked across the foyer at Peregrine, who was inelegantly propping up one of the columns, his eyes half closed. Now Peregrine, her dear "cousin," had been another story. He had bruited his blood ties to Cassandra about for so long in Society that he seemed to have begun to believe his own lies. He had taken Cassandra aside after dinner only a few days earlier, scratched his head, told her he knew she had been "compromised," and asked if she thought he'd really have to challenge Marcus to a duel.

"Wouldn't like it above half, Cousin, you understand," he'd told her. "Marcus is a deadly shot, and not too bad with his fives, now that I think on it, especially for a man who speaks Greek. But I'm honor bound to avenge your lost virginity, you see, so I suppose I shall just have to do it. Especially since Marcus says he ain't going to marry you because you're going to take a flit soon. Disappointed me, that did, on both heads. I will miss you, Cousin, but I have to support you in this time of trial. You won't mind my dying for you?"

It had taken Cassandra some time to convince Peregrine that he did not have to defend her honor, or the lack of it, as he seemed to see it, and he had given up his plans to die for her only when she explained about Brad the Bod.

Rather than be disenchanted with her on learning that she hadn't been a virgin for some time, Peregrine seemed to take heart at the news—a circumstance that was understandable, since it saved him from having to challenge his best friend to a duel. "But if you have your heart set on killing someone for me, Perry," Cassandra had said to him half-jokingly, "maybe you could try traveling through time with me at the end of the month. I'm sure we could find Brad's home address in my alumni directory. Would you like that?"

Cassandra watched now as Peregrine's eyes closed for a second and he nearly slid to the floor. Abruptly he awakened and scrambled to right himself, casting his eyes nervously in Marcus's direction. She remembered how he had paled at her suggestion. "Go with you? No, no, I don't think so," he answered hastily. "Not that it wouldn't be jolly good fun and all, seeing the airplanes, even if Marcus has reminded me that I don't much like my feet off the ground. But I think I should stay here. Got a mare running at Ascot soon, I do, and I've already promised Harry Atwood I'd make up one of his party this fall. Going to Scotland, you know, to chase salmon or some such thing. Couldn't disappoint Harry. No, no. Couldn't do it. Sorry."

Cassandra's stomach rumbled, bringing her back to attention (reminding her that she hadn't really had breakfast), and she chanced a look around. Seeing the foyer was nearly empty, she walked over to where Marcus stood, his eyes fixed on the front entrance. "I'm hungry, Marcus," she confided quietly, speaking out of the corner of her mouth as he had said they shouldn't look as if they were together. "Did you bring us anything to eat?"

He spoke without looking at her. "Goodfellow is stationed outside in the coach. He has a hamper on the box. I suggest you apply to him, my dear. Take your time."

"Oh, sure, take my time," she retorted, stung by his detached tone. "You'd just love that, wouldn't you? It's almost noon. You'd be in here, making a national hero of yourself, and I'd be outside, gnawing on a chicken leg. Well, no thank you. I can last as long as you can.

Longer!" She glanced at the doors to the chamber. "Shouldn't he be coming out soon?"

"Between noon and one, if he keeps to his schedule," Marcus answered, glancing down for a moment so that she saw he held his pocket watch in his left hand. "Perry!" he whispered loudly, "Stay alert."

Peregrine shuffled over to join them, his shirt points wilted, his green-and-white striped waistcoat open beneath his greatcoat. "What are you talking about, hmm? You know, I'm getting rather peckish. Does Goodfellow have any food with him out there? I already finished the strawberry tart I found in my pocket."

"In your pocket? Your *pistol* is supposed to be in your pocket," Marcus hissed.

Peregrine rolled his eyes. "I know that, Marcus. The pistol is in my *other* pocket. I have more than one, you understand." He leaned across Marcus to whisper to Cassandra. "You'd think he'd grasp that, wouldn't you, Cousin, him being so smart and all? If being in love makes a normally rational man this bosky, I'll remain heart whole, thank you."

Cassandra giggled. "I agree, Perry. At least you were smart enough to remember to bring a strawberry tart. Are you sure you don't have another one in your pocket? Any of your pockets?"

"If you two are quite through," Marcus said coldly, "I suggest you take up your posts once more. Perceval could appear at any moment. Hello, what's this? Perry—over there, right where you were standing. Where did that man come from?"

Perry whirled about, to look in the direction Marcus had pointed. "What man? Where?"

"Oh, my God," Cassandra said, springing to attention, her throat suddenly dry, her heart beginning to pound. Her fingers closed around the pistol in her pocket. She had begged Marcus to allow her to shoot it, for practice, but he had refused. Could she fire it now, or would she dissolve into feminine hysterics at the vital moment? Her expression hardened as she thought of Marcus's fate unless, today, this very moment, they could alter history. Could she fire the pistol? *Damn right, I can,* she thought resolutely, slipping her finger around the trigger. "Marcus, I hear voices. Perceval's coming!"

Peregrine, as planned, raced for the doors leading into the chamber, to position himself in front of the Prime Minister as he entered the foyer, hopefully blocking Perceval from view, while Marcus pushed Cassandra aside and lunged at the strange, wild-eyed man who was in the process of reaching into the pocket of his worn greatcoat.

It all happened so quickly.

One moment their end of the foyer was empty, and the next it was full, the members of the House of Commons all seeming to have decided to take their leave at the same moment. The foyer was alive with conversation; busy men strode toward the front doors while harried clerks, carrying sheaves of important-looking papers, tagged along like loyal puppies in their masters' wakes.

Cassandra could not take her eyes off Marcus. He had positioned himself directly in front of the strange man and was glaring down at him, as if daring him to move. The man seemed to shrink before her eyes—his weak smile was accompanied by nervous shrugs and wringing hands as he spoke to Marcus, who had begun to frown.

"What a crush of people. I say, lad, frightful day, isn't it?"

Cassandra wheeled about to see a pleasant-looking, well-dressed man of indeterminate years standing behind her. His frock coat glistened with raindrops as if he had just stepped into the foyer from the street.

"Yes, *um,* yes, it is," Cassandra answered, remembering to keep her voice low, and hopefully masculine, while continuing to shift her eyes toward Marcus. Did he have to stand so close to the murderer? The guy killed Perceval because he couldn't find his real target. What was Marcus planning—to change history by having the man kill *him* instead? "Frightful weather. *Um,* will you excuse me?"

She left the rain-soaked gentleman where he stood and skipped across the foyer to Marcus. "Are you nuts?" she whispered hoarsely, pretending to bump up against him "Why don't you just paint a target on your chest? 'Aim here, jerk.' Step back, for crying out loud."

Marcus silenced her with a look and turned away, watching Peregrine bravely walk no more than two feet in front of the Prime Minister as Perceval and his party headed for the front doors and the safety of the street. "Wrong man," he said quietly, scanning the faces in the crowd. "He's a petitioner, come to plead his case to one of the members."

Frowning, Cassandra looked at the man, who was holding the scrap of paper he had just taken from his pocket. "Christ," she mumbled, feeling suddenly sick.

Marcus inclined his head toward the front doors. "Who's that?"

"Over there? Just some guy. He's harmless." Cassandra turned about, just in time to see the pleasant-faced, well-dressed man of indeterminate years reach into his pocket and pull out a pistol. "Oh, my God! It's the shooter! Perry! *Look out!*"

Cassandra had been only four when President John Kennedy had been shot, but she had watched all the news stories shown on television on the anniversaries of the assassination, first because her parents had told her it was a part of history and she should know it, then because she had become fascinated with all the mistakes, all the errors of omission and moments of absolute

stupidity that, if only one of them could have been
averted, would have altered the course of the nation's
history.

One of the most intriguing segments, to Cassandra's
mind, had been the ease with which Jack Ruby made his
way to the basement of that Texas courthouse and shot
Lee Harvey Oswald while the whole world watched.

Now, as she stood, openmouthed, unable to move, it
was as if she was watching that scene all over again, in
agonizing slow motion.

The pleasant-faced man stepped into the center of the
foyer raising his arm, the deadly pistol pointed directly at
Spencer Perceval—and directly at Peregrine Walton.

He didn't shout, didn't say a word, this pleasant man
with neck cloth tied pristinely, boots polished to a high
gloss, who looked more like a banker than a crazed
killer. He had spoken to Cassandra, his voice educated
and well modulated. How could he be a killer? How
could she have known? Why hadn't she known? *Oh,
God, why hadn't she known?*

All these thoughts raced through Cassandra's mind as
Peregrine stepped squarely in front of the Prime Minister, his arms outflung, willing to sacrifice himself in the
name of English patriotism. That silly, lovable little man,
who hadn't bargained on any such thing when he agreed
to this scheme, was about to become a hero. A dead
hero.

It was too crowded now for Marcus to chance firing
his own pistol at the would-be assassin without possibly
harming innocent bystanders. To Cassandra's mind,
there was nothing they could do now but watch as their
friend fell.

"No!" Marcus's shout echoed in the high-ceilinged
foyer as he threw himself forward, tackling Peregrine
just as the pistol sparked fire and a single shot rang out,

the sharp report reverberating throughout the chamber, drowning out the sound of Marcus's desperate denial.

It had all happened so quickly.

It was still raining as the small group gathered in the drawing room of the mansion in Grosvenor Square. A fire burned in the fireplace to ward off the chill, and several candelabra were lit to help dispel the gloom.

"Poor Perry," Cassandra said, shaking her head. "He was so brave."

"I never thought he had it in him," Aunt Cornelia admitted. Fanning herself with her handkerchief, she took a seat beside the fireplace. Goodfellow had not as yet come into the room to position the fire screen. She could do it herself, or ask for her nephew's assistance, but she had already announced that she would much prefer to wait for Goodfellow. "Peregrine Walton, a hero. Who would have believed it? How cruelly I misjudged the boy."

Marcus busied himself at the drinks table. "Not a boy, Aunt. A man. A very brave man."

"A man, maybe, but being brave had nothing to do with it. Cousin Cassie, stop it," Peregrine protested impatiently from his reclining position on one of a pair of settees that faced each other. He brushed away Cassandra's hand as she tried to feel his forehead, as if checking him for fever. "And I'm not a hero. Not bloody well likely, pardon me for being so frank. Perceval's dead, ain't he, just as that book of yours said he would be? Now, if he was still alive, that would be different. Put a whole new light on the business. All I did was end up on the floor with Marcus sprawled all over me, and people either stepping on me as they ran to pelt that John Bellingham fella what shot the PM or running to catch poor Perceval as he fell." He shook his head. "Nope. I'm not a hero. Always wanted to be one, but there it is—I'm nothing of the sort. Pity."

Marcus handed his friend a generously filled snifter of brandy. "You did more than anyone could ask, Perry," he said, seating himself in a nearby chair once Cassandra who was still clad in those outrageous breeches, had collapsed on the second settee, across from Peregrine. "Knowing full well that you could die, you threw yourself into the breach. I cannot begin to tell you how much I admire your attempt. You are a man among men, Peregrine Walton, and I salute you."

Perry bobbed his head from side to side, smiling sheepishly. "Yes, well, if you say so, Marcus," he said, looking at Cassandra. "Sorry, Cousin. If you and Aunt Cornelia wish to call me a hero, I suppose I shouldn't be so cold as to naysay you. Go on," he said, waving his hands in a shooing motion as if urging them into speech. "I'm listening."

Cassandra looked over at Marcus, her violet eyes dancing, watching as he rose and began to pace. "Then it's settled, darling. We shall commission the statue tomorrow. Perry, you will consent to pose, won't you?"

Peregrine frowned, his chin collapsing into his wilted neckcloth. "Now you're making a May game out of me, aren't you, Cousin? I should have known you wouldn't be nice to me for long. Nobody is."

"And well they shouldn't be, you jackanapes," Aunt Cornelia scolded him. "A true hero is modest, Mr. Walton."

"I wonder what will happen now," Marcus said, looking into his snifter as he moved it in a lazy circle, watching the brandy swirl inside it like a small whirlpool. "Perceval wasn't a brilliant man, but he worked very hard, and he had the best interests of England at heart. Cassandra, do you think you could remember who is chosen to replace him? The Whigs are going to be running hotfoot to Prinny to convince him that fate has handed him a grand chance to trade a dead Tory for a live Whig, although I doubt Lord and Lady Hertford will allow it."

Cassandra frowned, shaking her head. "One of my authors went into a lot of detail on government figures, but I had to edit most of it out. That stuff's pretty boring unless you feed it to the readers in small doses. But I think I remember something about beef, or lamb, or—wait a minute! Liver! That's it. Liverpool. He was always around in Regency times. Could it be him—I mean *he*?"

"Liverpool?" Aunt Cornelia's handkerchief came into play once more. "Well, if that isn't above everything stupid! Why didn't the Prince Regent name Castlereagh in the first place and have done with it?" She turned to Cassandra. "You wouldn't understand this, my dear, but Liverpool is a stickler of a High Tory, but a born puppet, while Castlereagh is a master puppeteer. And quite possibly mad into the bargain," she added quietly, "although you did not hear me say that."

Marcus stifled a grin, enjoying his aunt's descent into gossip. "It is not that Lord Castlereagh is a bad man, Cassandra," he explained, tongue in cheek. "He works long and hard, studying each problem that comes before him, and then he comes down on precisely the incorrect side of every important argument. It's almost uncanny, how infallibly fallible he is. I believe I shall sleep nights thanks only to your information that we do eventually emerge victorious from this terrible war with France. Perhaps we'll be second-time-lucky, and Castlereagh himself is assassinated next year?"

Cassandra rose from her chair, to stand close beside Marcus, one arm slipped around his waist. "Bloodthirsty, aren't you? But I don't remember that happening. Sorry. Marcus—poor Perry still looks pale to me. Don't you think he should go upstairs and lie down on his bed? All in all, it's been a long day."

"Pale? *Me?* Nonsense," Peregrine blustered, jumping up to go and inspect himself in the gilded mirror that hung over a Sheraton side table. He grinned at his reflection, then lifted a hand to run it through his disheveled hair. "What is there to be pale about, I ask you? Heroes are never pale. Look at me—the picture of health! I say —what's this?"

As Peregrine began inspecting the skirt of his burgundy satin evening coat, just below the waist, Cassandra joined him in front of the mirror, leaning forward to see what was bothering him. "Perry!" she exclaimed, grabbing the material. "That's a bullet hole! My God, are you hurt?"

"Hurt?" Peregrine repeated, looking confused as he strained to see the hole. When he couldn't quite reach it, he pulled off the coat, turning the sleeves inside out in his rush. A moment later he was standing in front of Marcus, his pudgy index finger stuck straight through the hole. "Do you see this? Brand new, Marcus. Brand new from my tailor just last week—and not even paid for —and now it's ruined! Do you know what this coat cost? Oh, foul, foul! And Brummell complimented me on it just last night."

Marcus looked at his friend. "Beau complimented that coat?"

Perry pulled a face. "You know Beau, Marcus. He doesn't exactly go out of his way to make pretty speeches about anything. So, no, he didn't exactly *compliment* me. But he did say he greatly appreciated that I wasn't wearing that green thing m'tailor talked me into last month. It's almost the same thing as a compliment. And now," he added, waggling his index finger up at Marcus's face, "it's ruined!"

Cassandra snatched the coat from Peregrine's hands, quickly looking at the marquess. "Marcus will buy you another one—won't you, darling? I mean, it's the least you can do for our hero. But, Perry, you could have been killed! The bullet went straight through your open coat and into Perceval. The darned thing must have taken nearly as many turns as that "magic bullet" that supposedly killed Kennedy and then went on to hit Governor Connally. How about that! Why, if Marcus hadn't thought fast enough to tackle you at the last moment, we all could be sitting here right now, sadly toasting your memory for the sacrifice you made to your country."

Peregrine's eyes shifted from Marcus, to Cassandra, and lastly to Aunt Cornelia, who nodded solemnly. "Killed? Really?" he asked, taking back his coat, only to let it dangle from his fingertips, as if unwilling to really touch it. "My God! Marcus! I could have been killed! I *am* a hero, stap me if I ain't!" And then his complexion turned a sickly gray. "I don't think I feel so well, Cousin Cassie. I think I'll go lie down."

Cassandra kissed his pale cheek. "You do that, Perry. And then later, when you're feeling more up to it, perhaps you'll tell us again how you threw yourself in front of the Prime Minister, willingly sacrificing your own safety for the sake of the nation."

He looked at her queerly, as if she had lost her grip on reality. "Talk about it? I don't ever want to talk about it. I don't even want to *think* about it. Honestly, Cousin, you say the strangest things. Now, if you'll all excuse me?"

Marcus noticed that Cassandra was biting her bottom lip as she watched Peregrine depart the drawing room, but she waited until he was out of earshot before breaking into delighted laughter. "Marcus, did you see Perry's *face* when he finally realized he had nearly been shot? I thought he was going to faint. I think it's finally hit him that he *is* a hero, and now he doesn't know what to do about it."

"He will by this evening," Aunt Cornelia said, sniffing inelegantly. "And then we'll never hear the end of it.

Although I must say, I shouldn't have liked it if he had been shot. I've grown rather fond of the young nincompoop, although only the good Lord knows why." She rose from her chair near the fireplace and kissed Cassandra's cheek before heading for the foyer. "You were very brave today, my dear, what with seeing a bloody body and all. I should have swooned, I am sure. But now that you are home again, I suggest you rid yourself of those breeches. It isn't seemly. Besides," she added, already halfway to the doorway, "your legs are entirely too attractive. Marcus, behave yourself after I am gone, I beg you. The servants talk enough as it is."

Marcus bowed in Aunt Cornelia's direction. "I promise I shall do my best to control my animal instincts, dear lady," he said, delighting in the manner in which her rigidly erect spine slumped for only a second, then became ramrod straight once more as she exited the room. "However," he added once he believed Aunt Cornelia to be out of earshot, "I fear I cannot vouch for dearest Cassandra's powers of discretion."

"I *heard* that!" Aunt Cornelia called back to him as she disappeared down the hallway.

Cassandra collapsed against Marcus, giggling. "One of these days, darling, Corny is going to box your ears. She told me so just last week, when you teased her about showing a distinct preference for Goodfellow's companionship."

"Then you don't smell a romance in the air, my dear? Oh, you do. I can see your answer in that extremely self-satisfied smile." He dropped a kiss on the top of her head, then stepped away from her, knowing that they had to talk, but wishing to prolong this moment of happiness. "But back to business, for a moment, please, before you start planning their nuptials. Do you think I should compose a letter to the newspapers, recounting

Perry's bravery? He will insist upon having his coat preserved inside a glass dome, of course, once he realizes its worth. Oh, yes, he might be feeling a trifle upset now, but he'll soon see this entire episode in another light and begin dining out on his story. Why, I suppose—"

"That's enough, Marcus."

Cassandra retired to a nearby chair, to sit clutching at the arms with one slim leg tucked beneath her. She suddenly looked so alert, so alive, that he knew that he was going to have to keep his wits about him now or else lose control of this very important interview.

"All right, let's get on with it, shall we?" she said challengingly. "I tried to get rid of Perry and Corny earlier, and would have, if Perry hadn't seen that bullet hole. And I know you were hoping I would be so involved with Perry's lucky escape that I'd forget about what this all means—what Perceval's death means—but you're not going to get off that easy. We tried to change history today, Marcus, and we blew it. Your theory is shot to hell. So, *now* what do we do?"

Marcus picked up the snifter, not bothering to take a drink, but only held it in front of him, as a shield, if that indeed was the proper word. "You don't have to remind me of the obvious, Cassandra," he said wearily. "Although I suppose we might have changed history. But I could not allow Perry to make that sacrifice. I simply couldn't."

"Of course you couldn't, darling," Cassandra agreed quickly, "and I wouldn't have expected you to do anything differently. Perceval was meant to die today. It was fate—or *history*—if you look at it from my angle, my own time. But now we know we can't change *your* history, Marcus." She took a deep, shuddering breath. "We can't change your history, Marcus," she repeated, her violet eyes suddenly shimmering with tears. "You say

you're destined to die on the last day of May. You also
say I'm going to go back to my own time on that same
day—although it's only one of your theories, and we've
all just seen another of your theories go straight to hell.
I'm sorry, Marcus, but I can't fight it anymore. I'm
scared. I'm really, really scared. It's already almost May
twelfth. God! I feel like we're both trapped on a runaway
bus, and the bridge is out up ahead!''

Marcus rubbed a hand across his forehead. He hadn't
really been relying on saving Perceval—in fact, he had
given their chances to do it short shrift ever since coming up with the idea. But it had been worth a try. Perhaps now it was time to tell Cassandra everything—although he was loath to raise her hopes again, in the fear
his most important theory would come to nothing. But
she looked so small, tucked up on that chair, so vulnerable—so lovely.

"Cassandra—darling girl—" he began hesitantly. "I
must tell you something now. I didn't quite hang all my
hopes on saving the Prime Minister. You see, I haven't
been entirely honest with you about this dying business—" He broke off as Aunt Cornelia's scream echoed
loudly in the foyer and both he and Cassandra raced to
see what was wrong.

"Marcus, look here! *Marcus!*" Aunt Cornelia called in
near hysterics as she ran into the room, one hand holding her skirts above her bony ankles, her other hand
frantically waving what looked to be a letter over her
head. "This just arrived by messenger while I was in the
foyer, speaking with Goodfellow. We were just talking,
passing the time, but now he's dead, Marcus. Dead!"

The marquess frowned. "Goodfellow is dead?"

"Goodfellow?" Aunt Cornelia stopped in her tracks,
frowning as she mentally reviewed what she had said.
She shook her head. "No, no. Goodfellow isn't dead.

Richard is dead. It says so right here in this letter. You have no heir! It's happening—*it's all coming true!*''

"Sweet Jesus," Cassandra mumbled just before she fainted into Marcus's arms.

Chapter 15

 Cassandra awoke in her own bedchamber, Marcus's face hovering just above her head. "What happened?" she asked, struggling to sit up, only to find herself unpleasantly surprised by a roiling wave of nausea. "Oh, God," she groaned, one hand to her mouth as she slowly sank back against the pillows and willed her stomach to behave.

"You fainted," Aunt Cornelia trilled happily, appearing at Cassandra's left. "I wonder why."

"Of course you do, dear Aunt," Cassandra heard Marcus say. His voice sounded slightly fuzzy, as if she were on a trans-Atlantic call and the connection was bad. "You run screaming into the drawing room, announce that Richard broke his neck fox hunting, and you can't understand why Cassandra fainted? Perhaps I should take you downstairs and explain, but I fear I haven't the time right now. You will forgive me this lapse, won't you?"

Cassandra sliced a look toward Marcus, surprised at his sarcasm, and saw the telltale tic working in his cheek. Suddenly she remembered everything. Richard, Marcus's little-known and obviously not-very-much-lamented heir, was dead. The guidebook had been correct. Marcus's title, Marcus's entailed estates, and everything he had that he could not dispose of through his will would revert to the Crown at the time of his death—

May 31—exactly twenty days from now. In less than three weeks, Marcus would die. They didn't know how, they didn't know where, and they didn't know why. But they surely did know when. And there was nothing anybody could do to change it.

She reached up, clutching his forearm. "Marcus," she pleaded, "could we be alone? Just you and me? Please."

Aunt Cornelia sniffed indelicately, turned, and stomped toward the door. Cassandra smiled, realizing that if nothing else, Aunt Cornelia really knew how to make an exit. Her smile faded, however, as the older woman turned around just as her hand touched the door pull and announced flatly, "I don't require a red brick to fall on *my* head. I know when I'm not wanted. Very well, children, I will leave you alone for a while. Heaven only knows you can't cause any more damage, nephew. But you'll have to marry her now, to give that child a name."

"Child?" Marcus and Cassandra asked together, exchanging startled looks.

"Oh, the innocence of the pair," Aunt Cornelia lamented theatrically, raising her gaze to the ceiling as she opened the door and addressed only she knew (or cared) whom. "I never before saw the like!"

"Precisely what is Aunt Cornelia talking about, Cassandra?" Marcus asked once the door had closed behind the older woman. He seated himself on the side of the bed and took her hand in his. He looked at her searchingly, as if seeking outward signs of impending motherhood, as he might search for spots if Corny had mentioned the word *measles.* "You're pregnant?"

Cassandra fought down a sudden rising panic. "I don't know. Let me think."

"You're pregnant?" he repeated, his tone one of mingled amazement, and what else? Surely it couldn't be anger. Could it?

Cassandra's mind was whirling—rather like her stomach. She squeezed her eyes tightly shut as she performed some simple mathematics in her head. She had entered Regency England on March 12 while she was in the placebo cycle of her birth control pills. Okay, so she'd take it from there. Her fingers moved in Marcus's grasp as she mentally counted out the weeks from her last menstrual period until the night Marcus had first come to her bedchamber. The dates matched. Then she counted the days since her last period and discovered that that was exactly what it had been—her *last* period.

"*Uh,* Marcus?" she said after a few moments, wincing as she opened her eyes to look up at him. She took a deep breath and said quickly, "Do you remember those pills I was taking, but I'm not taking anymore because I didn't have them to take anymore even if I wanted to take them? Well, by rights I'm not supposed to be able to get pregnant right after I stop taking the pills, but I think I might have made a liar out of whoever wrote that package insert you read—at least if tossing my cookies this morning and fainting this afternoon mean anything, which I guess they do, if Aunt Cornelia thinks they do, although how she found out about any of this I'll never know. Wait a minute! *Yes,* I do. Rose told her. It's just like Rose to tell her. Well, how about that? Marcus—do you remember the first night you—*um*—you, well, *you* know what I mean—that first night? As close as I can figure, I was ovulating that night. Damn. It looks as if we might have had that earthquake after all."

"You're pregnant?"

Couldn't he think of anything else to ask? *You're pregnant? You're pregnant?* God, he sounded like a broken record. Bristling, she pulled her hand away from him. "Maybe," she said forcefully. "But I didn't do it alone—so stop looking at me as if I never warned you. I told you that all hell breaks loose every time I try to bend the rules."

And then she smiled. "Like I said—how about that? *A baby.*" She looked up at him, her heart melting, happy tears stinging her eyes as she saw that he was smiling too —even if he did look as if someone had just told him his pantaloons were on fire. "Marcus, we're going to have a *baby!*"

A baby.

Cassandra lay awake in the half-light that marked the imminent approach of night, Marcus lying beside her, as he had been all the rest of that fateful afternoon. Both of them were sans shoes but still dressed in their street clothes. She couldn't sleep, and she was fairly certain that Marcus wasn't sleeping either. Not that they had spoken much since he took her into his arms and held her, telling her how proud and happy he was that she carried his child.

Yet what else could they say to each other? There was nothing to be said. They were going to have a baby.

No. She corrected her own thinking. *She* was going to have a baby. And Marcus? *Nobody* knew what was going to happen to Marcus.

She and her unborn child would travel back to her own time on the last day of May, or if not then, sometime soon. She had to believe that. She just had to. There was no record of Marcus's heir in that guidebook. Just that afternoon, as Spencer Perceval had lain dying on the floor of the foyer of the House of Commons, they had learned once and for all that they couldn't alter history. And if they couldn't change history, their child could not survive in Regency England.

Their baby would have no future.

Oh, sure, the baby could be a girl, and that way there would be no mention of her in the guidebook, as she couldn't inherit. But this baby was a boy. She just knew it! She was carrying Marcus's son.

Cassandra stuffed a corner of the pillow into her mouth to stifle a sob. *Marcus's son. Oh, God. What happens now? Where's all that happy ending stuff that miraculously comes together in the last chapter of romance novels? This isn't fair. Love is supposed to conquer all, damn it!*

"Cassandra? Darling, are you awake?"

She turned on the bed to face him. He was so wonderful, so gloriously handsome, so caring. And she loved him so much her heart ached. "I'm awake, Marcus. Would you like me to ring for something to eat? We haven't had much of anything all day. Rose is probably hovering outside right now, wringing her hands and worrying. And, to tell you the truth, I think I'm hungry. You haven't invented peanut butter and marshmallow yet, have you? Pity. I know it's only psychological, but I think I'm having my first craving. Thank God you guys have pickles and ice cream."

She bit her bottom lip, realizing that she was babbling. Again. She shouldn't be babbling. She was going to be a mother. Mothers didn't babble. *Her* mother didn't babble. Nagged, maybe—but she never babbled. "Oh, God, Marcus," she howled, throwing herself into his arms, giving in to her mounting hysteria, "this is too much for one person—especially if that one person is me. I can't do this alone. I just can't!"

He made soothing sounds while she wept, while she hated herself for falling apart. But she seemed to have absolutely no control over her emotions. It was as if a sappy-switch had been flipped on in her brain, turning her into a mass of conflicting feelings. She wanted this baby, truly wanted it. But she wanted Marcus too. She wanted the life they had begun to build together, wanted the happiness they shared to go on and on, wanted the marriage she knew would be a happy one.

"Hic! Oh, damn," she wailed, sitting up and wiping

her tears with the back of one hand. "Now I have the hiccups. It, *hic,* it figures. I never was an eloquent crier. *Sheila's* a great crier. She has tears the size of quarters and looks adorable; her eyes are all sparkling and sympathetic. My nose runs and, *hic,* I get the hiccups." Her chin began to wobble again as Marcus smiled and handed her his handkerchief. "I'm, *hic*—oh, I'm a *mess!*"

"You're going to have my child, Cassandra," Marcus said in a teasing voice, interrupting her runaway train of self-pity just as she was getting up a full head of steam. "Therefore, I forbid you to be a mess."

She lustily blew her nose in the handkerchief, not caring if she didn't seem delicate or even particularly feminine. How dare Marcus interrupt her pity party? She had every right to feel sorry for herself, and he wasn't helping. And she had thought he was *sensitive?* Hah! Where *was* Alan Alda when a girl needed him?

"Oh, yeah, sure," she countered. "That's easy for you to say. You're not the one having this baby. What if I'm trapped back here in Regency England? I told you all about that breathing business to help control labor pains, but I've never really bought that theory. Nope. Not for a minute. I want *drugs,* Marcus—painkillers! And I want an obstetrician, and a first-rate hospital, and a million nurses, and—and Blue Cross and Blue Shield! What happens if something goes wrong? Is some ignorant Regency quack going to tell me to bite on a stick? Well, fat chance, buster!"

Cassandra slipped from his embrace and then from the bed itself. Jamming her hands on her hips, she confronted him, her tears replaced by a nearly white-hot anger. "I know I'm being unreasonable here, Marcus, but humor me, okay? I'm pregnant. You may have donned your damned English stiff upper lip now that we couldn't save Perceval, and accepted your fate, but I'm an American, and we Americans never give up. There's got to be some way to save you, to save this baby, to save *us.* There just has to be!''

Marcus slid from the bed on the far side and stood some distance from her, a small smile playing around his lips. She longed to hit him. Boy, being pregnant sure brought out the bitch in her, as well as the tears! But she didn't care. She had something to say, and she was going to say it. He opened his mouth to speak, but she cut him off.

"See this hand?'' she challenged, raising her right hand and wiggling her fingers. "It's not just a hand, you know. I can teach 'hand.' That's simple. But how do I teach hand, palm, finger, thumb, nail, knuckle? And eyes!'' she continued, nearly jabbing out one of her own. "What about eyes, Marcus? They've got upper lids, and lower lids, and lashes, and an iris, and a cornea—how in God's name am I supposed to teach a child all of that alone? *Sesame Street* doesn't cover everything, you know. And I haven't even gotten to mouths yet, with teeth, and gums, and a tongue, and lips and—''

"Cassandra, I think I have a plan—'' Marcus began, taking a step toward her, but she didn't hear him. She was too involved in her own thoughts.

"And what if it's a boy? I love baseball, but I can't play second base. I don't want him to be a sissy. A boy needs a father, Marcus, he needs—*what did you say*?''

He stepped even closer. "I said, I think I have a plan that will solve all our problems.'' He smiled, adding, "Except this business about *Sesame Street* and second base. Much as I love you, my pet, I haven't the faintest idea what you are talking about.''

Cassandra, immediately suspicious, narrowed her eyes and glared at him, glared at his gorgeous yet faintly mocking smile. "Never mind all that now, Marcus. You said you have a plan. What plan? When did you form it?

Why don't I know anything about it? Damn it, Marcus—
if you've been keeping secrets from me—"

He took hold of her elbow and steered her back to the
bed, helping her to boost herself up onto the high mattress. "I was planning to tell you about it—eventually,"
he explained, his calm rationality making her ache to
punch him.

"Go on," she said from between clenched teeth. And
she loved this man? This man was going to be the father
of her child? She might have been making great inroads
with Marcus since she'd landed in Regency England, but
she sure had a long way to go. "Tell me about this plan
you didn't want me to know about. I'm all ears, my lord.
Truly, I am."

He sat down beside her, nodding his agreement,
openly humoring her—and innocently setting her teeth
on edge. "Very well, Cassandra," he said, "but I will
have to preface my plan with some explanation."

"You've got that in one," she retorted belligerently,
folding her arms under her breasts. "And you'd better
make it good."

He kissed her cheek lightly, then retreated when she
held out her hands and glared at him, warning him off.
"You remember what I read in one of your guidebooks?"

She grimaced at the memory, the damning evidence
that had set them off to change history by saving the
Prime Minister. Only they hadn't saved him, and now
those words in the guidebook hovered over them all like
a sentence of death. "You told me that you read that the
fifth Marquess of Eastbourne died on the last day of May
in 1812. How could you think I'd forget?"

Marcus smiled sheepishly. "I hadn't thought that you
did, my sweet," he said, taking hold of her hands as if
she might want to slap him. "However, if you remember, I did not show you the page in the guidebook."

Cassandra frowned for a moment, then raised her eyebrows as she looked at him searchingly. "That's right. You never did show me the book. I remember thinking about that at the time. Are you trying to tell me that the guidebook did spell out how you're supposed to die? Is that your plan? To try again to change history?" Her heart sank to her toes. It wouldn't work. It hadn't worked today. What on earth made him believe it would work on the last day of May? Marcus had admitted he knew nothing about baseball. Obviously he also knew nothing about football. This wasn't the time to try what had already failed. It was time to drop back ten and punt! "Marcus—"

"I don't die, Cassandra, I disappear," he said quickly, so that her mouth remained open as she gaped at him, suddenly speechless. "I didn't want to get your hopes up earlier, which was why I tried to save Perceval—for Perceval's sake, yes, but mostly to keep you occupied—but I may not die on the last day of May. I think—I hope— that I, you and I both, travel through time on that day."

"Travel—travel through time?" Cassandra's head was spinning. So was her stomach, but she ignored it. This was too important a moment to interrupt simply because of a little nausea. Her mind still slightly muzzy, she opened her mouth and asked the obvious. "Marcus? Are you telling me that you're about to become a time traveler too?"

He released her hands and slipped an arm around her shoulders, drawing her against him. "If my theories are correct, yes, that's precisely what I'm telling you. As you might recall, I had been investigating time travel for nearly a year, and had finally centered my research on that room in the White Tower just weeks before you arrived so conveniently to prove my theory. I believe— and again, this is only another theory—that I was about to make an important breakthrough when you came to England unexpectedly."

"Well, it wasn't my idea," Cassandra interrupted him, beginning to hope. "All I was looking for that day was the way out of the place. But go on. I'm all ears."

"And quite lovely ears they are, imp. I have always been partial to them. But to continue. If you'll remember, you've already told me that you planned to be in England at the end of May. But you arrived early, upsetting all the preset schedules, and we were drawn to each other out of time. Using your calculator, I attempted to ascertain whether the intervening one hundred and eighty years affected the calendar, but the figures didn't quite add up. Rather than science, I believe our *fates* drew us together, our combined destinies, if you will, if you don't mind a descent into the poetic. And so, again, if I am correct, rather than to travel through time alone, madam, I will have the pleasure of my affianced wife and unborn child as my companions for the trip."

Cassandra was quiet for a long time, although she could feel Marcus's eyes boring into her.

He was waiting for her answer.

So was she.

She was numb. Completely and absolutely *numb*. She couldn't move—although her mind was racing at the speed of light. Marcus wasn't going to die on the last day of May. He was going to travel through time. To where? Would he travel to 1992 with her and their baby, or was his destination some other time, some other era? What if he were to zoom forward to 2057 or something, and meet her again when she was old enough to be his mother and his son was older than he? *No.* That wouldn't happen. Marcus appeared to be convinced their fates were intertwined. He would come back to 1992 with her. He had to.

But there were other questions.

Had they made love for the first time before or after he had told her about his impending death? And if it was after, wasn't he guilty of playing with her mind, her emotions? *No.* She had been falling in love with Marcus almost from the moment she'd first opened her eyes to see him standing in front of her, looking at her as if she was everything he'd always wanted for Christmas.

But he had lied to her, the rat! She wasn't going to forget that in a hurry. He had told her that he was going to die, then laughed when she immediately began making plans to save his life. No wonder he had thought she was so funny—he already knew he wasn't really going to die. Unless she killed him. That seemed like a pretty reasonable option at the moment—and she felt sure that there wouldn't be a jury in the world who'd convict her.

And then there was all that business about the Reverend Mr. Austin and Lady Blakewell, and that pompous nerd, Reginald Hawtrey. Had Marcus really been worried about her, or had he been scared that they might stumble onto his own secret, his own plans to experiment with time travel?

She was so confused! What did a person do when confronted with such a confounding mixture of righteous anger, astonished bewilderment, and blessed relief? On the one hand, she could kill Marcus for having kept a secret from her, while on the other hand, she had just been given new hope that they could have their "happily ever after" after all. Was she going to look a gift horse in the mouth—good Lord, but she was using a lot of trite sayings to examine her emotions—or was she going to grab at this new chance with both hands (yes, yet another cliché, but she was past editing herself), and the hell with placing blame or holding grudges?

Silly question, Kelley, she told herself, peeking through her lashes at Marcus. He was still staring at her, awaiting her reaction. Perceval was dead; her London guidebook's report of his demise had been neither faulty nor premature. Marcus's cousin Richard was dead, as implied by the second guidebook. And Marcus was going to disappear on the last day of May.

There were no questions. Not really. There were only facts—or at least as many facts as the editors of the guidebooks knew. History books, even the guide at the White Tower, declared that the Princes had died in the Bloody Tower, and Cassandra and Marcus both knew differently—or at least they had a darn good reason to doubt that particular theory.

And so, taking the guidebooks and the theories and the hopes and the promises all a step further—there would be a happy ending for Marcus and herself. *Bottom line, Kelley,* she told herself, beginning to smile. *It's time to cut to the chase. Where's your problem, lady? You, and Marcus, and your baby, are about to pack up and get the hell out of here!*

"Marcus?"

"Yes, Cassandra?"

Her bottom lip began to quiver, partly because she was crying again, but mostly because the whole thing was so ludicrously funny. He looked so adorably guilty, not at all the imperious marquess. He was just Marcus—her sweet, adorable, *fallible* Marcus. God, how she loved him!

"Marcus," she said, her smile wide as she began shaking her head in wonderment at her good fortune, at the lucky star that had appeared out of the blue just when all seemed lost. *Out of the blue. What a lovely thought!* "I love you, Marcus Pendelton."

His frown disappeared, to be replaced by what she could only call a boyish grin. "That does make it convenient, my dearest imp, as I positively adore you."

She pressed the back of her hand against her mouth, ineffectually trying to stifle her first escaping giggle. "I know," she said, delighted. She felt herself about to dissolve into hysterical laughter. It might not be the best time for laughing, but, hot damn, it sure beat the hell out of crying! "I love you. You love me. We're going to have a baby—conceived in 1812 and born in 1992. Technically, I'm about to have the longest pregnancy in history. Isn't it *marvelous*?"

Marcus took hold of her shoulders and gently pushed her down on her back on the mattress, swinging her legs onto the bed before stretching out his length beside her. "No, darling. *You're* marvelous," he said, smiling as she laughed and reached up to muss his hair. "You cannot know the times I have wanted to tell you all that I knew, all that I've hoped, but I foolishly held back, not wanting to raise your expectations in case I was wrong. For all my education, all my study, there are times, my sweet, when I can be remarkably obtuse. Can you ever forgive me?"

"That depends," Cassandra said, pulling at one end of his already disheveled neckcloth. "What's the Regency opinion on lovemaking during pregnancy?"

He frowned momentarily, then brightened. "I don't know. I could trot downstairs and beg all the pertinent information from Aunt Cornelia, I suppose, but is such a trip really necessary?"

"*Beep*," Cassandra replied, hooking one index finger beneath the knot of his neckcloth and pulling him down so that his face was only inches from hers and his warm breath caressed her cheek. "Wrong answer, Marcus. Sorry about that. Would you care to try again?"

"Indeed, yes," he replied, his smile so devilish that Cassandra knew he was enjoying their game as much as she. Maybe more. With his lips just above hers, he murmured, "As a matter of fact, I'm willing to try all night."

He got it right the second time.

And the third time.

And—being a very apt student—he even got it right a fourth time, just before dawn.

Chapter 16

"Okay, okay, that's it! Now don't move." Cassandra closed one eye and squinted into the viewfinder, making sure she wouldn't be cutting off Aunt Cornelia's and Peregrine's heads as she usually did when she took photographs. She had a whole album of pictures at home in Manhattan, full of feet, legs, torsos—but no heads. "Now say *cheese*!"

"Cheese?" Aunt Cornelia repeated in disgusted accents, stepping away from Peregrine and out of range of the viewfinder. "It is enough that I am standing here—*more* than enough—posing for a portrait that you have sworn will be magically painted within that little black box. I absolutely *refuse* to spout gibberish while I do so."

"It's a camera, Aunt Cornelia," Cassandra repeated for, she believed, the tenth time in as many minutes. "I had forgotten that I had stuck it in my purse that fateful day, but I promise you, it works. When Marcus and I get to my time, we just take the film inside it to any drugstore—apothecary, to you, Corny—and come back the next day to pick up the finished pictures. Now, come on, be a good sport and let me do this, okay? Marcus and I want to have something to remember you and Perry by after we're gone."

The older woman's chin quivered and Cassandra

sighed, knowing she had said precisely the wrong thing by reminding Aunt Cornelia of Marcus's imminent, and permanent, departure from Regency England. "Gone! My dearest Marcus—gone forever!"

Aunt Cornelia pulled a lace-edged handkerchief from her sleeve cuff and dabbed a corner of it at her tear-bright eyes before glaring at Cassandra and Peregrine in turn. "Never again to see my Marcus, never to see his little child—left behind here in the dithering, incapable hands of *this* grinning idiot. And it's all your fault, girl!" she ended, pointing an accusing finger in Cassandra's direction.

Cassandra lifted the camera once more, tempted to snap a candid photograph of Aunt Cornelia at her most memorable—her mouth open and her temper at full boil —then thought better of it. The woman was genuinely upset, and with good reason. It hadn't been easy, informing Peregrine and Aunt Cornelia that if all went as hoped, they would soon be bidding a final farewell to both Cassandra *and* Marcus—and their unborn child.

Even now, two days after Perceval's assassination, Cassandra was having difficulty comprehending that she and Marcus might be heading toward an actual happy, if somewhat bittersweet, ending after all. Especially now, with Marcus gone off into the country, to attend the funeral of his cousin and onetime heir. Left alone in the mansion, even though Peregrine and Aunt Cornelia were still in residence, she was feeling very much alone, and terrifyingly nervous. A happy ending might be in sight, but it was still more than two weeks in the future. She doubted she would truly believe it until she was back in the White Tower, Marcus by her side, reading the EXIT sign that hung above one of the stone archways.

But it would be exciting, seeing her own time through Marcus's eyes. No wonder he had been intrigued to hear her reactions to Regency England. She could hardly wait until she could introduce him to the myriad wonders of the twentieth century. Their first stop, if she had anything to say about it, would be the local McDonald's, where she would pig out on hamburgers, jumbo fries, and Coca-Cola—and the hell with cholesterol and saturated fat!

She watched helplessly as Aunt Cornelia tried to recover her composure. Although the fact that the old lady had perversely taken to wearing black these past two days—"and *not* in consideration of that neck-or-nothing fool, Richard, either"—was a tad disconcerting, Cassandra's heart still went out to the woman.

Laying down the camera, Cassandra went to Aunt Cornelia and put an arm around her shoulders. "Won't you reconsider Marcus's offer and come to the White Tower with us for a final farewell, Corny? Marcus feels you'll better understand what is happening if you can be there to see it. You've already read the guidebook, so you know this has to be done, and would be done whether I had dropped in for my little unexpected visit or not. If Marcus and our child are to survive at all, we have to leave."

"Yes, come along, do, Aunt Cornelia. I'll be there to see them off, you know. Wouldn't miss it," Peregrine broke in, picking up the camera and looking through the viewfinder, frowning at what he saw. "Now why would anyone want to paint a portrait of a fireplace, I ask you?" he questioned as he turned about slowly, still squinting into the viewfinder. "Or a chair? Or a mirror—I say, I can see m'self! Ain't that above everything wonderful? I could have this box make a portrait of myself, couldn't I, Cassandra?"

"Peregrine, put that down—keep your finger off that button!" Cassandra warned, without any real hope of being heeded. She was proved correct a moment later when the flash told her Peregrine had indeed just taken a picture of himself taking a picture.

"I did it! Just the same way you did it when you painted Rose's portrait this morning, Cousin Cassie—I made light!" Peregrine smiled sheepishly as he placed the camera in Cassandra's outstretched hand. "Well, I did," he asserted, thrusting out his bottom lip, just like a child who has been caught doing something naughty but who still feels proud of the accomplishment. "And I don't know why you think it is so wonderful that this box can paint portraits, when it can make light. I should think *that* would be more important by half."

"Perry," Cassandra said, leaning forward and giving him a quick kiss on the cheek, "I am going to miss you so much. You're the younger brother I never had."

Peregrine frowned. "*Younger* brother, Cousin Cassie? I'm the older by at least five years."

"Ten, you dolt," Aunt Cornelia remarked, stuffing her handkerchief back into her sleeve cuff.

Cassandra hid a smile, knowing the woman was correct. But to Cassandra, Peregrine would always be young, at least in his heart. And, soon, in her memories of him. Her wonderful, poignant memories of this extraordinary time in her life. "My apologies, Perry. You are just so handsome that I sometimes forget how truly ancient you really are."

"That's better!" Peregrine returned with a decisive nod of his head, then frowned. "Stap me, I think I've just been insulted."

Aunt Cornelia walked past him, cuffing his ear. "Really, Perry? Then there may be hope for you yet, you paper-skulled twit. I can see that I shall have to devote my declining years to making something out of you—if I don't wish to end up begging pennies on some corner after you've frittered away Marcus's funds. The man must be daft, thinking to put you in charge of his fortune."

Peregrine grinned. "A lot you know, Corny. Cousin Cassie has that all fig—" he began triumphantly before Cassandra cuffed his other ear, reminding him to keep his mouth shut. There'd be no holding Marcus back if he knew what she had done before she told him.

Cassandra picked up the camera, determined to give it one more try. "If you don't want to say *cheese,* Aunt Cornelia, would you be agreeable to standing beside Perry and smiling when *he* says it? I'd take separate pictures of you, except I have only twelve exposures—half of them gone—and I want to make them all count. We've already wasted one today," she added, winking at Peregrine to take the sting from her words.

"Exposures?" Aunt Cornelia looked at her cautiously. "These portraits you insist you are making of us, Cassandra—do they include clothing? I won't be painted like some of those odiously forward foreign ladies, exposing myself for the sake of art—lying on a bed, nibbling fruit. And I don't even *like* apples!"

A mental vision of Aunt Cornelia, her uncovered form reclining nude, an apple stuck in her mouth, nearly cost Cassandra her "photo opportunity," for she could barely keep a straight face as she assured the woman that she would, indeed, appear fully dressed in the "portrait."

A half hour later, once Aunt Cornelia had changed her funereal black for her favorite gown and turban ("Marcus has always said he likes me best in blue"), Cassandra succeeded in capturing her stern, unsmiling face and Peregrine's happy grin for posterity.

But she might have cut off their feet. She'd know once she got the pictures developed.

"*25 May 1812*
   "*Being sound of both mind and body, I, Marcus*

Aurelius Octavian Pendelton, Fifth Earl of East-bourne, declare this to be a true, accurate, and binding statement of intent."

"Marcus Aurelius Octavian Pendelton?" Cassandra interrupted from her seat on the other side of the desk, her chair placed between Peregrine's and Aunt Cornelia's. "You've *got* to be kidding!"

"It is a fine family name, girl," Aunt Cornelia broke in haughtily. "All the Pendeltons have Latin names. *My* full name is Cornelia Augusta Horatia."

"Yeah, well," Cassandra countered, giggling as she pointed to her still-flat stomach. "If you're thinking this kid is going to be christened Julius Caesar, you're all in for a sad disappointment."

Marcus, who privately shared his fiancée's dislike of ancient Latin names, hid a smile with his hand and pointedly cleared his throat, looking at Cassandra, Aunt Cornelia, and Peregrine in turn. "If I might continue? Or is anyone else determined to contribute something to this conversation?"

Peregrine tipped his head to one side. "Actually, Marcus," he said thoughtfully, "I was wondering why you have Rose locked up in the sewing room these past days. Nice girl, Rose. As a matter of fact, I've been liking her more and more each day. Taking this whole business very well, worlds better than Goodfellow, who's been walking round with a Friday face, barking at all the servants. Seems a shame to lock her up."

"Rose isn't locked up, Perry," Cassandra whispered fiercely before Marcus could answer. "She's making Marcus some clothes for the *trip.* I drew her some pictures and she's doing a splendid job, although we don't know what to do about shoes—unless we cover his boot tops with his slacks. After all, we can't have him walking around in pantaloons and a neckcloth. People will notice."

"Cover his boot tops?" Peregrine exclaimed, so that Marcus saw Cassandra wince. "Marcus, Hoby made those boots for you, and damn fine ones they are. They cost you a fistful of blunt. Why would you cover them up?" He turned in his chair, to look at Aunt Cornelia. "He's leaving all his boots and his clothing for me, you know, even if I don't know what I'll do with any of it, as we aren't of a size. Which boots are you taking, Marcus?" he asked, shifting back to look at Marcus once more. "Not your new black ones, I hope. If I stuff the toes with a pair of hose, they should do for me well enough. I'd hate to lose the black ones."

"Grave robber," Aunt Cornelia growled.

Marcus was glad he had thought to place Cassandra between Corny and his best friend. He could only hope they wouldn't kill each other once he was gone. He also hoped they wouldn't say anything too revealing. His solicitor and the man's clerk were standing in front of the window, listening to everything that was said, which explained Cassandra's attempt to whisper—not that Peregrine had seemed to take any notice of that fact.

"All right, that will be enough," Marcus declared finally, rising from his chair, the carefully written will in his right hand. "I will continue now whether you wish to listen or not. There is much left to do, and not much time in which to do it."

"Go on, darling," Cassandra said encouragingly, winking at him. "I'll make sure the peanut gallery behaves."

Marcus shook his head, putting this business of preparing for time travel aside for a moment as he gazed adoringly at the exasperatingly forward, daringly outspoken woman who had come to mean the world to him. He had been back from Richard's funeral for only three days, having needed all that time to put his cousin's af-

fairs in order, but Cassandra had made the days full ones
—turning the tables completely by giving *him* concentrated lessons on behavior in the twentieth century all
day and filling his nights with love.

He took a deep breath, sending up a silent prayer that
his theories would be proved correct and they would
have a lifetime together. Then he began to read aloud
once more.

*"Having decided to escort Miss Cassandra Kelley on
her return to America and then undertake a solitary,
lengthy, and inherently dangerous journey throughout Africa, commencing the last day of May, 1812, a
scientific expedition from which it is possible I shall
not return, and having no heir, I have undertaken to
dispose of my estate during my lifetime. I do so in
the form of this document, as advised by my trusted
solicitor, Mr. James Forquith. These wishes, which I
describe below, are to be carried out on 1 June 1812:*

*"All entailed lands and titles shall, by law and cus-
tom, be returned to the control of His Royal Highness, George III, including Eastbourne Crest in Sussex, Eastbourne Manor in Surrey, and Eastbourne
House in Hampshire, with all rents and income likewise reverting to the Crown. Personal items in these
domiciles, including jewelry, horseflesh, portraits,
etc., will be inventoried, made a part of my estate,
and distributed among my remaining properties.*

*"Unencumbered property, including Eastbourne
Mansion in Grosvenor Square, my hunting box in
Scotland, and Eastwind, my most beloved country
estate in Sussex, shall be administered, with the ad-
vice of but not the order of Mr. James Forquith or his
successors in the firm of Forquith, Jessup, and
Smythe, by my good friend Peregrine Walton. Said
Peregrine Walton shall have free use of these proper-*

*ties in his lifetime, including the enjoyment of all
benefits and liberties inherent in such husbandry.''*

"Ain't that pretty, Cousin Cassie? Almost poetic, even
if I can't understand it for the life of me. Marcus always
had a way with those jawbreaking words.''

"Perry—button it,'' Cassandra warned, speaking from
between clenched teeth.

Marcus continued:

*"All monies, rents, income, furnishings, investments,
etc., are likewise to be administered by and under
the complete control of Peregrine Walton, who is in
addition to be paid a quarterly allowance for his
private use, this allowance to consist of two thousand pounds.''*

This last statement brought Aunt Cornelia quickly to
her feet, as Marcus had supposed it would. "Two thousand pounds! What do you want him to do, nephew—
buy all of Mayfair and stick it in his pocket? You feed
him, you clothe him, you put a roof over his empty head
—and now you go and make him as rich as any nabob.
This is dangerous, nephew, very, very dangerous!''

"Please be seated, Aunt Cornelia. And remember, we
have guests,'' Marcus said quietly, his gaze on James Forquith's pinched, disapproving face, before reading from
the paper once more:

*"In the event that Peregrine Walton shall marry and
produce heirs, this quarterly allowance shall be in-
creased to three thousand pounds, to continue in
perpetuity at an increase of fifty pounds per annum
and divided equally among his descendants, for as
long as a single remaining Walton heir can be located.*

*"As to my cousin, Cornelia Haskins, she is to be
granted full use of all my properties and awarded an*

immediate settlement of fifty thousand pounds as well as a quarterly income of two thousand pounds for the remainder of her lifetime. These funds are hers to dispose of as she pleases."

"Happy now, Corny?" Peretrine whispered sotto voce, leaning across Cassandra, who promptly jabbed him in the ribs with her elbow. "I told you Marcus had the whole thing figured out."

Corny applied her handkerchief to her tear-filled eyes, a happenstance that unnerved Marcus no matter how often she'd so uncharacteristically had recourse to such displays of emotion since his announcement of his imminent departure. He continued reading:

"This disposition of property is to continue until the time of both Peregrine Walton's death and the demise of my cousin, Cornelia Haskins, upon which time my funds and income, except for the aforementioned Walton allowance, are to be placed in a trust, to be administered by appointed officers of Forquith, Jessup, and Smythe or another firm of their choosing if the partnership of Forquith, Jessup, and Smythe shall retire from business.

"My properties are to be kept fully staffed, and all buildings maintained and repaired, as to keep them in concert with the improvements of the passing years, and likewise updated, including the installation of modern inventions and conveniences, but expressly excluding adjustments to basic architecture and furnishings, which are to be maintained as closely as possible to existing style and substance.

"This mandate is to prevail until 5 June 2000, at which time, unless certain conditions are met, the entire inheritance, including accrued interest and all buildings, are to be turned over to and equally divided among English and American charities work-

ing on behalf of veterans of war, families without shelter, and victims of natural catastrophe."

Marcus looked up from the paper he was reading and saw that Cassandra was smiling. He had thought she'd like that last touch.

"The conditions alluded to above are as follows: that either a man named Marcus, or a woman named Cassandra, or both, shall introduce themselves at my Grosvenor Square mansion between the dates of 31 May and 5 June of any year, from 1830, and up to and including the year 2000, presenting a certain ring, an exact copy and description of which is enclosed with this Will. These rings are and will be absolute proof of ownership, and no other provisions, prerequisites, or conditions must be met by either Marcus or Cassandra in order to assume final, irrevocable title and control of my entire estate.

"This provision is made on the chance that I shall have indeed survived my expedition to Africa and wed, thereby occasioning the possibility of producing legitimate heirs to my unencumbered estates, although my renunciation of my title is absolute. Naming all firstborn offspring of each succeeding generation either Marcus or Cassandra will ensure that the proper persons inherit, if they so wish. Knowing that I do not enter into this agreement lightly, and aware that, although my wishes may seem frivolous to those not conversant with my penchant for scientific curiosities, I hereby affix my name and seal before God and the undersigned witnesses this twenty-fifth day of May, 1812.

"Mr. Forquith, if you will step forward to witness my signature?" Marcus asked, reaching for his quill. A moment later Forquith and his clerk had signed the paper

and the deed was done. Peregrine escorted the solicitor
and his assistant to the door. "Now, children," Marcus
said, spreading his hands as Peregrine returned to his
chair, "you may have at it."

"Marry? Marcus, do you really suppose I shall ever
marry?"

"That would depend, you twit. I would say your
chances are good, if you do your wooing among the
inmates in Bedlam," Aunt Cornelia answered swiftly, before apparently dismissing Peregrine and turning to Marcus. "My dear boy, how can I thank you for your generosity? It is too much. Entirely too much."

"Do you think they bought it, Marcus? I wouldn't
want to show up in 1992, sporting our rings, just to find
out this mansion has been turned into a parking lot. And
I loved that business about the charities. You have been
listening to me, haven't you?"

Marcus collapsed into his chair, exhausted. It had not
been easy, giving up his marquessate, giving up his unborn son's title, turning his back on his ancestry. But it
had to be done; there was no other way to secure his
and Cassandra's future. After all, he had nothing to offer
twentieth-century society, no talents that anyone living
in that enlightened time needed. He had to retain his
fortune, his properties, if he was to provide for his wife
and child. Besides, his greatest wish was to return to
university, where he could study his own history and,
one day, teach it.

"To answer your questions—yes, Perry, I do believe
you will marry one day, if only to assure yourself of some
company as you rattle around in this mansion. Aunt Cornelia, I do not deserve your thanks. It is I who should be
thanking you, for your company and caring over the
years, for your understanding of my eccentricities, and
for your generous help with Cassandra. And, yes, my
love, Mr. Forquith has, as you term the business, 'bought

it.' He is being extremely well paid to 'buy it.' Now, if you two good friends would leave us, I believe my fiancée is near to bursting with an overpowering need to kiss me. In her delicate condition, I have found that it is not wise to thwart her.''

Peregrine scratched his head. ''Cousin Cassie has a heart of gold, Marcus,'' he said, frowning, ''but I think you're right. All but bit off my head the other day when I chanced to eat the last sugar comfit. Made me personally run straight out and buy more—a full bag of pink ones. *Only* pink ones. And you think I'll marry? If there's nothing else for it, I suppose I might, but I'd much rather raise dogs, if you don't mind.''

Marcus watched as Aunt Cornelia, suppressed a smile, took hold of Peregrine's ear, and led him out of the room, firmly closing the door behind her.

Less than three seconds later Cassandra had made her way around the desk and deposited herself in his lap. ''You're a genius, do you know that? And it all sounded so legal. Dump me back in America and go off to Africa and marry, will you? I'm sure your prune-faced Mr. Forquith is convinced we're eloping. But tell me the truth now that we're alone, okay? Do you really think that document is going to stand up in court? And this identifying ring business—and the dates you stipulated—what are they all about?''

He kissed her cheek. ''The rings? They struck me as the simplest form of identification. As you have pointed out to me during our lessons, I have no birth certificate, no driver's license, no passport—no forms of identification that will have any meaning in your time. When we appear back in this house in 1992 I do not intend to be carrying the family Bible, showing my birth as it was dutifully recorded by my father back in the eighteenth century. Therefore, we will appear as my own descendants. I, in all modesty, considered it to be a master stroke.''

She snuggled closer, wrapping her arms around his neck. ''You're a genius, all right. And it's easy enough to buy you some fake identification—or at least that's what I've read in all those spy novels. It sure helps being filthy rich, doesn't it?''

She lay against him, content, then sat up again. ''But what's this business about the dates? You told me we'd travel to 1992. Are you just hedging your bets, or do you think we could end up in some other time?''

He avoided her eyes. ''I am positive we shall travel to your time, my darling,'' he said firmly. ''However, I could not consider myself thorough if I did not take other possibilities into account.''

Cassandra exhaled forcefully, as if his explanation had given credence to one of her worst fears. ''We've got to hold on tightly to each other once we're in that room, Marcus. I don't care anymore *where* I go, as long as I go with you.'' She laid her head against his chest once more. ''But I would like to have my mother around when this baby is born. She'll want to kill me when she first sees me, because I disappeared without telling her, but this baby is going to make me as welcome as the flowers in May, as she is so fond of saying.''

Now was the time for optimism, even if he had no basis in fact for that particular emotion. ''And so she shall be, my love. We will remain in London until your confinement, and you shall give birth to my son in one of those hospitals you are so fond of—although I certainly cannot see why, as our hospitals are nothing but pest-holes—and you shall have the king's own physicians in attendance.''

''The queen's physicians, Marcus, remember? And, if he was good enough for Princess Di, I suppose he'll be good enough for our little prince.'' She slid from his lap, taking hold of his hand, her mood taking another of its mercurial leaps. "Now, come on. Rose says she has your new clothes ready. I can't wait to see you in slacks, much as I've come to love those sexy legs of yours. And I'd better try my own clothes on as well, because I think I might be gaining some weight around my waist. God, my mom is going to be *so* happy!"

Marcus followed her willingly enough, also anxious to try on his new clothing, although the thought of eventually walking out in public with his shirt collar open and minus his neckcloth and curly brimmed beaver was decidedly unnerving—almost barbarian. Of course, he thought, smiling, he was rather eager to see Cassandra dressed once more in that short contraption she called a skirt.

Chapter 17

It's D-day. Departure day. De-part de-era, de-sooner de-better. Get out of town, clown; make some tracks, Zack; head for the Tower, Gower; just leave the scene, Jean— there must be fifty ways to leave your time warp!

Cassandra giggled at her own weak wit as she left the last step of the wide staircase and tiptoed across the tiled foyer, intent on taking a solitary walk, a farewell stroll around Grosvenor Square. She had grown to love the Square during these last weeks, as she had been confined to early-morning walks in the area with Rose thanks to both Marcus's stern admonitions against making herself too visible in London Society and her own lingering fears of Reginald Hawtrey— the creep—and his equally wifty aunt, Lady Blakewell. *Me and my big mouth! If I had behaved that day I drove out with Hawtrey, I might have had the run of London for the entirety of my visit to Regency England. Ah, well. I met Byron. After that, anything else could only be considered an anticlimax.*

Her camera was in her purse, and there was one last picture still to take. Already dressed in her own clothing, which were carefully hidden beneath a light, full-length cloak, she ventured out into the Square, debating as to which of the many possible shots she would like to preserve for posterity. Should she snap a picture of the ladies strolling along the flagway, or would a photograph of one of the open carriages making a circuit around the enclosed garden in the middle of the Square be better?

Finally, after making one full circuit around the large Square, she decided to use her last shot to capture the look of Marcus's mansion as he, she was sure, would prefer to remember it. He had been so cute, detailing in his legal statement that the mansion was not to be altered architecturally—making sure, she supposed, that he wouldn't come back to this place only to see his mansion had been turned into a "box."

Yet even if Marcus had failed to consider the possibility, Cassandra worried over the sobering thought that his wishes might not be carried out, through no fault of the persons in charge of his trust, and that he might find his beloved mansion had become a casualty of the blitz, the fierce bombing of London during World War II.

She walked, hopefully nonchalantly, to the center of the Square and looked all around her before sliding a hand under her cloak, opening her purse, which hung from her shoulder, and extracting the small camera. The wide brim of the bonnet she wore, a chip straw confection she would dearly miss, hid the camera when she raised it to her right eye. Squinting through the viewfinder, she attempted to fit as much of the tall mansion into the picture as possible, although she was already resigned to missing a few of the chimneys.

Cassandra had just snapped the picture and was in the process of returning the camera to her purse when she became aware of movement directly behind her. She must have piqued somebody's interest, standing here in the middle of the traffic lane. Quickly she dropped the camera into the purse and patted the flap closed, then withdrew her hands and pasted a polite smile on her face.

"Well, well, well," a definitely remembered and

dreaded voice drawled with sugary sweetness—cloying, saccharine sweetness. "If it isn't the elusive Miss Kelley. I had about given you up. You are a downy one, aren't you, giving out the information that you are indisposed, when here you are, looking fine as ninepence—and sadly lacking your chaperon. For shame, Miss Kelley. For shame, on both counts."

Cassandra slowly turned, reluctantly but not apprehensively, her lips curved in a sneer, her eyes raking the overdressed Reginald Hawtrey from his perfumed curls to his ridiculous red-heeled, gold-buckled shoes as he stood at his ease beside a closed coach she hadn't noticed until this moment. "Well, well, well," she retorted, "if it isn't the obnoxious Mr. Hawtrey. Your aunt has let you off your leash, I see. Or am I wrong, and you have turned your coach into a hack and are earning your daily bread by accepting fares from the *real* Quality? Go home, Reggie—I think I hear your auntie calling."

Hawtrey's patently insincere smile disappeared with the speed of a copper vanishing into a beggar's pocket. "Boglander peasant! You're very daring, standing not twenty yards from the safety of your paramour's front door. Oh, yes, I know the whole of it now. Keeping you to himself, Eastbourne is, using some of your talents to help him on the Exchange, while using the rest to warm his bed. Not that I blame him, for you've plenty of fire. Haven't you, my dear? But business first, I always say. Eastbourne's got some deep doings with Forquith. I know, because I have made it my business to know. The man has been fairly living in Grosvenor Square these past weeks. You're picking his investments, aren't you, you cunning Irish witch?"

"I don't know what you're talking about." Cassandra began backing toward the mansion. Something in Hawtrey's eyes told her that she would be wise to get out of his way as quickly as possible. He couldn't really hurt

Marcus and herself—things had progressed too far for anyone to thwart them—but the man didn't seem to be stable. Perhaps she had struck a nerve with her offhand remark, and his aunt *had* tossed him out on his money-grubbing rump.

Hawtrey moved quickly to grab her forearm and pull her close, to within inches of his face. "Witch!" he hissed, his eyes narrowed—any traces of his overblown good looks were transformed into a mask of evil, of jealousy, of vengeance. "My aunt has threatened to cut off my allowance if I cannot bring you round my thumb. I came within Ames ace of an heiress last week, but would she let me declare myself? No! It's *you* she wants; *you* she is determined to have. I've been haunting this Square for weeks, leaving my card, begging—yes, begging—for a word with you, but Eastbourne has denied me at every turn. Oh, what's this? You look surprised, Miss Kelley. Hasn't your master told you of my visits?"

No, Marcus didn't tell me, bless him. The mere thought that Reggie Hawtrey was asking for me would have turned my stomach more than my morning sickness. Not that it would be wise to mention any of this to friend Reggie, Cassandra swiftly decided. Instead, she attempted in vain to jerk her arm free, looking about her frantically in the hope of discovering a friendly face. But the Square, normally teeming with people, was nearly deserted, the only other occupants a few nannies herding their small charges. She had to help herself, but she also had to be careful. She had to consider her unborn child.

"Mr. Hawtrey," she began reasonably, employing her best Regency miss manners, "I am so very distressed to hear that you have been thwarted in your repeated attempts to contact me. And flattered as well. I promise, if you would care to present yourself tomorrow afternoon at two, I would be most happy to see you." *Yeah, right.*

*With any luck, I'll be years and years away from here
by then, bucko.*

Hawtrey sniffed indelicately. "How very generous of
you, Miss Kelley. But I think not. Tomorrow is too late.
My aunt has given me until midnight tonight to present
you to her—as her birthday gift. She plans to cage you, I
believe, trading food for secrets, drink for prophecies—
life for the prospect of fortune. Six weeks ago I believed
her mad—both her and that psalm-singing Austin who
has been draining her of money—but Eastbourne's
strange doings, and your own admissions, have changed
my mind.

"My aunt shall have her prophet at the stroke of
twelve, Miss Kelley, and I shall have my fortune all right
and tight. But, first, little witch—for the trouble you have
caused me—*I shall have you!*"

And then, before Cassandra could do more than realize that she had landed herself in big trouble, she was
being shoved headfirst into Reginald Hawtrey's closed
carriage. As the carriage pulled away, out of the Square,
headed for heaven only knew where, Cassandra's last
thought before she fainted (Lordy, how she hated fainting!) was simple and succinct: *Kelley, you've screwed up
again—big time. And to top it off, your timing was
impeccable!*

Marcus stood in front of the full-length mirror, shaking
his head. Could the image reflected in the glass truly be
his? He was dressed like a farm laborer, worse than the
lowest tenant in the fields. Cassandra had instructed
Rose that the sleeves of his new flowered shirt be
hemmed a good three inches above the elbow, exposing
his arms, and then told him he was under strict orders
not to button the top two buttons of the shirt.

His slacks—an apt name, for they were certainly slack
—fit him so loosely except at the waist that he could

have toothpicks for legs and no one would know it. Even worse, the material covered him to his ankles, nearly obscuring his new riding boots—the same boots Peregrine had coveted. Around his waist was a thin strip of leather strung through small loops on his slacks and fastened with a gold buckle that had last seen service on his black patent evening shoes.

In short, he felt ridiculous. He knew he *looked* ridiculous. But he would get used to it, he supposed. After all, if Cassandra could walk out in public in her state of near undress, he imagined he could face the world in *slacks*.

Cassandra. He smiled as he thought of her, as he thought of the adventure they were to have later this day. What would it be like, traveling in the midst of that intriguing blue mist? And what would it be like once they had completed their journey? Would they be in Cassandra's time? His theories all pointed to that happy event, but he could not be sure.

He touched the ring that encircled the third finger of his right hand, rubbing his thumb across the intricately carved surface, the Latin inscription that translated to "what is mine, I hold," the Eastbourne family motto. He had entrusted the third specially-made ring to Forquith yesterday before watching the mold being destroyed and had personally slipped the second on Cassandra's hand only this morning, before leaving her to complete some last-minute business with Peregrine.

Peregrine. That poor man was in a dither, caught between a reluctance to part with his best friend and the knowledge that he, Peregrine Walton, was soon to be in command of a vast estate. Marcus had found the fellow in the library only two hours earlier, reading—and valiantly attempting to understand—an essay on the benefits to be derived by seasonal crop rotation. Yes, the man would do a good job husbanding the Eastbourne estates.

Or, at least, he would do his best. Aunt Cornelia would see to that.

Corny. Marcus smiled as he turned away from the mirror. Dear Aunt Cornelia. Still sniffling into her handkerchief when she was sure no one was looking, she had rallied considerably in the past few days and promised to be a credit to the Pendelton family. She had also been observed whispering to Goodfellow a time or two. This was a growing association Marcus had been watching with some interest. With Marcus gone, and the title with him, perhaps Aunt Cornelia would throw propriety to the winds, bend her Pendelton consequence, and follow her heart. It was a soothing thought, and one he would enjoy sharing with Cassandra.

Cassandra. Marcus frowned, pulling out his watch and marking the time. He thought she would have come barging into his dressing room by now, showing off her modern clothes, flirting with him as she had a few days earlier, teasing him with glimpses of her long, straight legs.

He heard the door open behind him and smiled as he replaced the watch, turning to see his beloved Cassandra.

However, it was not Cassandra but Peregrine who had entered the room.

"Marcus? Is that really you? Dear me, and I thought Cousin Cassie said Rose had done a fine job. I shouldn't tell you this, I suppose, as it's too late to do anything about it, but you look terrible. I don't understand it, Marcus. Females in Cousin Cassie's time seem to go about in little more than scraps, while we men are forced to wear sacks. Can't even see your legs, you know, although I'm seeing more of your arms than I can countenance. Of course, Jack Sampson would like those slack things above half—he's been stuffing his hose with sawdust for years, to give himself a leg. Calves like sticks, Jack has, you know. Where's Cousin Cassie?"

"Cassandra?" Marcus frowned, giving his dressing room one last, assessing look—just to be sure he hadn't forgotten anything—before accompanying Peregrine into his bedchamber. "I suppose she is with Corny, trying yet again to persuade her to accompany us to the White Tower. We leave in less than an hour—at six, just as the traffic is thin."

"No, she ain't," Peregrine answered as Marcus caught him eyeing the wide tester bed—probably attempting to measure the comfort of the mattress he would sleep on for the first time that night. "Just there, Marcus. Didn't see her. Didn't linger either. Your aunt is dead set on making a man out of me, or so she says. Keeps telling me I mustn't eat so much, and learn to dance without tramping on m'partner's toes. Do you think she plans to marry me off? I can't say I like the idea. Oh, well, she'll show up."

"Who will show up, Perry," Marcus asked facetiously, already heading for the door, "Corny, your heretofore unlooked-for bride, or Cassandra?"

"Why, Cousin Cassie, of course," Peregrine answered testily, beginning to breathe heavily as he followed Marcus, who was striding down the hallway in the direction of Cassandra's bedchamber. "I saw her just after luncheon. She was looking for one last portrait to paint in her little black box."

Marcus halted so quickly that Peregrine cannoned into his back. "The camera, Perry?" he asked, beginning to feel uneasy. "She's already pointed that thing at everything and everyone inside the house. Are you telling me that Cassandra is taking pictures, as she terms it, somewhere? She didn't go outside dressed in her own clothing, did she?"

Peregrine stepped back a pace, shaking his head.

"Couldn't have. She could get into trouble going outside with no clothes on. Stands to reason, considering how she looked when I happened upon her earlier. I had forgotten how she looked when first we clapped eyes on her. Goodfellow blushed beet red to the top of his head when he brought us some tea in the drawing room. No, Cousin Cassie wouldn't go outside. Would she?"

Fifteen frantic minutes of searching and pointed questions later, Peregrine had his answer. Marcus was pacing the carpet in his study, cursing softly, fluently, endlessly, under his breath. Cassandra's blue cloak was missing. Rose had taken a quick inventory and discovered that fact. A few discreet inquiries in the servants' hall had disclosed the damning information that one of the underfootmen had seen Cassandra slipping out the front door dressed in that same missing cloak—although he couldn't recall seeing her slip back in again.

The underfootman also remembered hearing the clock in the drawing room strike two times as Cassandra closed the door behind her. She was nowhere to be found either in the mansion or in the garden leading to the mews. Now, just as the clock was rapidly moving toward the hour of six, it was obvious that the impetuous Miss Kelley had gone missing.

"Earthquakes! Always earthquakes!" Marcus exclaimed at last, slamming a fist into his palm. "I'll give her this much, Perry—the girl doesn't exaggerate. Come with me."

Peregrine scrambled out of the chair in which he had been sitting, having become faintly exhausted merely from watching Marcus pace. Crumbs of the strawberry tart he had been nibbling spilled from his waistcoat onto the floor. "Come with you where, Marcus? Where are we going? And shouldn't you tell Aunt Cornelia? She's that worried."

"No, I won't tell her, Perry. She'd be completely beside herself if I told her where we're going."

"I'll be the judge of that," Aunt Cornelia said as Marcus reached for the mahogany case containing his dueling pistols. "Hawtrey's got her, hasn't he? It's the only thing that makes sense. The gel didn't have time to make more than one enemy. Cassandra knows you must get to the White Tower before midnight. Procure a pistol for me as well, if you please. My father taught me to shoot. I may not be able to blow the pips out of a playing card at ten paces, but I should be able to hit that interfering, fat flawn of a Lady Blakewell if I put my mind to it."

"Hawtrey?" Peregrine asked, clearly aghast. Obviously that unpleasant thought had not occurred to him. "Oh, never say so, ma'am. He's evil. Marcus, what are we waiting for? We must rescue Cousin Cassie."

"Have Goodfellow bring the closed carriage around, Perry," Marcus ordered tightly. Locating a third pistol, he gingerly handed it to Corny, who took it with the air of a person who was familiar with firearms. Just as he was about to leave them forever, the members of his household were surprising him with depths of loyalty and affection he was having difficulty accepting without a nearly overwhelming gratitude. Rose, Goodfellow, Aunt Cornelia—even the emotional French cook—everyone had rallied around wonderfully, and no gossip of their resident time traveler had passed beyond the front door of the mansion.

"And, yes, Corny," he said now, "Cassandra must be in that chamber in the White Tower before midnight. I cannot vouch for her safety, or the future of our child, if she is not transported back to her own time tonight."

"And you, Marcus?" Aunt Cornelia asked as Peregrine raced from the room, a man with a mission. "Can you attest to your own safety if you rescue Cassandra from

Hawtrey's greedy clutches, only to miss your own opportunity, your own appointment with destiny?"

"I don't know, Aunt," Marcus said, taking her arm as he escorted her toward the foyer. "And, frankly, madam, without Cassandra by my side, I don't particularly care!"

Cassandra sat alone in the small, windowless room, still tightly wrapped in her cloak, wondering for the hundredth time what was keeping Marcus. Surely he had figured it out by now. She had been kidnapped, pure and simple.

Real simple.

Simple*minded*, that is.

How could she have been so stupid? Hadn't she read all the books? Hadn't she seen every plot twist imaginable, all of which had ended with the heroine stumbling into trouble by way of a villain straight out of Central Casting—and all just so that the hero could come riding to the rescue?

So why hadn't she used her head? Why had she set her wandering feet outside today, of all days, and allowed herself to be kidnapped by a man intent on—what? Ravishment? She shivered. The hell he would! Handing her over to his aunt was one thing, but satisfying his bruised ego by "having his wicked way with her" first was strictly *verboten*, not to mention terribly trite.

She had begun her imprisonment calmly enough, after rousing from her faint while still in the carriage and learning that their destination was well within the confines of London. Hawtrey, the twit (as Aunt Cornelia would call him), had obviously taken her to his own house. The guy wasn't exactly a brain trust—and Marcus should arrive at any moment, to punch his lights out and free her.

So thinking, Cassandra had passed the first hour singing "Ninety-nine Bottles of Beer on the Wall," but by the time she had wound down to fourteen bottles, her bravado had suffered a serious dent. Maybe Hawtrey hadn't taken her to his own house. Maybe she was being held in some anonymous building, and Marcus had been reduced to looking for the proverbial needle in a haystack.

She opened her purse and looked at her watch. Seven o'clock. If Marcus didn't show up on his white charger soon, she was going to have to take matters into her own hands and rescue herself.

Her stomach growled, reminding her that in her excitement she had barely touched her lunch. Coupling that fact with the knowledge that she hadn't been able to eat more than dry toast for breakfast in weeks, she knew she'd have to find some food soon or she'd be sick again.

And then she remembered her purse. Marcus had insisted that she pack everything she had brought, leaving nothing behind. That included the Hershey bar she hadn't eaten, as well as her remaining cigarettes, for although she had smoked one pack since her arrival in Regency England, she'd had none since discovering that she was pregnant.

"Let's all hear it for chocolate!" she said aloud, digging into her purse in an attempt to locate the candy.

Her fingers closed around her disposable lighter.

"Now this might prove helpful," she said, holding the lighter up in front of her and eyeing it speculatively. "I'll bet good old Reggie hasn't seen one of these. Bing Crosby might have had that handy eclipse in *A Connecticut Yankee in King Arthur's Court*, but I'll have to wing it." Laying the lighter in her lap, she dug through the rest of her belongings, finally locating the chocolate bar.

Cassandra munched on the chocolate bar, hating the fact that her hand trembled as she raised it to her mouth. She was putting up a brave front, mostly to benefit herself, and to protect her baby, but she was growing more frightened with each passing minute.

She had to get out of here!

She had to get to the White Tower.

De-part de-era, de-sooner de-better. Fifty ways to leave your time warp.

She'd settle for one. Now. Sooner if possible.

Cassandra flinched as the single door to the room opened and Reginald Hawtrey stepped inside, locked the door behind him, and slipped the key into his pocket. "Good evening, Miss Kelley. Please excuse my prolonged absence, but certain preparations had to be made, certain parties assembled. You will forgive me, *n'est-ce pas?*"

"I don't speak French, Reggie," Cassandra informed him coldly.

He launched himself into a torrent of that language, his tone more snide than romantic.

"Only Spanish."

That stopped him. "Spanish? No one speaks Spanish. What would a lady be doing speaking such a heathen tongue? Perhaps you are a spy after all, sent here by Bonaparte, and not Irish at all. And not a foreteller of futures either. What *is* Eastbourne up to?"

It worked once, Cassandra thought. *Besides, I'm too frightened to think up a good lie.* "What are we about, Reggie? Why, I thought you had guessed. We're time travelers—or at least I am. Marcus is going to make his first flight tonight. Want to come with us? There's a singles bar on East Forty-eighth Street that's right up your alley. I'll even buy you a gold chain."

"Enough!" Hawtrey ordered, covering his ears. "I won't listen to any more of your nonsense words. My aunt wants you, and that's good enough for me." He took the key from his pocket and opened the door. "One of your *handmaidens* will be attending you shortly, to prepare you. You'll be given a bath and a gown. Wrapping yourself in that cloak has not cooled my ardor, if that was your hope. Cooperate, Miss Kelley, and you might even find yourself enjoying the evening."

And then he threw back his head and laughed—a stock villain move, not that it was without effect.

Cassandra's panicked mind whirled back to that first evening she had encountered Reginald Hawtrey. Either Marcus or Peregrine—most probably Marcus, for Perry wouldn't be so outspoken—had said something about Reggie and orgies. She decided to call him on it. "You wouldn't be planning a Black Mass or anything, would you, Reggie? They're really not 'in' this season."

"Witch!" Hawtrey spat the word as he stabbed his index finger toward the center of her chest. "I'll soon see your arrogance silenced!"

And then he was gone, and she heard the key turn in the other side of the lock.

Cassandra slumped in the chair, totally defeated, and more frightened than she had been in her life. "Oh, God, he *is* planning a Black Mass. I don't believe this. I don't believe any of this. *Marcus!* Marcus, where are you?"

"I'll ask one last time. Where is she?"

Lady Blakewell fanned herself with her handkerchief, her usually sallow complexion strangely pink. "And I will answer you one last time, my lord. I haven't the faintest idea what you are talking about. My Reggie would never do such a thing. Kidnapping Peregrine Walton's nobody of a cousin? Why would Reggie stoop so low?"

"Why?" Marcus questioned, his dark eyes narrowing as he felt his temper threatening to explode beyond the boundaries of his rigid self-control. "Why not, madam? I've learned never to underestimate the ambition of stupidity—or the ruthlessness of greed. Hawtrey did it for *you,* madam. He did it for your money.''

He was losing time, precious, precious time. He had been forced to change his clothes before leaving Grosvenor Square—and he had wasted a frustrating half hour fighting the crush of vehicles surrounding Hyde Park before all but breaking down Hawtrey's door, just to be told that the man was not there.

Now he was forced to deal directly with Lady Blakewell, and the Reverend Ignatius Austin, who was hovering behind the settee like some oversize black crow. A wickedly grinning black crow, his yellowed teeth taking the place of that winged predator's beak.

''You have harbored one of Satan's own spawn in your bosom,'' the vicar said now, pointing a bony finger at Marcus. ''You have sown the wind, and ye have reaped the whirlwind!''

''Oh, stubble it, Ichabod,'' Aunt Cornelia snapped, reaching into the pocket of her cloak and pulling out the long-barreled pistol. ''Enough of this, Marcus. I say we shoot him.''

Marcus would have laughed out loud at this abrupt change of tactic, but Corny's actions seemed to have done the trick. Falling on his knees behind the settee, the vicar hid his head behind Lady Blakewell's turban and began loudly pleading for Aunt Cornelia to spare his life. ''Shoot her instead!'' he exclaimed, lifting a hand to point at Lady Blakewell's head. ''*She* made me tell what I knew. *She's* the one what wants to lock her up and make her tell the future. I know nothing of any kidnapping. I am innocent! I am a man of God!''

Lady Blakewell turned on the settee and began beating at the Reverend Mr. Austin's head with her ivory stick fan. ''Shoot me? *Shoot me?* How dare you, sirrah! Shoot him! Shoot *him*!''

''Pitiful, ain't it?'' Peregrine remarked sorrowfully,

drawing his own pistol as the vicar made a break for the hallway. "So, shall I take aim at this autem-bawler, Marcus? I will if you want me to, but I won't blow a hole in anyone just because Lady Blakewell here wants it done. I wouldn't want to do anything that might make *her* happy."

While Peregrine kept his pistol trained on the vicar, and Aunt Cornelia, clearly enjoying her role of Regency Boadicea, kept hers leveled at Lady Blakewell's ample bosom, Marcus looked at the mantel clock just as it struck the hour of nine. He didn't like what was happening—it was barely civilized and totally out of character for a gentleman—but Aunt Cornelia's tactics certainly seemed to be proving effective so far.

"Where is he, Lady Blakewell?" Marcus demanded again. "Where does your devious little nephew go when he wishes to indulge his basest whims? Speak up quickly, madam, for I cannot control my aunt much longer."

Less than two minutes later he, Peregrine, and his most remarkable aunt were back in the closed coach, the pertinent information in hand.

Goodfellow, who had volunteered—nay, demanded—to ride on the box (the French cook sitting beside him, a large, ugly meat cleaver in hand), sprang the horses. Corny discreetly covered her eyes, for Marcus was already pulling his slacks over his pantaloons and boots, before stripping off his jacket and neckcloth, to reveal the sprigged muslin shirt hidden beneath it.

"That was very good, Marcus, by the by," Aunt Cornelia said when she had been told she could uncover her eyes. "I never would have thought to tell that fat cow not to breathe a word of what just happened or I would inform Lady Hertford of her plans to usurp her in Prinny's affections—not to mention hinting that she had resorted to witchcraft in order to seduce our dearest

King. As for that twit, Austin, I do not believe he will stop running until he reaches John O' Groats.''

"That's for certain, Corny," Peregrine said. "That fellow will be playing least-in-sight for months, until his bony knees stop shaking."

"Needs must when the devil drives, my friends," Marcus countered, lifting the leather window flap to peer out into the foggy twilight. He could see that they were still a good three miles from their destination, a small house next to the World's End Tavern, which was an extremely congested four or more miles from the Tower. "Goodfellow!" he cried out, dropping the side window and sticking his head outside the coach. "Make haste, man!"

"I'll lay the whip on with a will, my lord!" Goodfellow bellowed back at him as the cook, raising the cleaver and swinging it above his head, called out loudly, *"Vive la Mademoiselle Kelley! Vive les french fries!"*

Chapter 18

Cassandra never did get that bath Hawtrey had promised her. A scant fifteen minutes after he had locked her in the windowless room once more, the door opened again, admitting a mismatched pair of painted ladies who looked as if they would feel very much at home lying on their backs.

Oh, yes, Hawtrey was planning mischief, that was for sure, even if it wouldn't quite be a Black Mass. Hawtrey couldn't really believe in the devil. His sort believed only in themselves.

"Strike me, Mab, but she's a pretty 'un," the first woman said, leaning against the doorjamb. "Oi'll be takin' 'er cloak fer m'pains."

"Oh, do ye say that, do ye? Well, the divil you will, Peg," Mab, a redhead of obvious Irish descent answered shortly. "And I say we draws for it, fair and square."

"And *I* say you can have it!" Cassandra announced quickly, seeing her chance for escape. "Here you go, ladies—now don't fight." With that, she untied the cloak and threw it at them, revealing her vee-necked sweater, run-filled panty hose, and—in her mind, the *pièce de résistance*—her miniskirt. "Who said I don't know any French?" she rhetorically asked out loud a moment later as the two women stood in front of her, transfixed, staring at what to them must have seemed to be extremely outlandish clothing.

Pulling the lighter from her skirt pocket, Cassandra then held it straight out in front of her, flicking it to life with a quick movement of her thumb. "That's right, ladies—stare! What's the matter, didn't good old Reggie tell you that I'm a witch? Well, I am. I'm a witch, and I can make fire with my fingers."

"Coo, Mab," Peg whispered, her eyes wide as saucers, "look-ee at dat, would ya? That gentry mort ain't paid us enuf to deal wit *dat*!"

"Bingo, Peg, you go to the head of the class. Now stand away from that door, before I show you the little trick I do with *this*!" She reached into her other skirt pocket and extracted the camera.

Mab jammed her beefy fists on her hips. "And what would that be, dearie? It's nothing but a bit of a box— ain't it, Peg? Nothin' ta be afeared of. And it's many a trick with fire I've seen back in County Cork. Ye can have the cloak, Peg. It's them clothes I wants, and don't ye know it."

Cassandra rolled her eyes. Leave it to a fellow Irishwoman to prove herself more brave than wise. There was no film left in the camera, but the flash still worked. It wasn't much in the way of magic, but it had certainly impressed Peregrine. Besides, she didn't have any more tricks up her sleeve.

Waiting until Mab made a swipe at the camera, Cassandra pushed the button. Quick as a flash the Irishwoman stopped in her tracks, looking like a deer caught in headlights. "Sweet Mither of Gawd!" Mab exclaimed with gratifying overreaction, covering her eyes with her hands. "It's blinded I am, Peg—blinded—with pretty blue lights everywhere! Run fer it, Peg, save yerself! I'm done fer, I'm done fer!"

"No wonder the critics say the best actors are all Irish," Cassandra murmured appreciatively. She walked boldly through the doorway, the camera still held high as

Peg flattened herself against the wall, making the sign against the evil eye.

Once outside the door, however, Cassandra felt her fears come back in a rush. She wasn't safe yet, not by a wide margin. She had to get out of this house, for one thing, and she had to find Marcus. Minus her cloak, for she hadn't dared to take the time to retrieve it, she would have a tough time walking through the streets or trying to hire a hack to return her to Grosvenor Square.

Glancing at the watch that she had strapped to her wrist once more, she felt her stomach do a small flip when she saw that it was past nine. She had to get to the White Tower before midnight. Get to it, get in it, and find her way to the small room where the blue mist would appear.

But how?

The muffled sound of men's voices came to her from behind a set of double doors on her right. Hawtrey! He was probably drinking with some of his cronies, getting themselves good and drunk before they got on with the "ceremony." She shivered, thankful for the miracles of modern technology that had saved her from such a fate.

Cassandra inched her way along the hallway, heading for the front door. At least she had lucked out a little. There was no way she could have forced herself to make her way downstairs, or past long hallways of doors—any of which could open at any moment, exposing the leering Hawtrey.

Her hand was on the handle when the front door was pushed open, sending her sprawling against a table, vainly clutching at a vase of wilted flowers and missing it, so that it crashed loudly to the floor.

"Marcus!" she shouted as the tall, powerful figure of her beloved took three giant steps into the foyer, followed closely by Peregrine, Aunt Cornelia, Goodfellow, and Jacques, the chef. They were all looking very stern,

and were armed to the teeth—even Aunt Cornelia. They
were also, Cassandra decided, more welcome than Su-
perman, or Batman, or the entire quartet of Teenage Mu-
tant Ninja Turtles—and their rat-faced friend. "Marcus!
You're here!" she cried.

"Cassandra!" Marcus exclaimed, dragging her into his
arms for a moment, then pushing her away, his eyes
searching her face and form as if for evidence of injury.
"He didn't hurt you, did he? The bastard! I'll kill him!"

Cassandra grabbed his bare forearms, some small part
of her mind realizing that he, too, was dressed for their
journey. "There isn't time for that, Marcus. We have to
get to the White Tower. How far away is it?"

"At this time of night, with carriages *to*ing and *fro*ing
to Carlton House, Almack's, and two dozen other
places?" Aunt Cornelia remarked, rubbing at her temple
with the barrel of an evil-looking pistol. "We'll be lucky
to do it in less than two hours."

"Two hours? Oh, no! No! That's cutting it too thin. We
have to go faster than that," Cassandra argued, trying to
take hold of Marcus's hand and drag him through the
door.

"In a moment, my dear," he answered with maddening calm before, elegantly lifting her hand to his lips, he
pressed a kiss in her palm. "It would appear we have
succeeded in rousing your host."

"Hawtrey." Peregrine growled the name low in his
throat and took a single step forward. "Let's get him!"

"Shoot him, Marcus!" Aunt Cornelia ordered, leveling
her own pistol at Reginald Hawtrey's diamond-studded
neckcloth.

"Yes, my lord," Goodfellow urged, "blast a hole in the
bounder!"

"Oui, monsieur, give to heem *une boule dans la
gorge*—ze ball in ze t'roat!" Jacques supplied, helpfully

translating his suggestion when he saw Cassandra's un-comprehending frown.

Cassandra could almost see the gears turning in Marcus's brain as he weighed the need for revenge against the rapidly diminishing window of opportunity that—according to his own theories—was the White Tower from now until the last stroke of the clock at midnight. "Marcus, no," she pleaded, tugging on his forearm again. "I'm fine, honestly I am. Let's just get out of here!"

Marcus looked at Hawtrey, who was showing signs that he would give a lot to be anyplace else, and then back at Cassandra. "Perry—take Miss Kelley away. All of you, get out of here. Wait for me in the coach. I believe I shall dispense with a second to stand by me at this time. No sense landing you in the basket with Bow Street if I kill my man."

"No! This is no time to play the macho man!" Cassandra cried as Peregrine lifted her bodily and carried her out into the foggy May night. "Perry, I'll murder you!" she vowed as he deposited her on one seat inside the coach and handed her his greatcoat. "We're wasting precious time—don't you men know that? Corny—*tell them*!"

But Aunt Cornelia shook her head. "You Americans never did quite understand, did you? This is a matter of honor, Cassandra, legal or not. Marcus can do no less than challenge Hawtrey to a duel. I suggest you make the best of this time, my dear, by shutting your mouth and offering up a silent prayer for your beloved's safety."

Cassandra fell silent, folding her hands in her lap and bowing her head. But no prayers would come, only the vision of her dearest Marcus lying on that dirty foyer floor among the shards of that ugly vase and those wilted blooms, a red stain slowly spreading on his chest.

A moment later two shots rang out, startling the

horses so that they reared and pulled against their leads before Goodfellow could bring them back under control.

The door to the coach opened and Marcus, his face split with what she could only describe as a devilish grin, vaulted inside, calling to Goodfellow to drive neck or nothing for the White Tower. He collapsed against the seat beside Cassandra as the horses began to move. "Well, that's done," he said, slipping the still slightly smoking dueling pistol into the holster built for it on the coach wall.

"You've killed him?" Cassandra couldn't believe it. Her Marcus. Her scientific, calm, collected Marcus had just blown a man away—just like in the movies. "You've actually *killed* Hawtrey?"

"No, more's the pity," he answered as Peregrine leaned forward on the facing seat as if unwilling to miss a single word of Marcus's explanation. "He fired early, on the count of two, and then ducked behind a potted plant to save himself. I fear I only wounded him. His 'friends' are supporting him now, in his time of need."

"Pity," Aunt Cornelia agreed, shaking her head. "But at least he will be out of commission for the remainder of the Season—and quite possibly forever, if Lady Blakewell has anything to say about the business. I don't believe she is best pleased with her nephew this evening."

And then, surprising Cassandra, and everyone else in the coach, Aunt Cornelia began to cry.

"For God's sake, Marcus, can't Goodfellow make this coach go any faster?"

"Hush, darling," he answered, kissing the top of her head. "He's doing the best he can. It's only eleven thirty. Even after being caught up in that crush of carriages near St. James's Park, we are sure to make the White Tower with minutes to spare. You are so full of impatience, my love. Impatient to be moving, impatient to arrive at your destination. I have my best cattle in the shafts, sixteen-miles-an-hour tits, if they can only be given their heads."

"Marcus," Cassandra countered testily as she shook herself free of his hold and lifted the leather window curtain to peer out into the night, "my *car* goes eighty-five miles per hour—and for God's sake, once we're in my time—and especially when my mother's around— *don't* call your horses 'tits.' Oh, look—there it is, there it is! The Tower of London! Marcus, we're going to make it!"

She leaned into his embrace once more, thankful he had yet to read her a lecture about the foolishness that had led to her being kidnapped in the first place. But that was just like Marcus—he didn't hold a grudge. Which was a good thing, now that she thought about it, because she had been giving him a hard time, one way or another, ever since she got to Regency England.

But now she was going home—back to her own time. "I've got my ring, Marcus," she said, pulling Peregrine's greatcoat more closely around her. "Do you have yours?"

"I do," he answered as Goodfellow pulled the horses to a halt just outside one of the main gates. Cassandra didn't know which, and couldn't have cared anyway, for in the near distance she could see the flambeaux lighting the White Tower. "Here, my darling, I want you to take these," he said, pushing a small cloth bag into her hands.

She held the pouch up to the faint light. It felt as if it was full of marbles. "What's in here?"

"A few gems, enough to keep you safe if—"

Cassandra's blood ran cold. "If, Marcus? You promised me there weren't going to be any 'ifs.' Do you still think we might be separated?"

The door to the coach opened and Goodfellow let down the folding stairs. "No, my love," Marcus answered, although his head was turned, so that she could not see his face, look into his dark eyes, and judge for herself whether or not he was lying to her. "Now come —we still have to bribe our way past the guards. Corny —Perry? Are you coming?"

It took forever, or at least it seemed so to Cassandra, but at last Marcus had persuaded the guards at the barred gate to allow them through. The hands on her watch read a quarter to twelve before they had mounted the huge flight of steps to the White Tower and were standing in the room holding that memorable Elizabethan chair.

"Hold there! In the name of the King!" The voice came from somewhere above them, perhaps the chapel that Cassandra had decided against visiting that fateful day so long ago—a whole lifetime ago.

"Now what?" Cassandra bleated plaintively. She knew she had bleated. But she didn't care. She was tired, and scared—and pregnant, dammit! She was allowed to bleat!

"Another guard," Aunt Cornelia whispered, stepping in front of Marcus. "I'll handle this. You wait until I have him distracted, and then slip by him and run as if the devil himself was after you. Godspeed, my darlings. All my love and prayers go with you."

"Corny—" Cassandra began, before her voice broke. This was it. They really were leaving. "Corny—I love you!" she vowed earnestly, taking a moment to fling her arms around the woman's ramrod-stiff back before Marcus pulled her away.

"Good-bye, Aunt," Marcus said solemnly, leaning down to kiss Corny's thin cheek. "Your name may be Haskins, but you are the *best* of the Pendeltons."

"Yes, yes, now go, children—go!"

Marcus grabbed Cassandra's hand, pulling her along behind him. Peregrine led the way, holding high a flaming torch that had been stuck in a holder on the stone wall. They raced toward the narrow hallway and the winding flight of steps that lay just a few feet along that hallway, tucked out of sight.

Cassandra's high heels made it nearly impossible for her to hurry. She pulled free of Marcus in order to slip them from her feet.

"Marcus?" she called loudly, the sound of her voice echoing off the ragstone walls. "Marcus? Where are you?"

"Just ahead of you, my love," she heard him call back to her. "Keep coming, Cassandra. I'll wait for you."

"Hurry, Cousin Cassie," Peregrine instructed, his voice sounding very far away—too far away. "The mist is already here!"

"Marcus! Don't wait for me!" she shouted, all thought for her own safety fading as she realized that Marcus was in real danger. "Go on! Go on! I'll catch up!" Her heart pounding, her arms outstretched so that her palms were scraped by the rough ragstone walls, she made her way toward the light of Peregrine's torch, toward the eerie blue light that she so longed to see.

"There you go, Cousin Cassie," Peregrine said at last, his smiling face welcome after her terrifyingly dark descent of the winding staircase. "Marcus is already there, waiting for you. He didn't want to go, but I pushed him in. Good luck—and I'll make you proud. I promise!"

"Good-bye, Cousin," Cassandra said, barely able to see him through her tears as Peregrine stood on the last step, carefully keeping himself away from the blue mist that now filled the small room. "I'll never forget you."

And then she plunged into the mist, blinded by it, her hands outstretched, searching for the solidness of Marcus's body—and found nothing.

Epilogue

Cassandra sat propped against a half dozen pillows in the middle of the big tester bed and wiped away the tears that she couldn't seem to keep from falling on the yellowed sheets of paper in her lap.

Peregrine had left his letter behind the picture in the upstairs hallway, just as he had promised. The letter was quite lengthy, begun in 1812 and added to over the years until 1853, and it told of many things, many wonderful things, that had happened since he had returned from the White Tower once she and Marcus had "done their flit."

But Peregrine was gone now, as were Aunt Cornelia, and Rose, and Goodfellow, and even Jacques—although it seemed strange to walk through the rooms of the Grosvenor Square mansion and not see them, not hear their voices.

She did have her pictures of them, of course, the pictures she had picked up only that morning at a small shop around the corner in Providence Street.

Their lives had been good, at least according to Peregrine, who had wed Rose a scant year after that fateful May night. Rose's main attractions, according to Peregrine, had been that she seemed to love him, and that she didn't expect him to learn to dance. Besides, he loved her too. It had only taken a year for most members of the usually prickly high-in-the-instep London Society to learn to love her homey good nature as well, and their life together had been good.

Jacques, Peregrine had written, had returned to France after Waterloo and had become the head chef for some French prince in Paris. Peregrine, or so he said, planned to mourn the man's loss until his own dying day.

To Cassandra's delight, Goodfellow and Aunt Cornelia had wed, although it had taken Corny nearly five years to unbend enough to post the bans with the Pendelton family butler. Aunt Cornelia had mellowed with the years (or at least as much as that dear lady could mellow), and had stayed on in the Grosvenor Square mansion even after she was eventually widowed, to alternately nag and dote on Peregrine and Rose's only child.

Cassandra already knew that Peregrine's son—he'd named the child Marcus Charles Walton—had gone on to found a dynasty in the railroads, an empire that later expanded to include the airline industry. Smart man, her "Cousin Perry." He had followed her directions to the letter, so that the Walton name, now carried by more than three dozen proud Englishmen, had become a real force in the world.

She took up the letter again.

It took a long time before people stopped speculating as to what happened to you, old friend, but in the end Aunt Cornelia took care of everything. According to Corny, who swore she had received a personal letter from you two years after your disappearance, you married Cassandra in America before the two of you went off to deepest Africa and discovered a lost civilization. Made you their king, this lost civilization did, and Cousin Cassie their queen. It has been forty years, and I still hear it talked about in the clubs, although the story has grown. You now are

*said to have discovered a lost diamond mine, rather
than a lost civilization, and everyone is quite sure
that one fine day one of your descendants will be
back, to claim this house and all your lands. Oh, and
by the by, Prinny refused to vacate the title, saying
that he was sure you'd return, although I think it's
probably that little bag of emeralds you had me drop
into his lap that made him so charitable. I told him
you found them in the White Tower, just as you said
for me to do.*

*Anyway, considering as how I also told Prinny a
couple of things I learned from dearest Cousin Cassie, and being as how those things came true, our
dearest Majesty (may he rest in peace) allowed for a
little fudging of rules, dear Marcus. Thanks to
Prinny—and some fancy footwork by a grateful
friend—if your male descendant (and you know just
whom I mean!) was to arrive in Grosvenor Square
anytime before 5 June 1992, wearing a certain ring
(yes, I confess that I bribed your solicitor and had a
copy made, then presented it to the King's Royal
Treasurer), that male descendent is to be named the
Sixth Marquess of Eastbourne. Just think, Marcus,
you have defied all the laws of nature you are so
proud of—you have succeeded yourself!*

*I dislike closing this letter for the last time, for it
will mean that I have to say my final good-bye to my
dearest friend, but I am old now, and Rose says it is
time. We adjourn to the country this week, so that I
may putter about in the garden, or whatever it is old
men do. As Corny said that last night, "Godspeed,"
Marcus and Cousin Cassie. You are the best of people
and the best of friends!*

After reading the letter for a third time, Cassandra
refolded it and tucked it in a drawer in the nightstand

and lay back against the pillows, turning the ring on the third finger of her left hand round and round nervously. It wouldn't do to let Marcus see that she was still so emotional.

Her dear, sweet Marcus. How frightened she had been when she couldn't find him in the blue mist! But then, just as she thought she would lose control completely, the mist had cleared and there he was, smiling at her, his arms spread wide, saying simply, "Come, my love. It's time to go home."

Together they had crept up the stone staircase and joined a tour group that was just then descending from the chapel. Marcus's smile wide as he pointed to the sign describing the history of the Elizabethan chair. Cassandra walked up to one woman and began to make an offhand query as to the date, saying that she always lost track of the days when on vacation, then exclaimed, "Miss Smithers! I don't believe it! It's as if I never left!"

"Why, yes, my dear, of course it is," the librarian from Omaha had answered. "We were only upstairs for a few minutes. So sorry you missed it. Are you feeling better now?"

"Better? Oh, oh yes, of course. I'm so much better you just wouldn't believe it! You will excuse me, won't you, Miss Smithers? I've, *um,* I've met a friend, and he has invited me to his home."

And what a home (by Marcus's quick count, one of only three original buildings left in the Square) they had come back to—a perfectly preserved, fully staffed Regency mansion, except for the fact that it was stocked from cellar to attic with VCRs, compact disc players, microwave ovens, dimmer switches for the chandeliers, and a wide-screen television set that Marcus immediately had moved upstairs into their bedchamber.

As to how she had left Regency England on the last day of May and still ended up back in her own time as if she had never left it, Cassandra had no idea. Marcus, however, said that he "had a theory," although he hadn't gotten to tell it to her before she silenced him with a kiss.

Cassandra smiled, remembering that she still had missed the London Book Fair, and would most probably be fired once she phoned the office in Manhattan—which she would do any day now. Yep, any day now. Or maybe next week.

But she couldn't care about her job anymore. She was through editing other people's work. She was going to write. Fiction. Lots of fiction. Really nifty historical romance fiction. As a matter of fact, she had a great idea for a time-travel romance!

"Daydreaming again, my love?" Marcus asked, walking from the dressing room that had been converted to a bathroom. A snowy white towel was about his hips and he used another to rub at his shower-wet hair. "I will never tire of that contraption, you know," he told her, grinning. And he was right. He was in the shower so much, Cassandra had teased him that his toes had become webbed.

"There are lots of things you don't seem to tire of, darling. Except to eat, I don't believe I've been out of this bed in three days. I wouldn't be surprised if our son ends up being born here."

"Our son," Marcus said, his expression so proud she would have teased him, except that she was just as proud as he about their child, the heir to the title Marcus had never had to relinquish. "Peregrine" might not be a Latin-based name, but she was going to get it into the list of middle names for the Seventh Marquess of Eastbourne if she had to wedge it in sideways!

Shrugging into his dressing gown—an exact replica of the dressing gown he had worn that first night when he'd come into her room—Marcus sat down beside her on the bed and used the remote control to switch on the television set. It still annoyed her that he had mastered the remote in a matter of minutes, when she still couldn't program the VCR in her apartment in Manhattan. But that was Marcus. He could fit in anywhere.

And he would. Although he could content himself being the marquess, and spend his days jet-setting around the world, Marcus had already told her that he planned to enroll in college as soon as they'd gotten his official passport and paid a visit to her parents—her parents, who phoned daily—her father, to ask about "this man you plan to marry," and her mother, whose conversation centered more on layettes and baby showers.

"Are we going to watch television again?" she asked now, pouting.

"Is that a complaint, my love?" Marcus asked, turning onto his stomach and propping his feet against the headboard. He flipped through the stations, finally deciding on a variety program being telecast on the BBC. "Or were you about to suggest an alternate means of entertainment?"

She pulled her feet out from beneath the covers and joined him at the foot of the bed, resting her chin on her forearms. "What do you think, darling?"

Putting down the remote control, he lightly pushed her onto her back, bringing his mouth down on hers, then untying the satin sash at her waist, inviting her back into the world of love they had rarely left these past few days.

From across the room the announcer's voice could be heard, introducing the next act on the program. "And now, ladies and gentlemen, the newest singing sensation to hit this marvelous island, and the proud holders of three platinum records—their album has just gone platinum as well. Allow me to introduce to you the medieval answer to rock 'n' roll—Ned and Dickon—*The King's Boys*!''

Marcus raised his head, a lock of dark hair falling forward onto his forehead. ''Ned and Dickon?''

The mood broken, Cassandra pushed him off her, turned onto her belly once more, and looked across the room to where two handsome, long-haired boys in their mid-twenties were playing guitar and singing hard rock lyrics that had something to do with ''treachery in the forest.''

''Marcus?'' Cassandra asked, looking at him. ''Do you suppose? I mean, could they possibly be—?''

He looked at the set, frowning, then looked at Cassandra. *''Nah!* That's impossible!'' they said together—but then, without another word, they turned their heads back to the television set and watched until the song was over.